John Carter of Mars
VOLUME THREE

John Carter of Mars
Volume Three

The Fifth Adventure
Chessmen of Mars

The Sixth Adventure
Mastermind of Mars

Edgar Rice Burroughs

John Carter of Mars Volume Three:
Chessmen of Mars and Mastermind of Mars
by Edgar Rice Burroughs

FIRST EDITION

Published by Leonaur Ltd

Material original to this edition and this editorial selection
copyright © 2007 Leonaur Ltd

ISBN (10 digit): 1-84677-158-7 (hardcover)
ISBN (13 digit): 978-1-84677-158-3 (hardcover)

ISBN (10 digit): 1-84677-152-8 (softcover)
ISBN (13 digit): 978-1-84677-152-1 (softcover)

http://www.leonaur.com

Publisher's Notes

In the interests of authenticity, the spellings, grammar and place names used by the author have been retained.

The views expressed in this book are not necessarily those of the publisher.

Contents

THE FIFTH ADVENTURE

Chessmen of Mars   7

THE SIXTH ADVENTURE

Mastermind of Mars   215

THE FIFTH ADVENTURE

Chessmen of Mars

Prelude

John Carter Comes to Earth

Shea had just beaten me at chess, as usual, and, also as usual, I had gleaned what questionable satisfaction I might by twitting him with this indication of failing mentality by calling his attention to the nth time to that theory, propounded by certain scientists, which is based upon the assertion that phenomenal chess players are always found to be from the ranks of children under twelve, adults over seventy-two or the mentally defective—a theory that is lightly ignored upon those rare occasions that I win. Shea had gone to bed and I should have followed suit, for we are always in the saddle here before sunrise; but instead I sat there before the chess table in the library, idly blowing smoke at the dishonoured head of my defeated king.

While thus profitably employed I heard the east door of the living-room open and someone enter. I thought it was Shea returning to speak with me on some matter of tomorrow's work; but when I raised my eyes to the doorway that connects the two rooms I saw framed there the figure of a bronzed giant, his otherwise naked body trapped with a jewel-encrusted harness from which there hung at one side an ornate short-sword and at the other a pistol of strange pattern. The black hair, the steel-grey eyes, brave and smiling, the noble features—I recognized them at once, and leaping to my feet I advanced with outstretched hand.

"John Carter!" I cried. "You?"

"None other, my son," he replied, taking my hand in one of his and placing the other upon my shoulder.

"And what are you doing here?" I asked. "It has been long years since you revisited Earth, and never before in the trappings of Mars. Lord! but it is good to see you—and not a day older in appearance than when you trotted me on your knee in my babyhood. How do you explain it, John Carter, Warlord of Mars, or do you try to explain it?"

"Why attempt to explain the inexplicable?" he replied. "As I have told you before, I am a very old man. I do not know how old I am. I recall no childhood; but recollect only having been always as you see me now and as you saw me first when you were five years old. You, yourself, have aged, though not as much as most men in a corresponding number of years, which may be accounted for by the fact that the same blood runs in our veins; but I have not aged at all. I have discussed the question with a noted Martian scientist, a friend of mine; but his theories are still only theories. However, I am content with the fact—I never age, and I love life and the vigour of youth.

"And now as to your natural question as to what brings me to Earth again and in this, to earthly eyes, strange habiliment. We may thank Kar Komak, the bowman of Lothar. It was he who gave me the idea upon which I have been experimenting until at last I have achieved success. As you know I have long possessed the power to cross the void in spirit, but never before have I been able to impart to inanimate things a similar power. Now, however, you see me for the first time precisely as my Martian fellows see me—you see the very short-sword that has tasted the blood of many a savage foeman; the harness with the devices of Helium and the insignia of my rank; the pistol that was presented to me by Tars Tarkas, Jeddak of Thark.

"Aside from seeing you, which is my principal reason for being here, and satisfying myself that I can transport inanimate things from Mars to Earth, and therefore animate things if I so desire, I have no purpose. Earth is not for me. My every interest is upon Barsoom—my wife, my children, my work; all are there. I will spend a quiet evening with you and then back to the world I love even better than I love life."

As he spoke he dropped into the chair upon the opposite side of the chess table.

"You spoke of children," I said. "Have you more than Carthoris?"

"A daughter," he replied, "only a little younger than Carthoris, and, barring one, the fairest thing that ever breathed the thin air of dying Mars. Only Dejah Thoris, her mother, could be more beautiful than Tara of Helium."

For a moment he fingered the chessmen idly. "We have a game on Mars similar to chess," he said, "very similar. And there is a race there that plays it grimly with men and naked swords. We call the game jetan. It is played on a board like yours, except that there are a hundred squares and we use twenty pieces on each side. I never see it played without thinking of Tara of Helium and what befell her among the chessmen of Barsoom. Would you like to hear her story?"

I said that I would and so he told it to me, and now I shall try to re-tell it for you as nearly in the words of The Warlord of Mars as I can recall them, but in the third person. If there be inconsistencies and errors, let the blame fall not upon John Carter, but rather upon my faulty memory, where it belongs. It is a strange tale and utterly Barsoomian.

Chapter 1

Tara in a Tantrum

Tara of Helium rose from the pile of silks and soft furs upon which she had been reclining, stretched her lithe body languidly, and crossed toward the centre of the room, where, above a large table, a bronze disc depended from the low ceiling. Her carriage was that of health and physical perfection—the effortless harmony of faultless coordination. A scarf of silken gossamer crossing over one shoulder was wrapped about her body; her black hair was piled high upon her head. With a wooden stick she tapped upon the bronze disc, lightly, and presently the summons was answered by a slave girl, who entered, smiling, to be greeted similarly by her mistress.

"Are my father's guests arriving?" asked the princess.

"Yes, Tara of Helium, they come," replied the slave. "I have seen Kantos Kan, Overlord of the Navy, and Prince Soran of Ptarth, and Djor Kantos, son of Kantos Kan," she shot a roguish glance at her mistress as she mentioned Djor Kantos' name, "and—oh, there were others, many have come."

"The bath, then, Uthia," said her mistress. "And why, Uthia," she added, "do you look thus and smile when you mention the name of Djor Kantos?"

The slave girl laughed gaily. "It is so plain to all that he worships you," she replied.

"It is not plain to me," said Tara of Helium. "He is the friend of my brother, Carthoris, and so he is here much; but not to see me. It is his friendship for Carthoris that brings him thus often to the palace of my father."

"But Carthoris is hunting in the north with Talu, Jeddak of Okar," Uthia reminded her.

"My bath, Uthia!" cried Tara of Helium. "That tongue of yours will bring you to some misadventure yet."

"The bath is ready, Tara of Helium," the girl responded, her eyes still twinkling with merriment, for she well knew that in the heart of her mistress was no anger that could displace the love of the princess for her slave. Preceding the daughter of The Warlord she opened the door of an adjoining room where lay the bath—a gleaming pool of scented water in a marble basin. Golden stanchions supported a chain of gold encircling it and leading down into the water on either side of marble steps. A glass dome let in the sun-light, which flooded the interior, glancing from the polished white of the marble walls and the procession of bathers and fishes, which, in conventional design, were inlaid with gold in a broad band that circled the room.

Tara of Helium removed the scarf from about her and handed it to the slave. Slowly she descended the steps to the water, the temperature of which she tested with a symmetrical foot, undeformed by tight shoes and high heels—a lovely foot, as God intended that feet should be and seldom are. Finding the water to her liking, the girl swam leisurely to and fro about the pool. With the silken ease of the seal she swam, now at the surface, now below, her smooth muscles rolling softly beneath her clear skin—a wordless song of health and happiness and grace. Presently she emerged and gave herself into the hands of the slave girl, who rubbed the body of her mistress with a sweet smelling semi-liquid substance contained in a golden urn, until the glowing skin was covered with a foamy lather, then a quick plunge into the pool, a drying with soft towels, and the bath was over. Typical of the life of the princess was the simple elegance of her bath—no retinue of useless slaves, no pomp, no idle waste of precious moments. In another half hour her hair was dried and built into the strange, but becoming, coiffure of her station; her leathern trappings, encrusted with gold and jewels, had been adjusted to her figure and she was ready to mingle with the guests that had been bidden to the midday function at the palace of The Warlord.

As she left her apartments to make her way to the gardens where the guests were congregating, two warriors, the insignia of the House of the Prince of Helium upon their harness, followed a few paces behind her, grim reminders that the assassin's blade may never be ignored upon Barsoom, where, in a measure, it counterbalances the great natural span of human life, which is estimated at not less than a thousand years.

As they neared the entrance to the garden another woman, similarly guarded, approached them from another quarter of the great palace. As she neared them Tara of Helium turned toward her with a smile and a happy greeting, while her guards knelt with bowed heads in willing and voluntary adoration of the beloved of Helium. Thus always, solely at the command of their own hearts, did the warriors of Helium greet Dejah Thoris, whose deathless beauty had more than once brought them to bloody warfare with other nations of Barsoom. So great was the love of the people of Helium for the mate of John Carter it amounted practically to worship, as though she were indeed the goddess that she looked.

The mother and daughter exchanged the gentle, Barsoomian, *kaor* of greeting and kissed. Then together they entered the gardens where the guests were. A huge warrior drew his short-sword and struck his metal shield with the flat of it, the brazen sound ringing out above the laughter and the speech.

"The Princess comes!" he cried. "Dejah Thoris! The Princess comes! Tara of Helium!" Thus always is royalty announced. The guests arose; the two women inclined their heads; the guards fell back upon either side of the entrance-way; a number of nobles advanced to pay their respects; the laughing and the talking were resumed and Dejah Thoris and her daughter moved simply and naturally among their guests, no suggestion of differing rank apparent in the bearing of any who were there, though there was more than a single Jeddak and many common warriors whose only title lay in brave deeds, or noble patriotism. Thus it is upon Mars where men are judged upon their own merits rather than upon those of their grandsires, even though pride of lineage be great.

Tara of Helium let her slow gaze wander among the throng of guests until presently it halted upon one she sought. Was the faint shadow of a frown that crossed her brow an indication of displeasure at the sight that met her eyes, or did the brilliant rays of the noonday sun distress her? Who may say! She had been reared to believe that one day she should wed Djor Kantos, son of her father's best friend. It had been the dearest wish of Kantos Kan and The Warlord that this should be, and Tara of Helium had accepted it as a matter of all but accomplished fact. Djor Kantos had seemed to accept the matter in the same way. They had spoken of it casually as something that would, as a matter of course, take place in the indefinite future, as, for instance, his promotion in the navy, in which he was now a padwar; or the set functions of the court of her grandfather, Tardos Mors, Jeddak of Helium; or Death. They had never spoken of love and that had puzzled Tara of Helium upon the rare occasions she gave it thought, for she knew that people who were to wed were usually much occupied with the matter of love and she had all of a woman's curiosity—she wondered what love was like. She was very fond of Djor Kantos and she knew that he was very fond of her. They liked to be together, for they liked the same things and the same people and the same books and their dancing was a joy, not only to themselves but to those who watched them. She could not imagine wanting to marry anyone other than Djor Kantos.

So perhaps it was only the sun that made her brows contract just the tiniest bit at the same instant that she discovered Djor Kantos sitting in earnest conversation with Olvia Marthis, daughter of the Jed of Hastor. It was Djor Kantos' duty immediately to pay his respects to Dejah Thoris and Tara of Helium; but he did not do so and presently the daughter of The Warlord frowned indeed. She looked long at Olvia Marthis, and though she had seen her many times before and knew her well, she looked at her today through new eyes that saw, apparently for the first time, that the girl from Hastor was noticeably beautiful even among those other beautiful women of Helium. Tara of Helium was disturbed. She attempted to analyze her emotions; but found it difficult. Olvia Marthis was her friend—she was very fond of her and she felt no anger toward her. Was she angry with Djor Kantos? No, she finally decided that she was not. It was merely surprise, then, that she felt—surprise that Djor Kantos could be more interested in another than in herself. She was about to cross the garden and join them when she heard her father's voice directly behind her.

"Tara of Helium!" he called, and she turned to see him approaching with a strange warrior whose harness and metal bore devices with which she was unfamiliar. Even among the gorgeous trappings of the men of Helium and the visitors from distant empires those of the stranger were remarkable for their barbaric splendour. The leather of his harness was completely hidden beneath ornaments of platinum thickly set with brilliant diamonds, as were the scabbards of his swords and the ornate holster that held his long, Martian pistol. Moving through the sunlit garden at the side of the great Warlord, the scintillant rays of his countless gems enveloping him as in an aureole of light imparted to his noble figure a suggestion of godliness.

"Tara of Helium, I bring you Gahan, Jed of Gathol," said John Carter, after the simple Barsoomian custom of presentation.

"Kaor! Gahan, Jed of Gathol," returned Tara of Helium.

"My sword is at your feet, Tara of Helium," said the young chieftain.

The Warlord left them and the two seated themselves upon an ersite bench beneath a spreading sorapus tree.

"Far Gathol," mused the girl. "Ever in my mind has it been connected with mystery and romance and the half-forgotten lore of the ancients. I cannot think of Gathol as existing today, possibly because I have never before seen a Gatholian."

"And perhaps too because of the great distance that separates Helium and Gathol, as well as the comparative insignificance of my little free city, which might easily be lost in one corner of mighty Helium," added Gahan. "But what we lack in power we make up in pride," he continued, laughing. "We believe ours the oldest inhabited city upon Barsoom. It is one of the few that has retained its freedom, and this despite the fact that its ancient diamond mines are the richest known and, unlike practically all the other fields, are today apparently as inexhaustible as ever."

"Tell me of Gathol," urged the girl. "The very thought fills me with interest," nor was it likely that the handsome face of the young jed detracted anything from the glamour of far Gathol.

Nor did Gahan seem displeased with the excuse for further monopolizing the society of his fair companion. His eyes seemed chained to her exquisite features, from which they moved no further than to a rounded breast, part hid beneath its jewelled covering, a naked shoulder or the symmetry of a perfect arm, resplendent in bracelets of barbaric magnificence.

"Your ancient history has doubtless told you that Gathol was built upon an island in Throxeus, mightiest of the five oceans of old Barsoom. As the ocean receded Gathol crept down the sides of the mountain, the summit of which was the island upon which she had been built, until today she covers the slopes from summit to base, while the bowels of the great hill are honeycombed with the galleries of her mines. Entirely surrounding us is a great salt marsh, which protects us from invasion by land, while the rugged and oft-times vertical topography of our mountain renders the landing of hostile airships a precarious undertaking."

"That, and your brave warriors?" suggested the girl.

Gahan smiled. "We do not speak of that except to enemies," he said, "and then with tongues of steel rather than of flesh."

"But what practice in the art of war has a people which nature has thus protected from attack?" asked Tara of Helium, who had liked the young Jed's answer to her previous question, but yet in whose mind persisted a vague conviction of the possible effeminacy of her companion, induced, doubtless, by the magnificence of his trappings and weapons which carried a suggestion of splendid show rather than grim utility.

"Our natural barriers, while they have doubtless saved us from defeat on countless occasions, have not by any means rendered us immune from attack," he explained, "for so great is the wealth of Gathol's diamond treasury that there yet may be found those who will risk almost certain defeat in an effort to loot our unconquered city; so thus we find occasional practice in the exercise of arms; but there is more to Gathol than the mountain city. My country extends from Polodona (Equator) north ten karads and from the tenth karad west of Horz to the twentieth west, including thus a million square haads, the greater proportion of which is fine grazing land where run our great herds of thoats and zitidars.

"Surrounded as we are by predatory enemies our herdsmen must indeed be warriors or we should have no herds, and you may be assured they get plenty of fighting. Then there is our constant need of workers in the mines. The Gatholians consider themselves a race of warriors and as such prefer not to labour in the mines. The law is, however, that each male Gatholian shall give an hour a day in labour to the government. That is practically the only tax that is levied upon them. They prefer however, to furnish a substitute to perform this labour, and as our own people will not hire out for labour in the mines it has been necessary to obtain slaves, and I do not need to tell you that slaves are not won without fighting. We sell these slaves in the public market, the proceeds going, half and half, to the government and the warriors who bring them in. The purchasers are credited with the amount of labour performed by their particular slaves. At the end of a year a good slave will have performed the labour tax of his master for six years, and if slaves are plentiful he is freed and permitted to return to his own people."

"You fight in platinum and diamonds?" asked Tara, indicating his gorgeous trappings with a quizzical smile.

Gahan laughed. "We are a vain people," he admitted, good-naturedly, "and it is possible that we place too much value on personal appearances. We vie with one another in the splendour of our accoutrements when trapped for the observance of the lighter duties of life, though when we take the field our leather is the plainest I ever have seen worn by fighting men of Barsoom. We pride ourselves, too, upon our physical beauty, and especially upon the beauty of our women. May I dare to say, Tara of Helium, that I am hoping for the day when you will visit Gathol that my people may see one who is really beautiful?"

"The women of Helium are taught to frown with displeasure upon the tongue of the flatterer," rejoined the girl, but Gahan, Jed of Gathol, observed that she smiled as she said it.

A bugle sounded, clear and sweet, above the laughter and the talk. "The Dance of Barsoom!" exclaimed the young warrior. "I claim you for it, Tara of Helium."

The girl glanced in the direction of the bench where she had last seen Djor Kantos. He was not in sight. She inclined her head in assent to the claim of the Gatholian. Slaves were passing among the guests, distributing small musical instruments of a single string. Upon each instrument were characters which indicated the pitch and length of its tone. The instruments were of skeel, the string of gut, and were shaped to fit the left forearm of the dancer, to which it was strapped. There was also a ring wound with gut which was worn between the first and second joints of the index finger of the right hand and which, when passed over the string of the instrument, elicited the single note required of the dancer.

The guests had risen and were slowly making their way toward the expanse of scarlet sward at the south end of the gardens where the dance was to be held, when Djor Kantos came hurriedly toward Tara of Helium. "I claim—" he exclaimed as he neared her; but she interrupted him with a gesture.

"You are too late, Djor Kantos," she cried in mock anger. "No laggard may claim Tara of Helium; but haste now lest thou lose also Olvia Marthis, whom I have never seen wait long to be claimed for this or any other dance."

"I have already lost her," admitted Djor Kantos ruefully.

"And you mean to say that you came for Tara of Helium only after having lost Olvia Marthis?" demanded the girl, still simulating displeasure.

"Oh, Tara of Helium, you know better than that," insisted the young man. "Was it not natural that I should assume that you would expect me, who alone has claimed you for the Dance of Barsoom for at least twelve times past?"

"And sit and play with my thumbs until you saw fit to come for me?" she questioned. "Ah, no, Djor Kantos; Tara of Helium is for no laggard," and she threw him a sweet smile and passed on toward the assembling dancers with Gahan, Jed of far Gathol.

The Dance of Barsoom bears a relation similar to the more formal dancing functions of Mars that The Grand March does to ours, though it is infinitely more intricate and more beautiful. Before a Martian youth of either sex may attend an important social function where there is dancing, he must have become proficient in at least three dances—The Dance of Barsoom, his national dance, and the dance of his city. In these three dances the dancers furnish their own music, which never varies; nor do the steps or figures vary, having been handed down from time immemorial. All Barsoomian dances are stately and beautiful, but The Dance of Barsoom is a wondrous epic of motion and harmony—there is no grotesque posturing, no vulgar or suggestive movements. It has been described as the interpretation of the highest ideals of a world that aspired to grace and beauty and chastity in woman, and strength and dignity and loyalty in man.

Today, John Carter, Warlord of Mars, with Dejah Thoris, his mate, led in the dancing, and if there was another couple that vied with them in possession of the silent admiration of the guests it was the resplendent Jed of Gathol and his beautiful partner. In the ever-changing figures of the dance the man found himself now with the girl's hand in his and again with an arm about the lithe body that the jewelled harness but inadequately covered, and the girl, though she had danced a thousand dances in the past, realized for the first time the personal contact of a man's arm against her naked flesh. It troubled her that she should notice it, and she looked up questioningly and almost with displeasure at the man as though it was his fault. Their eyes met and she saw in his that which she had never seen in the eyes of Djor Kantos. It was at the very end of the dance and they both stopped suddenly with the music and stood there looking straight into each other's eyes. It was Gahan of Gathol who spoke first.

"Tara of Helium, I love you!" he said.

The girl drew herself to her full height. "The Jed of Gathol forgets himself," she exclaimed haughtily.

"The Jed of Gathol would forget everything but you, Tara of Helium," he replied. Fiercely he pressed the soft hand that he still retained from the last position of the dance. "I love you, Tara of Helium," he repeated. "Why should your ears refuse to hear what your eyes but just now did not refuse to see—and answer?"

"What meanest thou?" she cried. "Are the men of Gathol such boors, then?"

"They are neither boors nor fools," he replied, quietly. "They know when they love a woman—and when she loves them."

Tara of Helium stamped her little foot in anger. "Go!" she said, "before it is necessary to acquaint my father with the dishonour of his guest."

She turned and walked away. "Wait!" cried the man. "Just another word."

"Of apology?" she asked.

"Of prophecy," he said.

"I do not care to hear it," replied Tara of Helium, and left him standing there. She was strangely unstrung and shortly thereafter returned to her own quarter of the palace, where she stood for a long time by a window looking out beyond the scarlet tower of Greater Helium toward the northwest.

Presently she turned angrily away. "I hate him!" she exclaimed aloud.

"Whom?" inquired the privileged Uthia.

Tara of Helium stamped her foot. "That ill-mannered boor, the Jed of Gathol," she replied.

Uthia raised her slim brows.

At the stamping of the little foot, a great beast rose from the corner of the room and crossed to Tara of Helium where it stood looking up into her face. She placed her hand upon the ugly head. "Dear old Woola," she said; "no love could be deeper than yours, yet it never offends. Would that men might pattern themselves after you!"

Chapter 2

At the Gale's Mercy

Tara of Helium did not return to her father's guests, but awaited in her own apartments the word from Djor Kantos which she knew must come, begging her to return to the gardens. She would then refuse, haughtily. But no appeal came from Djor Kantos. At first Tara of Helium was angry, then she was hurt, and always she was puzzled. She could not understand. Occasionally she thought of the Jed of Gathol and then she would stamp her foot, for she was very angry indeed with Gahan. The presumption of the man! He had insinuated that he read love for him in her eyes. Never had she been so insulted and humiliated. Never had she so thoroughly hated a man. Suddenly she turned toward Uthia.

"My flying leather!" she commanded.

"But the guests!" exclaimed the slave girl. "Your father, The Warlord, will expect you to return."

"He will be disappointed," snapped Tara of Helium.

The slave hesitated. "He does not approve of your flying alone," she reminded her mistress.

The young princess sprang to her feet and seized the unhappy slave by the shoulders, shaking her. "You are becoming unbearable, Uthia," she cried. "Soon there will be no alternative than to send you to the public slave-market. Then possibly you will find a master to your liking."

Tears came to the soft eyes of the slave girl. "It is because I love you, my princess," she said softly. Tara of Helium melted. She took the slave in her arms and kissed her.

"I have the disposition of a thoat, Uthia," she said. "Forgive me! I love you and there is nothing that I would not do for you and nothing would I do to harm you. Again, as I have so often in the past, I offer you your freedom."

"I do not wish my freedom if it will separate me from you, Tara of Helium," replied Uthia. "I am happy here with you—I think that I should die without you."

Again the girls kissed. "And you will not fly alone, then?" questioned the slave.

Tara of Helium laughed and pinched her companion. "You persistent little pest," she cried. "Of course I shall fly—does not Tara of Helium always do that which pleases her?"

Uthia shook her head sorrowfully. "Alas! she does," she admitted. "Iron is the Warlord of Barsoom to the influences of all but two. In the hands of Dejah Thoris and Tara of Helium he is as potters' clay."

"Then run and fetch my flying leather like the sweet slave you are," directed the mistress.

* * * * *

Far out across the ochre sea-bottoms beyond the twin cities of Helium raced the swift flier of Tara of Helium. Thrilling to the speed and the buoyancy and the obedience of the little craft the girl drove toward the northwest. Why she should choose that direction she did not pause to consider. Perhaps because in that direction lay the least known areas of Barsoom, and, ergo, Romance, Mystery, and Adventure. In that direction also lay far Gathol; but to that fact she gave no conscious thought.

She did, however, think occasionally of the jed of that distant kingdom, but the reaction to these thoughts was scarcely pleasurable. They still brought a flush of shame to her cheeks and a surge of angry blood to her heart. She was very angry with the Jed of Gathol, and though she should never see him again she was quite sure that hate of him would remain fresh in her memory forever. Mostly her thoughts revolved about another—Djor Kantos. And when she thought of him she thought also of Olvia Marthis of Hastor. Tara of Helium thought that she was jealous of the fair Olvia and it made her very angry to think that. She was angry with Djor Kantos and herself, but she was not angry at all with Olvia Marthis, whom she loved, and so of course she was not jealous really. The trouble was, that Tara of Helium had failed for once to have her own way. Djor Kantos had not come running like a willing slave when she had expected him, and, ah, here was the nub of the whole thing! Gahan, Jed of Gathol, a stranger, had been a witness to her humiliation. He had seen her unclaimed at the beginning of a great function and he had had to come to her rescue to save her, as he doubtless thought, from the inglorious fate of a wall-flower. At the recurring thought, Tara of

Helium could feel her whole body burning with scarlet shame and then she went suddenly white and cold with rage; whereupon she turned her flier about so abruptly that she was all but torn from her lashings upon the flat, narrow deck. She reached home just before dark. The guests had departed. Quiet had descended upon the palace. An hour later she joined her father and mother at the evening meal.

"You deserted us, Tara of Helium," said John Carter. "It is not what the guests of John Carter should expect."

"They did not come to see me," replied Tara of Helium. "I did not ask them."

"They were no less your guests," replied her father.

The girl rose, and came and stood beside him and put her arms about his neck.

"My proper old Virginian," she cried, rumpling his shock of black hair.

"In Virginia you would be turned over your father's knee and spanked," said the man, smiling.

She crept into his lap and kissed him. "You do not love me any more," she announced. "No one loves me," but she could not compose her features into a pout because bubbling laughter insisted upon breaking through.

"The trouble is there are too many who love you," he said. "And now there is another."

"Indeed!" she cried. "What do you mean?"

"Gahan of Gathol has asked permission to woo you."

The girl sat up very straight and tilted her chin in the air. "I would not wed with a walking diamond-mine," she said. "I will not have him."

"I told him as much," replied her father, "and that you were as good as betrothed to another. He was very courteous about it; but at the same time he gave me to understand that he was accustomed to getting what he wanted and that he wanted you very much. I suppose it will mean another war. Your mother's beauty kept Helium at war for many years, and—well, Tara of Helium, if I were a young man I should doubtless be willing to set all Barsoom afire to win you, as I still would to keep your divine mother," and he smiled across the sorapus table and its golden service at the undimmed beauty of Mars' most beautiful woman.

"Our little girl should not yet be troubled with such matters," said Dejah Thoris. "Remember, John Carter, that you are not dealing with an Earth child, whose span of life would be more than half completed before a daughter of Barsoom reached actual maturity." "But do not the daughters of Barsoom sometimes marry as early as twenty?" he insisted.

"Yes, but they will still be desirable in the eyes of men after forty generations of Earth folk have returned to dust—there is no hurry, at least, upon Barsoom. We do not fade and decay here as you tell me those of your planet do, though you, yourself, belie your own words. When the time seems proper Tara of Helium shall wed with Djor Kantos, and until then let us give the matter no further thought."

"No," said the girl, "the subject irks me, and I shall not marry Djor Kantos, or another—I do not intend to wed."

Her father and mother looked at her and smiled. "When Gahan of Gathol returns he may carry you off," said the former.

"He has gone?" asked the girl.

"His flier departs for Gathol in the morning," John Carter replied.

"I have seen the last of him then," remarked Tara of Helium with a sigh of relief.

"He says not," returned John Carter.

The girl dismissed the subject with a shrug and the conversation passed to other topics. A letter had arrived from Thuvia of Ptarth, who was visiting at her father's court while Carthoris, her mate, hunted in Okar. Word had been received that the Tharks and Warhoons were again at war, or rather that there had been an engagement, for war was their habitual state. In the memory of man there had been no peace between these two savage green hordes—only a single temporary truce. Two new battleships had been launched at Hastor. A little band of holy therns was attempting to revive the ancient and discredited religion of Issus, who they claimed still lived in spirit and had communicated with them. There were rumours of war from Dusar. A scientist claimed to have discovered human life on the further moon. A madman had attempted to destroy the atmosphere plant. Seven people had been assassinated in Greater Helium during the last ten zodes, (the equivalent of an Earth day).

Following the meal Dejah Thoris and The Warlord played at jetan, the Barsoomian game of chess, which is played upon a board of a hundred alternate black and orange squares. One player has twenty black pieces, the other, twenty orange pieces. A brief description of the game may interest those Earth readers who care for chess, and will not be lost upon those who pursue this narrative to its conclusion, since before they are done they will find that a knowledge of jetan will add to the interest and the thrills that are in store for them.

The men are placed upon the board as in chess upon the first two rows next the players. In order from left to right on the line of squares nearest the players, the jetan pieces are Warrior, Padwar, Dwar, Flier, Chief, Princess, Flier, Dwar, Padwar, Warrior. In the next line all are Panthans except the end pieces, which are called Thoats, and represent mounted warriors.

The Panthans, which are represented as warriors with one feather, may move one space in any direction except backward; the Thoats, mounted warriors with three feathers, may move one straight and one diagonal, and may jump intervening pieces; Warriors, foot soldiers with two feathers, straight in any direction, or diagonally, two spaces; Padwars, lieutenants wearing two feathers, two diagonal in any direction, or combination; Dwars, captains wearing three feathers, three spaces straight in any direction, or combination; Fliers, represented by a propellor with three blades, three spaces in any direction, or combination, diagonally, and may jump intervening pieces; the Chief, indicated by a diadem with ten jewels, three spaces in any direction, straight, or diagonal; Princess, diadem with a single jewel, same as Chief, and can jump intervening pieces.

The game is won when a player places any of his pieces on the same square with his opponent's Princess, or when a Chief takes a Chief. It is drawn when a Chief is taken by any opposing piece other than the opposing Chief; or when both sides have been reduced to three pieces, or less, of equal value, and the game is not terminated in the following ten moves, five apiece. This is but a general outline of the game, briefly stated.

It was this game that Dejah Thoris and John Carter were playing when Tara of Helium bid them good night, retiring to her own quarters and her sleeping silks and furs. "Until morning, my beloved," she called back to them as she passed from the apartment, nor little did she guess, nor her parents, that this might indeed be the last time that they would ever set eyes upon her.

The morning broke dull and grey. Ominous clouds billowed restlessly and low. Beneath them torn fragments scudded toward the northwest. From her window Tara of Helium looked out upon this unusual scene. Dense clouds seldom overcast the Barsoomian sky. At this hour of the day it was her custom to ride one of those small thoats that are the saddle animals of the red Martians, but the sight of the billowing clouds lured her to a new adventure. Uthia still slept and the girl did not disturb her. Instead, she dressed quietly and went to the hangar upon the roof of the palace directly above her quarters where her own swift flier was housed. She had never driven through the clouds. It was an adventure that always she had longed to experience. The wind was strong and it was with difficulty that she manoeuvred the craft from the hangar without accident, but once away it raced swiftly out above the twin cities. The buffeting winds caught and tossed it, and the girl laughed aloud in sheer joy of the resultant thrills. She handled the little ship like a veteran, though few veterans would have faced the menace of such a storm in so light a craft. Swiftly she rose toward the clouds, racing with the scudding streamers of the storm-swept fragments, and a moment later she was swallowed by the dense masses billowing above. Here was a new world, a world of chaos unpeopled except for herself; but it was a cold, damp, lonely world and she found it depressing after the novelty of it had been dissipated, by an overpowering sense of the magnitude of the forces surging about her. Suddenly she felt very lonely and very cold and very little. Hurriedly, therefore, she rose until presently her craft broke through into the glorious sunlight that transformed the upper surface of the sombre element into rolling masses of burnished silver. Here it was still cold, but without the dampness of the clouds, and in the eye of the brilliant sun her spirits rose with the mounting needle of her altimeter. Gazing at the clouds, now far beneath, the girl experienced the sensation of hanging stationary in mid-heaven; but the whirring of her propellor, the wind beating upon her, the high figures that rose and fell beneath the glass of her speedometer, these told her that her speed was terrific. It was then that she determined to turn back.

    The first attempt she made above the clouds, but it was unsuccessful. To her surprise she discovered that she could not even turn against the high wind, which rocked and buffeted the frail craft. Then she dropped swiftly to the dark and wind-swept zone between the hurtling clouds and the gloomy surface of the shadowed ground. Here she tried again to force the nose of the flier back toward Helium, but the tempest seized the frail thing and hurled it remorselessly about, rolling it over and over and tossing it as it were a cork in a cataract. At last the girl succeeded in righting the flier, perilously close to the ground. Never before had she been so close to death, yet she was not terrified. Her coolness had saved her, that and the strength of the deck lashings that held her. Travelling with the storm she was safe, but where was it bearing her? She pictured the apprehension of her father and mother when she failed to appear at the morning meal. They would find her flier missing and they would guess that somewhere in the path of the storm it lay a wrecked and tangled mass upon her dead body, and then brave men would go out in search of her, risking their lives; and that lives would be lost in the search, she knew, for she realized now that never in her life-time had such a tempest raged upon Barsoom.

She must turn back! She must reach Helium before her mad lust for thrills had cost the sacrifice of a single courageous life! She determined that greater safety and likelihood of success lay above the clouds, and once again she rose through the chilling, wind-tossed vapour. Her speed again was terrific, for the wind seemed to have increased rather than to have lessened. She sought gradually to check the swift flight of her craft, but though she finally succeeded in reversing her motor the wind but carried her on as it would. Then it was that Tara of Helium lost her temper. Had her world not always bowed in acquiescence to her every wish? What were these elements that they dared to thwart her? She would demonstrate to them that the daughter of The Warlord was not to be denied! They would learn that Tara of Helium might not be ruled even by the forces of nature!

And so she drove her motor forward again and then with her firm, white teeth set in grim determination she drove the steering lever far down to port with the intention of forcing the nose of her craft straight into the teeth of the wind, and the wind seized the frail thing and toppled it over upon its back, and twisted and turned it and hurled it over and over; the propellor raced for an instant in an air pocket and then the tempest seized it again and twisted it from its shaft, leaving the girl helpless upon an unmanageable atom that rose and fell, and rolled and tumbled—the sport of the elements she had defied. Tara of Helium's first sensation was one of surprise—that she had failed to have her own way. Then she commenced to feel concern—not for her own safety but for the anxiety of her parents and the dangers that the inevitable searchers must face. She reproached herself for the thoughtless selfishness that had jeopardized the peace and safety of others. She realized her own grave danger, too; but she was still unterrified, as befitted the daughter of Dejah Thoris and John Carter. She knew that her buoyancy tanks might keep her afloat indefinitely, but she had neither food nor water, and she was being borne toward the least-known area of Barsoom. Perhaps it would be better to land immediately and await the coming of the searchers, rather than to allow herself to be carried still further from Helium, thus greatly reducing the chances of early discovery; but when she dropped toward the ground she discovered that the violence of the wind rendered an attempt to land tantamount to destruction and she rose again, rapidly.

Carried along a few hundred feet above the ground she was better able to appreciate the Titanic proportions of the storm than when she had flown in the comparative serenity of the zone above the clouds, for now she could distinctly see the effect of the wind upon the surface of Barsoom. The air was filled with dust and flying bits of vegetation and when the storm carried her across an irrigated area of farm land she saw great trees and stone walls and buildings lifted high in air and scattered broadcast over the devastated country; and then she was carried swiftly on to other sights that forced in upon her consciousness a rapidly growing conviction that after all Tara of Helium was a very small and insignificant and helpless person. It was quite a shock to her self-pride while it lasted, and toward evening she was ready to believe that it was going to last forever. There had been no abatement in the ferocity of the tempest, nor was there indication of any. She could only guess at the distance she had been carried for she could not believe in the correctness of the high figures that had been piled upon the record of her odometer. They seemed unbelievable and yet, had she known it, they were quite true—in twelve hours she had flown and been carried by the storm full seven thousand haads. Just before dark she was carried over one of the deserted cities of ancient Mars. It was Torquas, but she did not know it. Had she, she might readily have been forgiven for abandoning the last vestige of hope, for to the people of Helium Torquas seems as remote as do the South Sea Islands to us. And still the tempest, its fury unabated, bore her on.

All that night she hurtled through the dark beneath the clouds, or rose to race through the moonlit void beneath the glory of Barsoom's two satellites. She was cold and hungry and altogether miserable, but her brave little spirit refused to admit that her plight was hopeless even though reason proclaimed the truth. Her reply to reason, sometime spoken aloud in sudden defiance, recalled the Spartan stubbornness of her sire in the face of certain annihilation: "I still live!"

That morning there had been an early visitor at the palace of The Warlord. It was Gahan, Jed of Gathol. He had arrived shortly after the absence of Tara of Helium had been noted, and in the excitement he had remained unannounced until John Carter had happened upon him in the great reception corridor of the palace as The Warlord was hurrying out to arrange for the dispatch of ships in search of his daughter.

Gahan read the concern upon the face of The Warlord. "Forgive me if I intrude, John Carter," he said. "I but came to ask the indulgence of another day since it would be fool-hardy to attempt to navigate a ship in such a storm."

"Remain, Gahan, a welcome guest until you choose to leave us," replied The Warlord; "but you must forgive any seeming inattention upon the part of Helium until my daughter is restored to us."

"You daughter! Restored! What do you mean?" exclaimed the Gatholian. "I do not understand."

"She is gone, together with her light flier. That is all we know. We can only assume that she decided to fly before the morning meal and was caught in the clutches of the tempest. You will pardon me, Gahan, if I leave you abruptly—I am arranging to send ships in search of her;" but Gahan, Jed of Gathol, was already speeding in the direction of the palace gate. There he leaped upon a waiting thoat and followed by two warriors in the metal of Gathol, he dashed through the avenues of Helium toward the palace that had been set aside for his entertainment.

Chapter 3

The Headless Humans

Above the roof of the palace that housed the Jed of Gathol and his entourage, the cruiser Vanator tore at her stout moorings. The groaning tackle bespoke the mad fury of the gale, while the worried faces of those members of the crew whose duties demanded their presence on the straining craft gave corroborative evidence of the gravity of the situation. Only stout lashings prevented these men from being swept from the deck, while those upon the roof below were constantly compelled to cling to rails and stanchions to save themselves from being carried away by each new burst of meteoric fury. Upon the prow of the Vanator was painted the device of Gathol, but no pennants were displayed in the upper works since the storm had carried away several in rapid succession, just as it seemed to the watching men that it must carry away the ship itself. They could not believe that any tackle could withstand for long this Titanic force. To each of the twelve lashings clung a brawny warrior with drawn short-sword. Had but a single mooring given to the power of the tempest eleven short-swords would have cut the others; since, partially moored, the ship was doomed, while free in the tempest it stood at least some slight chance for life.

"By the blood of Issus, I believe they will hold!" screamed one warrior to another.

"And if they do not hold may the spirits of our ancestors reward the brave warriors upon the Vanator," replied another of those upon the roof of the palace, "for it will not be long from the moment her cables part before her crew dons the leather of the dead; but yet, Tanus, I believe they will hold. Give thanks at least that we did not sail before the tempest fell, since now each of us has a chance to live."

"Yes," replied Tanus, "I should hate to be abroad today upon the stoutest ship that sails the Barsoomian sky."

It was then that Gahan the Jed appeared upon the roof. With him were the balance of his own party and a dozen warriors of Helium. The young chief turned to his followers.

"I sail at once upon the Vanator," he said, "in search of Tara of Helium who is thought to have been carried away upon a one-man flier by the storm. I do not need to explain to you the slender chances the Vanator has to withstand the fury of the tempest, nor will I order you to your deaths. Let those who wish remain behind without dishonour. The others will follow me," and he leaped for the rope ladder that lashed wildly in the gale.

The first man to follow him was Tanus and when the last reached the deck of the cruiser there remained upon the palace roof only the twelve warriors of Helium, who, with naked swords, had taken the posts of the Gatholians at the moorings.

Not a single warrior who had remained aboard the Vanator would leave her now.

"I expected no less," said Gahan, as with the help of those already on the deck he and the others found secure lashings. The commander of the Vanator shook his head. He loved his trim craft, the pride of her class in the little navy of Gathol. It was of her he thought—not of himself. He saw her lying torn and twisted upon the ochre vegetation of some distant sea-bottom, to be presently overrun and looted by some savage, green horde. He looked at Gahan.

"Are you ready, San Tothis?" asked the jed.

"All is ready."

"Then cut away!"

Word was passed across the deck and over the side to the Heliumetic warriors below that at the third gun they were to cut away. Twelve keen swords must strike simultaneously and with equal power, and each must sever completely and instantly three strands of heavy cable that no loose end fouling a block bring immediate disaster upon the Vanator.

Boom! The voice of the signal gun rolled down through the screaming wind to the twelve warriors upon the roof. Boom! Twelve swords were raised above twelve brawny shoulders. Boom! Twelve keen edges severed twelve complaining moorings, clean and as one.

The Vanator, her propellers whirling, shot forward with the storm. The tempest struck her in the stern as with a mailed fist and stood the great ship upon her nose, and then it caught her and spun her as a child's top spins; and upon the palace roof the twelve men looked on in silent helplessness and prayed for the souls of the brave warriors who were going to their death. And others saw, from Helium's lofty landing stages and from a thousand hangars upon a thousand roofs; but only for an instant did the preparations stop that would send other brave men into the frightful maelstrom of that apparently hopeless search, for such is the courage of the warriors of Barsoom.

But the Vanator did not fall to the ground, within sight of the city at least, though as long as the watchers could see her never for an instant did she rest upon an even keel. Sometimes she lay upon one side or the other, or again she hurtled along keel up, or rolled over and over, or stood upon her nose or her tail at the caprice of the great force that carried her along. And the watchers saw that this great ship was merely being blown away with the other bits of debris great and small that filled the sky. Never in the memory of man or the annals of recorded history had such a storm raged across the face of Barsoom.

And in another instant was the Vanator forgotten as the lofty, scarlet tower that had marked Lesser Helium for ages crashed to ground, carrying death and demolition upon the city beneath. Panic reigned. A fire broke out in the ruins. The city's every force seemed crippled, and it was then that The Warlord ordered the men that were about to set forth in search of Tara of Helium to devote their energies to the salvation of the city, for he too had witnessed the start of the Vanator and realized the futility of wasting men who were needed sorely if Lesser Helium was to be saved from utter destruction.

Shortly after noon of the second day the storm commenced to abate, and before the sun went down, the little craft upon which Tara of Helium had hovered between life and death these many hours drifted slowly before a gentle breeze above a landscape of rolling hills that once had been lofty mountains upon a Martian continent. The girl was exhausted from loss of sleep, from lack of food and drink, and from the nervous reaction consequent to the terrifying experiences through which she had passed. In the near distance, just topping an intervening hill, she caught a momentary glimpse of what appeared to be a dome-capped tower. Quickly she dropped the flier until the hill shut it off from the view of the possible occupants of the structure she had seen. The tower meant to her the habitation of man, suggesting the presence of water and, perhaps, of food. If the tower was the deserted relic of a bygone age she would scarcely find food there, but there was still a chance that there might be water. If it was inhabited, then must her approach be cautious, for only enemies might be expected to abide in so far distant a land. Tara of Helium knew that she must be far from the twin cities of her grandfather's empire, but had she guessed within even a thousand haads of the reality, she had been stunned by realization of the utter hopelessness of her state.

Keeping the craft low, for the buoyancy tanks were still intact, the girl skimmed the ground until the gently-moving wind had carried her to the side of the last hill that intervened between her and the structure she had thought a man-built tower. Here she brought the flier to the ground among some stunted trees, and dragging it beneath one where it might be somewhat hidden from craft passing above, she made it fast and set forth to reconnoitre. Like most women of her class she was armed only with a single slender blade, so that in such an emergency as now confronted her she must depend almost solely upon her cleverness in remaining undiscovered by enemies. With utmost caution she crept warily toward the crest of the hill, taking advantage of every natural screen that the landscape afforded to conceal her approach from possible observers ahead, while momentarily she cast quick glances rearward lest she be taken by surprise from that quarter.

She came at last to the summit, where, from the concealment of a low bush, she could see what lay beyond. Beneath her spread a beautiful valley surrounded by low hills. Dotting it were numerous circular towers, dome-capped, and surrounding each tower was a stone wall enclosing several acres of ground. The valley appeared to be in a high state of cultivation. Upon the opposite side of the hill and just beneath her was a tower and enclosure. It was the roof of the former that had first attracted her attention. In all respects it seemed identical in construction with those further out in the valley—a high, plastered wall of massive construction surrounding a similarly constructed tower, upon whose grey surface was painted in vivid colours a strange device. The towers were about forty sofads in diameter, approximately forty earth-feet, and sixty in height to the base of the dome. To an Earth man they would have immediately suggested the silos in which dairy farmers store ensilage for their herds; but closer scrutiny, revealing an occasional embrasured opening together with the strange construction of the domes, would have altered such a conclusion. Tara of Helium saw that the domes seemed to be faced with innumerable prisms of glass, those that were exposed to the declining sun scintillating so gorgeously as to remind her suddenly of the magnificent trappings of Gahan of Gathol. As she thought of the man she shook her head angrily, and moved cautiously forward a foot or two that she might get a less obstructed view of the nearer tower and its enclosure.

As Tara of Helium looked down into the enclosure surrounding the nearest tower, her brows contracted momentarily in frowning surprise, and then her eyes went wide in an expression of incredulity tinged with horror, for what she saw was a score or two of human bodies—naked and headless. For a long moment she watched, breathless; unable to believe the evidence of her own eyes—that these gruesome things moved and had life! She saw them crawling about on hands and knees over and across one another, searching about with their fingers. And she saw some of them at troughs, for which the others seemed to be searching, and those at the troughs were taking something from these receptacles and apparently putting it in a hole where their necks should have been. They were not far beneath her— she could see them distinctly and she saw that there were the bodies of both men and women, and that they were beautifully proportioned, and that their skin was similar to hers, but of a slightly lighter red. At first she had thought that she was looking upon a shambles and that the bodies, but recently decapitated, were moving under the impulse of muscular reaction; but presently she realized that this was their normal condition. The horror of them fascinated her, so that she could scarce take her eyes from them. It was evident from their groping hands that they were eyeless, and their sluggish movements suggested a rudimentary nervous system and a correspondingly minute brain. The girl wondered how they subsisted for she could not, even by the wildest stretch of imagination, picture these imperfect creatures as intelligent tillers of the soil. Yet that the soil of the valley was tilled was evident and that these things had food was equally so. But who tilled the soil? Who kept and fed these unhappy things, and for what purpose? It was an enigma beyond her powers of deduction.

The sight of food aroused again a consciousness of her own gnawing hunger and the thirst that parched her throat. She could see both food and water within the enclosure; but would she dare enter even should she find means of ingress? She doubted it, since the very thought of possible contact with these gruesome creatures sent a shudder through her frame.

Then her eyes wandered again out across the valley until presently they picked out what appeared to be a tiny stream winding its way through the centre of the farm lands—a strange sight upon Barsoom. Ah, if it were but water! Then might she hope with a real hope, for the fields would give her sustenance which she could gain by night, while by day she hid among the surrounding hills, and sometime, yes, sometime she knew, the searchers would come, for John Carter, Warlord of Barsoom, would never cease to search for his daughter until every square haad of the planet had been combed again and again. She knew him and she knew the warriors of Helium and so she knew that could she but manage to escape harm until they came, they would indeed come at last.

She would have to wait until dark before she dare venture into the valley, and in the meantime she thought it well to search out a place of safety nearby where she might be reasonably safe from savage beasts. It was possible that the district was free from carnivora, but one might never be sure in a strange land. As she was about to withdraw be hind the brow of the hill her attention was again attracted to the enclosure below. Two figures had emerged from the tower. Their beautiful bodies seemed identical with those of the headless creatures among which they moved, but the newcomers were not headless. Upon their shoulders were heads that seemed human, yet which the girl intuitively sensed were not human. They were just a trifle too far away for her to see them distinctly in the waning light of the dying day, but she knew that they were too large, they were out of proportion to the perfectly proportioned bodies, and they were oblate in form. She could see that the men wore some manner of harness to which were slung the customary long-sword and short-sword of the Barsoomian warrior, and that about their short necks were massive leather collars cut to fit closely over the shoulders and snugly to the lower part of the head. Their features were scarce discernible, but there was a suggestion of grotesqueness about them that carried to her a feeling of revulsion.

The two carried a long rope to which were fastened, at intervals of about two sofads, what she later guessed were light manacles, for she saw the warriors passing among the poor creatures in the enclosure and about the right wrist of each they fastened one of the manacles. When all had been thus fastened to the rope one of the warriors commenced to pull and tug at the loose end as though attempting to drag the headless company toward the tower, while the other went among them with a long, light whip with which he flicked them upon the naked skin. Slowly, dully, the creatures rose to their feet and between the tugging of the warrior in front and the lashing of him behind the hopeless band was finally herded within the tower. Tara of Helium shuddered as she turned away. What manner of creatures were these?

Suddenly it was night. The Barsoomian day had ended, and then the brief period of twilight that renders the transition from daylight to darkness almost as abrupt as the switching off of an electric light, and Tara of Helium had found no sanctuary. But perhaps there were no beasts to fear, or rather to avoid—Tara of Helium liked not the word fear. She would have been glad, however, had there been a cabin, even a very tiny cabin, upon her small flier; but there was no cabin. The interior of the hull was completely taken up by the buoyancy tanks. Ah, she had it! How stupid of her not to have thought of it before! She could moor the craft to the tree beneath which it rested and let it rise the length of the rope. Lashed to the deck rings she would then be safe from any roaming beast of prey that chanced along. In the morning she could drop to the ground again before the craft was discovered.

As Tara of Helium crept over the brow of the hill down toward the valley, her presence was hidden by the darkness of the night from the sight of any chance observer who might be loitering by a window in the nearby tower. Cluros, the farther moon, was just rising above the horizon to commence his leisurely journey through the heavens. Eight zodes later he would set—a trifle over nineteen and a half Earth hours—and during that time Thuria, his vivacious mate, would have circled the planet twice and be more than half way around on her third trip. She had but just set. It would be more than three and a half hours before she shot above the opposite horizon to hurtle, swift and low, across the face of the dying planet. During this temporary absence of the mad moon Tara of Helium hoped to find both food and water, and gain again the safety of her flier's deck.

She groped her way through the darkness, giving the tower and its enclosure as wide a berth as possible. Sometimes she stumbled, for in the long shadows cast by the rising Cluros objects were grotesquely distorted though the light from the moon was still not sufficient to be of much assistance to her. Nor, as a matter of fact, did she want light. She could find the stream in the dark, by the simple expedient of going down hill until she walked into it and she had seen that bearing trees and many crops grew throughout the valley, so that she would pass food in plenty ere she reached the stream. If the moon showed her the way more clearly and thus saved her from an occasional fall, he would, too, show her more clearly to the strange denizens of the towers, and that, of course, must not be. Could she have waited until the following night conditions would have been better, since Cluros would not appear in the heavens at all and so, during Thuria's absence, utter darkness would reign; but the pangs of thirst and the gnawing of hunger could be endured no longer with food and drink both in sight, and so she had decided to risk discovery rather than suffer longer.

Safely past the nearest tower, she moved as rapidly as she felt consistent with safety, choosing her way wherever possible so that she might take advantage of the shadows of the trees that grew at intervals and at the same time discover those which bore fruit. In this latter she met with almost immediate success, for the very third tree beneath which she halted was heavy with ripe fruit. Never, thought Tara of Helium, had aught so delicious impinged upon her palate, and yet it was naught else than the almost tasteless usa, which is considered to be palatable only after having been cooked and highly spiced. It grows easily with little irrigation and the trees bear abundantly. The fruit, which ranks high in food value, is one of the staple foods of the less well-to-do, and because of its cheapness and nutritive value forms one of the principal rations of both armies and navies upon Barsoom, a use which has won for it a Martian sobriquet which, freely translated into English, would be, The Fighting Potato. The girl was wise enough to eat but sparingly, but she filled her pocket-pouch with the fruit before she continued upon her way.

Two towers she passed before she came at last to the stream, and here again was she temperate, drinking but little and that very slowly, contenting herself with rinsing her mouth frequently and bathing her face, her hands, and her feet; and even though the night was cold, as Martian nights are, the sensation of refreshment more than compensated for the physical discomfort of the low temperature. Replacing her sandals she sought among the growing track near the stream for whatever edible berries or tubers might be planted there, and found a couple of varieties that could be eaten raw. With these she replaced some of the usa in her pocket-pouch, not only to insure a variety but because she found them more palatable. Occasionally she returned to the stream to drink, but each time moderately. Always were her eyes and ears alert for the first signs of danger, but she had neither seen nor heard aught to disturb her. And presently the time approached when she felt she must return to her flier lest she be caught in the revealing light of low swinging Thuria. She dreaded leaving the water for she knew that she must become very thirsty before she could hope to come again to the stream. If she only had some little receptacle in which to carry water, even a small amount would tide her over until the following night; but she had nothing and so she must content herself as best she could with the juices of the fruit and tubers she had gathered.

After a last drink at the stream, the longest and deepest she had allowed herself, she rose to retrace her steps toward the hills; but even as she did so she became suddenly tense with apprehension. What was that? She could have sworn that she saw something move in the shadows beneath a tree not far away. For a long minute the girl did not move—she scarce breathed. Her eyes remained fixed upon the dense shadows below the tree, her ears strained through the silence of the night. A low moaning came down from the hills where her flier was hidden. She knew it well—the weird note of the hunting banth. And the great carnivore lay directly in her path. But he was not so close as this other thing, hiding there in the shadows just a little way off. What was it? It was the strain of uncertainty that weighed heaviest upon her. Had she known the nature of the creature lurking there half its menace would have vanished. She cast quickly about her in search of some haven of refuge should the thing prove dangerous.

Again arose the moaning from the hills, but this time closer. Almost immediately it was answered from the opposite side of the valley, behind her, and then from the distance to the right of her, and twice upon her left. Her eyes had found a tree, quite near. Slowly, and without taking her eyes from the shadows of that other tree, she moved toward the overhanging branches that might afford her sanctuary in the event of need, and at her first move a low growl rose from the spot she had been watching and she heard the sudden moving of a big body. Simultaneously the creature shot into the moonlight in full charge upon her, its tail erect, its tiny ears laid flat, its great mouth with its multiple rows of sharp and powerful fangs already yawning for its prey, its ten legs carrying it forward in great leaps, and now from the beast's throat issued the frightful roar with which it seeks to paralyze its prey. It was a banth—the great, maned lion of Barsoom. Tara of Helium saw it coming and leaped for the tree toward which she had been moving, and the banth realized her intention and redoubled his speed. As his hideous roar awakened the echoes in the hills, so too it awakened echoes in the valley; but these echoes came from the living throats of others of his kind, until it seemed to the girl that Fate had thrown her into the midst of a countless multitude of these savage beasts.

Almost incredibly swift is the speed of a charging banth, and fortunate it was that the girl had not been caught farther in the open. As it was, her margin of safety was next to negligible, for as she swung nimbly to the lower branches the creature in pursuit of her crashed among the foliage almost upon her as it sprang upward to seize her. It was only a combination of good fortune and agility that saved her. A stout branch deflected the raking talons of the carnivore, but so close was the call that a giant forearm brushed her flesh in the instant before she scrambled to the higher branches.

Baffled, the banth gave vent to his rage and disappointment in a series of frightful roars that caused the very ground to tremble, and to these were added the roarings and the growlings and the moanings of his fellows as they approached from every direction, in the hope of wresting from him whatever of his kill they could take by craft or prowess. And now he turned snarling upon them as they circled the tree, while the girl, huddled in a crotch above them, looked down upon the gaunt, yellow monsters padding on noiseless feet in a restless circle about her. She wondered now at the strange freak of fate that had permitted her to come down this far into the valley by night unharmed, but even more she wondered how she was to return to the hills. She knew that she would not dare venture it by night and she guessed, too, that by day she might be confronted by even graver perils. To depend upon this valley for sustenance she now saw to be beyond the pale of possibility because of the banths that would keep her from food and water by night, while the dwellers in the towers would doubtless make it equally impossible for her to forage by day. There was but one solution of her difficulty and that was to return to her flier and pray that the wind would waft her to some less terrorful land; but when might she return to the flier? The banths gave little evidence of relinquishing hope of her, and even if they wandered out of sight would she dare risk the attempt? She doubted it.

Hopeless indeed seemed her situation—hopeless it was.

CHAPTER 4

Captured

As Thuria, swift racer of the night, shot again into the sky the scene changed. As by magic a new aspect fell athwart the face of Nature. It was as though in the instant one had been transported from one planet to another. It was the age-old miracle of the Martian nights that is always new, even to Martians—two moons resplendent in the heavens, where one had been but now; conflicting, fast-changing shadows that altered the very hills themselves; far Cluros, stately, majestic, almost stationary, shedding his steady light upon the world below; Thuria, a great and glorious orb, swinging swift across the vaulted dome of the blue-black night, so low that she seemed to graze the hills, a gorgeous spectacle that held the girl now beneath the spell of its enchantment as it always had and always would.

"Ah, Thuria, mad queen of heaven!" murmured Tara of Helium. "The hills pass in stately procession, their bosoms rising and falling; the trees move in restless circles; the little grasses describe their little arcs; and all is movement, restless, mysterious movement without sound, while Thuria passes." The girl sighed and let her gaze fall again to the stern realities beneath. There was no mystery in the huge banths. He who had discovered her squatted there looking hungrily up at her. Most of the others had wandered away in search of other prey, but a few remained hoping yet to bury their fangs in that soft body.

The night wore on. Again Thuria left the heavens to her lord and master, hurrying on to keep her tryst with the Sun in other skies. But a single banth waited impatiently beneath the tree which harboured Tara of Helium. The others had left, but their roars, and growls, and moans thundered or rumbled, or floated back to her from near and far. What prey found they in this little valley? There must be something that they were accustomed to find here that they should be drawn in so great numbers. The girl wondered what it could be.

How long the night! Numb, cold, and exhausted, Tara of Helium clung to the tree in growing desperation, for once she had dozed and almost fallen. Hope was low in her brave little heart. How much more could she endure? She asked herself the question and then, with a brave shake of her head, she squared her shoulders. "I still live!" she said aloud.

The banth looked up and growled.

Came Thuria again and after awhile the great Sun—a flaming lover, pursuing his heart's desire. And Cluros, the cold husband, continued his serene way, as placid as before his house had been violated by this hot Lothario. And now the Sun and both Moons rode together in the sky, lending their far mysteries to make weird the Martian dawn. Tara of Helium looked out across the fair valley that spread upon all sides of her. It was rich and beautiful, but even as she looked upon it she shuddered, for to her mind came a picture of the headless things that the towers and the walls hid. Those by day and the banths by night! Ah, was it any wonder that she shuddered?

With the coming of the Sun the great Barsoomian lion rose to his feet. He turned angry eyes upon the girl above him, voiced a single ominous growl, and slunk away toward the hills. The girl watched him, and she saw that he gave the towers as wide a berth as possible and that he never took his eyes from one of them while he was passing it. Evidently the inmates had taught these savage creatures to respect them. Presently he passed from sight in a narrow defile, nor in any direction that she could see was there another. Momentarily at least the landscape was deserted. The girl wondered if she dared to attempt to regain the hills and her flier. She dreaded the coming of the workmen to the fields as she was sure they would come. She shrank from again seeing the headless bodies, and found herself wondering if these things would come out into the fields and work. She looked toward the nearest tower. There was no sign of life there. The valley lay quiet now and deserted. She lowered herself stiffly to the ground. Her muscles were cramped and every move brought a twinge of pain. Pausing a moment to drink again at the stream she felt refreshed and then turned without more delay toward the hills. To cover the distance as quickly as possible seemed the only plan to pursue. The trees no longer offered concealment and so she did not go out of her way to be near them. The hills seemed very far away. She had not thought, the night before, that she had travelled so far. Really it had not been far, but now, with the three towers to pass in broad daylight, the distance seemed great indeed.

The second tower lay almost directly in her path. To make a detour would not lessen the chance of detection, it would only lengthen the period of her danger, and so she laid her course straight for the hill where her flier was, regardless of the tower. As she passed the first enclosure she thought that she heard the sound of movement within, but the gate did not open and she breathed more easily when it lay behind her. She came then to the second enclosure, the outer wall of which she must circle, as it lay across her route. As she passed close along it she distinctly heard not only movement within, but voices. In the world-language of Barsoom she heard a man issuing instructions—so many were to pick usa, so many were to irrigate this field, so many to cultivate that, and so on, as a foreman lay out the day's work for his crew.

Tara of Helium had just reached the gate in the outer wall. Without warning it swung open toward her. She saw that for a moment it would hide her from those within and in that moment she turned and ran, keeping close to the wall, until, passing out of sight beyond the curve of the structure, she came to the opposite side of the enclosure. Here, panting from her exertion and from the excitement of her narrow escape, she threw herself among some tall weeds that grew close to the foot of the wall. There she lay trembling for some time, not even daring to raise her head and look about. Never before had Tara of Helium felt the paralyzing effects of terror. She was shocked and angry at herself, that she, daughter of John Carter, Warlord of Barsoom, should exhibit fear. Not even the fact that there had been none there to witness it lessened her shame and anger, and the worst of it was she knew that under similar circumstances she would again be equally as craven. It was not the fear of death—she knew that. No, it was the thought of those headless bodies and that she might see them and that they might even touch her—lay hands upon her—seize her. She shuddered and trembled at the thought.

After a while she gained sufficient command of herself to raise her head and look about. To her horror she discovered that everywhere she looked she saw people working in the fields or preparing to do so. Workmen were coming from other towers. Little bands were passing to this field and that. They were even some already at work within thirty ads of her—about a hundred yards. There were ten, perhaps, in the party nearest her, both men and women, and all were beautiful of form and grotesque of face. So meagre were their trappings that they were practically naked; a fact that was in no way remarkable among the tillers of the fields of Mars. Each wore the peculiar, high leather collar that completely hid the neck, and each wore sufficient other leather to support a single sword and a pocket-pouch. The leather was very old and worn, showing long, hard service, and was absolutely plain with the exception of a single device upon the left shoulder. The heads, however, were covered with ornaments of precious metals and jewels, so that little more than eyes, nose, and mouth were discernible. These were hideously inhuman and yet grotesquely human at the same time. The eyes were far apart and protruding, the nose scarce more than two small, parallel slits set vertically above a round hole that was the mouth. The heads were peculiarly repulsive—so much so that it seemed unbelievable to the girl that they formed an integral part of the beautiful bodies below them.

So fascinated was Tara of Helium that she could scarce take her eyes from the strange creatures—a fact that was to prove her undoing, for in order that she might see them she was forced to expose a part of her own head and presently, to her consternation, she saw that one of the creatures had stopped his work and was staring directly at her. She did not dare move, for it was still possible that the thing had not seen her, or at least was only suspicious that some creature lay hid among the weeds. If she could allay this suspicion by remaining motionless the creature might believe that he had been mistaken and return to his work; but, alas, such was not to be the case. She saw the thing call the attention of others to her and almost immediately four or five of them started to move in her direction.

It was impossible now to escape discovery. Her only hope lay in flight. If she could elude them and reach the hills and the flier ahead of them she might escape, and that could be accomplished in but one way—flight, immediate and swift. Leaping to her feet she darted along the base of the wall which she must skirt to the opposite side, beyond which lay the hill that was her goal. Her act was greeted by strange whistling sounds from the things behind her, and casting a glance over her shoulder she saw them all in rapid pursuit.

There were also shrill commands that she halt, but to these she paid no attention. Before she had half circled the enclosure she discovered that her chances for successful escape were great, since it was evident to her that her pursuers were not so fleet as she. High indeed then were her hopes as she came in sight of the hill, but they were soon dashed by what lay before her, for there, in the fields that lay between, were fully a hundred creatures similar to those behind her and all were on the alert, evidently warned by the whistling of their fellows. Instructions and commands were shouted to and fro, with the result that those before her spread roughly into a great half circle to intercept her, and when she turned to the right, hoping to elude the net, she saw others coming from fields beyond, and to the left the same was true. But Tara of Helium would not admit defeat. Without once pausing she turned directly toward the centre of the advancing semi-circle, beyond which lay her single chance of escape, and as she ran she drew her long, slim dagger. Like her valiant sire, if die she must, she would die fighting. There were gaps in the thin line confronting her and toward the widest of one of these she directed her course. The things on either side of the opening guessed her intent for they closed in to place themselves in her path. This widened the openings on either side of them and as the girl appeared almost to rush into their arms she turned suddenly at right angles, ran swiftly in the new direction for a few yards, and then dashed quickly toward the hill again. Now only a single warrior, with a wide gap on either side of him, barred her clear way to freedom, though all the others were speeding as rapidly as they could to intercept her. If she could pass this one without too much delay she could escape, of that she was certain. Her every hope hinged on this. The creature before her realized it, too, for he moved cautiously, though swiftly, to intercept her, as a Rugby fullback might manoeuvre in the realization that he alone stood between the opposing team and a touchdown.

At first Tara of Helium had hoped that she might dodge him, for she could not but guess that she was not only more fleet but infinitely more agile than these strange creatures; but soon there came to her the realization that in the time consumed in an attempt to elude his grasp his nearer fellows would be upon her and escape then impossible, so she chose instead to charge straight for him, and when he guessed her decision he stood, half crouching and with outstretched arms, awaiting her. In one hand was his sword, but a voice arose, crying in tones of authority. "Take her alive! Do not harm her!" Instantly the fellow returned his sword to its scabbard and then Tara of Helium was upon him. Straight for that beautiful body she sprang and in the instant that the arms closed to seize her her sharp blade drove deep into the naked chest. The impact hurled them both to the ground and as Tara of Helium sprang to her feet again she saw, to her horror, that the loathsome head had rolled from the body and was now crawling away from her on six short, spider-like legs. The body struggled spasmodically and lay still. As brief as had been the delay caused by the encounter, it still had been of sufficient duration to undo her, for even as she rose two more of the things fell upon her and instantly thereafter she was surrounded. Her blade sank once more into naked flesh and once more a head rolled free and crawled away. Then they overpowered her and in another moment she was surrounded by fully a hundred of the creatures, all seeking to lay hands upon her. At first she thought that they wished to tear her to pieces in revenge for her having slain two of their fellows, but presently she realized that they were prompted more by curiosity than by any sinister motive.

"Come!" said one of her captors, both of whom had retained a hold upon her. As he spoke he tried to lead her away with him toward the nearest tower.

"She belongs to me," cried the other. "Did not I capture her? She will come with me to the tower of Moak."

"Never!" insisted the first. "She is Luud's. To Luud I will take her, and whosoever interferes may feel the keenness of my sword—in the head!" He almost shouted the last three words.

"Come! Enough of this," cried one who spoke with some show of authority. "She was captured in Luud's fields—she will go to Luud."

"She was discovered in Moak's fields, at the very foot of the tower of Moak," insisted he who had claimed her for Moak.

"You have heard the Nolach speak," cried the Luud. "It shall be as he says."

"Not while this Moak holds a sword," replied the other. "Rather will I cut her in twain and take my half to Moak than to relinquish her all to Luud," and he drew his sword, or rather he laid his hand upon its hilt in a threatening gesture; but before ever he could draw it the Luud had whipped his out and with a fearful blow cut deep into the head of his adversary. Instantly the big, round head collapsed, almost as a punctured balloon collapses, as a greyish, semi-fluid matter spurted from it. The protruding eyes, apparently lidless, merely stared, the sphincter-like muscle of the mouth opened and closed, and then the head toppled from the body to the ground. The body stood dully for a moment and then slowly started to wander aimlessly about until one of the others seized it by the arm.

One of the two heads crawling about on the ground now approached. "This rykor belongs to Moak," it said. "I am a Moak. I will take it," and without further discussion it commenced to crawl up the front of the headless body, using its six short, spider-like legs and two stout chelae which grew just in front of its legs and strongly resembled those of an Earthly lobster, except that they were both of the same size. The body in the meantime stood in passive indifference, its arms hanging idly at its sides. The head climbed to the shoulders and settled itself inside the leather collar that now hid its chelae and legs. Almost immediately the body gave evidence of intelligent animation. It raised its hands and adjusted the collar more comfortably, it took the head between its palms and settled it in place and when it moved around it did not wander aimlessly, but instead its steps were firm and to some purpose.

The girl watched all these things in growing wonder, and presently, no other of the Moaks seeming inclined to dispute the right of the Luud to her, she was led off by her captor toward the nearest tower. Several accompanied them, including one who carried the loose head under his arm. The head that was being carried conversed with the head upon the shoulders of the thing that carried it. Tara of Helium shivered. It was horrible! All that she had seen of these frightful creatures was horrible. And to be a prisoner, wholly in their power. Shadow of her first ancestor! What had she done to deserve so cruel a fate?

At the wall enclosing the tower they paused while one opened the gate and then they passed within the enclosure, which, to the girl's horror, she found filled with headless bodies. The creature who carried the bodiless head now set its burden upon the ground and the latter immediately crawled toward one of the bodies that was lying near by. Some wandered stupidly to and fro, but this one lay still. It was a female. The head crawled to it and made its way to the shoulders where it settled itself. At once the body sprang lightly erect. Another of those who had accompanied them from the fields approached with the harness and collar that had been taken from the dead body that the head had formerly topped. The new body now appropriated these and the hands deftly adjusted them. The creature was now as good as before Tara of Helium had struck down its former body with her slim blade. But there was a difference. Before it had been male—now it was female. That, however, seemed to make no difference to the head. In fact, Tara of Helium had noticed during the scramble and the fight about her that sex differences seemed of little moment to her captors. Males and females had taken equal part in her pursuit, both were identically harnessed and both carried swords, and she had seen as many females as males draw their weapons at the moment that a quarrel between the two factions seemed imminent.

The girl was given but brief opportunity for further observation of the pitiful creatures in the enclosure as her captor, after having directed the others to return to the fields, led her toward the tower, which they entered, passing into an apartment about ten feet wide and twenty long, in one end of which was a stairway leading to an upper level and in the other an opening to a similar stairway leading downward. The chamber, though on a level with the ground, was brilliantly lighted by windows in its inner wall, the light coming from a circular court in the centre of the tower. The walls of this court appeared to be faced with what resembled glazed, white tile and the whole interior of it was flooded with dazzling light, a fact which immediately explained to the girl the purpose of the glass prisms of which the domes were constructed. The stairways themselves were sufficient to cause remark, since in nearly all Barsoomian architecture inclined runways are utilized for purposes of communication between different levels, and especially is this true of the more ancient forms and of those of remote districts where fewer changes have come to alter the customs of antiquity.

Down the stairway her captor led Tara of Helium. Down and down through chambers still lighted from the brilliant well. Occasionally they passed others going in the opposite direction and these always stopped to examine the girl and ask questions of her captor.

"I know nothing but that she was found in the fields and that I caught her after a fight in which she slew two rykors and in which I slew a Moak, and that I take her to Luud, to whom, of course, she belongs. If Luud wishes to question her that is for Luud to do—not for me." Thus always he answered the curious.

Presently they reached a room from which a circular tunnel led away from the tower, and into this the creature conducted her. The tunnel was some seven feet in diameter and flattened on the bottom to form a walk. For a hundred feet from the tower it was lined with the same tile-like material of the light well and amply illuminated by reflected light from that source. Beyond it was faced with stone of various shapes and sizes, neatly cut and fitted together—a very fine mosaic without a pattern. There were branches, too, and other tunnels which crossed this, and occasionally openings not more than a foot in diameter; these latter being usually close to the floor. Above each of these smaller openings was painted a different device, while upon the walls of the larger tunnels at all intersections and points of convergence hieroglyphics appeared. These the girl could not read though she guessed that they were the names of the tunnels, or notices indicating the points to which they led. She tried to study some of them out, but there was not a character that was familiar to her, which seemed strange, since, while the written languages of the various nations of Barsoom differ, it still is true that they have many characters and words in common. She had tried to converse with her guard but he had not seemed inclined to talk with her and she had finally desisted. She could not but note that he had offered her no indignities, nor had he been either unnecessarily rough or in any way cruel. The fact that she had slain two of the bodies with her dagger had apparently aroused no animosity or desire for revenge in the minds of the strange heads that surmounted the bodies—even those whose bodies had been killed. She did not try to understand it, since she could not approach the peculiar relationship between the heads and the bodies of these creatures from the basis of any past knowledge or experience of her own. So far their treatment of her seemed to augur naught that might arouse her fears. Perhaps, after all, she had been fortunate to fall into the hands of these strange people, who might not only protect her from harm, but even aid her in returning to Helium. That they were repulsive and uncanny she could not forget, but if they meant her no harm she could, at least, overlook their repulsiveness. Renewed hope aroused within her a spirit of greater cheerfulness, and it was almost blithely now that she moved at the side of her weird companion. She even caught herself humming a gay little tune that was then popular in Helium. The creature at her side turned its expressionless eyes upon her.

"What is that noise that you are making?" it asked.

"I was but humming an air," she replied.

"'Humming an air,'" he repeated. "I do not know what you mean; but do it again, I like it."

This time she sang the words, while her companion listened intently. His face gave no indication of what was passing in that strange head. It was as devoid of expression as that of a spider. It reminded her of a spider. When she had finished he turned toward her again.

"That was different," he said. "I liked that better, even, than the other. How do you do it?"

"Why," she said, "it is singing. Do you not know what song is?"

"No," he replied. "Tell me how you do it."

"It is difficult to explain," she told him, "since any explanation of it presupposes some knowledge of melody and of music, while your very question indicates that you have no knowledge of either."

"No," he said, "I do not know what you are talking about; but tell me how you do it."

"It is merely the melodious modulations of my voice," she explained. "Listen!" and again she sang.

"I do not understand," he insisted; "but I like it. Could you teach me to do it?"

"I do not know, but I shall be glad to try."

"We will see what Luud does with you," he said. "If he does not want you I will keep you and you shall teach me to make sounds like that."

At his request she sang again as they continued their way along the winding tunnel, which was now lighted by occasional bulbs which appeared to be similar to the radium bulbs with which she was familiar and which were common to all the nations of Barsoom, insofar as she knew, having been perfected at so remote a period that their very origin was lost in antiquity. They consist, usually, of a hemispherical bowl of heavy glass in which is packed a compound containing what, according to John Carter, must be radium. The bowl is then cemented into a metal plate with a heavily insulated back and the whole affair set in the masonry of wall or ceiling as desired, where it gives off light of greater or less intensity, according to the composition of the filling material, for an almost incalculable period of time.

As they proceeded they met a greater number of the inhabitants of this underground world, and the girl noted that among many of these the metal and harness were more ornate than had been those of the workers in the fields above. The heads and bodies, however, were similar, even identical, she thought. No one offered her harm and she was now experiencing a feeling of relief almost akin to happiness, when her guide turned suddenly into an opening on the right side of the tunnel and she found herself in a large, well lighted chamber.

CHAPTER 5

The Perfect Brain

The song that had been upon her lips as she entered died there—frozen by the sight of horror that met her eyes. In the centre of the chamber a headless body lay upon the floor—a body that had been partially devoured—while over and upon it crawled a half a dozen heads upon their short, spider legs, and they tore at the flesh of the woman with their chelae and carried the bits to their awful mouths. They were eating human flesh—eating it raw!

Tara of Helium gasped in horror and turning away covered her eyes with her palms.

"Come!" said her captor. "What is the matter?"

"They are eating the flesh of the woman," she whispered in tones of horror.

"Why not?" he inquired. "Did you suppose that we kept the rykor for labour alone? Ah, no. They are delicious when kept and fattened. Fortunate, too, are those that are bred for food, since they are never called upon to do aught but eat."

"It is hideous!" she cried.

He looked at her steadily for a moment, but whether in surprise, in anger, or in pity his expressionless face did not reveal. Then he led her on across the room past the frightful thing, from which she turned away her eyes. Lying about the floor near the walls were half a dozen headless bodies in harness. These she guessed had been abandoned temporarily by the feasting heads until they again required their services. In the walls of this room there were many of the small, round openings she had noticed in various parts of the tunnels, the purpose of which she could not guess.

They passed through another corridor and then into a second chamber, larger than the first and more brilliantly illuminated. Within were several of the creatures with heads and bodies assembled, while many headless bodies lay about near the walls. Here her captor halted and spoke to one of the occupants of the chamber.

"I seek Luud," he said. "I bring to Luud a creature that I captured in the fields above."

The others crowded about to examine Tara of Helium. One of them whistled, whereupon the girl learned something of the smaller openings in the walls, for almost immediately there crawled from them, like giant spiders, a score or more of the hideous heads. Each sought one of the recumbent bodies and fastened itself in place. Immediately the bodies reacted to the intelligent direction of the heads. They arose, the hands adjusted the leather collars and put the balance of the harness in order, then the creatures crossed the room to where Tara of Helium stood. She noted that their leather was more highly ornamented than that worn by any of the others she had previously seen, and so she guessed that these must be higher in authority than the others. Nor was she mistaken. The demeanour of her captor indicated it. He addressed them as one who holds intercourse with superiors.

Several of those who examined her felt her flesh, pinching it gently between thumb and forefinger, a familiarity that the girl resented. She struck down their hands. "Do not touch me!" she cried, imperiously, for was she not a princess of Helium? The expression on those terrible faces did not change. She could not tell whether they were angry or amused, whether her action had filled them with respect for her, or contempt. Only one of them spoke immediately.

"She will have to be fattened more," he said.

The girl's eyes went wide with horror. She turned upon her captor. "Do these frightful creatures intend to devour me?" she cried.

"That is for Luud to say," he replied, and then he leaned closer so that his mouth was near her ear. "That noise you made which you called song pleased me," he whispered, "and I will repay you by warning you not to antagonize these kaldanes. They are very powerful. Luud listens to them. Do not call them frightful. They are very handsome. Look at their wonderful trappings, their gold, their jewels."

"Thank you," she said. "You called them kaldanes—what does that mean?"

"We are all kaldanes," he replied.

"You, too?" and she pointed at him, her slim finger directed toward his chest.

"No, not this," he explained, touching his body; "this is a rykor; but this," and he touched his head, "is a kaldane. It is the brain, the intellect, the power that directs all things. The rykor," he indicated his body, "is nothing. It is not so much even as the jewels upon our harness; no, not so much as the harness itself. It carries us about. It is true that we would find difficulty getting along without it; but it has less value than harness or jewels because it is less difficult to reproduce." He turned again to the other kaldanes. "Will you notify Luud that I am here?" he asked.

"Sept has already gone to Luud. He will tell him," replied one. "Where did you find this rykor with the strange kaldane that cannot detach itself?"

The girl's captor narrated once more the story of her capture. He stated facts just as they had occurred, without embellishment, his voice as expressionless as his face, and his story was received in the same manner that it was delivered. The creatures seemed totally lacking in emotion, or, at least, the capacity to express it. It was impossible to judge what impression the story made upon them, or even if they heard it. Their protruding eyes simply stared and occasionally the muscles of their mouths opened and closed. Familiarity did not lessen the horror the girl felt for them. The more she saw of them the more repulsive they seemed. Often her body was shaken by convulsive shudders as she looked at the kaldanes, but when her eyes wandered to the beautiful bodies and she could for a moment expunge the heads from her consciousness the effect was soothing and refreshing, though when the bodies lay, headless, upon the floor they were quite as shocking as the heads mounted on bodies. But by far the most gruesome and uncanny sight of all was that of the heads crawling about upon their spider legs. If one of these should approach and touch her Tara of Helium was positive that she should scream, while should one attempt to crawl up her person—ugh! the very idea induced a feeling of faintness.

Sept returned to the chamber. "Luud will see you and the captive. Come!" he said, and turned toward a door opposite that through which Tara of Helium had entered the chamber. "What is your name?" His question was directed to the girl's captor.

"I am Ghek, third foreman of the fields of Luud," he answered.

"And hers?"

"I do not know."

"It makes no difference. Come!"

The patrician brows of Tara of Helium went high. It made no difference, indeed! She, a princess of Helium; only daughter of The Warlord of Barsoom!

"Wait!" she cried. "It makes much difference who I am. If you are conducting me into the presence of your jed you may announce The Princess Tara of Helium, daughter of John Carter, The Warlord of Barsoom."

"Hold your peace!" commanded Sept. "Speak when you are spoken to. Come with me!"

The anger of Tara of Helium all but choked her. "Come," admonished Ghek, and took her by the arm, and Tara of Helium came. She was naught but a prisoner. Her rank and titles meant nothing to these inhuman monsters. They led her through a short, S-shaped passageway into a chamber entirely lined with the white, tile-like material with which the interior of the light wall was faced. Close to the base of the walls were numerous smaller apertures, circular in shape, but larger than those of similar aspect that she had noted elsewhere. The majority of these apertures were sealed. Directly opposite the entrance was one framed in gold, and above it a peculiar device was inlaid in the same precious metal.

Sept and Ghek halted just within the room, the girl between them, and all three stood silently facing the opening in the opposite wall. On the floor beside the aperture lay a headless male body of almost heroic proportions, and on either side of this stood a heavily armed warrior, with drawn sword. For perhaps five minutes the three waited and then something appeared in the opening. It was a pair of large chelae and immediately thereafter there crawled forth a hideous kaldane of enormous proportions. He was half again as large as any that Tara of Helium had yet seen and his whole aspect infinitely more terrible. The skin of the others was a bluish grey—this one was of a little bluer tinge and the eyes were ringed with bands of white and scarlet, as was its mouth.

From each nostril a band of white and one of scarlet extended outward horizontally the width of the face.

No one spoke or moved. The creature crawled to the prostrate body and affixed itself to the neck. Then the two rose as one and approached the girl. He looked at her and then he spoke to her captor.

"You are the third foreman of the fields of Luud?" he asked.

"Yes, Luud; I am called Ghek."

"Tell me what you know of this," and he nodded toward Tara of Helium.

Ghek did as he was bid and then Luud addressed the girl.

"What were you doing within the borders of Bantoom?" he asked.

"I was blown hither in a great storm that injured my flier and carried me I knew not where. I came down into the valley at night for food and drink. The banths came and drove me to the safety of a tree, and then your people caught me as I was trying to leave the valley. I do not know why they took me. I was doing no harm. All I ask is that you let me go my way in peace."

"None who enters Bantoom ever leaves," replied Luud.

"But my people are not at war with yours. I am a princess of Helium; my great-grandfather is a jeddak; my grandfather a jed; and my father is Warlord of all Barsoom. You have no right to keep me and I demand that you liberate me at once."

"None who enters Bantoom ever leaves," repeated the creature without expression. "I know nothing of the lesser creatures of Barsoom, of whom you speak. There is but one high race—the race of Bantoomians. All Nature exists to serve them. You shall do your share, but not yet—you are too skinny. We shall have to put some fat upon it, Sept. I tire of rykor. Perhaps this will have a different flavour. The banths are too rank and it is seldom that any other creature enters the valley. And you, Ghek; you shall be rewarded. I shall promote you from the fields to the burrows. Hereafter you shall remain underground as every Bantoomian longs to. No more shall you be forced to endure the hated sun, or look upon the hideous sky, or the hateful growing things that defile the surface. For the present you shall look after this thing that you have brought me, seeing that it sleeps and eats—and does nothing else. You understand me, Ghek; nothing else!"

"I understand, Luud," replied the other.

"Take it away!" commanded the creature.

Ghek turned and led Tara of Helium from the apartment. The girl was horrified by contemplation of the fate that awaited her—a fate from which it seemed, there was no escape. It was only too evident that these creatures possessed no gentle or chivalric sentiments to which she could appeal, and that she might escape from the labyrinthine mazes of their underground burrows appeared impossible.

Outside the audience chamber Sept overtook them and conversed with Ghek for a brief period, then her keeper led her through a confusing web of winding tunnels until they came to a small apartment.

"We are to remain here for a while. It may be that Luud will send for you again. If he does you will probably not be fattened—he will use you for another purpose." It was fortunate for the girl's peace of mind that she did not realize what he meant. "Sing for me," said Ghek, presently.

Tara of Helium did not feel at all like singing, but she sang, nevertheless, for there was always the hope that she might escape if given the opportunity and if she could win the friendship of one of the creatures, her chances would be increased proportionately. All during the ordeal, for such it was to the overwrought girl, Ghek stood with his eyes fixed upon her.

"It is wonderful," he said, when she had finished; "but I did not tell Luud—you noticed that I did not tell Luud about it. Had he known, he would have had you sing to him and that would have resulted in your being kept with him that he might hear you sing whenever he wished; but now I can have you all the time."

"How do you know he would like my singing?" she asked.

"He would have to," replied Ghek. "If I like a thing he has to like it, for are we not identical—all of us?"

"The people of my race do not all like the same things," said the girl.

"How strange!" commented Ghek. "All kaldanes like the same things and dislike the same things. If I discover something new and like it I know that all kaldanes will like it. That is how I know that Luud would like your singing. You see we are all exactly alike."

"But you do not look like Luud," said the girl.

"Luud is king. He is larger and more gorgeously marked; but otherwise he and I are identical, and why not? Did not Luud produce the egg from which I hatched?" "What?" queried the girl; "I do not understand you."

"Yes," explained Ghek, "all of us are from Luud's eggs, just as all the swarm of Moak are from Moak's eggs."

"Oh!" exclaimed Tara of Helium understandingly; "you mean that Luud has many wives and that you are the offspring of one of them."

"No, not that at all," replied Ghek. "Luud has no wife. He lays the eggs himself. You do not understand."

Tara of Helium admitted that she did not.

"I will try to explain, then," said Ghek, "if you will promise to sing to me later."

"I promise," she said.

"We are not like the rykors," he began. "They are creatures of a low order, like yourself and the banths and such things. We have no sex—not one of us except our king, who is bi-sexual. He produces many eggs from which we, the workers and the warriors, are hatched; and one in every thousand eggs is another king egg, from which a king is hatched. Did you notice the sealed openings in the room where you saw Luud? Sealed in each of those is another king.

If one of them escaped he would fall upon Luud and try to kill him and if he succeeded we should have a new king; but there would be no difference. His name would be Luud and all would go on as before, for are we not all alike? Luud has lived a long time and has produced many kings, so he lets only a few live that there may be a successor to him when he dies. The others he kills."

"Why does he keep more than one?" queried the girl.

"Sometimes accidents occur," replied Ghek, "and all the kings that a swarm has saved are killed. When this happens the swarm comes and obtains another king from a neighbouring swarm."

"Are all of you the children of Luud?" she asked.

"All but a few, who are from the eggs of the preceding king, as was Luud; but Luud has lived a long time and not many of the others are left."

"You live a long time, or short?" Tara asked.

"A very long time."

"And the rykors, too; they live a long time?"

"No; the rykors live for ten years, perhaps," he said, "if they remain strong and useful. When they can no longer be of service to us, either through age or sickness, we leave them in the fields and the banths come at night and get them."

"How horrible!" she exclaimed.

"Horrible?" he repeated. "I see nothing horrible about that. The rykors are but brainless flesh. They neither see, nor feel, nor hear. They can scarce move but for us. If we did not bring them food they would starve to death. They are less deserving of thought than our leather. All that they can do for themselves is to take food from a trough and put it in their mouths, but with us—look at them!" and he proudly exhibited the noble figure that he surmounted, palpitant with life and energy and feeling.

"How do you do it?" asked Tara of Helium. "I do not understand it at all."

"I will show you," he said, and lay down upon the floor. Then he detached himself from the body, which lay as a thing dead. On his spider legs he walked toward the girl. "Now look," he admonished her. "Do you see this thing?" and he extended what appeared to be a bundle of tentacles from the posterior part of his head. "There is an aperture just back of the rykor's mouth and directly over the upper end of his spinal column. Into this aperture I insert my tentacles and seize the spinal cord. Immediately I control every muscle of the rykor's body—it becomes my own, just as you direct the movement of the muscles of your body. I feel what the rykor would feel if he had a head and brain. If he is hurt, I would suffer if I remained connected with him; but the instant one of them is injured or becomes sick we desert it for another. As we would suffer the pains of their physical injuries, similarly do we enjoy the physical pleasures of the rykors. When your body becomes fatigued you are comparatively useless; it is sick, you are sick; if it is killed, you die. You are the slave of a mass of stupid flesh and bone and blood. There is nothing more wonderful about your carcass than there is about the carcass of a banth. It is only your brain that makes you superior to the banth, but your brain is bound by the limitations of your body. Not so, ours. With us brain is everything. Ninety per centum of our volume is brain. We have only the simplest of vital organs and they are very small for they do not have to assist in the support of a complicated system of nerves, muscles, flesh and bone. We have no lungs, for we do not require air. Far below the levels to which we can take the rykors is a vast network of burrows where the real life of the kaldane is lived. There the air-breathing rykor would perish as you would perish. There we have stored vast quantities of food in hermetically sealed chambers. It will last forever. Far beneath the surface is water that will flow for countless ages after the surface water is exhausted. We are preparing for the time we know must come—the time when the last vestige of the Barsoomian atmosphere is spent—when the waters and the food are gone. For this purpose were we created, that there might not perish from the planet Nature's divinest creation—the perfect brain."

"But what purpose can you serve when that time comes?" asked the girl.

"You do not understand," he said. "It is too big for you to grasp, but I will try to explain it. Barsoom, the moons, the sun, the stars, were created for a single purpose. From the beginning of time Nature has laboured arduously toward the consummation of this purpose. At the very beginning things existed with life, but with no brain. Gradually rudimentary nervous systems and minute brains evolved. Evolution proceeded. The brains became larger and more powerful. In us you see the highest development; but there are those of us who believe that there is yet another step—that some time in the far future our race shall develop into the super-thing—just brain. The incubus of legs and chelae and vital organs will be removed. The future kaldane will be nothing but a great brain. Deaf, dumb, and blind it will lie sealed in its buried vault far beneath the surface of Barsoom—just a great, wonderful, beautiful brain with nothing to distract it from eternal thought."

"You mean it will just lie there and think?" cried Tara of Helium.

"Just that!" he exclaimed. "Could aught be more wonderful?"

"Yes," replied the girl, "I can think of a number of things that would be infinitely more wonderful."

Chapter 6

In the Toils of Horror

What the creature had told her gave Tara of Helium food for thought. She had been taught that every created thing fulfilled some useful purpose, and she tried conscientiously to discover just what was the rightful place of the kaldane in the universal scheme of things. She knew that it must have its place but what that place was it was beyond her to conceive. She had to give it up. They recalled to her mind a little group of people in Helium who had forsworn the pleasures of life in the pursuit of knowledge. They were rather patronizing in their relations with those whom they thought not so intellectual. They considered themselves quite superior. She smiled at recollection of a remark her father had once made concerning them, to the effect that if one of them ever dropped his egotism and broke it it would take a week to fumigate Helium. Her father liked normal people—people who knew too little and people who knew too much were equally a bore. Tara of Helium was like her father in this respect and like him, too, she was both sane and normal.

Outside of her personal danger there was much in this strange world that interested her. The rykors aroused her keenest pity, and vast conjecture. How and from what form had they evolved? She asked Ghek.

"Sing to me again and I will tell you," he said. "If Luud would let me have you, you should never die. I should keep you always to sing to me."

The girl marvelled at the effect her voice had upon the creature. Somewhere in that enormous brain there was a chord that was touched by melody. It was the sole link between herself and the brain when detached from the rykor. When it dominated the rykor it might have other human instincts; but these she dreaded even to think of. After she had sung she waited for Ghek to speak. For a long time he was silent, just looking at her through those awful eyes.

"I wonder," he said presently, "if it might not be pleasant to be of your race. Do you all sing?"

"Nearly all, a little," she said; "but we do many other interesting and enjoyable things. We dance and play and work and love and sometimes we fight, for we are a race of warriors."

"Love!" said the kaldane. "I think I know what you mean; but we, fortunately, are above sentiment—when we are detached. But when we dominate the rykor—ah, that is different, and when I hear you sing and look at your beautiful body I know what you mean by love. I could love you."

The girl shrank from him. "You promised to tell me the origin of the rykor," she reminded him.

"Ages ago," he commenced, "our bodies were larger and our heads smaller. Our legs were very weak and we could not travel fast or far. There was a stupid creature that went upon four legs. It lived in a hole in the ground, to which it brought its food, so we ran our burrows into this hole and ate the food it brought; but it did not bring enough for all—for itself and all the kaldanes that lived upon it, so we had also to go abroad and get food. This was hard work for our weak legs. Then it was that we commenced to ride upon the backs of these primitive rykors. It took many ages, undoubtedly, but at last came the time when the kaldane had found means to guide the rykor, until presently the latter depended entirely upon the superior brain of his master to guide him to food. The brain of the rykor grew smaller as time went on. His ears went and his eyes, for he no longer had use for them—the kaldane saw and heard for him. By similar steps the rykor came to go upon its hind feet that the kaldane might be able to see farther. As the brain shrank, so did the head. The mouth was the only feature of the head that was used and so the mouth alone remains. Members of the red race fell into the hands of our ancestors from time to time. They saw the beauties and the advantages of the form that nature had given the red race over that which the rykor was developing into. By intelligent crossing the present rykor was achieved. He is really solely the product of the super-intelligence of the kaldane—he is our body, to do with as we see fit, just as you do what you see fit with your body, only we have the advantage of possessing an unlimited supply of bodies. Do you not wish that you were a kaldane?"

For how long they kept her in the subterranean chamber Tara of Helium did not know. It seemed a very long time. She ate and slept and watched the interminable lines of creatures that passed the entrance to her prison. There was a laden line passing from above carrying food, food, food. In the other line they returned empty handed. When she saw them she knew that it was daylight above. When they did not pass she knew it was night, and that the banths were about devouring the rykors that had been abandoned in the fields the previous day. She commenced to grow pale and thin. She did not like the food they gave her—it was not suited to her kind—nor would she have eaten overmuch palatable food, for the fear of becoming fat. The idea of plumpness had a new significance here—a horrible significance.

Ghek noted that she was growing thin and white. He spoke to her about it and she told him that she could not thrive thus beneath the ground—that she must have fresh air and sunshine, or she would wither and die. Evidently he carried her words to Luud, since it was not long after that he told her that the king had ordered that she be confined in the tower and to the tower she was taken. She had hoped against hope that this very thing might result from her conversation with Ghek. Even to see the sun again was something, but now there sprang to her breast a hope that she had not dared to nurse before, while she lay in the terrible labyrinth from which she knew she could never have found her way to the outer world; but now there was some slight reason to hope. At least she could see the hills and if she could see them might there not come also the opportunity to reach them? If she could have but ten minutes—just ten little minutes! The flier was still there—she knew that it must be. Just ten minutes and she would be free—free forever from this frightful place; but the days wore on and she was never alone, not even for half of ten minutes. Many times she planned her escape. Had it not been for the banths it had been easy of accomplishment by night. Ghek always detached his body then and sank into what seemed a semi-comatose condition. It could not be said that he slept, or at least it did not appear like sleep, since his lidless eyes were unchanged; but he lay quietly in a corner. Tara of Helium enacted a thousand times in her mind the scene of her escape. She would rush to the side of the rykor and seize the sword that hung in its harness. Before Ghek knew what she purposed, she would have this and then before he could give an alarm she would drive the blade through his hideous head. It would take but a moment to reach the enclosure. The rykors could not stop her, for they had no brains to tell them that she was escaping. She had watched from her window the opening and closing of the gate that led from the enclosure out into the fields and she knew how the great latch operated. She would pass through and make a quick dash for the hill. It was so near that they could not overtake her. It was so easy! Or it would have been but for the banths! The banths at night and the workers in the fields by day.

Confined to the tower and without proper exercise or food, the girl failed to show the improvement that her captors desired. Ghek questioned her in an effort to learn why it was that she did not grow round and plump; that she did not even look as well as when they had captured her. His concern was prompted by repeated inquiries on the part of Luud and finally resulted in suggesting to Tara of Helium a plan whereby she might find a new opportunity of escape.

"I am accustomed to walking in the fresh air and the sunlight," she told Ghek. "I cannot become as I was before if I am to be always shut away in this one chamber, breathing poor air and getting no proper exercise. Permit me to go out in the fields every day and walk about while the sun is shining. Then, I am sure, I shall become nice and fat."

"You would run away," he said.

"But how could I if you were always with me?" she asked. "And even if I wished to run away where could I go? I do not know even the direction of Helium. It must be very far. The very first night the banths would get me, would they not?"

"They would," said Ghek. "I will ask Luud about it."

The following day he told her that Luud had said that she was to be taken into the fields. He would try that for a time and see if she improved.

"If you do not grow fatter he will send for you anyway," said Ghek; "but he will not use you for food."

Tara of Helium shuddered.

That day and for many days thereafter she was taken from the tower, through the enclosure and out into the fields. Always was she alert for an opportunity to escape; but Ghek was always close by her side. It was not so much his presence that deterred her from making the attempt as the number of workers that were always between her and the hills where the flier lay. She could easily have eluded Ghek, but there were too many of the others. And then, one day, Ghek told her as he accompanied her into the open that this would be the last time.

"Tonight you go to Luud," he said. "I am sorry as I shall not hear you sing again."

"Tonight!" She scarce breathed the word, yet it was vibrant with horror.

She glanced quickly toward the hills. They were so close! Yet between were the inevitable workers—perhaps a score of them.

"Let us walk over there?" she said, indicating them. "I should like to see what they are doing."

"It is too far," said Ghek. "I hate the sun. It is much pleasanter here where I can stand beneath the shade of this tree."

"All right," she agreed; "then you stay here and I will walk over. It will take me but a minute."

"No," he answered. "I will go with you. You want to escape; but you are not going to."

"I cannot escape," she said.

"I know it," agreed Ghek; "but you might try. I do not wish you to try. Possibly it will be better if we return to the tower at once. It would go hard with me should you escape."

Tara of Helium saw her last chance fading into oblivion. There would never be another after today. She cast about for some pretext to lure him even a little nearer to the hills.

"It is very little that I ask," she said. "Tonight you will want me to sing to you. It will be the last time, if you do not let me go and see what those kaldanes are doing I shall never sing to you again."

Ghek hesitated. "I will hold you by the arm all the time, then," he said.

"Why, of course, if you wish," she assented. "Come!"

The two moved toward the workers and the hills. The little party was digging tubers from the ground. She had noted this and that nearly always they were stooped low over their work, the hideous eyes bent upon the upturned soil. She led Ghek quite close to them, pretending that she wished to see exactly how they did the work, and all the time he held her tightly by her left wrist.

"It is very interesting," she said, with a sigh, and then, suddenly; "Look, Ghek!" and pointed quickly back in the direction of the tower. The kaldane, still holding her turned half away from her to look in the direction she had indicated and simultaneously, with the quickness of a banth, she struck him with her right fist, backed by every ounce of strength she possessed—struck the back of the pulpy head just above the collar. The blow was sufficient to accomplish her design, dislodging the kaldane from its rykor and tumbling it to the ground. Instantly the grasp upon her wrist relaxed as the body, no longer controlled by the brain of Ghek, stumbled aimlessly about for an instant before it sank to its knees and then rolled over on its back; but Tara of Helium waited not to note the full results of her act. The instant the fingers loosened upon her wrist she broke away and dashed toward the hills. Simultaneously a warning whistle broke from Ghek's lips and in instant response the workers leaped to their feet, one almost in the girl's path. She dodged the outstretched arms and was away again toward the hills and freedom, when her foot caught in one of the hoe-like instruments with which the soil had been upturned and which had been left, half imbedded in the ground. For an instant she ran on, stumbling, in a mad effort to regain her equilibrium, but the upturned furrows caught her feet—again she stumbled and this time went down, and as she scrambled to rise again a heavy body fell upon her and seized her arms. A moment later she was surrounded and dragged to her feet and as she looked around she saw Ghek crawling to his prostrate rykor. A moment later he advanced to her side.

The hideous face, incapable of registering emotion, gave no clue to what was passing in the enormous brain. Was he nursing thoughts of anger, of hate, of revenge? Tara of Helium could not guess, nor did she care. The worst had happened. She had tried to escape and she had failed. There would never be another opportunity.

"Come!" said Ghek. "We will return to the tower." The deadly monotone of his voice was unbroken. It was worse than anger, for it revealed nothing of his intentions. It but increased her horror of these great brains that were beyond the possibility of human emotions.

And so she was dragged back to her prison in the tower and Ghek took up his vigil again, squatting by the doorway, but now he carried a naked sword in his hand and did not quit his rykor, only to change to another that he had brought to him when the first gave indications of weariness. The girl sat looking at him. He had not been unkind to her, but she felt no sense of gratitude, nor, on the other hand, any sense of hatred. The brains, incapable themselves of any of the finer sentiments, awoke none in her. She could not feel gratitude, or affection, or hatred of them. There was only the same unceasing sense of horror in their presence. She had heard great scientists discuss the future of the red race and she recalled that some had maintained that eventually the brain would entirely dominate the man. There would be no more instinctive acts or emotions, nothing would be done on impulse; but on the contrary reason would direct our every act. The propounder of the theory regretted that he might never enjoy the blessings of such a state, which, he argued, would result in the ideal life for mankind.

Tara of Helium wished with all her heart that this learned scientist might be here to experience to the full the practical results of the fulfilment of his prophecy. Between the purely physical rykor and the purely mental kaldane there was little choice; but in the happy medium of normal, and imperfect man, as she knew him, lay the most desirable state of existence. It would have been a splendid object lesson, she thought, to all those idealists who seek mass perfection in any phase of human endeavour, since here they might discover the truth that absolute perfection is as little to be desired as is its antithesis.

Gloomy were the thoughts that filled the mind of Tara of Helium as she awaited the summons from Luud—the summons that could mean for her but one thing; death. She guessed why he had sent for her and she knew that she must find the means for self-destruction before the night was over; but still she clung to hope and to life. She would not give up until there was no other way. She startled Ghek once by exclaiming aloud, almost fiercely: "I still live!"

"What do you mean?" asked the kaldane.

"I mean just what I say," she replied. "I still live and while I live I may still find a way. Dead, there is no hope."

"Find a way to what?" he asked.

"To life and liberty and mine own people," she responded.

"None who enters Bantoom ever leaves," he droned.

She did not reply and after a time he spoke again. "Sing to me," he said.

It was while she was singing that four warriors came to take her to Luud. They told Ghek that he was to remain where he was.

"Why?" asked Ghek.

"You have displeased Luud," replied one of the warriors.

"How?" demanded Ghek.

"You have demonstrated a lack of uncontaminated reasoning power. You have permitted sentiment to influence you, thus demonstrating that you are a defective. You know the fate of defectives."

"I know the fate of defectives, but I am no defective," insisted Ghek.

"You permitted the strange noises which issue from her throat to please and soothe you, knowing well that their origin and purpose had nothing whatever to do with logic or the powers of reason. This in itself constitutes an unimpeachable indictment of weakness. Then, influenced doubtless by an illogical feeling of sentiment, you permitted her to walk abroad in the fields to a place where she was able to make an almost successful attempt to escape. Your own reasoning power, were it not defective, would convince you that you are unfit. The natural, and reasonable, consequence is destruction. Therefore you will be destroyed in such a way that the example will be beneficial to all other kaldanes of the swarm of Luud. In the meantime you will remain where you are."

"You are right," said Ghek. "I will remain here until Luud sees fit to destroy me in the most reasonable manner."

Tara of Helium shot a look of amazement at him as they led her from the chamber. Over her shoulder she called back to him: "Remember, Ghek, you still live!" Then they led her along the interminable tunnels to where Luud awaited her.

When she was conducted into his presence he was squatting in a corner of the chamber upon his six spidery legs. Near the opposite wall lay his rykor, its beautiful form trapped in gorgeous harness—a dead thing without a guiding kaldane. Luud dismissed the warriors who had accompanied the prisoner. Then he sat with his terrible eyes fixed upon her and without speaking for some time. Tara of Helium could but wait. What was to come she could only guess. When it came would be sufficiently the time to meet it. There was no necessity for anticipating the end. Presently Luud spoke.

"You think to escape," he said, in the deadly, expressionless monotone of his kind—the only possible result of orally expressing reason uninfluenced by sentiment. "You will not escape. You are merely the embodiment of two imperfect things—an imperfect brain and an imperfect body. The two cannot exist together in perfection. There you see a perfect body." He pointed toward the rykor. "It has no brain. Here," and he raised one of his chelae to his head, "is the perfect brain. It needs no body to function perfectly and properly as a brain. You would pit your feeble intellect against mine! Even now you are planning to slay me. If you are thwarted in that you expect to slay yourself. You will learn the power of mind over matter. I am the mind. You are the matter. What brain you have is too weak and ill-developed to deserve the name of brain. You have permitted it to be weakened by impulsive acts dictated by sentiment. It has no value. It has practically no control over your existence. You will not kill me. You will not kill yourself. When I am through with you you shall be killed if it seems the logical thing to do. You have no conception of the possibilities for power which lie in a perfectly developed brain. Look at that rykor. He has no brain. He can move but slightly of his own volition. An inherent mechanical instinct that we have permitted to remain in him allows him to carry food to his mouth; but he could not find food for himself. We have to place it within his reach and always in the same place. Should we put food at his feet and leave him alone he would starve to death. But now watch what a real brain may accomplish."

He turned his eyes upon the rykor and squatted there glaring at the insensate thing. Presently, to the girl's horror, the headless body moved. It rose slowly to its feet and crossed the room to Luud; it stooped and took the hideous head in its hands; it raised the head and set it on its shoulders.

"What chance have you against such power?" asked Luud. "As I did with the rykor so can I do with you."

Tara of Helium made no reply. Evidently no vocal reply was necessary.

"You doubt my ability!" stated Luud, which was precisely the fact, though the girl had only thought it—she had not said it.

Luud crossed the room and lay down. Then he detached himself from the body and crawled across the floor until he stood directly in front of the circular opening through which she had seen him emerge the day that she had first been brought to his presence. He stopped there and fastened his terrible eyes upon her. He did not speak, but his eyes seemed to be boring straight to the centre of her brain. She felt an almost irresistible force urging her toward the kaldane. She fought to resist it; she tried to turn away her eyes, but she could not. They were held as in horrid fascination upon the glittering, lidless orbs of the great brain that faced her. Slowly, every step a painful struggle of resistance, she moved toward the horrific monster. She tried to cry aloud in an effort to awaken her numbing faculties, but no sound passed her lips. If those eyes would but turn away, just for an instant, she felt that she might regain the power to control her steps; but the eyes never left hers. They seemed but to burn deeper and deeper, gathering up every vestige of control of her entire nervous system.

As she approached the thing it backed slowly away upon its spider legs. She noticed that its chelae waved slowly to and fro before it as it backed, backed, backed, through the round aperture in the wall. Must she follow it there, too? What new and nameless horror lay concealed in that hidden chamber? No! she would not do it. Yet before she reached the wall she found herself down and crawling upon her hands and knees straight toward the hole from which the two eyes still clung to hers. At the very threshold of the opening she made a last, heroic stand, battling against the force that drew her on; but in the end she succumbed. With a gasp that ended in a sob Tara of Helium passed through the aperture into the chamber beyond.

The opening was but barely large enough to admit her. Upon the opposite side she found herself in a small chamber. Before her squatted Luud. Against the opposite wall lay a large and beautiful male rykor. He was without harness or other trappings.

"You see now," said Luud, "the futility of revolt."

The words seemed to release her momentarily from the spell. Quickly she turned away her eyes.

"Look at me!" commanded Luud.

Tara of Helium kept her eyes averted. She felt a new strength, or at least a diminution of the creature's power over her. Had she stumbled upon the secret of its uncanny domination over her will? She dared not hope. With eyes averted she turned toward the aperture through which those baleful eyes had drawn her. Again Luud commanded her to stop, but the voice alone lacked all authority to influence her. It was not like the eyes. She heard the creature whistle and knew that it was summoning assistance, but because she did not dare look toward it she did not see it turn and concentrate its gaze upon the great, headless body lying by the further wall.

The girl was still slightly under the spell of the creature's influence—she had not regained full and independent domination of her powers. She moved as one in the throes of some hideous nightmare—slowly, painfully, as though each limb was hampered by a great weight, or as she were dragging her body through a viscous fluid. The aperture was close, ah, so close, yet, struggle as she would, she seemed to be making no appreciable progress toward it.

Behind her, urged on by the malevolent power of the great brain, the headless body crawled upon all-fours toward her. At last she had reached the aperture. Something seemed to tell her that once beyond it the domination of the kaldane would be broken. She was almost through into the adjoining chamber when she felt a heavy hand close upon her ankle. The rykor had reached forth and seized her, and though she struggled the thing dragged her back into the room with Luud. It held her tight and drew her close, and then, to her horror, it commenced to caress her.

"You see now," she heard Luud's dull voice, "the futility of revolt—and its punishment."

Tara of Helium fought to defend herself, but pitifully weak were her muscles against this brainless incarnation of brute power. Yet she fought, fought on in the face of hopeless odds for the honour of the proud name she bore—fought alone, she whom the fighting men of a mighty empire, the flower of Martian chivalry, would gladly have lain down their lives to save.

Chapter 7

A Repellent Sight

The cruiser Vanator careened through the tempest. That she had not been dashed to the ground, or twisted by the force of the elements into tangled wreckage, was due entirely to the caprice of Nature. For all the duration of the storm she rode, a helpless derelict, upon those storm-tossed waves of wind. But for all the dangers and vicissitudes they underwent, she and her crew might have borne charmed lives up to within an hour of the abating of the hurricane. It was then that the catastrophe occurred—a catastrophe indeed to the crew of the Vanator and the kingdom of Gathol.

The men had been without food or drink since leaving Helium, and they had been hurled about and buffeted in their lashings until all were worn to exhaustion. There was a brief lull in the storm during which one of the crew attempted to reach his quarters, after releasing the lashings which had held him to the precarious safety of the deck. The act in itself was a direct violation of orders and, in the eyes of the other members of the crew, the effect, which came with startling suddenness, took the form of a swift and terrible retribution. Scarce had the man released the safety snaps ere a swift arm of the storm-monster encircled the ship, rolling it over and over, with the result that the foolhardy warrior went overboard at the first turn.

Unloosed from their lashing by the constant turning and twisting of the ship and the force of the wind, the boarding and landing tackle had been trailing beneath the keel, a tangled mass of cordage and leather. Upon the occasions that the Vanator rolled completely over, these things would be wrapped around her until another revolution in the opposite direction, or the wind itself, carried them once again clear of the deck to trail, whipping in the storm, beneath the hurtling ship.

Into this fell the body of the warrior, and as a drowning man clutches at a straw so the fellow clutched at the tangled cordage that caught him and arrested his fall. With the strength of desperation he clung to the cordage, seeking frantically to entangle his legs and body in it. With each jerk of the ship his hand holds were all but torn loose, and though he knew that eventually they would be and that he must be dashed to the ground beneath, yet he fought with the madness that is born of hopelessness for the pitiful second which but prolonged his agony.

It was upon this sight then that Gahan of Gathol looked, over the edge of the careening deck of the Vanator, as he sought to learn the fate of his warrior. Lashed to the gunwale close at hand a single landing leather that had not fouled the tangled mass beneath whipped free from the ship's side, the hook snapping at its outer end. The Jed of Gathol grasped the situation in a single glance. Below him one of his people looked into the eyes of Death. To the Jed's hand lay the means for succour.

There was no instant's hesitation. Casting off his deck lashings, he seized the landing leather and slipped over the ship's side. Swinging like a bob upon a mad pendulum he swung far out and back again, turning and twisting three thousand feet above the surface of Barsoom, and then, at last, the thing he had hoped for occurred. He was carried within reach of the cordage where the warrior still clung, though with rapidly diminishing strength. Catching one leg on a loop of the tangled strands Gahan pulled himself close enough to seize another quite near to the fellow. Clinging precariously to this new hold the jed slowly drew in the landing leather, down which he had clambered until he could grasp the hook at its end. This he fastened to a ring in the warrior's harness, just before the man's weakened fingers slipped from their hold upon the cordage.

Temporarily, at least, he had saved the life of his subject, and now he turned his attention toward insuring his own safety. Inextricably entangled in the mess to which he was clinging were numerous other landing hooks such as he had attached to the warrior's harness, and with one of these he sought to secure himself until the storm should abate sufficiently to permit him to climb to the deck, but even as he reached for one that swung near him the ship was caught in a renewed burst of the storm's fury, the thrashing cordage whipped and snapped to the lunging of the great craft and one of the heavy metal hooks, lashing through the air, struck the Jed of Gathol fair between the eyes.

Momentarily stunned, Gahan's fingers slipped from their hold upon the cordage and the man shot downward through the thin air of dying Mars toward the ground three thousand feet beneath, while upon the deck of the rolling Vanator his faithful warriors clung to their lashings all unconscious of the fate of their beloved leader; nor was it until more than an hour later, after the storm had materially subsided, that they realized he was lost, or knew the self-sacrificing heroism of the act that had sealed his doom. The Vanator now rested upon an even keel as she was carried along by a strong, though steady, wind. The warriors had cast off their deck lashings and the officers were taking account of losses and damage when a weak cry was heard from oversides, attracting their attention to the man hanging in the cordage beneath the keel. Strong arms hoisted him to the deck and then it was that the crew of the Vanator learned of the heroism of their jed and his end. How far they had travelled since his loss they could only vaguely guess, nor could they return in search of him in the disabled condition of the ship. It was a saddened company that drifted onward through the air toward whatever destination Fate was to choose for them.

And Gahan, Jed of Gathol—what of him? Plummet-like he fell for a thousand feet and then the storm seized him in its giant clutch and bore him far aloft again. As a bit of paper borne upon a gale he was tossed about in mid-air, the sport and plaything of the wind. Over and over it turned him and upward and downward it carried him, but after each new sally of the element he was brought nearer to the ground. The freaks of cyclonic storms are the rule of cyclonic storms, demolish giant trees, and in the same gust they transport frail infants for miles and deposit them unharmed in their wake.

And so it was with Gahan of Gathol. Expecting momentarily to be dashed to destruction he presently found himself deposited gently upon the soft, ochre moss of a dead sea-bottom, bodily no worse off for his harrowing adventure than in the possession of a slight swelling upon his forehead where the metal hook had struck him. Scarcely able to believe that Fate had dealt thus gently with him, the jed arose slowly, as though more than half convinced that he should discover crushed and splintered bones that would not support his weight. But he was intact. He looked about him in a vain effort at orientation. The air was filled with flying dust and debris. The Sun was obliterated. His vision was confined to a radius of a few hundred yards of ochre moss and dust-filled air. Five hundred yards away in any direction there might have arisen the walls of a great city and he not known it. It was useless to move from where he was until the air cleared, since he could not know in what direction he was moving, and so he stretched himself upon the moss and waited, pondering the fate of his warriors and his ship, but giving little thought to his own precarious situation.

Lashed to his harness were his swords, his pistols, and a dagger, and in his pocket-pouch a small quantity of the concentrated rations that form a part of the equipment of the fighting men of Barsoom. These things together with trained muscles, high courage, and an undaunted spirit sufficed him for whatever misadventures might lie between him and Gathol, which lay in what direction he knew not, nor at what distance.

The wind was falling rapidly and with it the dust that obscured the landscape. That the storm was over he was convinced, but he chafed at the inactivity the low visibility put upon him, nor did conditions better materially before night fell, so that he was forced to await the new day at the very spot at which the tempest had deposited him. Without his sleeping silks and furs he spent a far from comfortable night, and it was with feelings of unmixed relief that he saw the sudden dawn burst upon him. The air was now clear and in the light of the new day he saw an undulating plain stretching in all directions about him, while to the northwest there were barely discernible the outlines of low hills. Toward the southeast of Gathol was such a country, and as Gahan surmised the direction and the velocity of the storm to have carried him somewhere in the vicinity of the country he thought he recognized, he assumed that Gathol lay behind the hills he now saw, whereas, in reality, it lay far to the northeast.

It was two days before Gahan had crossed the plain and reached the summit of the hills from which he hoped to see his own country, only to meet at last with disappointment. Before him stretched another plain, of even greater proportions than that he had but just crossed, and beyond this other hills. In one material respect this plain differed from that behind him in that it was dotted with occasional isolated hills. Convinced, however, that Gathol lay somewhere in the direction of his search he descended into the valley and bent his steps toward the northwest.

For weeks Gahan of Gathol crossed valleys and hills in search of some familiar landmark that might point his way toward his native land, but the summit of each succeeding ridge revealed but another unfamiliar view. He saw few animals and no men, until he finally came to the belief that he had fallen upon that fabled area of ancient Barsoom which lay under the curse of her olden gods—the once rich and fertile country whose people in their pride and arrogance had denied the deities, and whose punishment had been extermination.

And then, one day, he scaled low hills and looked into an inhabited valley—a valley of trees and cultivated fields and plots of ground enclosed by stone walls surrounding strange towers. He saw people working in the fields, but he did not rush down to greet them. First he must know more of them and whether they might be assumed to be friends or enemies. Hidden by concealing shrubbery he crawled to a vantage point upon a hill that projected further into the valley, and here he lay upon his belly watching the workers closest to him. They were still quite a distance from him and he could not be quite sure of them, but there was something verging upon the unnatural about them. Their heads seemed out of proportion to their bodies—too large.

For a long time he lay watching them and ever more forcibly it was borne in upon his consciousness that they were not as he, and that it would be rash to trust himself among them. Presently he saw a couple appear from the nearest enclosure and slowly approach those who were working nearest to the hill where he lay in hiding. Immediately he was aware that one of these differed from all the others. Even at the greater distance he noted that the head was smaller and as they approached, he was confident that the harness of one of them was not as the harness of its companion or of that of any of those who tilled the fields.

The two stopped often, apparently in argument, as though one would proceed in the direction that they were going while the other demurred. But each time the smaller won reluctant consent from the other, and so they came closer and closer to the last line of workers toiling between the enclosure from which they had come and the hill where Gahan of Gathol lay watching, and then suddenly the smaller figure struck its companion full in the face. Gahan, horrified, saw the latter's head topple from its body, saw the body stagger and fall to the ground. The man half rose from his concealment the better to view the happening in the valley below. The creature that had felled its companion was dashing madly in the direction of the hill upon which he was hidden, it dodged one of the workers that sought to seize it. Gahan hoped that it would gain its liberty, why he did not know other than at closer range it had every appearance of being a creature of his own race. Then he saw it stumble and go down and instantly its pursuers were upon it. Then it was that Gahan's eyes chanced to return to the figure of the creature the fugitive had felled.

What horror was this that he was witnessing? Or were his eyes playing some ghastly joke upon him? No, impossible though it was—it was true—the head was moving slowly to the fallen body. It placed itself upon the shoulders, the body rose, and the creature, seemingly as good as new, ran quickly to where its fellows were dragging the hapless captive to its feet.

The watcher saw the creature take its prisoner by the arm and lead it back to the enclosure, and even across the distance that separated them from him he could note dejection and utter hopelessness in the bearing of the prisoner, and, too, he was half convinced that it was a woman, perhaps a red Martian of his own race. Could he be sure that this was true he must make some effort to rescue her even though the customs of his strange world required it only in case she was of his own country; but he was not sure; she might not be a red Martian at all, or, if she were, it was as possible that she sprang from an enemy people as not. His first duty was to return to his own people with as little personal risk as possible, and though the thought of adventure stirred his blood he put the temptation aside with a sigh and turned away from the peaceful and beautiful valley that he longed to enter, for it was his intention to skirt its eastern edge and continue his search for Gathol beyond.

As Gahan of Gathol turned his steps along the southern slopes of the hills that bound Bantoom upon the south and east, his attention was attracted toward a small cluster of trees a short distance to his right. The low sun was casting long shadows. It would soon be night. The trees were off the path that he had chosen and he had little mind to be diverted from his way; but as he looked again he hesitated. There was something there besides boles of trees, and underbrush. There were suggestions of familiar lines of the handicraft of man. Gahan stopped and strained his eyes in the direction of the thing that had arrested his attention. No, he must be mistaken—the branches of the trees and a low bush had taken on an unnatural semblance in the horizontal rays of the setting sun. He turned and continued upon his way; but as he cast another side glance in the direction of the object of his interest, the sun's rays were shot back into his eyes from a glistening point of radiance among the trees.

Gahan shook his head and walked quickly toward the mystery, determined now to solve it. The shining object still lured him on and when he had come closer to it his eyes went wide in surprise, for the thing they saw was naught else than the jewel-encrusted emblem upon the prow of a small flier. Gahan, his hand upon his short-sword, moved silently forward, but as he neared the craft he saw that he had naught to fear, for it was deserted. Then he turned his attention toward the emblem. As its significance was flashed to his understanding his face paled and his heart went cold—it was the insignia of the house of The Warlord of Barsoom. Instantly he saw the dejected figure of the captive being led back to her prison in the valley just beyond the hills. Tara of Helium! And he had been so near to deserting her to her fate. The cold sweat stood in beads upon his brow.

A hasty examination of the deserted craft unfolded to the young jed the whole tragic story. The same tempest that had proved his undoing had borne Tara of Helium to this distant country. Here, doubtless, she had landed in hope of obtaining food and water since, without a propellor, she could not hope to reach her native city, or any other friendly port, other than by the merest caprice of Fate. The flier seemed intact except for the missing propellor and the fact that it had been carefully moored in the shelter of the clump of trees indicated that the girl had expected to return to it, while the dust and leaves upon its deck spoke of the long days, and even weeks, since she had landed. Mute yet eloquent proofs, these things, that Tara of Helium was a prisoner, and that she was the very prisoner whose bold dash for liberty he had so recently witnessed he now had not the slightest doubt.

The question now revolved solely about her rescue. He knew to which tower she had been taken—that much and no more. Of the number, the kind, or the disposition of her captors he knew nothing; nor did he care—for Tara of Helium he would face a hostile world alone. Rapidly he considered several plans for succouring her; but the one that appealed most strongly to him was that which offered the greatest chance of escape for the girl should he be successful in reaching her. His decision reached he turned his attention quickly toward the flier. Casting off its lashings he dragged it out from beneath the trees, and, mounting to the deck tested out the various controls. The motor started at a touch and purred sweetly, the buoyancy tanks were well stocked, and the ship answered perfectly to the controls which regulated her altitude. There was nothing needed but a propellor to make her fit for the long voyage to Helium. Gahan shrugged impatiently—there must not be a propellor within a thousand haads. But what mattered it? The craft even without a propellor would still answer the purpose his plan required of it—provided the captors of Tara of Helium were a people without ships, and he had seen nothing to suggest that they had ships. The architecture of their towers and enclosures assured him that they had not.

The sudden Barsoomian night had fallen. Cluros rode majestically the high heavens. The rumbling roar of a banth reverberated among the hills. Gahan of Gathol let the ship rise a few feet from the ground, then, seizing a bow rope, he dropped over the side. To tow the little craft was now a thing of ease, and as Gahan moved rapidly toward the brow of the hill above Bantoom the flier floated behind him as lightly as a swan upon a quiet lake. Now down the hill toward the tower dimly visible in the moonlight the Gatholian turned his steps. Closer behind him sounded the roar of the hunting banth. He wondered if the beast sought him or was following some other spoor. He could not be delayed now by any hungry beast of prey, for what might that very instant be befalling Tara of Helium he could not guess; and so he hastened his steps. But closer and closer came the horrid screams of the great carnivore, and now he heard the swift fall of padded feet upon the hillside behind him. He glanced back just in time to see the beast break into a rapid charge. His hand leaped to the hilt of his long-sword, but he did not draw, for in the same instant he saw the futility of armed resistance, since behind the first banth came a herd of at least a dozen others. There was but a single alternative to a futile stand and that he grasped in the instant that he saw the overwhelming numbers of his antagonists.

Springing lightly from the ground he swarmed up the rope toward the bow of the flier. His weight drew the craft slightly lower and at the very instant that the man drew himself to the deck at the bow of the vessel, the leading banth sprang for the stern. Gahan leaped to his feet and rushed toward the great beast in the hope of dislodging it before it had succeeded in clambering aboard. At the same instant he saw that others of the banths were racing toward them with the quite evident intention of following their leader to the ship's deck. Should they reach it in any numbers he would be lost. There was but a single hope. Leaping for the altitude control Gahan pulled it wide. Simultaneously three banths leaped for the deck. The craft rose swiftly. Gahan felt the impact of a body against the keel, followed by the soft thuds of the great bodies as they struck the ground beneath. His act had not been an instant too soon. And now the leader had gained the deck and stood at the stern with glaring eyes and snarling jaws. Gahan drew his sword. The beast, possibly disconcerted by the novelty of its position, did not charge. Instead it crept slowly toward its intended prey. The craft was rising and Gahan placed a foot upon the control and stopped the ascent. He did not wish to chance rising to some higher air current that would bear him away. Already the craft was moving slowly toward the tower, carried thither by the impetus of the banth's heavy body leaping upon it from astern.

The man watched the slow approach of the monster, the slavering jowls, the malignant expression of the devilish face. The creature, finding the deck stable, appeared to be gaining confidence, and then the man leaped suddenly to one side of the deck and the tiny flier heeled as suddenly in response. The banth slipped and clutched frantically at the deck. Gahan leaped in with his naked sword; the great beast caught itself and reared upon its hind legs to reach forth and seize this presumptuous mortal that dared question its right to the flesh it craved; and then the man sprang to the opposite side of the deck. The banth toppled sideways at the same instant that it attempted to spring; a raking talon passed close to Gahan's head at the moment that his sword lunged through the savage heart, and as the warrior wrenched his blade from the carcass it slipped silently over the side of the ship.

A glance below showed that the vessel was drifting in the direction of the tower to which Gahan had seen the prisoner led. In another moment or two it would be directly over it. The man sprang to the control and let the craft drop quickly toward the ground where followed the banths, still hot for their prey. To land outside the enclosure spelled certain death, while inside he could see many forms huddled upon the ground as in sleep. The ship floated now but a few feet above the wall of the enclosure. There was nothing for it but to risk all on a bold bid for fortune, or drift helplessly past without hope of returning through the banth-infested valley, from many points of which he could now hear the roars and growls of these fierce Barsoomian lions.

Slipping over the side Gahan descended by the trailing anchor-rope until his feet touched the top of the wall, where he had no difficulty in arresting the slow drifting of the ship. Then he drew up the anchor and lowered it inside the enclosure. Still there was no movement upon the part of the sleepers beneath—they lay as dead men. Dull lights shone from openings in the tower; but there was no sign of guard or waking inmate. Clinging to the rope Gahan lowered himself within the enclosure, where he had his first close view of the creatures lying there in what he had thought sleep. With a half smothered exclamation of horror the man drew back from the headless bodies of the rykors. At first he thought them the corpses of decapitated humans like himself, which was quite bad enough; but when he saw them move and realized that they were endowed with life, his horror and disgust became even greater.

Here then was the explanation of the thing he had witnessed that afternoon, when Tara of Helium had struck the back to its body. And to think that the pearl of Helium was in the power of such hideous things as these. Again the man shuddered, but he hastened to make fast the flier, clamber again to its deck and lower it to the floor of the enclosure. Then he strode toward a door in the base of the tower, stepping lightly over the recumbent forms of the unconscious rykors, and crossing the threshold disappeared within.

Chapter 8

Close Work

Ghek, in his happier days third foreman of the fields of Luud, sat nursing his anger and his humiliation. Recently something had awakened within him the existence of which he had never before even dreamed. Had the influence of the strange captive woman aught to do with this unrest and dissatisfaction? He did not know. He missed the soothing influence of the noise she called singing. Could it be that there were other things more desirable than cold logic and undefiled brain power? Was well balanced imperfection more to be sought after then, than the high development of a single characteristic? He thought of the great, ultimate brain toward which all kaldanes were striving. It would be deaf, and dumb, and blind. A thousand beautiful strangers might sing and dance about it, but it could derive no pleasure from the singing or the dancing since it would possess no perceptive faculties. Already had the kaldanes shut themselves off from most of the gratifications of the senses. Ghek wondered if much was to be gained by denying themselves still further, and with the thought came a question as to the whole fabric of their theory. After all perhaps the girl was right; what purpose could a great brain serve sealed in the bowels of the earth?

And he, Ghek, was to die for this theory. Luud had decreed it. The injustice of it overwhelmed him with rage. But he was helpless. There was no escape. Beyond the enclosure the banths awaited him; within, his own kind, equally as merciless and ferocious. Among them there was no such thing as love, or loyalty, or friendship—they were just brains. He might kill Luud; but what would that profit him? Another king would be loosed from his sealed chamber and Ghek would be killed. He did not know it but he would not even have the poor satisfaction of satisfied revenge, since he was not capable of feeling so abstruse a sentiment.

Ghek, mounted upon his rykor, paced the floor of the tower chamber in which he had been ordered to remain. Ordinarily he would have accepted the sentence of Luud with perfect equanimity, since it was but the logical result of reason; but now it seemed different. The stranger woman had bewitched him. Life appeared a pleasant thing—there were great possibilities in it. The dream of the ultimate brain had receded into a tenuous haze far in the background of his thoughts.

At that moment there appeared in the doorway of the chamber a red warrior with naked sword. He was a male counterpart of the prisoner whose sweet voice had undermined the cold, calculating reason of the kaldane.

"Silence!" admonished the newcomer, his straight brows gathered in an ominous frown and the point of his long-sword playing menacingly before the eyes of the kaldane. "I seek the woman, Tara of Helium. Where is she? If you value your life speak quickly and speak the truth."

If he valued his life! It was a truth that Ghek had but just learned. He thought quickly. After all, a great brain is not without its uses. Perhaps here lay escape from the sentence of Luud.

"You are of her kind?" he asked. "You come to rescue her?"

"Yes."

"Listen, then. I have befriended her, and because of this I am to die. If I help you to liberate her, will you take me with you?"

Gahan of Gathol eyed the weird creature from crown to foot—the perfect body, the grotesque head, the expressionless face. Among such as these had the beautiful daughter of Helium been held captive for days and weeks.

"If she lives and is unharmed," he said, "I will take you with us."

"When they took her from me she was alive and unharmed," replied Ghek. "I cannot say what has befallen her since. Luud sent for her." "Who is Luud? Where is he? Lead me to him." Gahan spoke quickly in tones vibrant with authority.

"Come, then," said Ghek, leading the way from the apartment and down a stairway toward the underground burrows of the kaldanes. "Luud is my king. I will take you to his chambers."

"Hasten!" urged Gahan.

"Sheathe your sword," warned Ghek, "so that should we pass others of my kind I may say to them that you are a new prisoner with some likelihood of winning their belief."

Gahan did as he was bid, but warning the kaldane that his hand was ever ready at his dagger's hilt.

"You need have no fear of treachery," said Ghek "My only hope of life lies in you."

"And if you fail me," Gahan admonished him, "I can promise you as sure a death as even your king might guarantee you."

Ghek made no reply, but moved rapidly through the winding subterranean corridors until Gahan began to realize how truly was he in the hands of this strange monster. If the fellow should prove false it would profit Gahan nothing to slay him, since without his guidance the red man might never hope to retrace his way to the tower and freedom.

Twice they met and were accosted by other kaldanes; but in both instances Ghek's simple statement that he was taking a new prisoner to Luud appeared to allay all suspicion, and then at last they came to the ante-chamber of the king.

"Here, now, red man, thou must fight, if ever," whispered Ghek. "Enter there!" and he pointed to a doorway before them.

"And you?" asked Gahan, still fearful of treachery.

"My rykor is powerful," replied the kaldane. "I shall accompany you and fight at your side. As well die thus as in torture later at the will of Luud. Come!"

But Gahan had already crossed the room and entered the chamber beyond. Upon the opposite side of the room was a circular opening guarded by two warriors. Beyond this opening he could see two figures struggling upon the floor, and the fleeting glimpse he had of one of the faces suddenly endowed him with the strength of ten warriors and the ferocity of a wounded banth. It was Tara of Helium, fighting for her honour or her life.

The warriors, startled by the unexpected appearance of a red man, stood for a moment in dumb amazement, and in that moment Gahan of Gathol was upon them, and one was down, a sword-thrust through its heart.

"Strike at the heads," whispered the voice of Ghek in Gahan's ear. The latter saw the head of the fallen warrior crawl quickly within the aperture leading to the chamber where he had seen Tara of Helium in the clutches of a headless body. Then the sword of Ghek struck the kaldane of the remaining warrior from its rykor and Gahan ran his sword through the repulsive head.

Instantly the red warrior leaped for the aperture, while close behind him came Ghek.

"Look not upon the eyes of Luud," warned the kaldane, "or you are lost."

Within the chamber Gahan saw Tara of Helium in the clutches of a mighty body, while close to the wall upon the opposite side of the apartment crouched the hideous, spider-like Luud. Instantly the king realized the menace to himself and sought to fasten his eyes upon the eyes of Gahan, and in doing so he was forced to relax his concentration upon the rykor in whose embraces Tara struggled, so that almost immediately the girl found herself able to tear away from the awful, headless thing.

As she rose quickly to her feet she saw for the first time the cause of the interruption of Luud's plans. A red warrior! Her heart leaped in rejoicing and thanksgiving. What miracle of fate had sent him to her? She did not recognize him, though, this travel-worn warrior in the plain harness which showed no single jewel. How could she have guessed him the same as the scintillant creature of platinum and diamonds that she had seen for a brief hour under such different circumstances at the court of her august sire?

Luud saw Ghek following the strange warrior into the chamber. "Strike him down, Ghek!" commanded the king. "Strike down the stranger and your life shall be yours."

Gahan glanced at the hideous face of the king.

"Seek not his eyes," screamed Tara in warning; but it was too late. Already the horrid hypnotic gaze of the king kaldane had seized upon the eyes of Gahan. The red warrior hesitated in his stride. His sword point drooped slowly toward the floor. Tara glanced toward Ghek. She saw the creature glaring with his expressionless eyes upon the broad back of the stranger. She saw the hand of the creature's rykor creeping stealthily toward the hilt of its dagger.

And then Tara of Helium raised her eyes aloft and poured forth the notes of Mars' most beautiful melody, The Song of Love.

Ghek drew his dagger from its sheath. His eyes turned toward the singing girl. Luud's glance wavered from the eyes of the man to the face of Tara, and the instant that the latter's song distracted his attention from his victim, Gahan of Gathol shook himself and as with a supreme effort of will forced his eyes to the wall above Luud's hideous head. Ghek raised his dagger above his right shoulder, took a single quick step forward, and struck. The girl's song ended in a stifled scream as she leaped forward with the evident intention of frustrating the kaldane's purpose; but she was too late, and well it was, for an instant later she realized the purpose of Ghek's act as she saw the dagger fly from his hand, pass Gahan's shoulder, and sink full to the guard in the soft face of Luud.

"Come!" cried the assassin, "we have no time to lose," and started for the aperture through which they had entered the chamber; but in his stride he paused as his glance was arrested by the form of the mighty rykor lying prone upon the floor—a king's rykor; the most beautiful, the most powerful, that the breeders of Bantoom could produce. Ghek realized that in his escape he could take with him but a single rykor, and there was none in Bantoom that could give him better service than this giant lying here. Quickly he transferred himself to the shoulders of the great, inert hulk. Instantly the latter was transformed to a sentient creature, filled with pulsing life and alert energy.

"Now," said the kaldane, "we are ready. Let whoso would revert to nothingness impede me." Even as he spoke he stooped and crawled into the chamber beyond, while Gahan, taking Tara by the arm, motioned her to follow. The girl looked him full in the eyes for the first time. "The Gods of my people have been kind," she said; "you came just in time. To the thanks of Tara of Helium shall be added those of The Warlord of Barsoom and his people. Thy reward shall surpass thy greatest desires."

Gahan of Gathol saw that she did not recognize him, and quickly he checked the warm greeting that had been upon his lips.

"Be thou Tara of Helium or another," he replied, "is immaterial, to serve thus a red woman of Barsoom is in itself sufficient reward."

As they spoke the girl was making her way through the aperture after Ghek, and presently all three had quitted the apartments of Luud and were moving rapidly along the winding corridors toward the tower. Ghek repeatedly urged them to greater speed, but the red men of Barsoom were never keen for retreat, and so the two that followed him moved all too slowly for the kaldane.

"There are none to impede our progress," urged Gahan, "so why tax the strength of the Princess by needless haste?"

"I fear not so much opposition ahead, for there are none there who know the thing that has been done in Luud's chambers this night; but the kaldane of one of the warriors who stood guard before Luud's apartment escaped, and you may count it a truth that he lost no time in seeking aid. That it did not come before we left is due solely to the rapidity with which events transpired in the king's[*] room. Long

---

[*] I have used the word king in describing the rulers or chiefs of the Bantoomian swarms, since the word itself is unpronounceable in English, nor does jed or jeddak of the red Martian tongue have quite the same meaning as the Bantoomian word, which has practically the same significance as the English word queen as applied to the leader of a swarm of bees.—J. C.

before we reach the tower they will be upon us from behind, and that they will come in numbers far superior to ours and with great and powerful rykors I well know."

Nor was Ghek's prophecy long in fulfilment. Presently the sounds of pursuit became audible in the distant clanking of accoutrements and the whistling call to arms of the kaldanes.

"The tower is but a short distance now," cried Ghek. "Make haste while yet you may, and if we can barricade it until the sun rises we may yet escape."

"We shall need no barricades for we shall not linger in the tower," replied Gahan, moving more rapidly as he realized from the volume of sound behind them the great number of their pursuers.

"But we may not go further than the tower tonight," insisted Ghek. "Beyond the tower await the banths and certain death."

Gahan smiled. "Fear not the banths," he assured them. "Can we but reach the enclosure a little ahead of our pursuers we have naught to fear from any evil power within this accursed valley."

Ghek made no reply, nor did his expressionless face denote either belief or scepticism. The girl looked into the face of the man questioningly. She did not understand.

"Your flier," he said. "It is moored before the tower."

Her face lighted with pleasure and relief. "You found it!" she exclaimed. "What fortune!"

"It was fortune indeed," he replied. "Since it not only told that you were a prisoner here; but it saved me from the banths as I was crossing the valley from the hills to this tower into which I saw them take you this afternoon after your brave attempt at escape."

"How did you know it was I?" she asked, her puzzled brows scanning his face as though she sought to recall from past memories some scene in which he figured.

"Who is there but knows of the loss of the Princess Tara of Helium?" he replied. "And when I saw the device upon your flier I knew at once, though I had not known when I saw you among them in the fields a short time earlier. Too great was the distance for me to make certain whether the captive was man or woman. Had chance not divulged the hiding place of your flier I had gone my way, Tara of Helium. I shudder to think how close was the chance at that. But for the momentary shining of the sun upon the emblazoned device on the prow of your craft, I had passed on unknowing."

The girl shuddered. "The Gods sent you," she whispered reverently.

"The Gods sent me, Tara of Helium," he replied.

"But I do not recognize you," she said. "I have tried to recall you, but I have failed. Your name, what may it be?"

"It is not strange that so great a princess should not recall the face of every roving panthan of Barsoom," he replied with a smile.

"But your name?" insisted the girl.

"Call me Turan," replied the man, for it had come to him that if Tara of Helium recognized him as the man whose impetuous avowal of love had angered her that day in the gardens of The Warlord, her situation might be rendered infinitely less bearable than were she to believe him a total stranger. Then, too, as a simple panthan* he might win a greater degree of her confidence by his loyalty and faithfulness and a place in her esteem that seemed to have been closed to the resplendent Jed of Gathol.

They had reached the tower now, and as they entered it from the subterranean corridor a backward glance revealed the van of their pursuers—hideous kaldanes mounted upon swift and powerful rykors. As rapidly as might be the three ascended the stairways leading to the ground level, but after them, even more rapidly, came the minions of Luud. Ghek led the way, grasping one of Tara's hands the more easily to guide and assist her, while Gahan of Gathol followed a few paces in their rear, his bared sword ready for the assault that all realized must come upon them now before ever they reached the enclosure and the flier.

"Let Ghek drop behind to your side," said Tara, "and fight with you."

"There is but room for a single blade in these narrow corridors," replied the Gatholian. "Hasten on with Ghek and win to the deck of the flier. Have your hand upon the control, and if I come far enough ahead of these to reach the dangling cable you can rise at my word and I can clamber to the deck at my leisure; but if one of them emerges first into the enclosure you will know that I shall never come, and you will rise quickly and trust to the Gods of our ancestors to give you a fair breeze in the direction of a more hospitable people."

Tara of Helium shook her head. "We will not desert you, panthan," she said.

Gahan, ignoring her reply, spoke above her head to Ghek. "Take her to the craft moored within the enclosure," he commanded. "It is our only hope. Alone, I may win to its deck; but have I to wait upon you two at the last moment the chances are that none of us will escape. Do as I bid." His tone was haughty and arrogant—the tone of a

---

* Soldier of Fortune; free-lance warrior.

man who has commanded other men from birth, and whose will has been law. Tara of Helium was both angered and vexed. She was not accustomed to being either commanded or ignored, but with all her royal pride she was no fool, and she knew the man was right, that he was risking his life to save hers, so she hastened on with Ghek as she was bid, and after the first flush of anger she smiled, for the realization came to her that this fellow was but a rough untutored warrior, skilled not in the finer usages of cultured courts. His heart was right, though; a brave and loyal heart, and gladly she forgave him the offence of his tone and manner. But what a tone! Recollection of it gave her sudden pause. Panthans were rough and ready men. Often they rose to positions of high command, so it was not the note of authority in the fellow's voice that seemed remarkable; but something else—a quality that was indefinable, yet as distinct as it was familiar. She had heard it before when the voice of her great-grandsire, Tardos Mors, Jeddak of Helium, had risen in command; and in the voice of her grandfather, Mors Kajak, the jed; and in the ringing tones of her illustrious sire, John Carter, Warlord of Barsoom, when he addressed his warriors.

But now she had no time to speculate upon so trivial a thing, for behind her came the sudden clash of arms and she knew that Turan, the panthan, had crossed swords with the first of their pursuers. As she glanced back he was still visible beyond a turn in the stairway, so that she could see the quick swordplay that ensued. Daughter of a world's greatest swordsman, she knew well the finest points of the art. She saw the clumsy attack of the kaldane and the quick, sure return of the panthan. As she looked down from above upon his almost naked body, trapped only in the simplest of unadorned harness, and saw the play of the lithe muscles beneath the red-bronze skin, and witnessed the quick and delicate play of his sword point, to her sense of obligation was added a spontaneous admission of admiration that was but the natural tribute of a woman to skill and bravery and, perchance, some trifle to manly symmetry and strength.

Three times the panthan's blade changed its position—once to fend a savage cut; once to feint; and once to thrust. And as he withdrew it from the last position the kaldane rolled lifeless from its stumbling rykor and Turan sprang quickly down the steps to engage the next behind, and then Ghek had drawn Tara upward and a turn in the stairway shut the battling panthan from her view; but still she heard the ring of steel on steel, the clank of accoutrements and the shrill whistling of the kaldanes. Her heart moved her to turn back to the side of her brave defender; but her judgment told her that she could serve him best by being ready at the control of the flier at the moment he reached the enclosure.

Chapter 9

Adrift Over Strange Regions

Presently Ghek pushed aside a door that opened from the stairway, and before them Tara saw the moonlight flooding the walled court where the headless rykors lay beside their feeding-troughs. She saw the perfect bodies, muscled as the best of her father's fighting men, and the females whose figures would have been the envy of many of Helium's most beautiful women. Ah, if she could but endow these with the power to act! Then indeed might the safety of the panthan be assured; but they were only poor lumps of clay, nor had she the power to quicken them to life. Ever must they lie thus until dominated by the cold, heartless brain of the kaldane. The girl sighed in pity even as she shuddered in disgust as she picked her way over and among the sprawled creatures toward the flier.

Quickly she and Ghek mounted to the deck after the latter had cast off the moorings. Tara tested the control, raising and lowering the ship a few feet within the walled space. It responded perfectly. Then she lowered it to the ground again and waited. From the open doorway came the sounds of conflict, now nearing them, now receding. The girl, having witnessed her champion's skill, had little fear of the outcome. Only a single antagonist could face him at a time upon the narrow stairway, he had the advantage of position and of the defensive, and he was a master of the sword while they were clumsy bunglers by comparison. Their sole advantage was in their numbers, unless they might find a way to come upon him from behind.

She paled at the thought. Could she have seen him she might have been further perturbed, for he took no advantage of many opportunities to win nearer the enclosure. He fought coolly, but with a savage persistence that bore little semblance to purely defensive action. Often he clambered over the body of a fallen foe to leap against the next behind, and once there lay five dead kaldanes behind him, so far had he pushed back his antagonists. They did not know it; these kaldanes that he fought, nor did the girl awaiting him upon the flier, but Gahan of Gathol was engaged in a more alluring sport than winning to freedom, for he was avenging the indignities that had been put upon the woman he loved; but presently he realized that he might be jeopardizing her safety uselessly, and so he struck down another before him and turning leaped quickly up the stairway, while the leading kaldanes slipped upon the brain-covered floor and stumbled in pursuit.

Gahan reached the enclosure twenty paces ahead of them and raced toward the flier. "Rise!" he shouted to the girl. "I will ascend the cable."

Slowly the small craft rose from the ground as Gahan leaped the inert bodies of the rykors lying in his path. The first of the pursuers sprang from the tower just as Gahan seized the trailing rope.

"Faster!" he shouted to the girl above, "or they will drag us down!" But the ship seemed scarcely to move, though in reality she was rising as rapidly as might have been expected of a one-man flier carrying a load of three. Gahan swung free above the top of the wall, but the end of the rope still dragged the ground as the kaldanes reached it. They were pouring in a steady stream from the tower into the enclosure. The leader seized the rope.

"Quick!" he cried. "Lay hold and we will drag them down."

It needed but the weight of a few to accomplish his design. The ship was stopped in its flight and then, to the horror of the girl, she felt it being dragged steadily downward. Gahan, too, realized the danger and the necessity for instant action. Clinging to the rope with his left hand, he had wound a leg about it, leaving his right hand free for his long-sword which he had not sheathed. A downward cut clove the soft head of a kaldane, and another severed the taut rope beneath the panthan's feet. The girl heard a sudden renewal of the shrill whistling of her foes, and at the same time she realized that the craft was rising again. Slowly it drifted upward, out of reach of the enemy, and a moment later she saw the figure of Turan clamber over the side. For the first time in many weeks her heart was filled with the joy of thanksgiving; but her first thought was of another.

"You are not wounded?" she asked.

"No, Tara of Helium," he replied. "They were scarce worth the effort of my blade, and never were they a menace to me because of their swords."

"They should have slain you easily," said Ghek. "So great and highly developed is the power of reason among us that they should have known before you struck just where, logically, you must seek to strike, and so they should have been able to parry your every thrust and easily find an opening to your heart."

"But they did not, Ghek," Gahan reminded him. "Their theory of development is wrong, for it does not tend toward a perfectly balanced whole. You have developed the brain and neglected the body and you can never do with the hands of another what you can do with your own hands. Mine are trained to the sword—every muscle responds instantly and accurately, and almost mechanically, to the need of the instant. I am scarcely objectively aware that I think when I fight, so quickly does my point take advantage of every opening, or spring to my defence if I am threatened that it is almost as though the cold steel had eyes and brains. You, with your kaldane brain and your rykor body, never could hope to achieve in the same degree of perfection those things that I can achieve. Development of the brain should not be the sum total of human endeavour. The richest and happiest peoples will be those who attain closest to well-balanced perfection of both mind and body, and even these must always be short of perfection. In absolute and general perfection lies stifling monotony and death. Nature must have contrasts; she must have shadows as well as highlights; sorrow with happiness; both wrong and right; and sin as well as virtue."

"Always have I been taught differently," replied Ghek; "but since I have known this woman and you, of another race, I have come to believe that there may be other standards fully as high and desirable as those of the kaldanes. At least I have had a glimpse of the thing you call happiness and I realize that it may be good even though I have no means of expressing it. I cannot laugh nor smile, and yet within me is a sense of contentment when this woman sings—a sense that seems to open before me wondrous vistas of beauty and unguessed pleasure that far transcend the cold joys of a perfectly functioning brain. I would that I had been born of thy race."

Caught by a gentle current of air the flier was drifting slowly toward the northeast across the valley of Bantoom. Below them lay the cultivated fields, and one after another they passed over the strange towers of Moak and Nolach and the other kings of the swarms that inhabited this weird and terrible land. Within each enclosure surrounding the towers grovelled the rykors, repellent, headless things, beautiful yet hideous.

"A lesson, those," remarked Gahan, indicating the rykors in an enclosure above which they were drifting at the time, "to that fortunately small minority of our race which worships the flesh and makes a god of appetite. You know them, Tara of Helium; they can tell you exactly what they had at the midday meal two weeks ago, and how the loin of the thoat should be prepared, and what drink should be served with the rump of the zitidar."

Tara of Helium laughed. "But not one of them could tell you the name of the man whose painting took the Jeddak's Award in The Temple of Beauty this year," she said. "Like the rykors, their development has not been balanced."

"Fortunate indeed are those in which there is combined a little good and a little bad, a little knowledge of many things outside their own callings, a capacity for love and a capacity for hate, for such as these can look with tolerance upon all, unbiased by the egotism of him whose head is so heavy on one side that all his brains run to that point."

As Gahan ceased speaking Ghek made a little noise in his throat as one does who would attract attention. "You speak as one who has thought much upon many subjects. Is it, then, possible that you of the red race have pleasure in thought? Do you know aught of the joys of introspection? Do reason and logic form any part of your lives?"

"Most assuredly," replied Gahan, "but not to the extent of occupying all our time—at least not objectively. You, Ghek, are an example of the egotism of which I spoke. Because you and your kind devote your lives to the worship of mind, you believe that no other created beings think. And possibly we do not in the sense that you do, who think only of yourselves and your great brains. We think of many things that concern the welfare of a world. Had it not been for the red men of Barsoom even the kaldanes had perished from the planet, for while you may live without air the things upon which you depend for existence cannot, and there had been no air in sufficient quantities upon Barsoom these many ages had not a red man planned and built the great atmosphere plant which gave new life to a dying world.

"What have all the brains of all the kaldanes that have ever lived done to compare with that single idea of a single red man?"

Ghek was stumped. Being a kaldane he knew that brains spelled the sum total of universal achievement, but it had never occurred to him that they should be put to use in practical and profitable ways. He turned away and looked down upon the valley of his ancestors across which he was slowly drifting, into what unknown world? He should be a veritable god among the underlings, he knew; but somehow a doubt assailed him. It was evident that these two from that other world were ready to question his pre-eminence. Even through his great egotism was filtering a suspicion that they patronized him; perhaps even pitied him. Then he began to wonder what was to become of him. No longer would he have many rykors to do his bidding. Only this single one and when it died there could not be another. When it tired, Ghek must lie almost helpless while it rested. He wished that he had never seen this red woman. She had brought him only discontent and dishonour and now exile. Presently Tara of Helium commenced to hum a tune and Ghek, the kaldane, was content.

Gently they drifted beneath the hurtling moons above the mad shadows of a Martian night. The roaring of the banths came in diminishing volume to their ears as their craft passed on beyond the boundaries of Bantoom, leaving behind the terrors of that unhappy land. But to what were they being borne? The girl looked at the man sitting cross-legged upon the deck of the tiny flier, gazing off into the night ahead, apparently absorbed in thought.

"Where are we?" she asked. "Toward what are we drifting?"

Turan shrugged his broad shoulders. "The stars tell me that we are drifting toward the northeast," he replied, "but where we are, or what lies in our path I cannot even guess. A week since I could have sworn that I knew what lay behind each succeeding ridge that I approached; but now I admit in all humility that I have no conception of what lies a mile in any direction. Tara of Helium, I am lost, and that is all that I can tell you."

He was smiling and the girl smiled back at him. There was a slightly puzzled expression on her face—there was something tantalizingly familiar about that smile of his. She had met many a panthan—they came and went, following the fighting of a world—but she could not place this one.

"From what country are you, Turan?" she asked suddenly.

"Know you not, Tara of Helium," he countered, "that a panthan has no country? Today he fights beneath the banner of one master, tomorrow beneath that of another."

"But you must own allegiance to some country when you are not fighting," she insisted. "What banner, then, owns you now?"

He rose and stood before her, then, bowing low. "And I am acceptable," he said, "I serve beneath the banner of the daughter of The Warlord now—and forever."

She reached forth and touched his arm with a slim brown hand. "Your services are accepted," she said; "and if ever we reach Helium I promise that your reward shall be all that your heart could desire."

"I shall serve faithfully, hoping for that reward," he said; but Tara of Helium did not guess what was in his mind, thinking rather that he was mercenary. For how could the proud daughter of The Warlord guess that a simple panthan aspired to her hand and heart?

The dawn found them moving rapidly over an unfamiliar landscape. The wind had increased during the night and had borne them far from Bantoom. The country below them was rough and inhospitable. No water was visible and the surface of the ground was cut by deep gorges, while nowhere was any but the most meagre vegetation discernible. They saw no life of any nature, nor was there any indication that the country could support life. For two days they drifted over this horrid wasteland. They were without food or water and suffered accordingly. Ghek had temporarily abandoned his rykor after enlisting Turan's assistance in lashing it safely to the deck. The less he used it the less would its vitality be spent. Already it was showing the effects of privation. Ghek crawled about the vessel like a great spider—over the side, down beneath the keel, and up over the opposite rail. He seemed equally at home one place as another. For his companions, however, the quarters were cramped, for the deck of a one-man flier is not intended for three.

Turan sought always ahead for signs of water. Water they must have, or that water-giving plant which makes life possible upon many of the seemingly arid areas of Mars; but there was neither the one nor the other for these two days and now the third night was upon them. The girl did not complain, but Turan knew that she must be suffering and his heart was heavy within him. Ghek suffered least of all, and he explained to them that his kind could exist for long periods without food or water. Turan almost cursed him as he saw the form of Tara of Helium slowly wasting away before his eyes, while the hideous kaldane seemed as full of vitality as ever.

"There are circumstances," remarked Ghek, "under which a gross and material body is less desirable than a highly developed brain."

Turan looked at him, but said nothing. Tara of Helium smiled faintly. "One cannot blame him," she said, "were we not a bit boastful in the pride of our superiority? When our stomachs were filled," she added.

"Perhaps there is something to be said for their system," Turan admitted. "If we could but lay aside our stomachs when they cried for food and water I have no doubt but that we should do so."

"I should never miss mine now," assented Tara; "it is mighty poor company."

A new day had dawned, revealing a less desolate country and renewing again the hope that had been low within them. Suddenly Turan leaned forward, pointing ahead.

"Look, Tara of Helium!" he cried. "A city! As I am Ga—as I am Turan the panthan, a city."

Far in the distance the domes and walls and slender towers of a city shone in the rising sun. Quickly the man seized the control and the ship dropped rapidly behind a low range of intervening hills, for well Turan knew that they must not be seen until they could discover whether friend or foe inhabited the strange city. Chances were that they were far from the abode of friends and so must the panthan move with the utmost caution; but there was a city and where a city was, was water, even though it were a deserted city, and food if it were inhabited.

To the red man food and water, even in the citadel of an enemy, meant food and drink for Tara of Helium. He would accept it from friends or he would take it from enemies. Just so long as it was there he would have it—and there was shown the egotism of the fighting man, though Turan did not see it, nor Tara who came from a long line of fighting men; but Ghek might have smiled had he known how.

Turan permitted the flier to drift closer behind the screening hills, and then when he could advance no farther without fear of discovery, he dropped the craft gently to ground in a little ravine, and leaping over the side made her fast to a stout tree. For several moments they discussed their plans—whether it would be best to wait where they were until darkness hid their movements and then approach the city in search of food and water, or approach it now, taking advantage of what cover they could, until they could glean something of the nature of its inhabitants.

It was Turan's plan which finally prevailed. They would approach as close as safety dictated in the hope of finding water outside the city; food, too, perhaps. If they did not they could at least reconnoitre the ground by daylight, and then when night came Turan could quickly come close to the city and in comparative safety prosecute his search for food and drink.

Following the ravine upward they finally topped the summit of the ridge, from which they had an excellent view of that part of the city which lay nearest them, though themselves hidden by the brush behind which they crouched. Ghek had resumed his rykor, which had suffered less than either Tara or Turan through their enforced fast.

The first glance at the city, now much closer than when they had first discovered it, revealed the fact that it was inhabited. Banners and pennons broke from many a staff. People were moving about the gate before them. The high white walls were paced by sentinels at far intervals. Upon the roofs of higher buildings the women could be seen airing the sleeping silks and furs. Turan watched it all in silence for some time.

"I do not know them," he said at last. "I cannot guess what city this may be. But it is an ancient city. Its people have no fliers and no firearms. It must be old indeed."

"How do you know they have not these things?" asked the girl.

"There are no landing-stages upon the roofs—not one that can be seen from here; while were we looking similarly at Helium we would see hundreds. And they have no firearms because their defences are all built to withstand the attack of spear and arrow, with spear and arrow. They are an ancient people."

"If they are ancient perhaps they are friendly," suggested the girl. "Did we not learn as children in the history of our planet that it was once peopled by a friendly, peace-loving race?"

"But I fear they are not as ancient as that," replied Turan, laughing. "It has been long ages since the men of Barsoom loved peace."

"My father loves peace," returned the girl.

"And yet he is always at war," said the man.

She laughed. "But he says he likes peace."

"We all like peace," he rejoined; "peace with honour; but our neighbours will not let us have it, and so we must fight."

"And to fight well men must like to fight," she added.

"And to like to fight they must know how to fight," he said, "for no man likes to do the thing that he does not know how to do well."

"Or that some other man can do better than he."

"And so always there will be wars and men will fight," he concluded, "for always the men with hot blood in their veins will practice the art of war."

"We have settled a great question," said the girl, smiling; "but our stomachs are still empty."

"Your panthan is neglecting his duty," replied Turan; "and how can he with the great reward always before his eyes!"

She did not guess in what literal a sense he spoke.

"I go forthwith," he continued, "to wrest food and drink from the ancients."

"No," she cried, laying a hand upon his arm, "not yet. They would slay you or make you prisoner. You are a brave panthan and a mighty one, but you cannot overcome a city single-handed."

She smiled up into his face and her hand still lay upon his arm. He felt the thrill of hot blood coursing through his veins. He could have seized her in his arms and crushed her to him. There was only Ghek the kaldane there, but there was something stronger within him that restrained his hand. Who may define it—that inherent chivalry that renders certain men the natural protectors of women?

From their vantage point they saw a body of armed warriors ride forth from the gate, and winding along a well-beaten road pass from sight about the foot of the hill from which they watched. The men were red, like themselves, and they rode the small saddle thoats of the red race. Their trappings were barbaric and magnificent, and in their head-dress were many feathers as had been the custom of ancients. They were armed with swords and long spears and they rode almost naked, their bodies being painted in ochre and blue and white. There were, perhaps, a score of them in the party and as they galloped away on their tireless mounts they presented a picture at once savage and beautiful.

"They have the appearance of splendid warriors," said Turan. "I have a great mind to walk boldly into their city and seek service."

Tara shook her head. "Wait," she admonished. "What would I do without you, and if you were captured how could you collect your reward?"

"I should escape," he said. "At any rate I shall try it," and he started to rise.

"You shall not," said the girl, her tone all authority.

The man looked at her quickly—questioningly.

"You have entered my service," she said, a trifle haughtily.

"You have entered my service for hire and you shall do as I bid you."

Turan sank down beside her again with a half smile upon his lips. "It is yours to command, Princess," he said.

The day passed. Ghek, tiring of the sunlight, had deserted his rykor and crawled down a hole he had discovered close by. Tara and Turan reclined beneath the scant shade of a small tree. They watched the people coming and going through the gate. The party of horsemen did not return. A small herd of zitidars was driven into the city during the day, and once a caravan of broad-wheeled carts drawn by these huge animals wound out of the distant horizon and came down to the city. It, too, passed from their sight within the gateway. Then darkness came and Tara of Helium bid her panthan search for food and drink; but she cautioned him against attempting to enter the city. Before he left her he bent and kissed her hand as a warrior may kiss the hand of his queen.

CHAPTER 10

Entrapped

Turan the panthan approached the strange city under cover of the darkness. He entertained little hope of finding either food or water outside the wall, but he would try and then, if he failed, he would attempt to make his way into the city, for Tara of Helium must have sustenance and have it soon. He saw that the walls were poorly sentineled, but they were sufficiently high to render an attempt to scale them foredoomed to failure. Taking advantage of underbrush and trees, Turan managed to reach the base of the wall without detection. Silently he moved north past the gateway which was closed by a massive gate which effectively barred even the slightest glimpse within the city beyond. It was Turan's hope to find upon the north side of the city away from the hills a level plain where grew the crops of the inhabitants, and here too water from their irrigating system, but though he travelled far along that seemingly interminable wall he found no fields nor any water. He searched also for some means of ingress to the city, yet here, too, failure was his only reward, and now as he went keen eyes watched him from above and a silent stalker kept pace with him for a time upon the summit of the wall; but presently the shadower descended to the pavement within and hurrying swiftly raced ahead of the stranger without.

He came presently to a small gate beside which was a low building and before the doorway of the building a warrior standing guard. He spoke a few quick words to the warrior and then entered the building only to return almost immediately to the street, followed by fully forty warriors. Cautiously opening the gate the fellow peered carefully along the wall upon the outside in the direction from which he had come. Evidently satisfied, he issued a few words of instruction to those behind him, whereupon half the warriors returned to the interior of the building, while the other half followed the man stealthily through the gateway where they crouched low among the shrubbery in a half circle just north of the gateway which they had left open. Here they waited in utter silence, nor had they long to wait before Turan the panthan came cautiously along the base of the wall. To the very gate he came and when he found it and that it was open he paused for a moment, listening; then he approached and looked within. Assured that there was none within sight to apprehend him he stepped through the gateway into the city.

He found himself in a narrow street that paralleled the wall. Upon the opposite side rose buildings of an architecture unknown to him, yet strangely beautiful. While the buildings were packed closely together there seemed to be no two alike and their fronts were of all shapes and heights and of many hues. The skyline was broken by spire and dome and minaret and tall, slender towers, while the walls supported many a balcony and in the soft light of Cluros, the farther moon, now low in the west, he saw, to his surprise and consternation, the figures of people upon the balconies. Directly opposite him were two women and a man. They sat leaning upon the rail of the balcony looking, apparently, directly at him; but if they saw him they gave no sign.

Turan hesitated a moment in the face of almost certain discovery and then, assured that they must take him for one of their own people, he moved boldly into the avenue. Having no idea of the direction in which he might best hope to find what he sought, and not wishing to arouse suspicion by further hesitation, he turned to the left and stepped briskly along the pavement with the intention of placing himself as quickly as possible beyond the observation of those nocturnal watchers. He knew that the night must be far spent; and so he could not but wonder why people should sit upon their balconies when they should have been asleep among their silks and furs. At first he had thought them the late guests of some convivial host; but the windows behind them were shrouded in darkness and utter quiet prevailed, quite upsetting such a theory. And as he proceeded he passed many another group sitting silently upon other balconies. They paid no attention to him, seeming not even to note his passing. Some leaned with a single elbow upon the rail, their chins resting in their palms; others leaned upon both arms across the balcony, looking down into the street, while several that he saw held musical instruments in their hands, but their fingers moved not upon the strings.

And then Turan came to a point where the avenue turned to the right, to skirt a building that jutted from the inside of the city wall, and as he rounded the corner he came full upon two warriors standing upon either side of the entrance to a building upon his right. It was impossible for them not to be aware of his presence, yet neither moved, nor gave other evidence that they had seen him. He stood there waiting, his hand upon the hilt of his long-sword, but they neither challenged nor halted him. Could it be that these also thought him one of their own kind? Indeed upon no other grounds could he explain their inaction.

As Turan had passed through the gateway into the city and taken his unhindered way along the avenue, twenty warriors had entered the city and closed the gate behind them, and then one had taken to the wall and followed along its summit in the rear of Turan, and another had followed him along the avenue, while a third had crossed the street and entered one of the buildings upon the opposite side.

The balance of them, with the exception of a single sentinel beside the gate, had re-entered the building from which they had been summoned. They were well built, strapping, painted fellows, their naked figures covered now by gorgeous robes against the chill of night. As they spoke of the stranger they laughed at the ease with which they had tricked him, and were still laughing as they threw themselves upon their sleeping silks and furs to resume their broken slumber. It was evident that they constituted a guard detailed for the gate beside which they slept, and it was equally evident that the gates were guarded and the city watched much more carefully than Turan had believed. Chagrined indeed had been the Jed of Gathol had he dreamed that he was being so neatly tricked.

As Turan proceeded along the avenue he passed other sentries beside other doors but now he gave them small heed, since they neither challenged nor otherwise outwardly noted his passing; but while at nearly every turn of the erratic avenue he passed one or more of these silent sentinels he could not guess that he had passed one of them many times and that his every move was watched by silent, clever stalkers. Scarce had he passed a certain one of these rigid guardsmen before the fellow awoke to sudden life, bounded across the avenue, entered a narrow opening in the outer wall where he swiftly followed a corridor built within the wall itself until presently he emerged a little distance ahead of Turan, where he assumed the stiff and silent attitude of a soldier upon guard. Nor did Turan know that a second followed in the shadows of the buildings behind him, nor of the third who hastened ahead of him upon some urgent mission.

And so the panthan moved through the silent streets of the strange city in search of food and drink for the woman he loved. Men and women looked down upon him from shadowy balconies, but spoke not; and sentinels saw him pass and did not challenge. Presently from along the avenue before him came the familiar sound of clanking accoutrements, the herald of marching warriors, and almost simultaneously he saw upon his right an open doorway dimly lighted from within. It was the only available place where he might seek to hide from the approaching company, and while he had passed several sentries unquestioned he could scarce hope to escape scrutiny and questioning from a patrol, as he naturally assumed this body of men to be.

Inside the doorway he discovered a passage turning abruptly to the right and almost immediately thereafter to the left. There was none in sight within and so he stepped cautiously around the second turn the more effectually to be hidden from the street. Before him stretched a long corridor, dimly lighted like the entrance. Waiting there he heard the party approach the building, he heard someone at the entrance to his hiding place, and then he heard the door past which he had come slam to. He laid his hand upon his sword, expecting momentarily to hear footsteps approaching along the corridor; but none came. He approached the turn and looked around it; the corridor was empty to the closed door. Whoever had closed it had remained upon the outside.

Turan waited, listening. He heard no sound. Then he advanced to the door and placed an ear against it. All was silence in the street beyond. A sudden draft must have closed the door, or perhaps it was the duty of the patrol to see to such things. It was immaterial. They had evidently passed on and now he would return to the street and continue upon his way. Somewhere there would be a public fountain where he could obtain water, and the chance of food lay in the strings of dried vegetables and meat which hung before the doorways of nearly every Barsoomian home of the poorer classes that he had ever seen. It was this district he was seeking, and it was for this reason his search had led him away from the main gate of the city which he knew would not be located in a poor district.

He attempted to open the door only to find that it resisted his every effort—it was locked upon the outside. Here indeed was a sorry contretemps. Turan the panthan scratched his head. "Fortune frowns upon me," he murmured; but beyond the door, Fate, in the form of a painted warrior, stood smiling. Neatly had he tricked the unwary stranger. The lighted doorway, the marching patrol—these had been planned and timed to a nicety by the third warrior who had sped ahead of Turan along another avenue, and the stranger had done precisely what the fellow had thought he would do—no wonder, then, that he smiled.

This exit barred to him Turan turned back into the corridor. He followed it cautiously and silently. Occasionally there was a door on one side or the other. These he tried only to find each securely locked. The corridor wound more erratically the farther he advanced. A locked door barred his way at its end, but a door upon his right opened and he stepped into a dimly-lighted chamber, about the walls of which were three other doors, each of which he tried in turn. Two were locked; the other opened upon a runway leading downward. It was spiral and he could see no farther than the first turn. A door in the corridor he had quitted opened after he had passed, and the third warrior stepped out and followed after him. A faint smile still lingered upon the fellow's grim lips.

Turan drew his short-sword and cautiously descended. At the bottom was a short corridor with a closed door at the end. He approached the single heavy panel and listened. No sound came to him from beyond the mysterious portal. Gently he tried the door, which swung easily toward him at his touch. Before him was a low-ceiled chamber with a dirt floor. Set in its walls were several other doors and all were closed. As Turan stepped cautiously within, the third warrior descended the spiral runway behind him. The panthan crossed the room quickly and tried a door. It was locked. He heard a muffled click behind him and turned about with ready sword. He was alone; but the door through which he had entered was closed—it was the click of its lock that he had heard.

With a bound he crossed the room and attempted to open it; but to no avail. No longer did he seek silence, for he knew now that the thing had gone beyond the sphere of chance. He threw his weight against the wooden panel; but the thick skeel of which it was constructed would have withstood a battering ram. From beyond came a low laugh.

Rapidly Turan examined each of the other doors. They were all locked. A glance about the chamber revealed a wooden table and a bench. Set in the walls were several heavy rings to which rusty chains were attached—all too significant of the purpose to which the room was dedicated. In the dirt floor near the wall were two or three holes resembling the mouths of burrows—doubtless the habitat of the giant Martian rat. He had observed this much when suddenly the dim light was extinguished, leaving him in darkness utter and complete. Turan, groping about, sought the table and the bench. Placing the latter against the wall he drew the table in front of him and sat down upon the bench, his long-sword gripped in readiness before him. At least they should fight before they took him.

For some time he sat there waiting for he knew not what. No sound penetrated to his subterranean dungeon. He slowly revolved in his mind the incidents of the evening—the open, unguarded gate; the lighted doorway—the only one he had seen thus open and lighted along the avenue he had followed; the advance of the warriors at precisely the moment that he could find no other avenue of escape or concealment; the corridors and chambers that led past many locked doors to this underground prison leaving no other path for him to pursue.

"By my first ancestor!" he swore; "but it was simple and I a simpleton. They tricked me neatly and have taken me without exposing themselves to a scratch; but for what purpose?"

He wished that he might answer that question and then his thoughts turned to the girl waiting there on the hill beyond the city for him—and he would never come. He knew the ways of the more savage peoples of Barsoom. No, he would never come, now. He had disobeyed her. He smiled at the sweet recollection of those words of command that had fallen from her dear lips. He had disobeyed her and now he had lost the reward.

But what of her? What now would be her fate—starving before a hostile city with only an inhuman kaldane for company? Another thought—a horrid thought—obtruded itself upon him. She had told him of the hideous sights she had witnessed in the burrows of the kaldanes and he knew that they ate human flesh. Ghek was starving. Should he eat his rykor he would be helpless; but—there was sustenance there for them both, for the rykor and the kaldane. Turan cursed himself for a fool. Why had he left her? Far better to have remained and died with her, ready always to protect her, than to have left her at the mercy of the hideous Bantoomian.

Now Turan detected a heavy door in the air. It oppressed him with a feeling of drowsiness. He would have risen to fight off the creeping lethargy, but his legs seemed weak, so that he sank again to the bench. Presently his sword slipped from his fingers and he sprawled forward upon the table his head resting upon his arms.

★ ★ ★ ★ ★

Tara of Helium, as the night wore on and Turan did not return, became more and more uneasy, and when dawn broke with no sign of him she guessed that he had failed. Something more than her own unhappy predicament brought a feeling of sorrow to her heart—of sorrow and loneliness. She realized now how she had come to depend upon this panthan not only for protection but for companionship as well. She missed him, and in missing him realized suddenly that he had meant more to her than a mere hired warrior. It was as though a friend had been taken from her—an old and valued friend. She rose from her place of concealment that she might have a better view of the city.

U-Dor, dwar of the 8th Utan of O-Tar, Jeddak of Manator, rode back in the early dawn toward Manator from a brief excursion to a neighbouring village. As he was rounding the hills south of the city, his keen eyes were attracted by a slight movement among the shrubbery close to the summit of the nearest hill. He halted his vicious mount and watched more closely. He saw a figure rise facing away from him and peer down toward Manator beyond the hill.

"Come!" he signalled to his followers, and with a word to this thoat turned the beast at a rapid gallop up the hillside. In his wake swept his twenty savage warriors, the padded feet of their mounts soundless upon the soft turf. It was the rattle of side-arms and harness that brought Tara of Helium suddenly about, facing them. She saw a score of warriors with couched lances bearing down upon her.

She glanced at Ghek. What would the spiderman do in this emergency? She saw him crawl to his rykor and attach himself. Then he arose, the beautiful body once again animated and alert. She thought that the creature was preparing for flight. Well, it made little difference to her. Against such as were streaming up the hill toward them a single mediocre swordsman such as Ghek was worse than no defence at all.

"Hurry, Ghek!" she admonished him. "Back into the hills! You may find there a hiding-place;" but the creature only stepped between her and the oncoming riders, drawing his long-sword.

"It is useless, Ghek," she said, when she saw that he intended to defend her. "What can a single sword accomplish against such odds?"

"I can die but once," replied the kaldane. "You and your panthan saved me from Luud and I but do what your panthan would do were he here to protect you."

"It is brave, but it is useless," she replied. "Sheathe your sword. They may not intend us harm."

Ghek let the point of his weapon drop to the ground, but he did not sheathe it, and thus the two stood waiting as U-Dor the dwar stopped his thoat before them while his twenty warriors formed a rough circle about. For a long minute U-Dor sat his mount in silence, looking searchingly first at Tara of Helium and then at her hideous companion.

"What manner of creature are you?" he asked presently. "And what do you before the gates of Manator?"

"We are from far countries," replied the girl, "and we are lost and starving. We ask only food and rest and the privilege to go our way seeking our own homes." U-Dor smiled a grim smile. "Manator and the hills which guard it alone know the age of Manator," he said; "yet in all the ages that have rolled by since Manator first was, there be no record in the annals of Manator of a stranger departing from Manator."

"But I am a princess," cried the girl haughtily, "and my country is not at war with yours. You must give me and my companions aid and assist us to return to our own land. It is the law of Barsoom."

"Manator knows only the laws of Manator," replied U-Dor; "but come. You shall go with us to the city, where you, being beautiful, need have no fear. I, myself, will protect you if O-Tar so decrees. And as for your companion—but hold! You said 'companions'—there are others of your party then?" "You see what you see," replied Tara haughtily.

"Be that as it may," said U-Dor. "If there be more they shall not escape Manator; but as I was saying, if your companion fights well he too may live, for O-Tar is just, and just are the laws of Manator. Come!"

Ghek demurred.

"It is useless," said the girl, seeing that he would have stood his ground and fought them. "Let us go with them. Why pit your puny blade against their mighty ones when there should lie in your great brain the means to outwit them?" She spoke in a low whisper, rapidly.

"You are right, Tara of Helium," he replied and sheathed his sword.

And so they moved down the hillside toward the gates of Manator—Tara, Princess of Helium, and Ghek, the kaldane of Bantoom—and surrounding them rode the savage, painted warriors of U-Dor, dwar of the 8th Utan of O-Tar, Jeddak of Manator.

Chapter 11

The Choice of Tara

The dazzling sunlight of Barsoom clothed Manator in an aureole of splendour as the girl and her captors rode into the city through The Gate of Enemies. Here the wall was some fifty feet thick, and the sides of the passageway within the gate were covered with parallel shelves of masonry from bottom to top. Within these shelves, or long, horizontal niches, stood row upon row of small figures, appearing like tiny, grotesque statuettes of men, their long, black hair falling below their feet and sometimes trailing to the shelf beneath. The figures were scarce a foot in height and but for their diminutive proportions might have been the mummified bodies of once living men. The girl noticed that as they passed, the warriors saluted the figures with their spears after the manner of Barsoomian fighting men in extending a military courtesy, and then they rode on into the avenue beyond, which ran, wide and stately, through the city toward the east.

On either side were great buildings wondrously wrought. Paintings of great beauty and antiquity covered many of the walls, their colours softened and blended by the suns of ages. Upon the pavement the life of the newly-awakened city was already afoot. Women in brilliant trappings, befeathered warriors, their bodies daubed with paint; artisans, armed but less gaily caparisoned, took their various ways upon the duties of the day. A giant zitidar, magnificent in rich harness, rumbled its broad-wheeled cart along the stone pavement toward The Gate of Enemies. Life and colour and beauty wrought together a picture that filled the eyes of Tara of Helium with wonder and with admiration, for here was a scene out of the dead past of dying Mars. Such had been the cities of the founders of her race before Throxeus, mightiest of oceans, had disappeared from the face of a world. And from balconies on either side men and women looked down in silence upon the scene below.

The people in the street looked at the two prisoners, especially at the hideous Ghek, and called out in question or comment to their guard; but the watchers upon the balconies spoke not, nor did one so much as turn a head to note their passing. There were many balconies on each building and not a one that did not hold its silent party of richly trapped men and women, with here and there a child or two, but even the children maintained the uniform silence and immobility of their elders. As they approached the centre of the city the girl saw that even the roofs bore companies of these idle watchers, harnessed and bejewelled as for some gala-day of laughter and music, but no laughter broke from those silent lips, nor any music from the strings of the instruments that many of them held in jewelled fingers.

And now the avenue widened into an immense square, at the far end of which rose a stately edifice gleaming white in virgin marble among the gaily painted buildings surrounding it and its scarlet sward and gaily-flowering, green-foliaged shrubbery. Toward this U-Dor led his prisoners and their guard to the great arched entrance before which a line of fifty mounted warriors barred the way. When the commander of the guard recognized U-Dor the guardsmen fell back to either side leaving a broad avenue through which the party passed. Directly inside the entrance were inclined runways leading upward on either side. U-Dor turned to the left and led them upward to the second floor and down a long corridor. Here they passed other mounted men and in chambers upon either side they saw more. Occasionally there was another runway leading either up or down. A warrior, his steed at full gallop, dashed into sight from one of these and raced swiftly past them upon some errand.

Nowhere as yet had Tara of Helium seen a man afoot in this great building; but when at a turn, U-Dor led them to the third floor she caught glimpses of chambers in which many riderless thoats were penned and others adjoining where dismounted warriors lolled at ease or played games of skill or chance and many there were who played at jetan, and then the party passed into a long, wide hall of state, as magnificent an apartment as even a princess of mighty Helium ever had seen. The length of the room ran an arched ceiling ablaze with countless radium bulbs. The mighty spans extended from wall to wall leaving the vast floor unbroken by a single column. The arches were of white marble, apparently quarried in single, huge blocks from which each arch was cut complete. Between the arches, the ceiling was set solid about the radium bulbs with precious stones whose scintillant fire and colour and beauty filled the whole apartment. The stones were carried down the walls in an irregular fringe for a few feet, where they appeared to hang like a beautiful and gorgeous drapery against the white marble of the wall. The marble ended some six or seven feet from the floor, the walls from that point down being wainscoted in solid gold. The floor itself was of marble richly inlaid with gold. In that single room was a vast treasure equal to the wealth of many a large city.

But what riveted the girl's attention even more than the fabulous treasure of decorations were the files of gorgeously harnessed warriors who sat their thoats in grim silence and immobility on either side of the central aisle, rank after rank of them to the farther walls, and as the party passed between them she could not note so much as the flicker of an eyelid, or the twitching of a thoat's ear.

"The Hall of Chiefs," whispered one of her guard, evidently noting her interest. There was a note of pride in the fellow's voice and something of hushed awe. Then they passed through a great doorway into the chamber beyond, a large, square room in which a dozen mounted warriors lolled in their saddles.

As U-Dor and his party entered the room, the warriors came quickly erect in their saddles and formed a line before another door upon the opposite side of the wall. The padwar commanding them saluted U-Dor who, with his party, had halted facing the guard.

"Send one to O-Tar announcing that U-Dor brings two prisoners worthy of the observation of the great jeddak," said U-Dor; "one because of her extreme beauty, the other because of his extreme ugliness."

"O-Tar sits in council with the lesser chiefs," replied the lieutenant; "but the words of U-Dor the dwar shall be carried to him," and he turned and gave instructions to one who sat his thoat behind him.

"What manner of creature is the male?" he asked of U-Dor. "It cannot be that both are of one race."

"They were together in the hills south of the city," explained U-Dor, "and they say that they are lost and starving."

"The woman is beautiful," said the padwar. "She will not long go begging in the city of Manator," and then they spoke of other matters—of the doings of the palace, of the expedition of U-Dor, until the messenger returned to say that O-Tar bade them bring the prisoners to him.

They passed then through a massive doorway, which, when opened, revealed the great council chamber of O-Tar, Jeddak of Manator, beyond. A central aisle led from the doorway the full length of the great hall, terminating at the steps of a marble dais upon which a man sat in a great throne-chair. Upon either side of the aisle were ranged rows of highly carved desks and chairs of skeel, a hard wood of great beauty. Only a few of the desks were occupied—those in the front row, just below the rostrum.

At the entrance U-Dor dismounted with four of his followers who formed a guard about the two prisoners who were then conducted toward the foot of the throne, following a few paces behind U-Dor. As they halted at the foot of the marble steps, the proud gaze of Tara of Helium rested upon the enthroned figure of the man above her. He sat erect without stiffness—a commanding presence trapped in the barbaric splendour that the Barsoomian chieftain loves. He was a large man, the perfection of whose handsome face was marred only by the hauteur of his cold eyes and the suggestion of cruelty imparted by too thin lips. It needed no second glance to assure the least observing that here indeed was a ruler of men—a fighting jeddak whose people might worship but not love, and for whose slightest favour warriors would vie with one another to go forth and die. This was O-Tar, Jeddak of Manator, and as Tara of Helium saw him for the first time she could not but acknowledge a certain admiration for this savage chieftain who so virilely personified the ancient virtues of the God of War.

U-Dor and the jeddak interchanged the simple greetings of Barsoom, and then the former recounted the details of the discovery and capture of the prisoners. O-Tar scrutinized them both intently during U-Dor's narration of events, his expression revealing naught of what passed in the brain behind those inscrutable eyes. When the officer had finished the jeddak fastened his gaze upon Ghek.

"And you," he asked, "what manner of thing are you? From what country? Why are you in Manator?"

"I am a kaldane," replied Ghek; "the highest type of created creature upon the face of Barsoom; I am mind, you are matter. I come from Bantoom. I am here because we were lost and starving."

"And you!" O-Tar turned suddenly on Tara. "You, too, are a kaldane?"

"I am a princess of Helium," replied the girl. "I was a prisoner in Bantoom. This kaldane and a warrior of my own race rescued me. The warrior left us to search for food and water. He has doubtless fallen into the hands of your people. I ask you to free him and give us food and drink and let us go upon our way. I am a granddaughter of a jeddak, the daughter of a jeddak of jeddaks, The Warlord of Barsoom. I ask only the treatment that my people would accord you or yours."

"Helium," repeated O-Tar. "I know naught of Helium, nor does the Jeddak of Helium rule Manator. I, O-Tar, am Jeddak of Manator. I alone rule. I protect my own. You have never seen a woman or a warrior of Manator captive in Helium! Why should I protect the people of another jeddak? It is his duty to protect them. If he cannot, he is weak, and his people must fall into the hands of the strong. I, O-Tar, am strong. I will keep you. That—" he pointed at Ghek—"can it fight?"

"It is brave," replied Tara of Helium, "but it has not the skill at arms which my people possess."

"There is none then to fight for you?" asked O-Tar. "We are a just people," he continued without waiting for a reply, "and had you one to fight for you he might win to freedom for himself and you as well."

"But U-Dor assured me that no stranger ever had departed from Manator," she answered.

O-Tar shrugged. "That does not disprove the justice of the laws of Manator," replied O-Tar, "but rather that the warriors of Manator are invincible. Had there come one who could defeat our warriors that one had won to liberty."

"And you fetch my warrior," cried Tara haughtily, "you shall see such swordplay as doubtless the crumbling walls of your decaying city never have witnessed, and if there be no trick in your offer we are already as good as free."

O-Tar smiled more broadly than before and U-Dor smiled, too, and the chiefs and warriors who looked on nudged one another and whispered, laughing. And Tara of Helium knew then that there was trickery in their justice; but though her situation seemed hopeless she did not cease to hope, for was she not the daughter of John Carter, Warlord of Barsoom, whose famous challenge to Fate, "I still live!" remained the one irreducible defence against despair? At thought of her noble sire the patrician chin of Tara of Helium rose a shade higher. Ah! if he but knew where she was there were little to fear then. The hosts of Helium would batter at the gates of Manator, the great green warriors of John Carter's savage allies would swarm up from the dead sea bottoms lusting for pillage and for loot, the stately ships of her beloved navy would soar above the unprotected towers and minarets of the doomed city which only capitulation and heavy tribute could then save.

But John Carter did not know! There was only one other to whom she might hope to look—Turan the panthan; but where was he? She had seen his sword in play and she knew that it had been wielded by a master hand, and who should know swordplay better than Tara of Helium, who had learned it well under the constant tutorage of John Carter himself. Tricks she knew that discounted even far greater physical prowess than her own, and a method of attack that might have been at once the envy and despair of the cleverest of warriors. And so it was that her thoughts turned to Turan the panthan, though not alone because of the protection he might afford her. She had realized, since he had left her in search of food, that there had grown between them a certain comradeship that she now missed. There had been that about him which seemed to have bridged the gulf between their stations in life. With him she had failed to consider that he was a panthan or that she was a princess—they had been comrades. Suddenly she realized that she missed him for himself more than for his sword. She turned toward O-Tar.

"Where is Turan, my warrior?" she demanded.

"You shall not lack for warriors," replied the jeddak. "One of your beauty will find plenty ready to fight for her. Possibly it shall not be necessary to look farther than the jeddak of Manator. You please me, woman. What say you to such an honour?"

Through narrowed lids the Princess of Helium scrutinized the Jeddak of Manator, from feathered headdress to sandaled foot and back to feathered headdress.

"'Honour'!" she mimicked in tones of scorn. "I please thee, do I? Then know, swine, that thou pleaseth me not—that the daughter of John Carter is not for such as thou!"

A sudden, tense silence fell upon the assembled chiefs. Slowly the blood receded from the sinister face of O-Tar, Jeddak of Manator, leaving him a sickly purple in his wrath. His eyes narrowed to two thin slits, his lips were compressed to a bloodless line of malevolence. For a long moment there was no sound in the throne room of the palace at Manator. Then the jeddak turned toward U-Dor.

"Take her away," he said in a level voice that belied his appearance of rage. "Take her away, and at the next games let the prisoners and the common warriors play at Jetan for her."

"And this?" asked U-Dor, pointing at Ghek.

"To the pits until the next games," replied O-Tar.

"So this is your vaunted justice!" cried Tara of Helium; "that two strangers who have not wronged you shall be sentenced without trial? And one of them is a woman. The swine of Manator are as just as they are brave."

"Away with her!" shouted O-Tar, and at a sign from U-Dor the guards formed about the two prisoners and conducted them from the chamber.

Outside the palace, Ghek and Tara of Helium were separated. The girl was led through long avenues toward the centre of the city and finally into a low building, topped by lofty towers of massive construction. Here she was turned over to a warrior who wore the insignia of a dwar, or captain.

"It is O-Tar's wish," explained U-Dor to this one, "that she be kept until the next games, when the prisoners and the common warriors shall play for her. Had she not the tongue of a thoat she had been a worthy stake for our noblest steel," and U-Dor sighed. "Perhaps even yet I may win a pardon for her. It were too bad to see such beauty fall to the lot of some common fellow. I would have honoured her myself."

"If I am to be imprisoned, imprison me," said the girl. "I do not recall that I was sentenced to listen to the insults of every low-born boor who chanced to admire me."

"You see, A-Kor," cried U-Dor, "the tongue that she has. Even so and worse spoke she to O-Tar the jeddak."

"I see," replied A-Kor, whom Tara saw was with difficulty restraining a smile. "Come, then, with me, woman," he said, "and we shall find a safe place within The Towers of Jetan—but stay! what ails thee?"

The girl had staggered and would have fallen had not the man caught her in his arms. She seemed to gather herself then and bravely sought to stand erect without support. A-Kor glanced at U-Dor. "Knew you the woman was ill?" he asked.

"Possibly it is lack of food," replied the other. "She mentioned, I believe, that she and her companions had not eaten for several days."

"Brave are the warriors of O-Tar," sneered A-Kor; "lavish their hospitality. U-Dor, whose riches are uncounted, and the brave O-Tar, whose squealing thoats are stabled within marble halls and fed from troughs of gold, can spare no crust to feed a starving girl."

The black haired U-Dor scowled. "Thy tongue will yet pierce thy heart, son of a slave!" he cried. "Once too often mayst thus try the patience of the just O-Tar. Hereafter guard thy speech as well as thy towers."

"Think not to taunt me with my mother's state," said A-Kor. "'Tis the blood of the slave woman that fills my veins with pride, and my only shame is that I am also the son of thy jeddak."

"And O-Tar heard this?" queried U-Dor.

"O-Tar has already heard it from my own lips," replied A-Kor; "this, and more."

He turned upon his heel, a supporting arm still around the waist of Tara of Helium and thus he half led, half carried her into The Towers of Jetan, while U-Dor wheeled his thoat and galloped back in the direction of the palace.

Within the main entrance to The Tower of Jetan lolled a half-dozen warriors. To one of these spoke A-Kor, keeper of the towers. "Fetch Lan-O, the slave girl, and bid her bring food and drink to the upper level of the Thurian tower," then he lifted the half-fainting girl in his arms and bore her along the spiral, inclined runway that led upward within the tower.

Somewhere in the long ascent Tara lost consciousness. When it returned she found herself in a large, circular chamber, the stone walls of which were pierced by windows at regular intervals about the entire circumference of the room. She was lying upon a pile of sleeping silks and furs while there knelt above her a young woman who was forcing drops of some cooling beverage between her parched lips. Tara of Helium half rose upon an elbow and looked about. In the first moments of returning consciousness there were swept from the screen of recollection the happenings of many weeks. She thought that she awoke in the palace of The Warlord at Helium. Her brows knit as she scrutinized the strange face bending over her.

"Who are you?" she asked, and, "Where is Uthia?"

"I am Lan-O the slave girl," replied the other. "I know none by the name of Uthia."

Tara of Helium sat erect and looked about her. This rough stone was not the marble of her father's halls. "Where am I?" she asked.

"In The Thurian Tower," replied the girl, and then seeing that the other still did not understand she guessed the truth. "You are a prisoner in The Towers of Jetan in the city of Manator," she explained. "You were brought to this chamber, weak and fainting, by A-Kor, Dwar of The Towers of Jetan, who sent me to you with food and drink, for kind is the heart of A-Kor."

"I remember, now," said Tara, slowly. "I remember; but where is Turan, my warrior? Did they speak of him?"

"I heard naught of another," replied Lan-O; "you alone were brought to the towers. In that you are fortunate, for there be no nobler man in Manator than A-Kor. It is his mother's blood that makes him so. She was a slave girl from Gathol."

"Gathol!" exclaimed Tara of Helium. "Lies Gathol close by Manator?"

"Not close, yet still the nearest country," replied Lan-O. "About twenty-two degrees* east, it lies."

"Gathol!" murmured Tara, "Far Gathol!"

"But you are not from Gathol," said the slave girl; "your harness is not of Gathol."

"I am from Helium," said Tara

"It is far from Helium to Gathol," said the slave girl, "but in our studies we learned much of the greatness of Helium, we of Gathol, so it seems not so far away."

"You, too, are from Gathol?" asked Tara.

"Many of us are from Gathol who are slaves in Manator," replied the girl. "It is to Gathol, nearest country, that the Manatorians look for slaves most often. They go in great numbers at intervals of three or seven years and haunt the roads that lead to Gathol, and thus they capture whole caravans leaving none to bear warning to Gathol of their fate. Nor do any ever escape from Manator to carry word of us back to Gahan our jed."

Tara of Helium ate slowly and in silence. The girl's words aroused memories of the last hours she had spent in her father's palace and the great midday function at which she had met Gahan of Gathol. Even now she flushed as she recalled his daring words.

Upon her reveries the door opened and a burly warrior appeared in the opening—a hulking fellow, with thick lips and an evil, leering face. The slave girl sprang to her feet, facing him.

"What does this mean, E-Med?" she cried, "was it not the will of A-Kor that this woman be not disturbed?"

"The will of A-Kor, indeed!" and the man sneered. "The will of A-Kor is without power in The Towers of Jetan, or elsewhere, for A-Kor lies now in the pits of O-Tar, and E-Med is dwar of the Towers."

Tara of Helium saw the face of the slave girl pale and the terror in her eyes.

---

* Approximately 814 Earth Miles.

Chapter 12

Ghek Plays Pranks

While Tara of Helium was being led to The Towers of Jetan, Ghek was escorted to the pits beneath the palace where he was imprisoned in a dimly-lighted chamber. Here he found a bench and a table standing upon the dirt floor near the wall, and set in the wall several rings from which depended short lengths of chain. At the base of the walls were several holes in the dirt floor. These, alone, of the several things he saw, interested him. Ghek sat down upon the bench and waited in silence, listening. Presently the lights were extinguished. If Ghek could have smiled he would have then, for Ghek could see as well in the dark as in the light—better, perhaps. He watched the dark openings of the holes in the floor and waited. Presently he detected a change in the air about him—it grew heavy with a strange door, and once again might Ghek have smiled, could he have smiled.

Let them replace all the air in the chamber with their most deadly fumes; it would be all the same to Ghek, the kaldane, who, having no lungs, required no air. With the rykor it might be different. Deprived of air it would die; but if only a sufficient amount of the gas was introduced to stupefy an ordinary creature it would have no effect upon the rykor, who had no objective mind to overcome. So long as the excess of carbon dioxide in the blood was not sufficient to prevent heart action, the rykor would suffer only a diminution of vitality; but would still respond to the exciting agency of the kaldane's brain.

Ghek caused the rykor to assume a sitting position with its back against the wall where it might remain without direction from his brain. Then he released his contact with its spinal cord; but remained in position upon its shoulders, waiting and watching, for the kaldane's curiosity was aroused. He had not long to wait before the lights were flashed on and one of the locked doors opened to admit a half-dozen warriors. They approached him rapidly and worked quickly. First they removed all his weapons and then, snapping a fetter about one of the rykor's ankles, secured him to the end of one of the chains hanging from the walls. Next they dragged the long table to a new position and there bolted it to the floor so that an end, instead of the middle, was directly before the prisoner. On the table before him they set food and water and upon the opposite end of the table they laid the key to the fetter. Then they unlocked and opened all the doors and departed.

* * * * *

When Turan the panthan regained consciousness it was to the realization of a sharp pain in one of his forearms. The effects of the gas departed as rapidly as they had overcome him so that as he opened his eyes he was in full possession of all his faculties. The lights were on again and in their glow there was revealed to the man the figure of a giant Martian rat crouching upon the table and gnawing upon his arm. Snatching his arm away he reached for his short-sword, while the rat, growling, sought to seize his arm again. It was then that Turan discovered that his weapons had been removed—short-sword, long-sword, dagger, and pistol. The rat charged him then and striking the creature away with his hand the man rose and backed off, searching for something with which to strike a harder blow. Again the rat charged and as Turan stepped quickly back to avoid the menacing jaws, something seemed to jerk suddenly upon his right ankle, and as he drew his left foot back to regain his equilibrium his heel caught upon a taut chain and he fell heavily backward to the floor just as the rat leaped upon his breast and sought his throat.

The Martian rat is a fierce and unlovely thing. It is many-legged and hairless, its hide resembling that of a newborn mouse in repulsiveness. In size and weight it is comparable to a large Airedale terrier. Its eyes are small and close-set, and almost hidden in deep, fleshy apertures. But its most ferocious and repulsive feature is its jaws, the entire bony structure of which protrudes several inches beyond the flesh, revealing five sharp, spade-like teeth in the upper jaw and the same number of similar teeth in the lower, the whole suggesting the appearance of a rotting face from which much of the flesh has sloughed away.

It was such a thing that leaped upon the breast of the panthan to tear at his jugular. Twice Turan struck it away as he sought to regain his feet, but both times it returned with increased ferocity to renew the attack. Its only weapons are its jaws since its broad, splay feet are armed with blunt talons. With its protruding jaws it excavates its winding burrows and with its broad feet it pushes the dirt behind it. To keep the jaws from his flesh then was Turan's only concern and this he succeeded in doing until chance gave him a hold upon the creature's throat. After that the end was but a matter of moments. Rising at last he flung the lifeless thing from him with a shudder of disgust.

Now he turned his attention to a hurried inventory of the new conditions which surrounded him since the moment of his incarceration. He realized vaguely what had happened. He had been anaesthetized and stripped of his weapons, and as he rose to his feet he saw that one ankle was fettered to a chain in the wall. He looked about the room. All the doors swung wide open! His captors would render his imprisonment the more cruel by leaving ever before him tempting glimpses of open aisles to the freedom he could not attain. Upon the end of the table and within easy reach was food and drink. This at least was attainable and at sight of it his starved stomach seemed almost to cry aloud for sustenance. It was with difficulty that he ate and drank in moderation.

As he devoured the food his eyes wandered about the confines of his prison until suddenly they seized upon a thing that lay on the table at the end farthest from him. It was a key. He raised his fettered ankle and examined the lock. There could be no doubt of it! The key that lay there on the table before him was the key to that very lock. A careless warrior had laid it there and departed, forgetting.

Hope surged high in the breast of Gahan of Gathol, of Turan the panthan. Furtively his eyes sought the open doorways. There was no one in sight. Ah, if he could but gain his freedom! He would find some way from this odious city back to her side and never again would he leave her until he had won safety for her or death for himself.

He rose and moved cautiously toward the opposite end of the table where lay the coveted key. The fettered ankle halted his first step, but he stretched at full length along the table, extending eager fingers toward the prize. They almost laid hold upon it—a little more and they would touch it. He strained and stretched, but still the thing lay just beyond his reach. He hurled himself forward until the iron fetter bit deep into his flesh, but all futilely. He sat back upon the bench then and glared at the open doors and the key, realizing now that they were part of a well-laid scheme of refined torture, none the less demoralizing because it inflicted no physical suffering.

For just a moment the man gave way to useless regret and foreboding, then he gathered himself together, his brows cleared, and he returned to his unfinished meal. At least they should not have the satisfaction of knowing how sorely they had hit him. As he ate it occurred to him that by dragging the table along the floor he could bring the key within his reach, but when he essayed to do so, he found that the table had been securely bolted to the floor during the period of his unconsciousness. Again Gahan smiled and shrugged and resumed his eating.

*****

When the warriors had departed from the prison in which Ghek was confined, the kaldane crawled from the shoulders of the rykor to the table. Here he drank a little water and then directed the hands of the rykor to the balance of it and to the food, upon which the brainless thing fell with avidity. While it was thus engaged Ghek took his spider-like way along the table to the opposite end where lay the key to the fetter. Seizing it in a chela he leaped to the floor and scurried rapidly toward the mouth of one of the burrows against the wall, into which he disappeared. For long had the brain been contemplating these burrow entrances. They appealed to his kaldanean tastes, and further, they pointed a hiding place for the key and a lair for the only kind of food that the kaldane relished—flesh and blood.

Ghek had never seen an ulsio, since these great Martian rats had long ago disappeared from Bantoom, their flesh and blood having been greatly relished by the kaldanes; but Ghek had inherited, almost unimpaired, every memory of every ancestor, and so he knew that ulsio inhabited these lairs and that ulsio was good to eat, and he knew what ulsio looked like and what his habits were, though he had never seen him nor any picture of him. As we breed animals for the transmission of physical attributes, so the Kaldanes breed themselves for the transmission of attributes of the mind, including memory and the power of recollection, and thus have they raised what we term instinct, above the level of the threshold of the objective mind where it may be commanded and utilized by recollection. Doubtless in our own subjective minds lie many of the impressions and experiences of our forebears. These may impinge upon our consciousness in dreams only, or in vague, haunting suggestions that we have before experienced some transient phase of our present existence. Ah, if we had but the power to recall them! Before us would unfold the forgotten story of the lost eons that have preceded us. We might even walk with God in the garden of His stars while man was still but a budding idea within His mind.

Ghek descended into the burrow at a steep incline for some ten feet, when he found himself in an elaborate and delightful network of burrows! The kaldane was elated. This indeed was life! He moved rapidly and fearlessly and he went as straight to his goal as you could to the kitchen of your own home. This goal lay at a low level in a spheroidal cavity about the size of a large barrel. Here, in a nest of torn bits of silk and fur lay six baby ulsios.

When the mother returned there were but five babies and a great spider-like creature, which she immediately sprang to attack only to be met by powerful chelae which seized and held her so that she could not move. Slowly they dragged her throat toward a hideous mouth and in a little moment she was dead.

Ghek might have remained in the nest for a long time, since there was ample food for many days; but he did not do so. Instead he explored the burrows. He followed them into many subterranean chambers of the city of Manator, and upward through walls to rooms above the ground. He found many ingeniously devised traps, and he found poisoned food and other signs of the constant battle that the inhabitants of Manator waged against these repulsive creatures that dwelt beneath their homes and public buildings.

His exploration revealed not only the vast proportions of the network of runways that apparently traversed every portion of the city, but the great antiquity of the majority of them. Tons upon tons of dirt must have been removed, and for a long time he wondered where it had been deposited, until in following downward a tunnel of great size and length he sensed before him the thunderous rush of subterranean waters, and presently came to the bank of a great, underground river, tumbling onward, no doubt, the length of a world to the buried sea of Omean. Into this torrential sewer had unthinkable generations of ulsios pushed their few handfuls of dirt in the excavating of their vast labyrinth.

For only a moment did Ghek tarry by the river, for his seemingly aimless wanderings were in reality prompted by a definite purpose, and this he pursued with vigour and singleness of design. He followed such runways as appeared to terminate in the pits or other chambers of the inhabitants of the city, and these he explored, usually from the safety of a burrow's mouth, until satisfied that what he sought was not there. He moved swiftly upon his spider legs and covered remarkable distances in short periods of time.

His search not being rewarded with immediate success, he decided to return to the pit where his rykor lay chained and look to its wants. As he approached the end of the burrow that terminated in the pit he slackened his pace, stopping just within the entrance of the runway that he might scan the interior of the chamber before entering it. As he did so he saw the figure of a warrior appear suddenly in an opposite doorway. The rykor sprawled upon the table, his hands groping blindly for more food. Ghek saw the warrior pause and gaze in sudden astonishment at the rykor; he saw the fellow's eyes go wide and an ashen hue replace the copper bronze of his cheek. He stepped back as though someone had struck him in the face. For an instant only he stood thus as in a paralysis of fear, then he uttered a smothered shriek and turned and fled. Again was it a catastrophe that Ghek, the kaldane, could not smile.

Quickly entering the room he crawled to the table top and affixed himself to the shoulders of his rykor, and there he waited; and who may say that Ghek, though he could not smile, possessed not a sense of humour? For a half-hour he sat there, and then there came to him the sound of men approaching along corridors of stone. He could hear their arms clank against the rocky walls and he knew that they came at a rapid pace; but just before they reached the entrance to his prison they paused and advanced more slowly. In the lead was an officer, and just behind him, wide-eyed and perhaps still a little ashen, the warrior who had so recently departed in haste. At the doorway they halted and the officer turned sternly upon the warrior. With upraised finger he pointed at Ghek.

"There sits the creature! Didst thou dare lie, then, to thy dwar?"

"I swear," cried the warrior, "that I spoke the truth. But a moment since the thing grovelled, headless, upon this very table! And may my first ancestor strike me dead upon the spot if I speak other than a true word!"

The officer looked puzzled. The men of Mars seldom if ever lie. He scratched his head. Then he addressed Ghek. "How long have you been here?" he asked.

"Who knows better than those who placed me here and chained me to a wall?" he returned in reply.

"Saw you this warrior enter here a few minutes since?"

"I saw him," replied Ghek. "And you sat there where you sit now?" continued the officer.

"Look thou to my chain and tell me then where else might I sit!" cried Ghek. "Art the people of thy city all fools?"

Three other warriors pressed behind the two in front, craning their necks to view the prisoner while they grinned at the discomfiture of their fellow. The officer scowled at Ghek.

"Thy tongue is as venomous as that of the she-banth O-Tar sent to The Towers of Jetan," he said.

"You speak of the young woman who was captured with me?" asked Ghek, his expressionless monotone and face revealing naught of the interest he felt.

"I speak of her," replied the dwar, and then turning to the warrior who had summoned him: "return to thy quarters and remain there until the next games. Perhaps by that time thy eyes may have learned not to deceive thee."

The fellow cast a venomous glance at Ghek and turned away. The officer shook his head. "I do not understand it," he muttered. "Always has U-Van been a true and dependable warrior. Could it be—?" he glanced piercingly at Ghek. "Thou hast a strange head that misfits thy body, fellow," he cried. "Our legends tell us of those ancient creatures that placed hallucinations upon the mind of their fellows. If thou be such then maybe U-Van suffered from thy forbidden powers. If thou be such O-Tar will know well how to deal with thee." He wheeled about and motioned his warriors to follow him.

"Wait!" cried Ghek. "Unless I am to be starved, send me food."

"You have had food," replied the warrior.

"Am I to be fed but once a day?" asked Ghek. "I require food oftener than that. Send me food."

"You shall have food," replied the officer. "None may say that the prisoners of Manator are ill-fed. Just are the laws of Manator," and he departed.

No sooner had the sounds of their passing died away in the distance than Ghek clambered from the shoulders of his rykor, and scurried to the burrow where he had hidden the key. Fetching it he unlocked the fetter from about the creature's ankle, locked it empty and carried the key farther down into the burrow. Then he returned to his place upon his brainless servitor. After a while he heard footsteps approaching, whereupon he rose and passed into another corridor from that down which he knew the warrior was coming. Here he waited out of sight, listening. He heard the man enter the chamber and halt. He heard a muttered exclamation, followed by the jangle of metal dishes as a salver was slammed upon a table; then rapidly retreating footsteps, which quickly died away in the distance.

Ghek lost no time in returning to the chamber, recovering the key, relocking the rykor to his chain. Then he replaced the key in the burrow and squatting on the table beside his headless body, directed its hands toward the food. While the rykor ate Ghek sat listening for the scraping sandals and clattering arms that he knew soon would come. Nor had he long to wait. Ghek scrambled to the shoulders of his rykor as he heard them coming. Again it was the officer who had been summoned by U-Van and with him were three warriors. The one directly behind him was evidently the same who had brought the food, for his eyes went wide when he saw Ghek sitting at the table and he looked very foolish as the dwar turned his stern glance upon him.

"It is even as I said," he cried. "He was not here when I brought his food."

"But he is here now," said the officer grimly, "and his fetter is locked about his ankle. Look! it has not been opened—but where is the key? It should be upon the table at the end opposite him. Where is the key, creature?" he shouted at Ghek.

"How should I, a prisoner, know better than my jailer the whereabouts of the key to my fetters?" he retorted.

"But it lay here," cried the officer, pointing to the other end of the table.

"Did you see it?" asked Ghek.

The officer hesitated. "No but it must have been there," he parried.

"Did you see the key lying there?" asked Ghek, pointing to another warrior.

The fellow shook his head negatively. "And you? and you?" continued the kaldane addressing the others.

They both admitted that they never had seen the key. "And if it had been there how could I have reached it?" he continued.

"No, he could not have reached it," admitted the officer; "but there shall be no more of this! I-Zav, you will remain here on guard with this prisoner until you are relieved."

I-Zav looked anything but happy as this intelligence was transmitted to him, and he eyed Ghek suspiciously as the dwar and the other warriors turned and left him to his unhappy lot.

Chapter 13

A Desperate Deed

E-Med crossed the tower chamber toward Tara of Helium and the slave girl, Lan-O. He seized the former roughly by a shoulder. "Stand!" he commanded. Tara struck his hand from her and rising, backed away.

"Lay not your hand upon the person of a princess of Helium, beast!" she warned.

E-Med laughed. "Think you that I play at jetan for you without first knowing something of the stake for which I play?" he demanded. "Come here!"

The girl drew herself to her full height, folding her arms across her breast, nor did E-Med note that the slim fingers of her right hand were inserted beneath the broad leather strap of her harness where it passed over her left shoulder.

"And O-Tar learns of this you shall rue it, E-Med," cried the slave girl; "there be no law in Manator that gives you this girl before you shall have won her fairly."

"What cares O-Tar for her fate?" replied E-Med. "Have I not heard? Did she not flout the great jeddak, heaping abuse upon him? By my first ancestor, I think O-Tar might make a jed of the man who subdued her," and again he advanced toward Tara.

"Wait!" said the girl in low, even tone. "Perhaps you know not what you do. Sacred to the people of Helium are the persons of the women of Helium. For the honour of the humblest of them would the great jeddak himself unsheathe his sword. The greatest nations of Barsoom have trembled to the thunders of war in defence of the person of Dejah Thoris, my mother. We are but mortal and so may die; but we may not be defiled. You may play at jetan for a princess of Helium, but though you may win the match, never may you claim the reward. If thou wouldst possess a dead body press me too far, but know, man of Manator, that the blood of The Warlord flows not in the veins of Tara of Helium for naught. I have spoken."

"I know naught of Helium and O-Tar is our warlord," replied E-Med; "but I do know that I would examine more closely the prize that I shall play for and win. I would test the lips of her who is to be my slave after the next games; nor is it well, woman, to drive me too far to anger." His eyes narrowed as he spoke, his visage taking on the semblance of that of a snarling beast. "If you doubt the truth of my words ask Lan-O, the slave girl."

"He speaks truly, O woman of Helium," interjected Lan-O. "Try not the temper of E-Med, if you value your life."

But Tara of Helium made no reply. Already had she spoken. She stood in silence now facing the burly warrior who approached her. He came close and then quite suddenly he seized her and, bending, tried to draw her lips to his.

Lan-O saw the woman from Helium half turn, and with a quick movement jerk her right hand from where it had lain upon her breast. She saw the hand shoot from beneath the arm of E-Med and rise behind his shoulder and she saw in the hand a long, slim blade. The lips of the warrior were drawing closer to those of the woman, but they never touched them, for suddenly the man straightened, stiffly, a shriek upon his lips, and then he crumpled like an empty fur and lay, a shrunken heap, upon the floor. Tara of Helium stooped and wiped her blade upon his harness.

Lan-O, wide-eyed, looked with horror upon the corpse. "For this we shall both die," she cried.

"And who would live a slave in Manator?" asked Tara of Helium.

"I am not so brave as thou," said the slave girl, "and life is sweet and there is always hope."

"Life is sweet," agreed Tara of Helium, "but honour is sacred. But do not fear. When they come I shall tell them the truth—that you had no hand in this and no opportunity to prevent it."

For a moment the slave girl seemed to be thinking deeply. Suddenly her eyes lighted. "There is a way, perhaps," she said, "to turn suspicion from us. He has the key to this chamber upon him. Let us open the door and drag him out—maybe we shall find a place to hide him."

"Good!" exclaimed Tara of Helium, and the two immediately set about the matter Lan-O had suggested. Quickly they found the key and unlatched the door and then, between them, they half carried, half dragged, the corpse of E-Med from the room and down the stairway to the next level where Lan-O said there were vacant chambers. The first door they tried was unlatched, and through this the two bore their grisly burden into a small room lighted by a single window. The apartment bore evidence of having been utilized as a living-room rather than as a cell, being furnished with a degree of comfort and even luxury. The walls were panelled to a height of about seven feet from the floor, while the plaster above and the ceiling were decorated with faded paintings of another day.

As Tara's eyes ran quickly over the interior her attention was drawn to a section of panelling that seemed to be separated at one edge from the piece next adjoining it. Quickly she crossed to it, discovering that one vertical edge of an entire panel projected a half-inch beyond the others. There was a possible explanation which piqued her curiosity, and acting upon its suggestion she seized upon the projecting edge and pulled outward. Slowly the panel swung toward her, revealing a dark aperture in the wall behind.

"Look, Lan-O!" she cried. "See what I have found—a hole in which we may hide the thing upon the floor."

Lan-O joined her and together the two investigated the dark aperture, finding a small platform from which a narrow runway led downward into Stygian darkness. Thick dust covered the floor within the doorway, indicating that a great period of time had elapsed since human foot had trod it—a secret way, doubtless, unknown to living Manatorians. Here they dragged the corpse of E-Med, leaving it upon the platform, and as they left the dark and forbidden closet Lan-O would have slammed to the panel had not Tara prevented.

"Wait!" she said, and fell to examining the door frame and the stile.

"Hurry!" whispered the slave girl. "If they come we are lost."

"It may serve us well to know how to open this place again," replied Tara of Helium, and then suddenly she pressed a foot against a section of the carved base at the right of the open panel. "Ah!" she breathed, a note of satisfaction in her tone, and closed the panel until it fitted snugly in its place. "Come!" she said and turned toward the outer doorway of the chamber.

They reached their own cell without detection, and closing the door Tara locked it from the inside and placed the key in a secret pocket in her harness.

"Let them come," she said. "Let them question us! What could two poor prisoners know of the whereabouts of their noble jailer? I ask you, Lan-O, what could they?"

"Nothing," admitted Lan-O, smiling with her companion.

"Tell me of these men of Manator," said Tara presently. "Are they all like E-Med, or are some of them like A-Kor, who seemed a brave and chivalrous character?"

"They are not unlike the peoples of other countries," replied Lan-O. "There be among them both good and bad. They are brave warriors and mighty. Among themselves they are not without chivalry and honour, but in their dealings with strangers they know but one law—the law of might. The weak and unfortunate of other lands fill them with contempt and arouse all that is worst in their natures, which doubtless accounts for their treatment of us, their slaves."

"But why should they feel contempt for those who have suffered the misfortune of falling into their hands?" queried Tara.

"I do not know," said Lan-O; "A-Kor says that he believes that it is because their country has never been invaded by a victorious foe. In their stealthy raids never have they been defeated, because they have never waited to face a powerful force; and so they have come to believe themselves invincible, and the other peoples are held in contempt as inferior in valour and the practice of arms."

"Yet A-Kor is one of them," said Tara.

"He is a son of O-Tar, the jeddak," replied Lan-O; "but his mother was a high born Gatholian, captured and made slave by O-Tar, and A-Kor boasts that in his veins runs only the blood of his mother, and indeed is he different from the others. His chivalry is of a gentler form, though not even his worst enemy has dared question his courage, while his skill with the sword, and the spear, and the thoat is famous throughout the length and breadth of Manator."

"What think you they will do with him?" asked Tara of Helium.

"Sentence him to the games," replied Lan-O. "If O-Tar be not greatly angered he may be sentenced to but a single game, in which case he may come out alive; but if O-Tar wishes really to dispose of him he will be sentenced to the entire series, and no warrior has ever survived the full ten, or rather none who was under a sentence from O-Tar."

"What are the games? I do not understand," said Tara "I have heard them speak of playing at jetan, but surely no one can be killed at jetan. We play it often at home."

"But not as they play it in the arena at Manator," replied Lan-O. "Come to the window," and together the two approached an aperture facing toward the east.

Below her Tara of Helium saw a great field entirely surrounded by the low building, and the lofty towers of which that in which she was imprisoned was but a unit. About the arena were tiers of seats; but the a thing that caught her attention was a gigantic jetan board laid out upon the floor of the arena in great squares of alternate orange and black.

"Here they play at jetan with living pieces. They play for great stakes and usually for a woman—some slave of exceptional beauty. O-Tar himself might have played for you had you not angered him, but now you will be played for in an open game by slaves and criminals, and you will belong to the side that wins—not to a single warrior, but to all who survive the game."

The eyes of Tara of Helium flashed, but she made no comment.

"Those who direct the play do not necessarily take part in it," continued the slave girl, "but sit in those two great thrones which you see at either end of the board and direct their pieces from square to square."

"But where lies the danger?" asked Tara of Helium. "If a piece be taken it is merely removed from the board—this is a rule of jetan as old almost as the civilization of Barsoom."

"But here in Manator, when they play in the great arena with living men, that rule is altered," explained Lan-O. "When a warrior is moved to a square occupied by an opposing piece, the two battle to the death for possession of the square and the one that is successful advantages by the move. Each is caparisoned to simulate the piece he represents and in addition he wears that which indicates whether he be slave, a warrior serving a sentence, or a volunteer. If serving a sentence the number of games he must play is also indicated, and thus the one directing the moves knows which pieces to risk and which to conserve, and further than this, a man's chances are affected by the position that is assigned him for the game. Those whom they wish to die are always Panthans in the game, for the Panthan has the least chance of surviving."

"Do those who direct the play ever actually take part in it?" asked Tara.

"Oh, yes," said Lan-O. "Often when two warriors, even of the highest class, hold a grievance against one another O-Tar compels them to settle it upon the arena. Then it is that they take active part and with drawn swords direct their own players from the position of Chief. They pick their own players, usually the best of their own warriors and slaves, if they be powerful men who possess such, or their friends may volunteer, or they may obtain prisoners from the pits. These are games indeed—the very best that are seen. Often the great chiefs themselves are slain."

"It is within this amphitheatre that the justice of Manator is meted, then?" asked Tara.

"Very largely," replied Lan-O.

"How, then, through such justice, could a prisoner win his liberty?" continued the girl from Helium.

"If a man, and he survived ten games his liberty would be his," replied Lan-O.

"But none ever survives?" queried Tara. "And if a woman?"

"No stranger within the gates of Manator ever has survived ten games," replied the slave girl. "They are permitted to offer themselves into perpetual slavery if they prefer that to fighting at jetan. Of course they may be called upon, as any warrior, to take part in a game, but their chances then of surviving are increased, since they may never again have the chance of winning to liberty."

"But a woman," insisted Tara; "how may a woman win her freedom?"

Lan-O laughed. "Very simply," she cried, derisively. "She has but to find a warrior who will fight through ten consecutive games for her and survive."

"'Just are the laws of Manator,'" quoted Tara, scornfully.

Then it was that they heard footsteps outside their cell and a moment later a key turned in the lock and the door opened. A warrior faced them.

"Hast seen E-Med the dwar?" he asked.

"Yes," replied Tara, "he was here some time ago."

The man glanced quickly about the bare chamber and then searchingly first at Tara of Helium and then at the slave girl, Lan-O. The puzzled expression upon his face increased. He scratched his head. "It is strange," he said. "A score of men saw him ascend into this tower; and though there is but a single exit, and that well guarded, no man has seen him pass out."

Tara of Helium hid a yawn with the back of a shapely hand. "The Princess of Helium is hungry, fellow," she drawled; "tell your master that she would eat."

It was an hour later that food was brought, an officer and several warriors accompanying the bearer. The former examined the room carefully, but there was no sign that aught amiss had occurred there. The wound that had sent E-Med the dwar to his ancestors had not bled, fortunately for Tara of Helium.

"Woman," cried the officer, turning upon Tara, "you were the last to see E-Med the dwar. Answer me now and answer me truthfully. Did you see him leave this room?"

"I did," answered Tara of Helium.

"Where did he go from here?"

"How should I know? Think you that I can pass through a locked door of skeel?" the girl's tone was scornful.

"Of that we do not know," said the officer. "Strange things have happened in the cell of your companion in the pits of Manator. Perhaps you could pass through a locked door of skeel as easily as he performs seemingly more impossible feats."

"Whom do you mean," she cried; "Turan the panthan? He lives, then? Tell me, is he here in Manator unharmed?"

"I speak of that thing which calls itself Ghek the kaldane," replied the officer.

"But Turan! Tell me, padwar, have you heard aught of him?" Tara's tone was insistent and she leaned a little forward toward the officer, her lips slightly parted in expectancy.

Into the eyes of the slave girl, Lan-O, who was watching her, there crept a soft light of understanding; but the officer ignored Tara's question—what was the fate of another slave to him? "Men do not disappear into thin air," he growled, "and if E-Med be not found soon O-Tar himself may take a hand in this. I warn you, woman, if you be one of those horrid Corphals that by commanding the spirits of the wicked dead gains evil mastery over the living, as many now believe the thing called Ghek to be, that lest you return E-Med, O-Tar will have no mercy on you."

"What foolishness is this?" cried the girl. "I am a princess of Helium, as I have told you all a score of times. Even if the fabled Corphals existed, as none but the most ignorant now believes, the lore of the ancients tells us that they entered only into the bodies of wicked criminals of the lowest class. Man of Manator, thou art a fool, and thy jeddak and all his people," and she turned her royal back upon the padwar, and gazed through the window across the Field of Jetan and the roofs of Manator through the low hills and the rolling country and freedom.

"And you know so much of Corphals, then," he cried, "you know that while no common man dare harm them they may be slain by the hand of a jeddak with impunity!"

The girl did not reply, nor would she speak again, for all his threats and rage, for she knew now that none in all Manator dared harm her save O-Tar, the jeddak, and after a while the padwar left, taking his men with him. And after they had gone Tara stood for long looking out upon the city of Manator, and wondering what more of cruel wrongs Fate held in store for her. She was standing thus in silent meditation when there rose to her the strains of martial music from the city below—the deep, mellow tones of the long war trumpets of mounted troops, the clear, ringing notes of foot-soldiers' music. The girl raised her head and looked about, listening, and Lan-O, standing at an opposite window, looking toward the west, motioned Tara to join her. Now they could see across roofs and avenues to The Gate of Enemies, through which troops were marching into the city.

"The Great Jed is coming," said Lan-O, "none other dares enter thus, with blaring trumpets, the city of Manator. It is U-Thor, Jed of Manatos, second city of Manator. They call him The Great Jed the length and breadth of Manator, and because the people love him, O-Tar hates him. They say, who know, that it would need but slight provocation to inflame the two to war. How such a war would end no one could guess; for the people of Manator worship the great O-Tar, though they do not love him. U-Thor they love, but he is not the jeddak," and Tara understood, as only a Martian may, how much that simple statement encompassed.

The loyalty of a Martian to his jeddak is almost an instinct, and second not even to the instinct of self-preservation at that. Nor is this strange in a race whose religion includes ancestor worship, and where families trace their origin back into remote ages and a jeddak sits upon the same throne that his direct progenitors have occupied for, perhaps, hundreds of thousands of years, and rules the descendants of the same people that his forebears ruled. Wicked jeddaks have been dethroned, but seldom are they replaced by other than members of the imperial house, even though the law gives to the jeds the right to select whom they please.

"U-Thor is a just man and good, then?" asked Tara of Helium.

"There be none nobler," replied Lan-O. "In Manatos none but wicked criminals who deserve death are forced to play at jetan, and even then the play is fair and they have their chance for freedom. Volunteers may play, but the moves are not necessarily to the death—a wound, and even sometimes points in swordplay, deciding the issue. There they look upon jetan as a martial sport—here it is but butchery. And U-Thor is opposed to the ancient slave raids and to the policy that keeps Manator forever isolated from the other nations of Barsoom; but U-Thor is not jeddak and so there is no change."

The two girls watched the column moving up the broad avenue from The Gate of Enemies toward the palace of O-Tar. A gorgeous, barbaric procession of painted warriors in jewel-studded harness and waving feathers; vicious, squealing thoats caparisoned in rich trappings; far above their heads the long lances of their riders bore fluttering pennons; foot-soldiers swinging easily along the stone pavement, their sandals of zitidar hide giving forth no sound; and at the rear of each utan a train of painted chariots, drawn by mammoth zitidars, carrying the equipment of the company to which they were attached. Utan after utan entered through the great gate, and even when the head of the column reached the palace of O-Tar they were not all within the city.

"I have been here many years," said the girl, Lan-O; "but never have I seen even The Great Jed bring so many fighting men into the city of Manator."

Through half-closed eyes Tara of Helium watched the warriors marching up the broad avenue, trying to imagine them the fighting men of her beloved Helium coming to the rescue of their princess. That splendid figure upon the great thoat might be John Carter, himself, Warlord of Barsoom, and behind him utan after utan of the veterans of the empire, and then the girl opened her eyes again and saw the host of painted, befeathered barbarians, and sighed. But yet she watched, fascinated by the martial scene, and now she noted again the groups of silent figures upon the balconies. No waving silks; no cries of welcome; no showers of flowers and jewels such as would have marked the entry of such a splendid, friendly pageant into the twin cities of her birth.

"The people do not seem friendly to the warriors of Manatos," she remarked to Lan-O; "I have not seen a single welcoming sign from the people on the balconies." The slave girl looked at her in surprise. "It cannot be that you do not know!" she exclaimed. "Why, they are—" but she got no further. The door swung open and an officer stood before them.

"The slave girl, Tara, is summoned to the presence of O-Tar, the jeddak!" he announced.

Chapter 14

At Ghek's Command

Turan the panthan chafed in his chains. Time dragged; silence and monotony prolonged minutes into hours. Uncertainty of the fate of the woman he loved turned each hour into an eternity of hell. He listened impatiently for the sound of approaching footsteps that he might see and speak to some living creature and learn, perchance, some word of Tara of Helium.

After torturing hours his ears were rewarded by the rattle of harness and arms. Men were coming! He waited breathlessly. Perhaps they were his executioners; but he would welcome them notwithstanding. He would question them. But if they knew naught of Tara he would not divulge the location of the hiding place in which he had left her.

Now they came—a half-dozen warriors and an officer, escorting an unarmed man; a prisoner, doubtless. Of this Turan was not left long in doubt, since they brought the newcomer and chained him to an adjoining ring. Immediately the panthan commenced to question the officer in charge of the guard.

"Tell me," he demanded, "why I have been made prisoner, and if other strangers were captured since I entered your city."

"What other prisoners?" asked the officer.

"A woman, and a man with a strange head," replied Turan.

"It is possible," said the officer; "but what were their names?"

"The woman was Tara, Princess of Helium, and the man was Ghek, a kaldane, of Bantoom."

"These were your friends?" asked the officer.

"Yes," replied Turan.

"It is what I would know," said the officer, and with a curt command to his men to follow him he turned and left the cell.

"Tell me of them!" cried Turan after him. "Tell me of Tara of Helium! Is she safe?" but the man did not answer and soon the sound of their departure died in the distance.

"Tara of Helium was safe, but a short time since," said the prisoner chained at Turan's side.

The panthan turned toward the speaker, seeing a large man, handsome of face and with a manner both stately and dignified. "You have seen her?" he asked. "They captured her then? She is in danger?"

"She is being held in The Towers of Jetan as a prize for the next games," replied the stranger.

"And who are you?" asked Turan. "And why are you here, a prisoner?"

"I am A-Kor the dwar, keeper of The Towers of Jetan," replied the other. "I am here because I dared speak the truth of O-Tar the jeddak, to one of his officers."

"And your punishment?" asked Turan.

"I do not know. O-Tar has not yet spoken. Doubtless the games—perhaps the full ten, for O-Tar does not love A-Kor, his son."

"You are the jeddak's son?" asked Turan.

"I am the son of O-Tar and of a slave, Haja of Gathol, who was a princess in her own land."

Turan looked searchingly at the speaker. A son of Haja of Gathol! A son of his mother's sister, this man, then, was his own cousin. Well did Gahan remember the mysterious disappearance of the Princess Haja and an entire utan of her personal troops. She had been upon a visit far from the city of Gathol and returning home had vanished with her whole escort from the sight of man. So this was the secret of the seeming mystery? Doubtless it explained many other similar disappearances that extended nearly as far back as the history of Gathol. Turan scrutinized his companion, discovering many evidences of resemblance to his mother's people. A-Kor might have been ten years younger than he, but such differences in age are scarce accounted among a people who seldom or never age outwardly after maturity and whose span of life may be a thousand years.

"And where lies Gathol?" asked Turan.

"Almost due east of Manator," replied A-Kor.

"And how far?"

"Some twenty-one degrees it is from the city of Manator to the city of Gathol," replied A-Kor; "but little more than ten degrees between the boundaries of the two countries. Between them, though, there lies a country of torn rocks and yawning chasms."

Well did Gahan know this country that bordered his upon the

west—even the ships of the air avoided it because of the treacherous currents that rose from the deep chasms, and the almost total absence of safe landings. He knew now where Manator lay and for the first time in long weeks the way to his own Gathol, and here was a man, a fellow prisoner, in whose veins flowed the blood of his own ancestors—a man who knew Manator; its people, its customs and the country surrounding it—one who could aid him, with advice at least, to find a plan for the rescue of Tara of Helium and for escape. But would A-Kor—could he dare broach the subject? He could do no less than try.

"And O-Tar you think will sentence you to death?" he asked; "and why?"

"He would like to," replied A-Kor, "for the people chafe beneath his iron hand and their loyalty is but the loyalty of a people to the long line of illustrious jeddaks from which he has sprung. He is a jealous man and has found the means of disposing of most of those whose blood might entitle them to a claim upon the throne, and whose place in the affections of the people endowed them with any political significance. The fact that I was the son of a slave relegated me to a position of minor importance in the consideration of O-Tar, yet I am still the son of a jeddak and might sit upon the throne of Manator with as perfect congruity as O-Tar himself. Combined with this is the fact that of recent years the people, and especially many of the younger warriors, have evinced a growing affection for me, which I attribute to certain virtues of character and training derived from my mother, but which O-Tar assumes to be the result of an ambition upon my part to occupy the throne of Manator.

"And now, I am firmly convinced, he has seized upon my criticism of his treatment of the slave girl Tara as a pretext for ridding himself of me."

"But if you could escape and reach Gathol," suggested Turan.

"I have thought of that," mused A-Kor; "but how much better off would I be? In the eyes of the Gatholians I would be, not a Gatholian; but a stranger and doubtless they would accord me the same treatment that we of Manator accord strangers."

"Could you convince them that you are the son of the Princess Haja your welcome would be assured," said Turan; "while on the other hand you could purchase your freedom and citizenship with a brief period of labour in the diamond mines."

"How know you all these things?" asked A-Kor. "I thought you were from Helium."

"I am a panthan," replied Turan, "and I have served many countries, among them Gathol."

"It is what the slaves from Gathol have told me," said A-Kor, thoughtfully, "and my mother, before O-Tar sent her to live at Manatos. I think he must have feared her power and influence among the slaves from Gathol and their descendants, who number perhaps a million people throughout the land of Manator."

"Are these slaves organized?" asked Turan.

A-Kor looked straight into the eyes of the panthan for a long moment before he replied. "You are a man of honour," he said; "I read it in your face, and I am seldom mistaken in my estimate of a man; but—" and he leaned closer to the other—"even the walls have ears," he whispered, and Turan's question was answered.

It was later in the evening that warriors came and unlocked the fetter from Turan's ankle and led him away to appear before O-Tar, the jeddak. They conducted him toward the palace along narrow, winding streets and broad avenues; but always from the balconies there looked down upon them in endless ranks the silent people of the city. The palace itself was filled with life and activity. Mounted warriors galloped through the corridors and up and down the runways connecting adjacent floors. It seemed that no one walked within the palace other than a few slaves. Squealing, fighting thoats were stabled in magnificent halls while their riders, if not upon some duty of the palace, played at jetan with small figures carved from wood.

Turan noted the magnificence of the interior architecture of the palace, the lavish expenditure of precious jewels and metals, the gorgeous mural decorations which depicted almost exclusively martial scenes, and principally duels which seemed to be fought upon jetan boards of heroic size. The capitals of many of the columns supporting the ceilings of the corridors and chambers through which they passed were wrought into formal likenesses of jetan pieces—everywhere there seemed a suggestion of the game. Along the same path that Tara of Helium had been led Turan was conducted toward the throne room of O-Tar the jeddak, and when he entered the Hall of Chiefs his interest turned to wonder and admiration as he viewed the ranks of statuesque thoatmen decked in their gorgeous, martial panoply. Never, he thought, had he seen upon Barsoom more soldierly figures or thoats so perfectly trained to perfection of immobility as these. Not a muscle quivered, not a tail lashed, and the riders were as motionless as their mounts—each warlike eye straight to the front, the great spears inclined at the same angle. It was a picture to fill the breast of a fighting man with awe and reverence. Nor did it fail in its effect upon Turan as they conducted him the length of the chamber, where he waited before great doors until he should be summoned into the presence of the ruler of Manator.

*****

When Tara of Helium was ushered into the throne room of O-Tar she found the great hall filled with the chiefs and officers of O-Tar and U-Thor, the latter occupying the place of honour at the foot of the throne, as was his due. The girl was conducted to the foot of the aisle and halted before the jeddak, who looked down upon her from his high throne with scowling brows and fierce, cruel eyes.

"The laws of Manator are just," said O-Tar, addressing her; "thus is it that you have been summoned here again to be judged by the highest authority of Manator. Word has reached me that you are suspected of being a Corphal. What word have you to say in refutation of the charge?"

Tara of Helium could scarce restrain a sneer as she answered the ridiculous accusation of witchcraft. "So ancient is the culture of my people," she said, "that authentic history reveals no defence for that which we know existed only in the ignorant and superstitious minds of the most primitive peoples of the past. To those who are yet so untutored as to believe in the existence of Corphals, there can be no argument that will convince them of their error—only long ages of refinement and culture can accomplish their release from the bondage of ignorance. I have spoken."

"Yet you do not deny the accusation," said O-Tar.

"It is not worthy the dignity of a denial," she responded haughtily.

"And I were you, woman," said a deep voice at her side, "I should, nevertheless, deny it."

Tara of Helium turned to see the eyes of U-Thor, the great jed of Manatos, upon her. Brave eyes they were, but neither cold nor cruel. O-Tar rapped impatiently upon the arm of his throne. "U-Thor forgets," he cried, "that O-Tar is the jeddak."

"U-Thor remembers," replied the jed of Manatos, "that the laws of Manator permit any who may be accused to have advice and counsel before their judge."

Tara of Helium saw that for some reason this man would have assisted her, and so she acted upon his advice.

"I deny the charge," she said, "I am no Corphal."

"Of that we shall learn," snapped O-Tar. "U-Dor, where are those who have knowledge of the powers of this woman?"

And U-Dor brought several who recounted the little that was known of the disappearance of E-Med, and others who told of the capture of Ghek and Tara, suggesting by deduction that having been found together they had sufficient in common to make it reasonably certain that one was as bad as the other, and that, therefore, it remained but to convict one of them of Corphalism to make certain the guilt of both. And then O-Tar called for Ghek, and immediately the hideous kaldane was dragged before him by warriors who could not conceal the fear in which they held this creature.

"And you!" said O-Tar in cold accusing tones. "Already have I been told enough of you to warrant me in passing through your heart the jeddak's steel—of how you stole the brains from the warrior U-Van so that he thought he saw your headless body still endowed with life; of how you caused another to believe that you had escaped, making him to see naught but an empty bench and a blank wall where you had been."

"Ah, O-Tar, but that is as nothing!" cried a young padwar who had come in command of the escort that brought Ghek. "The thing which he did to I-Zav, here, would prove his guilt alone."

"What did he to the warrior I-Zav?" demanded O-Tar. "Let I-Zav speak!"

The warrior I-Zav, a great fellow of bulging muscles and thick neck, advanced to the foot of the throne. He was pale and still trembling visibly as from a nervous shock.

"Let my first ancestor be my witness, O-Tar, that I speak the truth," he began. "I was left to guard this creature, who sat upon a bench, shackled to the wall. I stood by the open doorway at the opposite side of the chamber. He could not reach me, yet, O-Tar, may Iss engulf me if he did not drag me to him helpless as an unhatched egg. He dragged me to him, greatest of jeddaks, with his eyes! With his eyes he seized upon my eyes and dragged me to him and he made me lay my swords and dagger upon the table and back off into a corner, and still keeping his eyes upon my eyes his head quitted his body and crawling upon six short legs it descended to the floor and backed part way into the hole of an ulsio, but not so far that the eyes were not still upon me and then it returned with the key to its fetter and after resuming its place upon its own shoulders it unlocked the fetter and again dragged me across the room and made me to sit upon the bench where it had been and there it fastened the fetter about my ankle, and I could do naught for the power of its eyes and the fact that it wore my two swords and my dagger. And then the head disappeared down the hole of the ulsio with the key, and when it returned, it resumed its body and stood guard over me at the doorway until the padwar came to fetch it hither."

"It is enough!" said O-Tar, sternly. "Both shall receive the jeddak's steel," and rising from his throne he drew his long sword and descended the marble steps toward them, while two brawny warriors seized Tara by either arm and two seized Ghek, holding them facing the naked blade of the jeddak.

"Hold, just O-Tar!" cried U-Dor. "There be yet another to be judged. Let us confront him who calls himself Turan with these his fellows before they die."

"Good!" exclaimed O-Tar, pausing half way down the steps. "Fetch Turan, the slave!"

When Turan had been brought into the chamber he was placed a little to Tara's left and a step nearer the throne. O-Tar eyed him menacingly.

"You are Turan," he asked, "friend and companion of these?"

The panthan was about to reply when Tara of Helium spoke. "I know not this fellow," she said. "Who dares say that he be a friend and companion of the Princess Tara of Helium?"

Turan and Ghek looked at her in surprise, but at Turan she did not look, and to Ghek she passed a quick glance of warning, as to say: "Hold thy peace."

The panthan tried not to fathom her purpose for the head is useless when the heart usurps its functions, and Turan knew only that the woman he loved had denied him, and though he tried not even to think it his foolish heart urged but a single explanation—that she refused to recognize him lest she be involved in his difficulties.

O-Tar looked first at one and then at another of them; but none of them spoke.

"Were they not captured together?" he asked of U-Dor.

"No," replied the dwar. "He who is called Turan was found seeking entrance to the city and was enticed to the pits. The following morning I discovered the other two upon the hill beyond The Gate of Enemies."

"But they are friends and companions," said a young padwar, "for this Turan inquired of me concerning these two, calling them by name and saying that they were his friends."

"It is enough," stated O-Tar, "all three shall die," and he took another step downward from the throne.

"For what shall we die?" asked Ghek. "Your people prate of the just laws of Manator, and yet you would slay three strangers without telling them of what crime they are accused."

"He is right," said a deep voice. It was the voice of U-Thor, the great jed of Manatos. O-Tar looked at him and scowled; but there came voices from other portions of the chamber seconding the demand for justice.

"Then know, though you shall die anyway," cried O-Tar, "that all three are convicted of Corphalism and that as only a jeddak may slay such as you in safety you are about to be honoured with the steel of O-Tar."

"Fool!" cried Turan. "Know you not that in the veins of this woman flows the blood of ten thousand jeddaks—that greater than yours is her power in her own land? She is Tara, Princess of Helium, great-granddaughter of Tardos Mors, daughter of John Carter, Warlord of Barsoom. She cannot be a Corphal. Nor is this creature Ghek, nor am I. And you would know more, I can prove my right to be heard and to be believed if I may have word with the Princess Haja of Gathol, whose son is my fellow prisoner in the pits of O-Tar, his father."

At this U-Thor rose to his feet and faced O-Tar. "What means this?" he asked. "Speaks the man the truth? Is the son of Haja a prisoner in thy pits, O-Tar?"

"And what is it to the jed of Manatos who be the prisoners in the pits of his jeddak?" demanded O-Tar, angrily.

"It is this to the jed of Manatos," replied U-Thor in a voice so low as to be scarce more than a whisper and yet that was heard the whole length and breadth of the great throne room of O-Tar, Jeddak of Manator. "You gave me a slave woman, Haja, who had been a princess in Gathol, because you feared her influence among the slaves from Gathol. I have made of her a free woman, and I have married her and made her thus a princess of Manatos. Her son is my son, O-Tar, and though thou be my jeddak, I say to you that for any harm that befalls A-Kor you shall answer to U-Thor of Manatos."

O-Tar looked long at U-Thor, but he made no reply. Then he turned again to Turan. "If one be a Corphal," he said, "then all of you be Corphals, and we know well from the things that this creature has done," he pointed at Ghek, "that he is a Corphal, for no mortal has such powers as he. And as you are all Corphals you must all die." He took another step downward, when Ghek spoke.

"These two have no such powers as I," he said. "They are but ordinary, brainless things such as yourself. I have done all the things that your poor, ignorant warriors have told you; but this only demonstrates that I am of a higher order than yourselves, as is indeed the fact. I am a kaldane, not a Corphal. There is nothing supernatural or mysterious about me, other than that to the ignorant all things which they cannot understand are mysterious. Easily might I have eluded your warriors and escaped your pits; but I remained in the hope that I might help these two foolish creatures who have not the brains to escape without help. They befriended me and saved my life. I owe them this debt. Do not slay them—they are harmless. Slay me if you will. I offer my life if it will appease your ignorant wrath. I cannot return to Bantoom and so I might as well die, for there is no pleasure in intercourse with the feeble intellects that cumber the face of the world outside the valley of Bantoom."

"Hideous egotist," said O-Tar, "prepare to die and assume not to dictate to O-Tar the jeddak. He has passed sentence and all three of you shall feel the jeddak's naked steel. I have spoken!"

He took another step downward and then a strange thing happened. He paused, his eyes fixed upon the eyes of Ghek. His sword slipped from nerveless fingers, and still he stood there swaying forward and back. A jed rose to rush to his side; but Ghek stopped him with a word.

"Wait!" he cried. "The life of your jeddak is in my hands. You believe me a Corphal and so you believe, too, that only the sword of a jeddak may slay me, therefore your blades are useless against me. Offer harm to any one of us, or seek to approach your jeddak until I have spoken, and he shall sink lifeless to the marble. Release the two prisoners and let them come to my side—I would speak to them, privately. Quick! do as I say; I would as lief as not slay O-Tar. I but let him live that I may gain freedom for my friends—obstruct me and he dies."

The guards fell back, releasing Tara and Turan, who came close to Ghek's side.

"Do as I tell you and do it quickly," whispered the kaldane. "I cannot hold this fellow long, nor could I kill him thus. There are many minds working against mine and presently mine will tire and O-Tar will be himself again. You must make the best of your opportunity while you may. Behind the arras that you see hanging in the rear of the throne above you is a secret opening. From it a corridor leads to the pits of the palace, where there are storerooms containing food and drink. Few people go there. From these pits lead others to all parts of the city. Follow one that runs due west and it will bring you to The Gate of Enemies. The rest will then lie with you. I can do no more; hurry before my waning powers fail me—I am not as Luud, who was a king. He could have held this creature forever. Make haste! Go!"

Chapter 15

The Old Man of the Pits

"I shall not desert you, Ghek," said Tara of Helium, simply.

"Go! Go!" whispered the kaldane. "You can do me no good. Go, or all I have done is for naught."

Tara shook her head. "I cannot," she said.

"They will slay her," said Ghek to Turan, and the panthan, torn between loyalty to this strange creature who had offered its life for him, and love of the woman, hesitated but a moment, then he swept Tara from her feet and lifting her in his arms leaped up the steps that led to the throne of Manator. Behind the throne he parted the arras and found the secret opening. Into this he bore the girl and down a long, narrow corridor and winding runways that led to lower levels until they came to the pits of the palace of O-Tar. Here was a labyrinth of passages and chambers presenting a thousand hiding-places.

As Turan bore Tara up the steps toward the throne a score of warriors rose as though to rush forward to intercept them. "Stay!" cried Ghek, "or your jeddak dies," and they halted in their tracks, waiting the will of this strange, uncanny creature.

Presently Ghek took his eyes from the eyes of O-Tar and the jeddak shook himself as one who would be rid of a bad dream and straightened up, half dazed still.

"Look," said Ghek, then, "I have given your jeddak his life, nor have I harmed one of those whom I might easily have slain when they were in my power. No harm have I or my friends done in the city of Manator. Why then should you persecute us? Give us our lives. Give us our liberty."

O-Tar, now in command of his faculties, stooped and regained his sword. In the room was silence as all waited to hear the jeddak's answer.

"Just are the laws of Manator," he said at last. "Perhaps, after all, there is truth in the words of the stranger. Return him then to the pits and pursue the others and capture them. Through the mercy of O-Tar they shall be permitted to win their freedom upon the Field of Jetan, in the coming games."

Still ashen was the face of the jeddak as Ghek was led away and his appearance was that of a man who had been snatched from the brink of eternity into which he has gazed, not with the composure of great courage, but with fear. There were those in the throne room who knew that the execution of the three prisoners had but been delayed and the responsibility placed upon the shoulders of others, and one of those who knew was U-Thor, the great jed of Manatos. His curling lip betokened his scorn of the jeddak who had chosen humiliation rather than death. He knew that O-Tar had lost more of prestige in those few moments than he could regain in a lifetime, for the Martians are jealous of the courage of their chiefs—there can be no evasions of stern duty, no temporizing with honour. That there were others in the room who shared U-Thor's belief was evidenced by the silence and the grim scowls.

O-Tar glanced quickly around. He must have sensed the hostility and guessed its cause, for he went suddenly angry, and as one who seeks by the vehemence of his words to establish the courage of his heart he roared forth what could be considered as naught other than a challenge.

"The will of O-Tar, the jeddak, is the law of Manator," he cried, "and the laws of Manator are just—they cannot err. U-Dor, dispatch those who will search the palace, the pits, and the city, and return the fugitives to their cells.

"And now for you, U-Thor of Manatos! Think you with impunity to threaten your jeddak—to question his right to punish traitors and instigators of treason? What am I to think of your own loyalty, who takes to wife a woman I have banished from my court because of her intrigues against the authority of her jeddak and her master? But O-Tar is just. Make your explanations and your peace, then, before it is too late."

"U-Thor has nothing to explain," replied the jed of Manatos; "nor is he at war with his jeddak; but he has the right that every jed and every warrior enjoys, of demanding justice at the hands of the jeddak for whomsoever he believes to be persecuted. With increasing rigor has the jeddak of Manator persecuted the slaves from Gathol since he took to himself the unwilling Princess Haja. If the slaves from Gathol have harboured thoughts of vengeance and escape 'tis no more than might be expected from a proud and courageous people. Ever have I counselled greater fairness in our treatment of our slaves, many of whom, in their own lands, are people of great distinction and power; but always has O-Tar, the jeddak, flouted with arrogance my every suggestion. Though it has been through none of my seeking that the question has arisen now I am glad that it has, for the time was bound to come when the jeds of Manator would demand from O-Tar the respect and consideration that is their due from the man who holds his high office at their pleasure. Know, then, O-Tar, that you must free A-Kor, the dwar, forthwith or bring him to fair trial before the assembled jeds of Manator. I have spoken."

"You have spoken well and to the point, U-Thor," cried O-Tar, "for you have revealed to your jeddak and your fellow jeds the depth of the disloyalty that I have long suspected. A-Kor already has been tried and sentenced by the supreme tribunal of Manator—O-Tar, the jeddak; and you too shall receive justice from the same unfailing source. In the meantime you are under arrest. To the pits with him! To the pits with U-Thor the false jed!" He clapped his hands to summon the surrounding warriors to do his bidding. A score leaped forward to seize U-Thor. They were warriors of the palace, mostly; but two score leaped to defend U-Thor, and with ringing steel they fought at the foot of the steps to the throne of Manator where stood O-Tar, the jeddak, with drawn sword ready to take his part in the melee.

At the clash of steel, palace guards rushed to the scene from other parts of the great building until those who would have defended U-Thor were outnumbered two to one, and then the jed of Manatos slowly withdrew with his forces, and fighting his way through the corridors and chambers of the palace came at last to the avenue. Here he was reinforced by the little army that had marched with him into Manator. Slowly they retreated toward The Gate of Enemies between the rows of silent people looking down upon them from the balconies and there, within the city walls, they made their stand.

In a dimly-lighted chamber beneath the palace of O-Tar the jeddak, Turan the panthan lowered Tara of Helium from his arms and faced her. "I am sorry, Princess," he said, "that I was forced to disobey your commands, or to abandon Ghek; but there was no other way. Could he have saved you I would have stayed in his place. Tell me that you forgive me."

"How could I do less?" she replied graciously. "But it seemed cowardly to abandon a friend."

"Had we been three fighting men it had been different," he said.

"We could only have remained and died together, fighting; but you know, Tara of Helium, that we may not jeopardize a woman's safety even though we risk the loss of honour."

"I know that, Turan," she said; "but no one may say that you have risked honour, who knows the honour and bravery that are yours."

He heard her with surprise for these were the first words that she had spoken to him that did not savour of the attitude of a princess to a panthan—though it was more in her tone than the actual words that he apprehended the difference. How at variance were they to her recent repudiation of him! He could not fathom her, and so he blurted out the question that had been in his mind since she had told O-Tar that she did not know him.

"Tara of Helium," he said, "your words are balm to the wound you gave me in the throne room of O-Tar. Tell me, Princess, why you denied me."

She turned her great, deep eyes up to his and in them was a little of reproach.

"You did not guess," she asked, "that it was my lips alone and not my heart that denied you? O-Tar had ordered that I die, more because I was a companion of Ghek than because of any evidence against me, and so I knew that if I acknowledged you as one of us, you would be slain, too."

"It was to save me, then?" he cried, his face suddenly lighting.

"It was to save my brave panthan," she said in a low voice.

"Tara of Helium," said the warrior, dropping to one knee, "your words are as food to my hungry heart," and he took her fingers in his and pressed them to his lips.

Gently she raised him to his feet. "You need not tell me, kneeling," she said, softly.

Her hand was still in his as he rose and they were very close, and the man was still flushed with the contact of her body since he had carried her from the throne room of O-Tar. He felt his heart pounding in his breast and the hot blood surging through his veins as he looked at her beautiful face, with its downcast eyes and the half-parted lips that he would have given a kingdom to possess, and then he swept her to him and as he crushed her against his breast his lips smothered hers with kisses.

But only for an instant. Like a tigress the girl turned upon him, striking him, and thrusting him away. She stepped back, her head high and her eyes flashing fire. "You would dare?" she cried. "You would dare thus defile a princess of Helium?"

His eyes met hers squarely and there was no shame and no remorse in them.

"Yes, I would dare," he said. "I would dare love Tara of Helium; but I would not dare defile her or any woman with kisses that were not prompted by love of her alone." He stepped closer to her and laid his hands upon her shoulders. "Look into my eyes, daughter of The Warlord," he said, "and tell me that you do not wish the love of Turan, the panthan."

"I do not wish your love," she cried, pulling away. "I hate you!" and then turning away she bent her head into the hollow of her arm, and wept.

The man took a step toward her as though to comfort her when he was arrested by the sound of a crackling laugh behind him. Wheeling about, he discovered a strange figure of a man standing in a doorway. It was one of those rarities occasionally to be seen upon Barsoom—an old man with the signs of age upon him. Bent and wrinkled, he had more the appearance of a mummy than a man.

"Love in the pits of O-Tar!" he cried, and again his thin laughter jarred upon the silence of the subterranean vaults. "A strange place to woo! A strange place to woo, indeed! When I was a young man we roamed in the gardens beneath giant pimalias and stole our kisses in the brief shadows of hurtling Thuria. We came not to the gloomy pits to speak of love; but times have changed and ways have changed, though I had never thought to live to see the time when the way of a man with a maid, or a maid with a man would change. Ah, but we kissed them then! And what if they objected, eh? What if they objected? Why, we kissed them more. Ey, ey, those were the days!" and he cackled again. "Ey, well do I recall the first of them I ever kissed, and I've kissed an army of them since; she was a fine girl, but she tried to slip a dagger into me while I was kissing her. Ey, ey, those were the days! But I kissed her. She's been dead over a thousand years now, but she was never kissed again like that while she lived, I'll swear, not since she's been dead, either. And then there was that other—" but Turan, seeing a thousand or more years of osculatory memoirs portending, interrupted.

"Tell me, ancient one," he said, "not of thy loves but of thyself. Who are you? What do you here in the pits of O-Tar?"

"I might ask you the same, young man," replied the other. "Few there are who visit the pits other than the dead, except my pupils—ey! That is it—you are new pupils! Good! But never before have they sent a woman to learn the great art from the greatest artist. But times have changed. Now, in my day the women did no work—they were just for kissing and loving. Ey, those were the women. I mind the one we captured in the south—ey! she was a devil, but how she could love. She had breasts of marble and a heart of fire. Why, she—"

"Yes, yes," interrupted Turan; "we are pupils, and we are anxious to get to work. Lead on and we will follow."

"Ey, yes! Ey, yes! Come! All is rush and hurry as though there were not another countless myriad of ages ahead. Ey, yes! as many as lie behind. Two thousand years have passed since I broke my shell and always rush, rush, rush, yet I cannot see that aught has been accomplished. Manator is the same today as it was then—except the girls. We had the girls then. There was one that I gained upon The Fields of Jetan. Ey, but you should have seen —"

"Lead on!" cried Turan. "After we are at work you shall tell us of her."

"Ey, yes," said the old fellow and shuffled off down a dimly lighted passage. "Follow me!"

"You are going with him?" asked Tara.

"Why not?" replied Turan. "We know not where we are, or the way from these pits; for I know not east from west; but he doubtless knows and if we are shrewd we may learn from him that which we would know. At least we cannot afford to arouse his suspicions"; and so they followed him—followed along winding corridors and through many chambers, until they came at last to a room in which there were several marble slabs raised upon pedestals some three feet above the floor and upon each slab lay a human corpse.

"Here we are," exclaimed the old man. "These are fresh and we shall have to get to work upon them soon. I am working now on one for The Gate of Enemies. He slew many of our warriors. Truly is he entitled to a place in The Gate. Come, you shall see him."

He led them to an adjoining apartment. Upon the floor were many fresh, human bones and upon a marble slab a mass of shapeless flesh.

"You will learn this later," announced the old man; "but it will not harm you to watch me now, for there are not many thus prepared, and it may be long before you will have the opportunity to see another prepared for The Gate of Enemies. First, you see, I remove all the bones, carefully that the skin may be damaged as little as possible. The skull is the most difficult, but it can be removed by a skilful artist. You see, I have made but a single opening. This I now sew up, and that done, the body is hung so," and he fastened a piece of rope to the hair of the corpse and swung the horrid thing to a ring in the ceiling.

Directly below it was a circular manhole in the floor from which he removed the cover revealing a well partially filled with a reddish liquid. "Now we lower it into this, the formula for which you shall learn in due time. We fasten it thus to the bottom of the cover, which we now replace. In a year it will be ready; but it must be examined often in the meantime and the liquid kept above the level of its crown. It will be a very beautiful piece, this one, when it is ready.

"And you are fortunate again, for there is one to come out today." He crossed to the opposite side of the room and raised another cover, reached in and dragged a grotesque looking figure from the hole. It was a human body, shrunk by the action of the chemical in which it had been immersed, to a little figure scarce a foot high.

"Ey! is it not fine?" cried the little old man. "Tomorrow it will take its place in The Gate of Enemies." He dried it off with cloths and packed it away carefully in a basket. "Perhaps you would like to see some of my life work," he suggested, and without waiting for their assent led them to another apartment, a large chamber in which were forty or fifty people. All were sitting or standing quietly about the walls, with the exception of one huge warrior who bestrode a great thoat in the very centre of the room, and all were motionless. Instantly there sprang to the minds of Tara and Turan the rows of silent people upon the balconies that lined the avenues of the city, and the noble array of mounted warriors in The Hall of Chiefs, and the same explanation came to both but neither dared voice the question that was in his mind, for fear of revealing by his ignorance the fact that they were strangers in Manator and therefore impostors in the guise of pupils.

"It is very wonderful," said Turan. "It must require great skill and patience and time."

"That it does," replied the old man, "though having done it so long I am quicker than most; but mine are the most natural. Why, I would defy the wife of that warrior to say that insofar as appearances are concerned he does not live," and he pointed at the man upon the thoat. "Many of them, of course, are brought here wasted or badly wounded and these I have to repair. That is where great skill is required, for everyone wants his dead to look as they did at their best in life; but you shall learn—to mount them and paint them and repair them and sometimes to make an ugly one look beautiful. And it will be a great comfort to be able to mount your own. Why, for fifteen hundred years no one has mounted my own dead but myself.

"I have many, my balconies are crowded with them; but I keep a great room for my wives. I have them all, as far back as the first one, and many is the evening I spend with them—quiet evenings and very pleasant. And then the pleasure of preparing them and making them even more beautiful than in life partially recompenses one for their loss. I take my time with them, looking for a new one while I am working on the old. When I am not sure about a new one I bring her to the chamber where my wives are, and compare her charms with theirs, and there is always a great satisfaction at such times in knowing that they will not object. I love harmony."

"Did you prepare all the warriors in The Hall of Chiefs?" asked Turan.

"Yes, I prepare them and repair them," replied the old man. "O-Tar will trust no other. Even now I have two in another room who were damaged in some way and brought down to me. O-Tar does not like to have them gone long, since it leaves two riderless thoats in the Hall; but I shall have them ready presently. He wants them all there in the event any momentous question arises upon which the living jeds cannot agree, or do not agree with O-Tar. Such questions he carries to the jeds in The Hall of Chiefs. There he shuts himself up alone with the great chiefs who have attained wisdom through death. It is an excellent plan and there is never any friction or misunderstandings. O-Tar has said that it is the finest deliberative body upon Barsoom—much more intelligent than that composed of the living jeds. But come, we must get to work; come into the next chamber and I will begin your instruction."

He led the way into the chamber in which lay the several corpses upon their marble slabs, and going to a cabinet he donned a pair of huge spectacles and commenced to select various tools from little compartments. This done he turned again toward his two pupils.

"Now let me have a look at you," he said. "My eyes are not what they once were, and I need these powerful lenses for my work, or to see distinctly the features of those around me."

He turned his eyes upon the two before him. Turan held his breath for he knew that now the man must discover that they wore not the harness or insignia of Manator. He had wondered before why the old fellow had not noticed it, for he had not known that he was half blind. The other examined their faces, his eyes lingering long upon the beauty of Tara of Helium, and then they drifted to the harness of the two. Turan thought that he noted an appreciable start of surprise on the part of the taxidermist, but if the old man noticed anything his next words did not reveal it.

"Come with I-Gos," he said to Turan, "I have materials in the next room that I would have you fetch hither. Remain here, woman, we shall be gone but a moment."

He led the way to one of the numerous doors opening into the chamber and entered ahead of Turan. Just inside the door he stopped, and pointing to a bundle of silks and furs upon the opposite side of the room directed Turan to fetch them. The latter had crossed the room and was stooping to raise the bundle when he heard the click of a lock behind him. Wheeling instantly he saw that he was alone in the room and that the single door was closed. Running rapidly to it he strove to open it, only to find that he was a prisoner.

I-Gos, stepping out and locking the door behind him, turned toward Tara.

"Your leather betrayed you," he said, laughing his cackling laugh. "You sought to deceive old I-Gos, but you found that though his eyes are weak his brain is not. But it shall not go ill with you. You are beautiful and I-Gos loves beautiful women. I might not have you elsewhere in Manator, but here there is none to deny old I-Gos. Few come to the pits of the dead—only those who bang the dead and they hasten away as fast as they can. No one will know that I-Gos has a beautiful woman locked with his dead. I shall ask you no questions and then I will not have to give you up, for I will not know to whom you belong, eh? And when you die I shall mount you beautifully and place you in the chamber with my other women. Will not that be fine, eh?" He had approached until he stood close beside the horrified girl. "Come!" he cried, seizing her by the wrist. "Come to I-Gos!"

Chapter 16

Another Change of Name

Turan dashed himself against the door of his prison in a vain effort to break through the solid skeel to the side of Tara whom he knew to be in grave danger, but the heavy panels held and he succeeded only in bruising his shoulders and his arms. At last he desisted and set about searching his prison for some other means of escape. He found no other opening in the stone walls, but his search revealed a heterogeneous collection of odds and ends of arms and apparel, of harness and ornaments and insignia, and sleeping silks and furs in great quantities. There were swords and spears and several large, two-bladed battle-axes, the heads of which bore a striking resemblance to the propellor of a small flier. Seizing one of these he attacked the door once more with great fury. He expected to hear something from I-Gos at this ruthless destruction, but no sound came to him from beyond the door, which was, he thought, too thick for the human voice to penetrate; but he would have wagered much that I-Gos heard him. Bits of the hard wood splintered at each impact of the heavy axe, but it was slow work and heavy. Presently he was compelled to rest, and so it went for what seemed hours—working almost to the verge of exhaustion and then resting for a few minutes; but ever the hole grew larger though he could see nothing of the interior of the room beyond because of the hanging that I-Gos had drawn across it after he had locked Turan within.

At last, however, the panthan had hewn an opening through which his body could pass, and seizing a long-sword that he had brought close to the door for the purpose he crawled through into the next room. Flinging aside the arras he stood ready, sword in hand, to fight his way to the side of Tara of Helium—but she was not there. In the centre of the room lay I-Gos, dead upon the floor; but Tara of Helium was nowhere to be seen.

Turan was nonplussed. It must have been her hand that had struck down the old man, yet she had made no effort to release Turan from his prison. And then he thought of those last words of hers: "I do not want your love! I hate you," and the truth dawned upon him—she had seized upon this first opportunity to escape him. With downcast heart Turan turned away. What should he do? There could be but one answer. While he lived and she lived he must still leave no stone unturned to effect her escape and safe return to the land of her people. But how? How was he even to find his way from this labyrinth? How was he to find her again? He walked to the nearest doorway. It chanced to be that which led into the room containing the mounted dead, awaiting transportation to balcony or grim room or whatever place was to receive them. His eyes travelled to the great, painted warrior on the thoat and as they ran over the splendid trappings and the serviceable arms a new light came into the pain-dulled eyes of the panthan. With a quick step he crossed to the side of the dead warrior and dragged him from his mount. With equal celerity he stripped him of his harness and his arms, and tearing off his own, donned the regalia of the dead man. Then he hastened back to the room in which he had been trapped, for there he had seen that which he needed to make his disguise complete. In a cabinet he found them—pots of paint that the old taxidermist had used to place the war-paint in its wide bands across the cold faces of dead warriors.

A few moments later Gahan of Gathol emerged from the room a warrior of Manator in every detail of harness, equipment, and ornamentation. He had removed from the leather of the dead man the insignia of his house and rank so that he might pass, with the least danger of arousing suspicion, as a common warrior.

To search for Tara of Helium in the vast, dim labyrinth of the pits of O-Tar seemed to the Gatholian a hopeless quest, foredoomed to failure. It would be wiser to seek the streets of Manator where he might hope to learn first if she had been recaptured and, if not, then he could return to the pits and pursue the hunt for her. To find egress from the maze he must perforce travel a considerable distance through the winding corridors and chambers, since he had no idea as to the location or direction of any exit. In fact, he could not have retraced his steps a hundred yards toward the point at which he and Tara had entered the gloomy caverns, and so he set out in the hope that he might find by accident either Tara of Helium or a way to the street level above.

For a time he passed room after room filled with the cunningly preserved dead of Manator, many of which were piled in tiers after the manner that firewood is corded, and as he moved through corridor and chamber he noticed hieroglyphics painted upon the walls above every opening and at each fork or crossing of corridors, until by observation he reached the conclusion that these indicated the designations of passageways, so that one who understood them might travel quickly and surely through the pits; but Turan did not understand them. Even could he have read the language of Manator they might not materially have aided one unfamiliar with the city; but he could not read them at all since, though there is but one spoken language upon Barsoom, there are as many different written languages as there are nations. One thing, however, soon became apparent to him—the hieroglyphic of a corridor remained the same until the corridor ended.

It was not long before Turan realized from the distance that he had travelled that the pits were part of a vast system undermining, possibly, the entire city. At least he was convinced that he had passed beyond the precincts of the palace. The corridors and chambers varied in appearance and architecture from time to time. All were lighted, though usually quite dimly, with radium bulbs. For a long time he saw no signs of life other than an occasional ulsio, then quite suddenly he came face to face with a warrior at one of the numerous crossings. The fellow looked at him, nodded, and passed on. Turan breathed a sigh of relief as he realized that his disguise was effective, but he was caught in the middle of it by a hail from the warrior who had stopped and turned toward him. The panthan was glad that a sword hung at his side, and glad too that they were buried in the dim recesses of the pits and that there would be but a single antagonist, for time was precious.

"Heard you any word of the other?" called the warrior to him.

"No," replied Turan, who had not the faintest idea to whom or what the fellow referred.

"He cannot escape," continued the warrior. "The woman ran directly into our arms, but she swore that she knew not where her companion might be found."

"They took her back to O-Tar?" asked Turan, for now he knew whom the other meant, and he would know more.

"They took her back to The Towers of Jetan," replied the warrior. "Tomorrow the games commence and doubtless she will be played for, though I doubt if any wants her, beautiful as she is. She fears not even O-Tar. By Cluros! but she would make a hard slave to subdue—a regular she-banth she is. Not for me," and he continued on his way shaking his head.

Turan hurried on searching for an avenue that led to the level of the streets above when suddenly he came to the open doorway of a small chamber in which sat a man who was chained to the wall. Turan voiced a low exclamation of surprise and pleasure as he recognized that the man was A-Kor, and that he had stumbled by accident upon the very cell in which he had been imprisoned. A-Kor looked at him questioningly. It was evident that he did not recognize his fellow prisoner. Turan crossed to the table and leaning close to the other whispered to him.

"I am Turan the panthan," he said, "who was chained beside you."

A-Kor looked at him closely. "Your own mother would never know you!" he said; "but tell me, what has transpired since they took you away?"

Turan recounted his experiences in the throne room of O-Tar and in the pits beneath, "and now," he continued, "I must find these Towers of Jetan and see what may be done toward liberating the Princess of Helium."

A-Kor shook his head. "Long was I dwar of the Towers," he said, "and I can say to you, stranger, that you might as well attempt to reduce Manator, single handed, as to rescue a prisoner from The Towers of Jetan."

"But I must," replied Turan.

"Are you better than a good swordsman?" asked A-Kor presently.

"I am accounted so," replied Turan.

"Then there is a way—sst!" he was suddenly silent and pointing toward the base of the wall at the end of the room.

Turan looked in the direction the other's forefinger indicated, to see projecting from the mouth of an ulsio's burrow two large chelae and a pair of protruding eyes.

"Ghek!" he cried and immediately the hideous kaldane crawled out upon the floor and approached the table. A-Kor drew back with a half-stifled ejaculation of repulsion. "Do not fear," Turan reassured him. "It is my friend—he whom I told you held O-Tar while Tara and I escaped."

Ghek climbed to the table top and squatted between the two warriors. "You are safe in assuming," he said addressing A-Kor, "that Turan the panthan has no master in all Manator where the art of sword-play is concerned. I overheard your conversation—go on."

"You are his friend," continued A-Kor, "and so I may explain safely in your presence the only plan I know whereby he may hope to rescue the Princess of Helium. She is to be the stake of one of the games and it is O-Tar's desire that she be won by slaves and common warriors, since she repulsed him. Thus would he punish her. Not a single man, but all who survive upon the winning side are to possess her. With money, however, one may buy off the others before the game. That you could do, and if your side won and you survived she would become your slave."

"But how may a stranger and a hunted fugitive accomplish this?" asked Turan.

"No one will recognize you. You will go tomorrow to the keeper of the Towers and enlist in that game for which the girl is to be the stake, telling the keeper that you are from Manataj, the farthest city of Manator. If he questions you, you may say that you saw her when she was brought into the city after her capture. If you win her, you will find thoats stabled at my palace and you will carry from me a token that will place all that is mine at your disposal."

"But how can I buy off the others in the game without money?" asked Turan. "I have none—not even of my own country."

A-Kor opened his pocket-pouch and drew forth a packet of Manatorian money.

"Here is sufficient to buy them off twice over," he said, handing a portion of it to Turan.

"But why do you do this for a stranger?" asked the panthan.

"My mother was a captive princess here," replied A-Kor. "I but do for the Princess of Helium what my mother would have me do."

"Under the circumstances, then, Manatorian," replied Turan, "I cannot but accept your generosity on behalf of Tara of Helium and live in hope that some day I may do for you something in return."

"Now you must be gone," advised A-Kor. "At any minute a guard may come and discover you here. Go directly to the Avenue of Gates, which circles the city just within the outer wall. There you will find many places devoted to the lodging of strangers. You will know them by the thoat's head carved above the doors. Say that you are here from Manataj to witness the games. Take the name of U-Kal—it will arouse no suspicion, nor will you if you can avoid conversation. Early in the morning seek the keeper of The Towers of Jetan. May the strength and fortune of all your ancestors be with you!"

Bidding good-bye to Ghek and A-Kor, the panthan, following directions given him by A-Kor, set out to find his way to the Avenue of Gates, nor had he any great difficulty. On the way he met several warriors, but beyond a nod they gave him no heed. With ease he found a lodging place where there were many strangers from other cities of

Manator. As he had had no sleep since the previous night he threw himself among the silks and furs of his couch to gain the rest which he must have, was he to give the best possible account of himself in the service of Tara of Helium the following day.

It was already morning when he awoke, and rising he paid for his lodgings, sought a place to eat, and a short time later was on his way toward The Towers of Jetan, which he had no difficulty in finding owing to the great crowds that were winding along the avenues toward the games. The new keeper of The Towers who had succeeded E-Med was too busy to scrutinize entries closely, for in addition to the many volunteer players there were scores of slaves and prisoners being forced into the games by their owners or the government. The name of each must be recorded as well as the position he was to play and the game or games in which he was to be entered, and then there were the substitutes for each that was entered in more than a single game—one for each additional game that an individual was entered for, that no succeeding game might be delayed by the death or disablement of a player.

"Your name?" asked a clerk as Turan presented himself.

"U-Kal," replied the panthan.

"Your city?"

"Manataj."

The keeper, who was standing beside the clerk, looked at Turan. "You have come a great way to play at jetan," he said. "It is seldom that the men of Manataj attend other than the decennial games. Tell me of O-Zar! Will he attend next year? Ah, but he was a noble fighter. If you be half the swordsman, U-Kal, the fame of Manataj will increase this day. But tell me, what of O-Zar?"

"He is well," replied Turan, glibly, "and he sent greetings to his friends in Manator."

"Good!" exclaimed the keeper, "and now in what game would you enter?"

"I would play for the Heliumetic princess, Tara," replied Turan.

"But man, she is to be the stake of a game for slaves and criminals," cried the keeper. "You would not volunteer for such a game!"

"But I would," replied Turan. "I saw here when she was brought into the city and even then I vowed to possess her."

"But you will have to share her with the survivors even if your colour wins," objected the other.

"They may be brought to reason," insisted Turan.

"And you will chance incurring the wrath of O-Tar, who has no love for this savage barbarian," explained the keeper.

"And I win her O-Tar will be rid of her," said Turan.

The keeper of The Towers of Jetan shook his head. "You are rash," he said. "I would that I might dissuade the friend of my friend O-Zar from such madness."

"Would you favour the friend of O-Zar?" asked Turan.

"Gladly!" exclaimed the other. "What may I do for him?"

"Make me chief of the Black and give me for my pieces all slaves from Gathol, for I understand that those be excellent warriors," replied the panthan.

"It is a strange request," said the keeper, "but for my friend O-Zar I would do even more, though of course—" he hesitated—"it is customary for one who would be chief to make some slight payment."

"Certainly," Turan hastened to assure him; "I had not forgotten that. I was about to ask you what the customary amount is."

"For the friend of my friend it shall be nominal," replied the keeper, naming a figure that Gahan, accustomed to the high price of wealthy Gathol, thought ridiculously low.

"Tell me," he said, handing the money to the keeper, "when the game for the Heliumite is to be played."

"It is the second in order of the day's games; and now if you will come with me you may select your pieces."

Turan followed the keeper to a large court which lay between the towers and the jetan field, where hundreds of warriors were assembled. Already chiefs for the games of the day were selecting their pieces and assigning them to positions, though for the principal games these matters had been arranged for weeks before. The keeper led Turan to a part of the courtyard where the majority of the slaves were assembled.

"Take your choice of those not assigned," said the keeper, "and when you have your quota conduct them to the field. Your place will be assigned you by an officer there, and there you will remain with your pieces until the second game is called. I wish you luck, U-Kal, though from what I have heard you will be more lucky to lose than to win the slave from Helium."

After the fellow had departed Turan approached the slaves. "I seek the best swordsmen for the second game," he announced. "Men from Gathol I wish, for I have heard that these be noble fighters."

A slave rose and approached him. "It is all the same in which game we die," he said. "I would fight for you as a panthan in the second game."

Another came. "I am not from Gathol," he said. "I am from Helium, and I would fight for the honour of a princess of Helium."

"Good!" exclaimed Turan. "Art a swordsman of repute in Helium?"

"I was a dwar under the great Warlord, and I have fought at his side in a score of battles from The Golden Cliffs to The Carrion Caves. My name is Val Dor. Who knows Helium, knows my prowess."

The name was well known to Gahan, who had heard the man spoken of on his last visit to Helium, and his mysterious disappearance discussed as well as his renown as a fighter.

"How could I know aught of Helium?" asked Turan; "but if you be such a fighter as you say no position could suit you better than that of Flier. What say you?"

The man's eyes denoted sudden surprise. He looked keenly at Turan, his eyes running quickly over the other's harness. Then he stepped quite close so that his words might not be overheard.

"Methinks you may know more of Helium than of Manator," he whispered.

"What mean you, fellow?" demanded Turan, seeking to cudgel his brains for the source of this man's knowledge, guess, or inspiration.

"I mean," replied Val Dor, "that you are not of Manator and that if you wish to hide the fact it is well that you speak not to a Manatorian as you did just speak to me of—Fliers! There be no Fliers in Manator and no piece in their game of Jetan bearing that name. Instead they call him who stands next to the Chief or Princess, Odwar. The piece has the same moves and power that the Flier has in the game as played outside Manator. Remember this then and remember, too, that if you have a secret it be safe in the keeping of Val Dor of Helium."

Turan made no reply but turned to the task of selecting the remainder of his pieces. Val Dor, the Heliumite, and Floran, the volunteer from Gathol, were of great assistance to him, since one or the other of them knew most of the slaves from whom his selection was to be made. The pieces all chosen, Turan led them to the place beside the playing field where they were to wait their turn, and here he passed the word around that they were to fight for more than the stake he offered for the princess should they win. This stake they accepted, so that Turan was sure of possessing Tara if his side was victorious, but he knew that these men would fight even more valorously for chivalry than for money, nor was it difficult to enlist the interest even of the Gatholians in the service of the princess. And now he held out the possibility of a still further reward.

"I cannot promise you," he explained, "but I may say I have heard that this day which makes it possible that should we win this game we may even win your freedom!"

They leaped to their feet and crowded around him with many questions.

"It may not be spoken of aloud," he said; "but Floran and Val Dor know and they assure me that you may all be trusted. Listen! What I would tell you places my life in your hands, but you must know that every man will realize that he is fighting today the greatest battle of his life—for the honour and the freedom of Barsoom's most wondrous princess and for his own freedom as well—for the chance to return each to his own country and to the woman who awaits him there.

"First, then, is my secret. I am not of Manator. Like yourselves I am a slave, though for the moment disguised as a Manatorian from Mantaj. My country and my identity must remain undisclosed for reasons that have no bearing upon our game today. I, then, am one of you. I fight for the same things that you will fight for.

"And now for that which I have but just learned. U-Thor, the great jed of Manatos, quarrelled with O-Tar in the palace the day before yesterday and their warriors set upon one another. U-Thor was driven as far as The Gate of Enemies, where he now lies encamped. At any moment the fight may be renewed; but it is thought that U-Thor has sent to Manatos for reinforcements. Now, men of Gathol, here is the thing that interests you. U-Thor has recently taken to wife the Princess Haja of Gathol, who was slave to O-Tar and whose son, A-Kor, was dwar of The Towers of Jetan. Haja's heart is filled with loyalty for Gathol and compassion for her sons who are here enslaved, and this latter sentiment she has to some extent transmitted to U-Thor. Aid me, therefore, in freeing the Princess Tara of Helium and I believe that I can aid you and her and myself to escape the city. Bend close your ears, slaves of O-Tar, that no cruel enemy may hear my words," and Gahan of Gathol whispered in low tones the daring plan he had conceived. "And now," he demanded, when he had finished, "let him who does not dare speak now." None replied. "Is there none?"

"And it would not betray you should I cast my sword at thy feet, it had been done ere this," said one in low tones pregnant with suppressed feeling.

"And I!" "And I!" "And I!" chorused the others in vibrant whispers.

Chapter 17

A Play to the Death

Clear and sweet a trumpet spoke across The Fields of Jetan. From The High Tower its cool voice floated across the city of Manator and above the babble of human discords rising from the crowded mass that filled the seats of the stadium below. It called the players for the first game, and simultaneously there fluttered to the peaks of a thousand staffs on tower and battlement and the great wall of the stadium the rich, gay pennons of the fighting chiefs of Manator. Thus was marked the opening of The Jeddak's Games, the most important of the year and second only to the Grand Decennial Games.

Gahan of Gathol watched every play with eagle eye. The match was an unimportant one, being but to settle some petty dispute between two chiefs, and was played with professional jetan players for points only. No one was killed and there was but little blood spilled. It lasted about an hour and was terminated by the chief of the losing side deliberately permitting himself to be out-pointed, that the game might be called a draw.

Again the trumpet sounded, this time announcing the second and last game of the afternoon. While this was not considered an important match, those being reserved for the fourth and fifth days of the games, it promised to afford sufficient excitement since it was a game to the death. The vital difference between the game played with living men and that in which inanimate pieces are used, lies in the fact that while in the latter the mere placing of a piece upon a square occupied by an opponent piece terminates the move, in the former the two pieces thus brought together engage in a duel for possession of the square. Therefore there enters into the former game not only the strategy of jetan but the personal prowess and bravery of each individual piece, so that a knowledge not only of one's own men but of each player upon the opposing side is of vast value to a chief.

In this respect was Gahan handicapped, though the loyalty of his players did much to offset his ignorance of them, since they aided him in arranging the board to the best advantage and told him honestly the faults and virtues of each. One fought best in a losing game; another was too slow; another too impetuous; this one had fire and a heart of steel, but lacked endurance. Of the opponents, though, they knew little or nothing, and now as the two sides took their places upon the black and orange squares of the great jetan board Gahan obtained, for the first time, a close view of those who opposed him. The Orange Chief had not yet entered the field, but his men were all in place. Val Dor turned to Gahan. "They are all criminals from the pits of Manator," he said. "There is no slave among them. We shall not have to fight against a single fellow-countryman and every life we take will be the life of an enemy."

"It is well," replied Gahan; "but where is their Chief, and where the two Princesses?"

"They are coming now, see?" and he pointed across the field to where two women could be seen approaching under guard.

As they came nearer Gahan saw that one was indeed Tara of Helium, but the other he did not recognize, and then they were brought to the centre of the field midway between the two sides and there waited until the Orange Chief arrived.

Floran voiced an exclamation of surprise when he recognized him. "By my first ancestor if it is not one of their great chiefs," he said, "and we were told that slaves and criminals were to play for the stake of this game."

His words were interrupted by the keeper of The Towers whose duty it was not only to announce the games and the stakes, but to act as referee as well.

"Of this, the second game of the first day of the Jeddak's Games in the four hundred and thirty-third year of O-Tar, Jeddak of Manator, the Princesses of each side shall be the sole stakes and to the survivors of the winning side shall belong both the Princesses, to do with as they shall see fit. The Orange Princess is the slave woman Lan-O of Gathol; the Black Princess is the slave woman Tara, a princess of Helium. The Black Chief is U-Kal of Manataj, a volunteer player; the Orange Chief is the dwar U-Dor of the 8th Utan of the jeddak of Manator, also a volunteer player. The squares shall be contested to the death. Just are the laws of Manator! I have spoken."

The initial move was won by U-Dor, following which the two Chiefs escorted their respective Princesses to the square each was to occupy. It was the first time Gahan had been alone with Tara since she had been brought upon the field. He saw her scrutinizing him closely as he approached to lead her to her place and wondered if she recognized him: but if she did she gave no sign of it. He could not but remember her last words—"I hate you!" and her desertion of him when he had been locked in the room beneath the palace by I-Gos, the taxidermist, and so he did not seek to enlighten her as to his identity. He meant to fight for her—to die for her, if necessary—and if he did not die to go on fighting to the end for her love. Gahan of Gathol was not easily to be discouraged, but he was compelled to admit that his chances of winning the love of Tara of Helium were remote. Already had she repulsed him twice. Once as jed of Gathol and again as Turan the panthan. Before his love, however, came her safety and the former must be relegated to the background until the latter had been achieved.

Passing among the players already at their stations the two took their places upon their respective squares. At Tara's left was the Black Chief, Gahan of Gathol; directly in front of her the Princess' Panthan, Floran of Gathol; and at her right the Princess' Odwar, Val Dor of Helium. And each of these knew the part that he was to play, win or lose, as did each of the other Black players. As Tara took her place Val Dor bowed low. "My sword is at your feet, Tara of Helium," he said.

She turned and looked at him, an expression of surprise and incredulity upon her face. "Val Dor, the dwar!" she exclaimed. "Val Dor of Helium—one of my father's trusted captains! Can it be possible that my eyes speak the truth?"

"It is Val Dor, Princess," the warrior replied, "and here to die for you if need be, as is every wearer of the Black upon this field of jetan today. Know Princess," he whispered, "that upon this side is no man of Manator, but each and every is an enemy of Manator."

She cast a quick, meaning glance toward Gahan. "But what of him?" she whispered, and then she caught her breath quickly in surprise. "Shade of the first jeddak!" she exclaimed. "I did but just recognize him through his disguise."

"And you trust him?" asked Val Dor. "I know him not; but he spoke fairly, as an honourable warrior, and we have taken him at his word."

"You have made no mistake," replied Tara of Helium. "I would trust him with my life—with my soul; and you, too, may trust him."

Happy indeed would have been Gahan of Gathol could he have heard those words; but Fate, who is usually unkind to the lover in such matters, ordained it otherwise, and then the game was on.

U-Dor moved his Princess' Odwar three squares diagonally to the right, which placed the piece upon the Black Chief's Odwar's seventh. The move was indicative of the game that U-Dor intended playing—a game of blood, rather than of science—and evidenced his contempt for his opponents.

Gahan followed with his Odwar's Panthan one square straight forward, a more scientific move, which opened up an avenue for himself through his line of Panthans, as well as announcing to the players and spectators that he intended having a hand in the fighting himself even before the exigencies of the game forced it upon him. The move elicited a ripple of applause from those sections of seats reserved for the common warriors and their women, showing perhaps that U-Dor was none too popular with these, and, too, it had its effect upon the morale of Gahan's pieces. A Chief may, and often does, play almost an entire game without leaving his own square, where, mounted upon a thoat, he may overlook the entire field and direct each move, nor may he be reproached for lack of courage should he elect thus to play the game since, by the rules, were he to be slain or so badly wounded as to be compelled to withdraw, a game that might otherwise have been won by the science of his play and the prowess of his men would be drawn. To invite personal combat, therefore, denotes confidence in his own swordsmanship, and great courage, two attributes that were calculated to fill the Black players with hope and valour when evinced by their Chief thus early in the game.

U-Dor's next move placed Lan-O's Odwar upon Tara's Odwar's fourth—within striking distance of the Black Princess.

Another move and the game would be lost to Gahan unless the Orange Odwar was overthrown, or Tara moved to a position of safety; but to move his Princess now would be to admit his belief in the superiority of the Orange. In the three squares allowed him he could not place himself squarely upon the square occupied by the Odwar of U-Dor's Princess. There was only one player upon the Black side that might dispute the square with the enemy and that was the Chief's Odwar, who stood upon Gahan's left. Gahan turned upon his thoat and looked at the man. He was a splendid looking fellow, resplendent in the gorgeous trappings of an Odwar, the five brilliant feathers which denoted his position rising defiantly erect from his thick, black hair. In common with every player upon the field and every spectator in the crowded stands he knew what was passing in his Chief's mind. He dared not speak, the ethics of the game forbade it, but what his lips might not voice his eyes expressed in martial fire, and eloquently: "The honour of the Black and the safety of our Princess are secure with me!"

Gahan hesitated no longer. "Chief's Odwar to Princess' Odwar's fourth!" he commanded. It was the courageous move of a leader who had taken up the gauntlet thrown down by his opponent.

The warrior sprang forward and leaped into the square occupied by U-Dor's piece. It was the first disputed square of the game. The eyes of the players were fastened upon the contestants, the spectators leaned forward in their seats after the first applause that had greeted the move, and silence fell upon the vast assemblage. If the Black went down to defeat, U-Dor could move his victorious piece on to the square occupied by Tara of Helium and the game would be over—over in four moves and lost to Gahan of Gathol. If the Orange lost U-Dor would have sacrificed one of his most important pieces and more than lost what advantage the first move might have given him.

Physically the two men appeared perfectly matched and each was fighting for his life, but from the first it was apparent that the Black Odwar was the better swordsman, and Gahan knew that he had another and perhaps a greater advantage over his antagonist. The latter was fighting for his life only, without the spur of chivalry or loyalty. The Black Odwar had these to strengthen his arm, and besides these the knowledge of the thing that Gahan had whispered into the ears of his players before the game, and so he fought for what is more than life to the man of honour.

It was a duel that held those who witnessed it in spellbound silence. The weaving blades gleamed in the brilliant sunlight, ringing to the parries of cut and thrust. The barbaric harness of the duellists lent splendid colour to the savage, martial scene. The Orange Odwar, forced upon the defensive, was fighting madly for his life. The Black, with cool and terrible efficiency, was forcing him steadily, step by step, into a corner of the square—a position from which there could be no escape. To abandon the square was to lose it to his opponent and win for himself ignoble and immediate death before the jeering populace. Spurred on by the seeming hopelessness of his plight, the Orange Odwar burst into a sudden fury of offence that forced the Black back a half dozen steps, and then the sword of U-Dor's piece leaped in and drew first blood, from the shoulder of his merciless opponent. An ill-smothered cry of encouragement went up from U-Dor's men; the Orange Odwar, encouraged by his single success, sought to bear down the Black by the rapidity of his attack. There was a moment in which the swords moved with a rapidity that no man's eye might follow, and then the Black Odwar made a lightning parry of a vicious thrust, leaned quickly forward into the opening he had effected, and drove his sword through the heart of the Orange Odwar—to the hilt he drove it through the body of the Orange Odwar.

A shout arose from the stands, for wherever may have been the favour of the spectators, none there was who could say that it had not been a pretty fight, or that the better man had not won. And from the Black players came a sigh of relief as they relaxed from the tension of the past moments.

I shall not weary you with the details of the game—only the high features of it are necessary to your understanding of the outcome. The fourth move after the victory of the Black Odwar found Gahan upon U-Dor's fourth; an Orange Panthan was on the adjoining square diagonally to his right and the only opposing piece that could engage him other than U-Dor himself.

It had been apparent to both players and spectators for the past two moves, that Gahan was moving straight across the field into the enemy's country to seek personal combat with the Orange Chief—that he was staking all upon his belief in the superiority of his own swordsmanship, since if the two Chiefs engage, the outcome decides the game. U-Dor could move out and engage Gahan, or he could move his Princess' Panthan upon the square occupied by Gahan in he hope that the former would defeat the Black Chief and thus draw the game, which is the outcome if any other than a Chief slays the opposing Chief, or he could move away and escape, temporarily, the necessity for personal combat, or at least that is evidently what he had in mind as was obvious to all who saw him scanning the board about him; and his disappointment was apparent when he finally discovered that Gahan had so placed himself that there was no square to which U-Dor could move that it was not within Gahan's power to reach at his own next move.

U-Dor had placed his own Princess four squares east of Gahan when her position had been threatened, and he had hoped to lure the Black Chief after her and away from U-Dor; but in that he had failed. He now discovered that he might play his own Odwar into personal combat with Gahan; but he had already lost one Odwar and could ill spare the other. His position was a delicate one, since he did not wish to engage Gahan personally, while it appeared that there was little likelihood of his being able to escape. There was just one hope and that lay in his Princess' Panthan, so, without more deliberation he ordered the piece onto the square occupied by the Black Chief.

The sympathies of the spectators were all with Gahan now. If he lost, the game would be declared a draw, nor do they think better of drawn games upon Barsoom than do Earth men. If he won, it would doubtless mean a duel between the two Chiefs, a development for which they all were hoping. The game already bade fair to be a short one and it would be an angry crowd should it be decided a draw with only two men slain. There were great, historic games on record where of the forty pieces on the field when the game opened only three survived—the two Princesses and the victorious Chief.

They blamed U-Dor, though in fact he was well within his rights in directing his play as he saw fit, nor was a refusal on his part to engage the Black Chief necessarily an imputation of cowardice. He was a great chief who had conceived a notion to possess the slave Tara. There was no honour that could accrue to him from engaging in combat with slaves and criminals, or an unknown warrior from Manataj, nor was the stake of sufficient import to warrant the risk.

But now the duel between Gahan and the Orange Panthan was on and the decision of the next move was no longer in other hands than theirs. It was the first time that these Manatorians had seen Gahan of Gathol fight, but Tara of Helium knew that he was master of his sword. Could he have seen the proud light in her eyes as he crossed blades with the wearer of the Orange, he might easily have wondered if they were the same eyes that had flashed fire and hatred at him that time he had covered her lips with mad kisses, in the pits of the palace of O-Tar. As she watched him she could not but compare his swordplay with that of the greatest swordsman of two worlds—her father, John Carter, of Virginia, a Prince of Helium, Warlord of Barsoom—and she knew that the skill of the Black Chief suffered little by the comparison.

Short and to the point was the duel that decided possession of the Orange Chief's fourth. The spectators had settled themselves for an interesting engagement of at least average duration when they were brought almost standing by a brilliant flash of rapid swordplay that was over ere one could catch his breath. They saw the Black Chief step quickly back, his point upon the ground, while his opponent, his sword slipping from his fingers, clutched his breast, sank to his knees and then lunged forward upon his face.

And then Gahan of Gathol turned his eyes directly upon U-Dor of Manator, three squares away. Three squares is a Chief's move—three squares in any direction or combination of directions, only provided that he does not cross the same square twice in a given move. The people saw and guessed Gahan's intention. They rose and roared forth their approval as he moved deliberately across the intervening squares toward the Orange Chief.

O-Tar, in the royal enclosure, sat frowning upon the scene. O-Tar was angry. He was angry with U-Dor for having entered this game for possession of a slave, for whom it had been his wish only slaves and criminals should strive. He was angry with the warrior from Manataj for having so far out-generaled and out-fought the men from Manator. He was angry with the populace because of their open hostility toward one who had basked in the sunshine of his favour for long years. O-Tar the jeddak had not enjoyed the afternoon. Those who surrounded him were equally glum—they, too, scowled upon the field, the players, and the people. Among them was a bent and wrinkled old man who gazed through weak and watery eyes upon the field and the players.

As Gahan entered his square, U-Dor leaped toward him with drawn sword with such fury as might have overborne a less skilled and powerful swordsman. For a minute the fighting was fast and furious and by comparison reducing to insignificance all that had gone before. Here indeed were two magnificent swordsmen, and here was to be a battle that bade fair to make up for whatever the people felt they had been defrauded of by the shortness of the game. Nor had it continued long before many there were who would have prophesied that they were witnessing a duel that was to become historic in the annals of jetan at Manator. Every trick, every subterfuge, known to the art of fence these men employed. Time and again each scored a point and brought blood to his opponent's copper hide until both were red with gore; but neither seemed able to administer the coup de grace.

From her position upon the opposite side of the field Tara of Helium watched the long-drawn battle. Always it seemed to her that the Black Chief fought upon the defensive, or when he assumed to push his opponent, he neglected a thousand openings that her practiced eye beheld. Never did he seem in real danger, nor never did he appear to exert himself to quite the pitch needful for victory. The duel already had been long contested and the day was drawing to a close. Presently the sudden transition from daylight to darkness which, owing to the tenuity of the air upon Barsoom, occurs almost without the warning twilight of Earth, would occur. Would the fight never end? Would the game be called a draw after all? What ailed the Black Chief?

Tara wished that she might answer at least the last of these questions for she was sure that Turan the panthan, as she knew him, while fighting brilliantly, was not giving of himself all that he might. She could not believe that fear was restraining his hand, but that there was something beside inability to push U-Dor more fiercely she was confident. What it was, however, she could not guess.

Once she saw Gahan glance quickly up toward the sinking sun. In thirty minutes it would be dark. And then she saw and all those others saw a strange transition steal over the swordplay of the Black Chief. It was as though he had been playing with the great dwar, U-Dor, all these hours, and now he still played with him but there was a difference. He played with him terribly as a carnivore plays with its victim in the instant before the kill. The Orange Chief was helpless now in the hands of a swordsman so superior that there could be no comparison, and the people sat in open-mouthed wonder and awe as Gahan of Gathol cut his foe to ribbons and then struck him down with a blow that cleft him to the chin.

In twenty minutes the sun would set. But what of that?

Chapter 18

A Task for Loyalty

Long and loud was the applause that rose above the Field of Jetan at Manator, as The Keeper of the Towers summoned the two Princesses and the victorious Chief to the centre of the field and presented to the latter the fruits of his prowess, and then, as custom demanded, the victorious players, headed by Gahan and the two Princesses, formed in procession behind The Keeper of the Towers and were conducted to the place of victory before the royal enclosure that they might receive the commendation of the jeddak. Those who were mounted gave up their thoats to slaves as all must be on foot for this ceremony. Directly beneath the royal enclosure are the gates to one of the tunnels that, passing beneath the seats, give ingress or egress to or from the Field. Before this gate the party halted while O-Tar looked down upon them from above. Val Dor and Floran, passing quietly ahead of the others, went directly to the gates, where they were hidden from those who occupied the enclosure with O-Tar. The Keeper of the Towers may have noticed them, but so occupied was he with the formality of presenting the victorious Chief to the jeddak that he paid no attention to them.

"I bring you, O-Tar, Jeddak of Manator, U-Kal of Manataj," he cried in a loud voice that might be heard by as many as possible, "victor over the Orange in the second of the Jeddak's Games of the four hundred and thirty-third year of O-Tar, and the slave woman Tara and the slave woman Lan-O that you may bestow these, the stakes, upon U-Kal."

As he spoke, a little, wrinkled, old man peered over the rail of the enclosure down upon the three who stood directly behind The Keeper, and strained his weak and watery eyes in an effort to satisfy the curiosity of old age in a matter of no particular import, for what were two slaves and a common warrior from Manataj to any who sat with O-Tar the jeddak?

"U-Kal of Manataj," said O-Tar, "you have deserved the stakes. Seldom have we looked upon more noble swordplay. And you tire of Manataj there be always here in the city of Manator a place for you in The Jeddak's Guard."

While the jeddak was speaking the little, old man, failing clearly to discern the features of the Black Chief, reached into his pocket-pouch and drew forth a pair of thick-lensed spectacles, which he placed upon his nose. For a moment he scrutinized Gahan closely, then he leaped to his feet and addressing O-Tar pointed a shaking finger it Gahan. As he rose Tara of Helium clutched the Black Chief's arm.

"Turan!" she whispered. "It is I-Gos, whom I thought to have slain in the pits of O-Tar. It is I-Gos and he recognizes you and will—"

But what I-Gos would do was already transpiring. In his falsetto voice he fairly screamed: "It is the slave Turan who stole the woman Tara from your throne room, O-Tar. He desecrated the dead chief I-Mal and wears his harness now!"

Instantly all was pandemonium. Warriors drew their swords and leaped to their feet. Gahan's victorious players rushed forward in a body, sweeping The Keeper of the Towers from his feet. Val Dor and Floran threw open the gates beneath the royal enclosure, opening the tunnel that led to the avenue in the city beyond the Towers. Gahan, surrounded by his men, drew Tara and Lan-O into the passageway, and at a rapid pace the party sought to reach the opposite end of the tunnel before their escape could be cut off. They were successful and when they emerged into the city the sun had set and darkness had come, relieved only by an antiquated and ineffective lighting system, which cast but a pale glow over the shadowy streets.

Now it was that Tara of Helium guessed why the Black Chief had drawn out his duel with U-Dor and realized that he might have slain his man at almost any moment he had elected. The whole plan that Gahan had whispered to his players before the game was thoroughly understood. They were to make their way to The Gate of Enemies and there offer their services to U-Thor, the great Jed of Manatos. The fact that most of them were Gatholians and that Gahan could lead rescuers to the pit where A-Kor, the son of U-Thor's wife, was confined, convinced the Jed of Gathol that they would meet with no rebuff at the hands of U-Thor. But even should he refuse them, still were they bound together to go on toward freedom, if necessary cutting their way through the forces of U-Thor at The Gate of Enemies—twenty men against a small army; but of such stuff are the warriors of Barsoom.

They had covered a considerable distance along the almost deserted avenue before signs of pursuit developed and then there came upon them suddenly from behind a dozen warriors mounted on thoats—a detachment, evidently, from The Jeddak's Guard. Instantly the avenue was a pandemonium of clashing blades, cursing warriors, and squealing thoats. In the first onslaught life blood was spilled upon both sides. Two of Gahan's men went down, and upon the enemies' side three riderless thoats attested at least a portion of their casualties.

Gahan was engaged with a fellow who appeared to have been selected to account for him only, since he rode straight for him and sought to cut him down without giving the slightest heed to several who slashed at him as he passed them. The Gatholian, practiced in the art of combating a mounted warrior from the ground, sought to reach the left side of the fellow's thoat a little to the rider's rear, the only position in which he would have any advantage over his antagonist, or rather the position that would most greatly reduce the advantage of the mounted man, and, similarly, the Manatorian strove to thwart his design. And so the guardsman wheeled and turned his vicious, angry mount while Gahan leaped in and out in an effort to reach the coveted vantage point, but always seeking some other opening in his foe's defence.

And while they jockeyed for position a rider swept swiftly past them. As he passed behind Gahan the latter heard a cry of alarm.

"Turan, they have me!" came to his ears in the voice of Tara of Helium.

A quick glance across his shoulder showed him the galloping thoatman in the act of dragging Tara to the withers of the beast, and then, with the fury of a demon, Gahan of Gathol leaped for his own man, dragged him from his mount and as he fell smote his head from his shoulders with a single cut of his keen sword. Scarce had the body touched the pavement when the Gatholian was upon the back of the dead warrior's mount, and galloping swiftly down the avenue after the diminishing figures of Tara and her abductor, the sounds of the fight waning in the distance as he pursued his quarry along the avenue that passes the palace of O-Tar and leads to The Gate of Enemies.

Gahan's mount, carrying but a single rider, gained upon that of the Manatorian, so that as they neared the palace Gahan was scarce a hundred yards behind, and now, to his consternation, he saw the fellow turn into the great entrance-way. For a moment only was he halted by the guards and then he disappeared within. Gahan was almost upon him then, but evidently he had warned the guards, for they leaped out to intercept the Gatholian. But no! the fellow could not have known that he was pursued, since he had not seen Gahan seize a mount, nor would he have thought that pursuit would come so soon. If he had passed then, so could Gahan pass, for did he not wear the trappings of a Manatorian? The Gatholian thought quickly, and stopping his thoat called to the guardsmen to let him pass, "In the name of O-Tar!" They hesitated a moment.

"Aside!" cried Gahan. "Must the jeddak's messenger parley for the right to deliver his message?"

"To whom would you deliver it?" asked the padwar of the guard.

"Saw you not him who just entered?" cried Gahan, and without waiting for a reply urged his thoat straight past them into the palace, and while they were deliberating what was best to be done, it was too late to do anything—which is not unusual.

Along the marble corridors Gahan guided his thoat, and because he had gone that way before, rather than because he knew which way Tara had been taken, he followed the runways and passed through the chambers that led to the throne room of O-Tar. On the second level he met a slave.

"Which way went he who carried the woman before him?" he asked.

The slave pointed toward a nearby runway that led to the third level and Gahan dashed rapidly on in pursuit. At the same moment a thoatman, riding at a furious pace, approached the palace and halted his mount at the gate.

"Saw you aught of a warrior pursuing one who carried a woman before him on his thoat?" he shouted to the guard.

"He but just passed in," replied the padwar, "saying that he was O-Tar's messenger."

"He lied," cried the newcomer. "He was Turan, the slave, who stole the woman from the throne room two days since. Arouse the palace! He must be seized, and alive if possible. It is O-Tar's command."

Instantly warriors were dispatched to search for the Gatholian and warn the inmates of the palace to do likewise. Owing to the games there were comparatively few retainers in the great building, but those whom they found were immediately enlisted in the search, so that presently at least fifty warriors were seeking through the countless chambers and corridors of the palace of O-Tar.

As Gahan's thoat bore him to the third Level the man glimpsed the hind quarters of another thoat disappearing at the turn of a corridor far ahead. Urging his own animal forward he raced swiftly in pursuit and making the turn discovered only an empty corridor ahead. Along this he hurried to discover near its farther end a runway to the fourth level, which he followed upward. Here he saw that he had gained upon his quarry who was just turning through a doorway fifty yards ahead. As Gahan reached the opening he saw that the warrior had dismounted and was dragging Tara toward a small door on the opposite side of the chamber. At the same instant the clank of harness to his rear caused him to cast a glance behind where, along the corridor he had just traversed, he saw three warriors approaching on foot at a run. Leaping from his thoat Gahan sprang into the chamber where Tara was struggling to free herself from the grasp of her captor, slammed the door behind him, shot the great bolt into its seat, and drawing his sword crossed the room at a run to engage the Manatorian. The fellow, thus menaced, called aloud to Gahan to halt, at the same time thrusting Tara at arm's length and threatening her heart with the point of his short-sword.

"Stay!" he cried, "or the woman dies, for such is the command of O-Tar, rather than that she again fall into your hands."

Gahan stopped. But a few feet separated him from Tara and her captor, yet he was helpless to aid her. Slowly the warrior backed toward the open doorway behind him, dragging Tara with him. The girl struggled and fought, but the warrior was a powerful man and having seized her by the harness from behind was able to hold her in a position of helplessness.

"Save me, Turan!" she cried. "Let them not drag me to a fate worse than death. Better that I die now while my eyes behold a brave friend than later, fighting alone among enemies in defence of my honour."

He took a step nearer. The warrior made a threatening gesture with his sword close to the soft, smooth skin of the princess, and Gahan halted.

"I cannot, Tara of Helium," he cried. "Think not ill of me that I am weak—that I cannot see you die. Too great is my love for you, daughter of Helium."

The Manatorian warrior, a derisive grin upon his lips, backed steadily away. He had almost reached the doorway when Gahan saw another warrior in the chamber toward which Tara was being borne—a fellow who moved silently, almost stealthily, across the marble floor as he approached Tara's captor from behind. In his right hand he grasped a long-sword.

"Two to one," thought Gahan, and a grim smile touched his lips, for he had no doubt that once they had Tara safely in the adjoining chamber the two would set upon him. If he could not save her, he could at least die for her.

And then, suddenly, Gahan's eyes fastened with amazement upon the figure of the warrior behind the grinning fellow who held Tara and was forcing her to the doorway. He saw the newcomer step almost within arm's reach of the other. He saw him stop, an expression of malevolent hatred upon his features. He saw the great sword swing through the arc of a great circle, gathering swift and terrific momentum from its own weight backed by the brawn of the steel thews that guided it; he saw it pass through the feathered skull of the Manatorian, splitting his sardonic grin in twain, and open him to the middle of his breast bone.

As the dead hand relaxed its grasp upon Tara's wrist the girl leaped forward, without a backward glance, to Gahan's side. His left arm encircled her, nor did she draw away, as with ready sword the Gatholian awaited Fate's next decree. Before them Tara's deliverer was wiping the blood from his sword upon the hair of his victim. He was evidently a Manatorian, his trappings those of the Jeddak's Guard, and so his act was inexplicable to Gahan and to Tara. Presently he sheathed his sword and approached them.

"When a man chooses to hide his identity behind an assumed name," he said, looking straight into Gahan's eyes, "whatever friend pierces the deception were no friend if he divulged the other's secret."

He paused as though awaiting a reply.

"Your integrity has perceived and your lips voiced an unalterable truth," replied Gahan, whose mind was filled with wonder if the implication could by any possibility be true—that this Manatorian had guessed his identity.

"We are thus agreed," continued the other, "and I may tell you that though I am here known as A-Sor, my real name is Tasor." He paused and watched Gahan's face intently for any sign of the effect of this knowledge and was rewarded with a quick, though guarded expression of recognition.

Tasor! Friend of his youth. The son of that great Gatholian noble who had given his life so gloriously, however futilely, in an attempt to defend Gahan's sire from the daggers of the assassins. Tasor an underpadwar in the guard of O-Tar, Jeddak of Manator! It was inconceivable—and yet it was he; there could be no doubt of it. "Tasor," Gahan repeated aloud. "But it is no Manatorian name." The statement was half interrogatory, for Gahan's curiosity was aroused. He would know how his friend and loyal subject had become a Manatorian. Long years had passed since Tasor had disappeared as mysteriously as the Princess Haja and many other of Gahan's subjects. The Jed of Gathol had long supposed him dead.

"No," replied Tasor, "nor is it a Manatorian name. Come, while I search for a hiding place for you in some forgotten chamber in one of the untenanted portions of the palace, and as we go I will tell you briefly how Tasor the Gatholian became A-Sor the Manatorian.

"It befell that as I rode with a dozen of my warriors along the western border of Gathol searching for zitidars that had strayed from my herds, we were set upon and surrounded by a great company of Manatorians. They overpowered us, though not before half our number was slain and the balance helpless from wounds. And so I was brought a prisoner to Manataj, a distant city of Manator, and there sold into slavery. A woman bought me—a princess of Manataj whose wealth and position were unequalled in the city of her birth. She loved me and when her husband discovered her infatuation she beseeched me to slay him, and when I refused she hired another to do it. Then she married me; but none would have aught to do with her in Manataj, for they suspected her guilty knowledge of her husband's murder. And so we set out from Manataj for Manatos accompanied by a great caravan bearing all her worldly goods and jewels and precious metals, and on the way she caused the rumour to be spread that she and I had died. Then we came to Manator instead, she taking a new name and I the name A-Sor, that we might not be traced through our names. With her great wealth she bought me a post in The Jeddak's Guard and none knows that I am not a Manatorian, for she is dead. She was beautiful, but she was a devil."

"And you never sought to return to your native city?" asked Gahan.

"Never has the hope been absent from my heart, or my mind empty of a plan," replied Tasor. "I dream of it by day and by night, but always must I return to the same conclusion—that there can be but a single means for escape. I must wait until Fortune favours me with a place in a raiding party to Gathol. Then, once within the boundaries of my own country, they shall see me no more."

"Perhaps your opportunity lies already within your grasp," said Gahan, "has not your fealty to your own Jed been undermined by years of association with the men of Manator." The statement was half challenge.

"And my Jed stood before me now," cried Tasor, "and my avowal could be made without violating his confidence, I should cast my sword at his feet and beg the high privilege of dying for him as my sire died for his sire."

There could be no doubt of his sincerity nor any that he was cognizant of Gahan's identity. The Jed of Gathol smiled. "And if your Jed were here there is little doubt but that he would command you to devote your talents and your prowess to the rescue of the Princess Tara of Helium," he said, meaningly. "And he possessed the knowledge I have gained during my captivity he would say to you, 'Go, Tasor, to the pit where A-kor, son of Haja of Gathol, is confined and set him free and with him arouse the slaves from Gathol and march to The Gate of Enemies and offer your services to U-Thor of Manataj, who is wed to Haja of Gathol, and ask of him in return that he attack the palace of O-Tar and rescue Tara of Helium and when that thing is accomplished that he free the slaves of Gathol and furnish them with the arms and the means to return to their own country.' That, Tasor of Gathol, is what Gahan your Jed would demand of you."

"And that, Turan the slave, is what I shall bend my every effort to accomplish after I have found a safe refuge for Tara of Helium and her panthan," replied Tasor.

Gahan's glance carried to Tasor an intimation of his Jed's gratification and filled him with a chivalrous determination to do the thing required of him, or die, for he considered that he had received from the lips of his beloved ruler a commission that placed upon his shoulders a responsibility that encompassed not alone the life of Gahan and Tara but the welfare, perhaps the whole future, of Gathol. And so he hastened them onward through the musty corridors of the old palace where the dust of ages lay undisturbed upon the marble tiles. Now and again he tried a door until he found one that was unlocked. Opening it he ushered them into a chamber, heavy with dust. Crumbling silks and furs adorned the walls, with ancient weapons, and great paintings whose colours were toned by age to wondrous softness.

"This be as good as any place," he said. "No one comes here. Never have I been here before, so I know no more of the other chambers than you; but this one, at least, I can find again when I bring you food and drink. O-Mai the Cruel occupied this portion of the palace during his reign, five thousand years before O-Tar. In one of these apartments he was found dead, his face contorted in an expression of fear so horrible that it drove to madness those who looked upon it; yet there was no mark of violence upon him. Since then the quarters of O-Mai have been shunned for the legends have it that the ghosts of Corphals pursue the spirit of the wicked Jeddak nightly through these chambers, shrieking and moaning as they go. But," he added, as though to reassure himself as well as his companions, "such things may not be countenanced by the culture of Gathol or Helium."

Gahan laughed. "And if all who looked upon him were driven mad, who then was there to perform the last rites or prepare the body of the Jeddak for them?"

"There was none," replied Tasor. "Where they found him they left him and there to this very day his mouldering bones lie hid in some forgotten chamber of this forbidden suite."

Tasor left them then assuring them that he would seek the first opportunity to speak with A-Kor, and upon the following day he would bring them food and drink.*

Martians in A Princess of Mars will recall that these strange people could exist for considerable periods of time without food or water, and to a lesser degree is the same true of all Martians.

After Tasor had gone Tara turned to Gahan and approaching laid a hand upon his arm. "So swiftly have events transpired since I recognized you beneath your disguise," she said, "that I have had no opportunity to assure you of my gratitude and the high esteem that your valour has won for you in my consideration. Let me now acknowledge my indebtedness; and if promises be not vain from one whose life and liberty are in grave jeopardy, accept my assurance of the great reward that awaits you at the hand of my father in Helium."

"I desire no reward," he replied, "other than the happiness of knowing that the woman I love is happy."

For an instant the eyes of Tara of Helium blazed as she drew herself haughtily to her full height, and then they softened and her attitude relaxed as she shook her head sadly.

"I have it not in my heart to reprimand you, Turan," she said, "however great your fault, for you have been an honourable and a loyal friend to Tara of Helium; but you must not say what my ears must not hear."

"You mean," he asked, "that the ears of a Princess must not listen to words of love from a panthan?"

"It is not that, Turan," she replied; "but rather that I may not in honour listen to words of love from another than him to whom I am betrothed—a fellow countryman, Djor Kantos."

---

*Those who have read John Carter's description of the Green Martians in A Princess of Mars will recall that these strange people could exist for considerable periods of time without food or water, and to a lesser degree is the same true of all Martians.

"You mean, Tara of Helium," he cried, "that were it not for that you would—"

"Stop!" she commanded. "You have no right to assume aught else than my lips testify."

"The eyes are ofttimes more eloquent than the lips, Tara," he replied; "and in yours I have read that which is neither hatred nor contempt for Turan the panthan, and my heart tells me that your lips bore false witness when they cried in anger: 'I hate you!'"

"I do not hate you, Turan, nor yet may I love you," said the girl, simply.

"When I broke my way out from the chamber of I-Gos I was indeed upon the verge of believing that you did hate me," he said, "for only hatred, it seemed to me, could account for the fact that you had gone without making an effort to liberate me; but presently both my heart and my judgment told me that Tara of Helium could not have deserted a companion in distress, and though I still am in ignorance of the facts I know that it was beyond your power to aid me."

"It was indeed," said the girl. "Scarce had I-Gos fallen at the bite of my dagger than I heard the approach of warriors. I ran then to hide until they had passed, thinking to return and liberate you; but in seeking to elude the party I had heard I ran full into the arms of another. They questioned me as to your whereabouts, and I told them that you had gone ahead and that I was following you and thus I led them from you."

"I knew," was Gahan's only comment, but his heart was glad with elation, as a lover's must be who has heard from the lips of his divinity an avowal of interest and loyalty, however little tinged by a suggestion of warmer regard it may be. To be abused, even, by the mistress of one's heart is better than to be ignored.

As the two conversed in the ill-lit chamber, the dim bulbs of which were encrusted with the accumulated dust of centuries, a bent and withered figure traversed slowly the gloomy corridors without, his weak and watery eyes peering through thick lenses at the signs of passage written upon the dusty floor.

CHAPTER 19

The Menace of the Dead

The night was still young when there came one to the entrance of the banquet hall where O-Tar of Manator dined with his chiefs, and brushing past the guards entered the great room with the insolence of a privileged character, as in truth he was. As he approached the head of the long board O-Tar took notice of him.

"Well, hoary one!" he cried. "What brings you out of your beloved and stinking burrow again this day. We thought that the sight of the multitude of living men at the games would drive you back to your corpses as quickly as you could go."

The cackling laugh of I-Gos acknowledged the royal sally. "Ey, ey, O-Tar," squeaked the ancient one, "I-Gos goes out not upon pleasure bound; but when one does ruthlessly desecrate the dead of I-Gos, vengeance must be had!"

"You refer to the act of the slave Turan?" demanded O-Tar.

"Turan, yes, and the slave Tara, who slipped beneath my hide a murderous blade. Another fraction of an inch, O-Tar, and I-Gos' ancient and wrinkled covering were even now in some apprentice tanner's hands, ey, ey!"

"But they have again eluded us," cried O-Tar. "Even in the palace of the great jeddak twice have they escaped the stupid knaves I call The Jeddak's Guard." O-Tar had risen and was angrily emphasizing his words with heavy blows upon the table, dealt with a golden goblet.

"Ey, O-Tar, they elude thy guard but not the wise old calot, I-Gos."

"What mean you? Speak!" commanded O-Tar.

"I know where they are hid," said the ancient taxidermist. "In the dust of unused corridors their feet have betrayed them."

"You followed them? You have seen them?" demanded the jeddak.

"I followed them and I heard them speaking beyond a closed door," replied I-Gos; "but I did not see them."

"Where is that door?" cried O-Tar. "We will send at once and fetch them," he looked about the table as though to decide to whom he would entrust this duty. A dozen warrior chiefs arose and laid their hands upon their swords.

"To the chambers of O-Mai the Cruel I traced them," squeaked I-Gos. "There you will find them where the moaning Corphals pursue the shrieking ghost of O-Mai; ey!" and he turned his eyes from O-Tar toward the warriors who had arisen, only to discover that, to a man, they were hurriedly resuming their seats.

The cackling laughter of I-Gos broke derisively the hush that had fallen on the room. The warriors looked sheepishly at the food upon their plates of gold. O-Tar snapped his fingers impatiently.

"Be there only cravens among the chiefs of Manator?" he cried. "Repeatedly have these presumptuous slaves flouted the majesty of your jeddak. Must I command one to go and fetch them?"

Slowly a chief arose and two others followed his example, though with ill-concealed reluctance. "All, then, are not cowards," commented O-Tar. "The duty is distasteful. Therefore all three of you shall go, taking as many warriors as you wish."

"But do not ask for volunteers," interrupted I-Gos, "or you will go alone."

The three chiefs turned and left the banquet hall, walking slowly like doomed men to their fate.

Gahan and Tara remained in the chamber to which Tasor had led them, the man brushing away the dust from a deep and comfortable bench where they might rest in comparative comfort. He had found the ancient sleeping silks and furs too far gone to be of any service, crumbling to powder at a touch, thus removing any chance of making a comfortable bed for the girl, and so the two sat together, talking in low tones, of the adventures through which they already had passed and speculating upon the future; planning means of escape and hoping Tasor would not be long gone. They spoke of many things—of Hastor, and Helium, and Ptarth, and finally the conversation reminded Tara of Gathol.

"You have served there?" she asked.

"Yes," replied Turan.

"I met Gahan the Jed of Gathol at my father's palace," she said, "the very day before the storm snatched me from Helium—he was a presumptuous fellow, magnificently trapped in platinum and diamonds. Never in my life saw I so gorgeous a harness as his, and you must well know, Turan, that the splendour of all Barsoom passes through the court at Helium; but in my mind I could not see so resplendent a creature drawing that jewelled sword in mortal combat. I fear me that the Jed of Gathol, though a pretty picture of a man, is little else."

In the dim light Tara did not perceive the wry expression upon the half-averted face of her companion.

"You thought little then of the Jed of Gathol?" he asked.

"Then or now," she replied, and with a little laugh; "how it would pique his vanity to know, if he might, that a poor panthan had won a higher place in the regard of Tara of Helium," and she laid her fingers gently upon his knee.

He seized the fingers in his and carried them to his lips. "O, Tara of Helium," he cried. "Think you that I am a man of stone?" One arm slipped about her shoulders and drew the yielding body toward him.

"May my first ancestor forgive me my weakness," she cried, as her arms stole about his neck and she raised her panting lips to his. For long they clung there in love's first kiss and then she pushed him away, gently. "I love you, Turan," she half sobbed; "I love you so! It is my only poor excuse for having done this wrong to Djor Kantos, whom now I know I never loved, who knew not the meaning of love. And if you love me as you say, Turan, your love must protect me from greater dishonour, for I am but as clay in your hands."

Again he crushed her to him and then as suddenly released her, and rising, strode rapidly to and fro across the chamber as though he endeavoured by violent exercise to master and subdue some evil spirit that had laid hold upon him. Ringing through his brain and heart and soul like some joyous paean were those words that had so altered the world for Gahan of Gathol: "I love you, Turan; I love you so!" And it had come so suddenly. He had thought that she felt for him only gratitude for his loyalty and then, in an instant, her barriers were all down, she was no longer a princess; but instead a—his reflections were interrupted by a sound from beyond the closed door. His sandals of zitidar hide had given forth no sound upon the marble floor he strode, and as his rapid pacing carried him past the entrance to the chamber there came faintly from the distance of the long corridor the sound of metal on metal—the unmistakable herald of the approach of armed men.

For a moment Gahan listened intently, close to the door, until there could be no doubt but that a party of warriors was approaching. From what Tasor had told him he guessed correctly that they would be coming to this portion of the palace but for a single purpose—to search for Tara and himself—and it behoved him therefore to seek immediate means for eluding them. The chamber in which they were had other doorways beside that at which they had entered, and to one of these he must look for some safer hiding place. Crossing to Tara he acquainted her with his suspicion, leading her to one of the doors which they found unsecured. Beyond it lay a dimly-lighted chamber at the threshold of which they halted in consternation, drawing back quickly into the chamber they had just quitted, for their first glance revealed four warriors seated around a jetan board.

That their entrance had not been noted was attributed by Gahan to the absorption of the two players and their friends in the game. Quietly closing the door the fugitives moved silently to the next, which they found locked. There was now but another door which they had not tried, and this they approached quickly as they knew that the searching party must be close to the chamber. To their chagrin they found this avenue of escape barred.

Now indeed were they in a sorry plight, for should the searchers have information leading them to this room they were lost. Again leading Tara to the door behind which were the jetan players Gahan drew his sword and waited, listening. The sound of the party in the corridor came distinctly to their ears—they must be quite close, and doubtless they were coming in force. Beyond the door were but four warriors who might be readily surprised. There could, then, be but one choice and acting upon it Gahan quietly opened the door again, stepped through into the adjoining chamber, Tara's hand in his, and closed the door behind them. The four at the jetan board evidently failed to hear them. One player had either just made or was contemplating a move, for his fingers grasped a piece that still rested upon the board. The other three were watching his move. For an instant Gahan looked at them, playing jetan there in the dim light of this forgotten and forbidden chamber, and then a slow smile of understanding lighted his face.

"Come!" he said to Tara. "We have nothing to fear from these. For more than five thousand years they have sat thus, a monument to the handiwork of some ancient taxidermist."

As they approached more closely they saw that the lifelike figures were coated with dust, but that otherwise the skin was in as fine a state of preservation as the most recent of I-Gos' groups, and then they heard the door of the chamber they had quitted open and knew that the searchers were close upon them. Across the room they saw the opening of what appeared to be a corridor and which investigation proved to be a short passageway, terminating in a chamber in the centre of which was an ornate sleeping dais. This room, like the others, was but poorly lighted, time having dimmed the radiance of its bulbs and coated them with dust. A glance showed that it was hung with heavy goods and contained considerable massive furniture in addition to the sleeping platform, a second glance at which revealed what appeared to be the form of a man lying partially on the floor and partially on the dais. No doorways were visible other than that at which they had entered, though both knew that others might be concealed by the hangings.

Gahan, his curiosity aroused by the legends surrounding this portion of the palace, crossed to the dais to examine the figure that apparently had fallen from it, to find the dried and shrivelled corpse of a man lying upon his back on the floor with arms outstretched and fingers stiffly outspread. One of his feet was doubled partially beneath him, while the other was still entangled in the sleeping silks and furs upon the dais. After five thousand years the expression of the withered face and the eyeless sockets retained the aspect of horrid fear to such an extent, that Gahan knew that he was looking upon the body of O-Mai the Cruel.

Suddenly Tara, who stood close beside him, clutched his arm and pointed toward a far corner of the room. Gahan looked and looking felt the hairs upon his neck rising. He threw his left arm about the girl and with bared sword stood between her and the hangings that they watched, and then slowly Gahan of Gathol backed away, for in this grim and sombre chamber, which no human foot had trod for five thousand years and to which no breath of wind might enter, the heavy hangings in the far corner had moved. Not gently had they moved as a draught might have moved them had there been a draught, but suddenly they had bulged out as though pushed against from behind. To the opposite corner backed Gahan until they stood with their backs against the hangings there, and then hearing the approach of their pursuers across the chamber beyond Gahan pushed Tara through the hangings and, following her, kept open with his left hand, which he had disengaged from the girl's grasp, a tiny opening through which he could view the apartment and the doorway upon the opposite side through which the pursuers would enter, if they came this far.

Behind the hangings there was a space of about three feet in width between them and the wall, making a passageway entirely around the room, broken only by the single entrance opposite them; this being a common arrangement especially in the sleeping apartments of the rich and powerful upon Barsoom. The purposes of this arrangement were several. The passageway afforded a station for guards in the same room with their master without intruding entirely upon his privacy; it concealed secret exits from the chamber; it permitted the occupant of the room to hide eavesdroppers and assassins for use against enemies that he might lure to his chamber.

The three chiefs with a dozen warriors had had no difficulty in following the tracks of the fugitives through the dust of the corridors and chambers they had traversed. To enter this portion of the palace at all had required all the courage they possessed, and now that they were within the very chambers of O-Mai their nerves were pitched to the highest key—another turn and they would snap; for the people of Manator are filled with weird superstitions. As they entered the outer chamber they moved slowly, with drawn swords, no one seeming anxious to take the lead, and the twelve warriors hanging back in unconcealed and shameless terror, while the three chiefs, spurred on by fear of O-Tar and by pride, pressed together for mutual encouragement as they slowly crossed the dimly-lighted room.

Following the tracks of Gahan and Tara they found that though each doorway had been approached only one threshold had been crossed and this door they gingerly opened, revealing to their astonished gaze the four warriors at the jetan table. For a moment they were on the verge of flight, for though they knew what they were, coming as they did upon them in this mysterious and haunted suite, they were as startled as though they had beheld the very ghosts of the departed. But they presently regained their courage sufficiently to cross this chamber too and enter the short passageway that led to the ancient sleeping apartment of O-Mai the Cruel. They did not know that this awful chamber lay just before them, or it were doubtful that they would have proceeded farther; but they saw that those they sought had come this way and so they followed, but within the gloomy interior of the chamber they halted, the three chiefs urging their followers, in low whispers, to close in behind them, and there just within the entrance they stood until, their eyes becoming accustomed to the dim light, one of them pointed suddenly to the thing lying upon the floor with one foot tangled in the coverings of the dais.

"Look!" he gasped. "It is the corpse of O-Mai! Ancestor of ancestors! we are in the forbidden chamber." Simultaneously there came from behind the hangings beyond the gruesome dead a hollow moan followed by a piercing scream, and the hangings shook and bellied before their eyes.

With one accord, chieftains and warriors, they turned and bolted for the doorway; a narrow doorway, where they jammed, fighting and screaming in an effort to escape. They threw away their swords and clawed at one another to make a passage for escape; those behind climbed upon the shoulders of those in front; and some fell and were trampled upon; but at last they all got through, and, the swiftest first, they bolted across the two intervening chambers to the outer corridor beyond, nor did they halt their mad retreat before they stumbled, weak and trembling, into the banquet hall of O-Tar. At sight of them the warriors who had remained with the jeddak leaped to their feet with drawn swords, thinking that their fellows were pursued by many enemies; but no one followed them into the room, and the three chieftains came and stood before O-Tar with bowed heads and trembling knees.

"Well?" demanded the jeddak. "What ails you? Speak!"

"O-Tar," cried one of them when at last he could master his voice. "When have we three failed you in battle or combat? Have our swords been not always among the foremost in defence of your safety and your honour?"

"Have I denied this?" demanded O-Tar. "Listen, then, O Jeddak, and judge us with leniency. We followed the two slaves to the apartments of O-Mai the Cruel. We entered the accursed chambers and still we did not falter. We came at last to that horrid chamber no human eye had scanned before in fifty centuries and we looked upon the dead face of O-Mai lying as he has lain for all this time. To the very death chamber of O-Mai the Cruel we came and yet we were ready to go farther; when suddenly there broke upon our horrified ears the moans and the shrieking that mark these haunted chambers and the hangings moved and rustled in the dead air. O-Tar, it was more than human nerves could endure. We turned and fled. We threw away our swords and fought with one another to escape. With sorrow, but without shame, I tell it, for there be no man in all Manator that would not have done the same. If these slaves be Corphals they are safe among their fellow ghosts. If they be not Corphals, then already are they dead in the chambers of O-Mai, and there may they rot for all of me, for I would not return to that accursed spot for the harness of a jeddak and the half of Barsoom for an empire. I have spoken."

O-Tar knitted his scowling brows. "Are all my chieftains cowards and cravens?" he demanded presently in sneering tones.

From among those who had not been of the searching party a chieftain arose and turned a scowling face upon O-Tar.

"The jeddak knows," he said, "that in the annals of Manator her jeddaks have ever been accounted the bravest of her warriors. Where my jeddak leads I will follow, nor may any jeddak call me a coward or a craven unless I refuse to go where he dares to go. I have spoken."

After he had resumed his seat there was a painful silence, for all knew that the speaker had challenged the courage of O-Tar the Jeddak of Manator and all awaited the reply of their ruler. In every mind was the same thought—O-Tar must lead them at once to the chamber of O-Mai the Cruel, or accept forever the stigma of cowardice, and there could be no coward upon the throne of Manator. That they all knew and that O-Tar knew, as well.

But O-Tar hesitated. He looked about upon the faces of those around him at the banquet board; but he saw only the grim visages of relentless warriors. There was no trace of leniency in the face of any. And then his eyes wandered to a small entrance at one side of the great chamber. An expression of relief expunged the scowl of anxiety from his features.

"Look!" he exclaimed. "See who has come!"

CHAPTER 20

The Charge of Cowardice

Gahan, watching through the aperture between the hangings, saw the frantic flight of their pursuers. A grim smile rested upon his lips as he viewed the mad scramble for safety and saw them throw away their swords and fight with one another to be first from the chamber of fear, and when they were all gone he turned back toward Tara, the smile still upon his lips; but the smile died the instant that he turned, for he saw that Tara had disappeared.

"Tara!" he called in a loud voice, for he knew that there was no danger that their pursuers would return; but there was no response, unless it was a faint sound as of cackling laughter from afar. Hurriedly he searched the passageway behind the hangings finding several doors, one of which was ajar. Through this he entered the adjoining chamber which was lighted more brilliantly for the moment by the soft rays of hurtling Thuria taking her mad way through the heavens. Here he found the dust upon the floor disturbed, and the imprint of sandals. They had come this way—Tara and whatever the creature was that had stolen her.

But what could it have been? Gahan, a man of culture and high intelligence, held few if any superstitions. In common with nearly all races of Barsoom he clung, more or less inherently, to a certain exalted form of ancestor worship, though it was rather the memory or legends of the virtues and heroic deeds of his forebears that he deified rather than themselves. He never expected any tangible evidence of their existence after death; he did not believe that they had the power either for good or for evil other than the effect that their example while living might have had upon following generations; he did not believe therefore in the materialization of dead spirits. If there was a life hereafter he knew nothing of it, for he knew that science had demonstrated the existence of some material cause for every seemingly supernatural phenomenon of ancient religions and superstitions. Yet he was at a loss to know what power might have removed Tara so suddenly and mysteriously from his side in a chamber that had not known the presence of man for five thousand years.

In the darkness he could not see whether there were the imprints of other sandals than Tara's—only that the dust was disturbed—and when it led him into gloomy corridors he lost the trail altogether. A perfect labyrinth of passages and apartments were now revealed to him as he hurried on through the deserted quarters of O-Mai. Here was an ancient bath—doubtless that of the jeddak himself, and again he passed through a room in which a meal had been laid upon a table five thousand years before—the untasted breakfast of O-Mai, perhaps. There passed before his eyes in the brief moments that he traversed the chambers, a wealth of ornaments and jewels and precious metals that surprised even the Jed of Gathol whose harness was of diamonds and platinum and whose riches were the envy of a world. But at last his search of O-Mai's chambers ended in a small closet in the floor of which was the opening to a spiral runway leading straight down into Stygian darkness. The dust at the entrance of the closet had been freshly disturbed, and as this was the only possible indication that Gahan had of the direction taken by the abductor of Tara it seemed as well to follow on as to search elsewhere. So, without hesitation, he descended into the utter darkness below. Feeling with a foot before taking a forward step his descent was necessarily slow, but Gahan was a Barsoomian and so knew the pitfalls that might await the unwary in such dark, forbidden portions of a jeddak's palace.

He had descended for what he judged might be three full levels and was pausing, as he occasionally did, to listen, when he distinctly heard a peculiar shuffling, scraping sound approaching him from below. Whatever the thing was it was ascending the runway at a steady pace and would soon be near him. Gahan laid his hand upon the hilt of his sword and drew it slowly from its scabbard that he might make no noise that would apprise the creature of his presence. He wished that there might be even the slightest lessening of the darkness. If he could see but the outline of the thing that approached him he would feel that he had a fairer chance in the meeting; but he could see nothing, and then because he could see nothing the end of his scabbard struck the stone side of the runway, giving off a sound that the stillness and the narrow confines of the passage and the darkness seemed to magnify to a terrific clatter.

Instantly the shuffling sound of approach ceased. For a moment Gahan stood in silent waiting, then casting aside discretion he moved on again down the spiral. The thing, whatever it might be, gave forth no sound now by which Gahan might locate it. At any moment it might be upon him and so he kept his sword in readiness. Down, ever downward the steep spiral led. The darkness and the silence of the tomb surrounded him, yet somewhere ahead was something. He was not alone in that horrid place—another presence that he could not hear or see hovered before him—of that he was positive. Perhaps it was the thing that had stolen Tara. Perhaps Tara herself, still in the clutches of some nameless horror, was just ahead of him. He quickened his pace—it became almost a run at the thought of the danger that threatened the woman he loved, and then he collided with a wooden door that swung open to the impact. Before him was a lighted corridor. On either side were chambers. He had advanced but a short distance from the bottom of the spiral when he recognized that he was in the pits below the palace. A moment later he heard behind him the shuffling sound that had attracted his attention in the spiral runway. Wheeling about he saw the author of the sound emerging from a doorway he had just passed. It was Ghek the kaldane.

"Ghek!" exclaimed Gahan. "It was you in the runway? Have you seen Tara of Helium?"

"It was I in the spiral," replied the kaldane; "but I have not seen Tara of Helium. I have been searching for her. Where is she?"

"I do not know," replied the Gatholian; "but we must find her and take her from this place."

"We may find her," said Ghek; "but I doubt our ability to take her away. It is not so easy to leave Manator as it is to enter it. I may come and go at will, through the ancient burrows of the ulsios; but you are too large for that and your lungs need more air than may be found in some of the deeper runways."

"But U-Thor!" exclaimed Gahan. "Have you heard aught of him or his intentions?"

"I have heard much," replied Ghek. "He camps at The Gate of Enemies. That spot he holds and his warriors lie just beyond The Gate; but he has not sufficient force to enter the city and take the palace. An hour since and you might have made your way to him; but now every avenue is strongly guarded since O-Tar learned that A-Kor had escaped to U-Thor."

"A-Kor has escaped and joined U-Thor!" exclaimed Gahan.

"But little more than an hour since. I was with him when a warrior came—a man whose name is Tasor—who brought a message from you. It was decided that Tasor should accompany A-Kor in an attempt to reach the camp of U-Thor, the great jed of Manatos, and exact from him the assurances you required. Then U-Thor was to return and take food to you and the Princess of Helium. I accompanied them. We won through easily and found U-Thor more than willing to respect your every wish, but when Tasor would have returned to you the way was blocked by the warriors of O-Tar. Then it was that I volunteered to come to you and report and find food and drink and then go forth among the Gatholian slaves of Manator and prepare them for their part in the plan that U-Thor and Tasor conceived."

"And what was this plan?"

"U-Thor has sent for reinforcements. To Manatos he has sent and to all the outlying districts that are his. It will take a month to collect and bring them hither and in the meantime the slaves within the city are to organize secretly, stealing and hiding arms against the day that the reinforcements arrive. When that day comes the forces of U-Thor will enter the Gate of Enemies and as the warriors of O-Tar rush to repulse them the slaves from Gathol will fall upon them from the rear with the majority of their numbers, while the balance will assault the palace. They hope thus to divert so many from The Gate that U-Thor will have little difficulty in forcing an entrance to the city."

"Perhaps they will succeed," commented Gahan; "but the warriors of O-Tar are many, and those who fight in defence of their homes and their jeddak have always an advantage. Ah, Ghek, would that we had the great warships of Gathol or of Helium to pour their merciless fire into the streets of Manator while U-Thor marched to the palace over the corpses of the slain." He paused, deep in thought, and then turned his gaze again upon the kaldane. "Heard you aught of the party that escaped with me from The Field of Jetan—of Floran, Val Dor, and the others? What of them?"

"Ten of these won through to U-Thor at The Gate of Enemies and were well received by him. Eight fell in the fighting upon the way. Val Dor and Floran live, I believe, for I am sure that I heard U-Thor address two warriors by these names."

"Good!" exclaimed Gahan. "Go then, through the burrows of the ulsios, to The Gate of Enemies and carry to Floran the message that I shall write in his own language. Come, while I write the message."

In a nearby room they found a bench and table and there Gahan sat and wrote in the strange, stenographic characters of Martian script a message to Floran of Gathol. "Why," he asked, when he had finished it, "did you search for Tara through the spiral runway where we nearly met?"

"Tasor told me where you were to be found, and as I have explored the greater part of the palace by means of the ulsio runways and the darker and less frequented passages I knew precisely where you were and how to reach you. This secret spiral ascends from the pits to the roof of the loftiest of the palace towers. It has secret openings at every level; but there is no living Manatorian, I believe, who knows of its existence. At least never have I met one within it and I have used it many times. Thrice have I been in the chamber where O-Mai lies, though I knew nothing of his identity or the story of his death until Tasor told it to us in the camp of U-Thor."

"You know the palace thoroughly then?" Gahan interrupted.

"Better than O-Tar himself or any of his servants."

"Good! And you would serve the Princess Tara, Ghek, you may serve her best by accompanying Floran and following his instructions. I will write them here at the close of my message to him, for the walls have ears, Ghek, while none but a Gatholian may read what I have written to Floran. He will transmit it to you. Can I trust you?"

"I may never return to Bantoom," replied Ghek. "Therefore I have but two friends in all Barsoom. What better may I do than serve them faithfully? You may trust me, Gatholian, who with a woman of your kind has taught me that there be finer and nobler things than perfect mentality uninfluenced by the unreasoning tuitions of the heart. I go."

*****

As O-Tar pointed to the little doorway all eyes turned in the direction he indicated and surprise was writ large upon the faces of the warriors when they recognized the two who had entered the banquet hall. There was I-Gos, and he dragged behind him one who was gagged and whose hands were fastened behind with a ribbon of tough silk. It was the slave girl. I-Gos' cackling laughter rose above the silence of the room.

"Ey, ey!" he shrilled. "What the young warriors of O-Tar cannot do, old I-Gos does alone."

"Only a Corphal may capture a Corphal," growled one of the chiefs who had fled from the chambers of O-Mai.

I-Gos laughed. "Terror turned your heart to water," he replied; "and shame your tongue to libel. This be no Corphal, but only a woman of Helium; her companion a warrior who can match blades with the best of you and cut your putrid hearts. Not so in the days of I-Gos' youth. Ah, then were there men in Manator. Well do I recall that day that I—"

"Peace, doddering fool!" commanded O-Tar. "Where is the man?"

"Where I found the woman—in the death chamber of O-Mai. Let your wise and brave chieftains go thither and fetch him. I am an old man, and could bring but one."

"You have done well, I-Gos," O-Tar hastened to assure him, for when he learned that Gahan might still be in the haunted chambers he wished to appease the wrath of I-Gos, knowing well the vitriolic tongue and temper of the ancient one. "You think she is no Corphal, then, I-Gos?" he asked, wishing to carry the subject from the man who was still at large.

"No more than you," replied the ancient taxidermist.

O-Tar looked long and searchingly at Tara of Helium. All the beauty that was hers seemed suddenly to be carried to every fibre of his consciousness. She was still garbed in the rich harness of a Black Princess of Jetan, and as O-Tar the Jeddak gazed upon her he realized that never before had his eyes rested upon a more perfect figure—a more beautiful face.

"She is no Corphal," he murmured to himself. "She is no Corphal and she is a princess—a princess of Helium, and, by the golden hair of the Holy Hekkador, she is beautiful. Take the gag from her mouth and release her hands," he commanded aloud. "Make room for the Princess Tara of Helium at the side of O-Tar of Manator. She shall dine as becomes a princess."

Slaves did as O-Tar bid and Tara of Helium stood with flashing eyes behind the chair that was offered her. "Sit!" commanded O-Tar.

The girl sank into the chair. "I sit as a prisoner," she said; "not as a guest at the board of my enemy, O-Tar of Manator."

O-Tar motioned his followers from the room. "I would speak alone with the Princess of Helium," he said. The company and the slaves withdrew and once more the Jeddak of Manator turned toward the girl. "O-Tar of Manator would be your friend," he said.

Tara of Helium sat with arms folded upon her small, firm breasts, her eyes flashing from behind narrowed lids, nor did she deign to answer his overture. O-Tar leaned closer to her. He noted the hostility of her bearing and he recalled his first encounter with her. She was a she-banth, but she was beautiful. She was by far the most desirable woman that O-Tar had ever looked upon and he was determined to possess her. He told her so.

"I could take you as my slave," he said to her; "but it pleases me to make you my wife. You shall be Jeddara of Manator. You shall have seven days in which to prepare for the great honour that O-Tar is conferring upon you, and at this hour of the seventh day you shall become an empress and the wife of O-Tar in the throne room of the jeddaks of Manator." He struck a gong that stood beside him upon the table and when a slave appeared he bade him recall the company. Slowly the chiefs filed in and took their places at the table. Their faces were grim and scowling, for there was still unanswered the question of their jeddak's courage. If O-Tar had hoped they would forget he had been mistaken in his men.

O-Tar arose. "In seven days," he announced, "there will be a great feast in honour of the new Jeddara of Manator," and he waved his hand toward Tara of Helium. "The ceremony will occur at the beginning of the seventh zode* in the throne room. In the meantime the Princess of Helium will be cared for in the tower of the women's quarters of the palace. Conduct her thither, E-Thas, with a suitable guard of honour and see to it that slaves and eunuchs be placed at her disposal, who shall attend upon all her wants and guard her carefully from harm."

Now E-Thas knew that the real meaning concealed in these fine words was that he should conduct the prisoner under a strong guard to the women's quarters and confine her there in the tower for seven days, placing about her trustworthy guards who would prevent her escape or frustrate any attempted rescue.

As Tara was departing from the chamber with E-Thas and the guard, O-Tar leaned close to her ear and whispered: "Consider well during these seven days the high honour I have offered you, and—its sole alternative." As though she had not heard him the girl passed out of the banquet hall, her head high and her eyes straight to the front.

After Ghek had left him Gahan roamed the pits and the ancient corridors of the deserted portions of the palace seeking some clue to the whereabouts or the fate of Tara of Helium. He utilized the spiral runway in passing from level to level until he knew every foot of it from the pits to the summit of the high tower, and into what apartments it opened at the various levels as well as the ingenious and hidden mechanism that operated the locks of the cleverly concealed doors leading to it. For food he drew upon the stores he found in the pits and when he slept he lay upon the royal couch of O-Mai in the forbidden chamber sharing the dais with the dead foot of the ancient jeddak.

---

* About 8:30 p. m. Earth Time.

In the palace about him seethed, all unknown to Gahan, a vast unrest. Warriors and chieftains pursued the duties of their vocations with dour faces, and little knots of them were collecting here and there and with frowns of anger discussing some subject that was uppermost in the minds of all. It was upon the fourth day following Tara's incarceration in the tower that E-Thas, the major-domo of the palace and one of O-Tar's creatures, came to his master upon some trivial errand. O-Tar was alone in one of the smaller chambers of his personal suite when the major-domo was announced, and after the matter upon which E-Thas had come was disposed of the jeddak signed him to remain.

"From the position of an obscure warrior I have elevated you, E-Thas, to the honours of a chief. Within the confines of the palace your word is second only to mine. You are not loved for this, E-Thas, and should another jeddak ascend the throne of Manator what would become of you, whose enemies are among the most powerful of Manator?"

"Speak not of it, O-Tar," begged E-Thas. "These last few days I have thought upon it much and I would forget it; but I have sought to appease the wrath of my worst enemies. I have been very kind and indulgent with them."

"You, too, read the voiceless message in the air?" demanded the jeddak.

E-Thas was palpably uneasy and he did not reply.

"Why did you not come to me with your apprehensions?" demanded O-Tar. "Be this loyalty?"

"I feared, O mighty jeddak!" replied E-Thas. "I feared that you would not understand and that you would be angry."

"What know you? Speak the whole truth!" commanded O-Tar.

"There is much unrest among the chieftains and the warriors," replied E-Thas. "Even those who were your friends fear the power of those who speak against you."

"What say they?" growled the jeddak.

"They say that you are afraid to enter the apartments of O-Mai in search of the slave Turan—oh, do not be angry with me, Jeddak; it is but what they say that I repeat. I, your loyal E-Thas, believe no such foul slander."

"No, no; why should I fear?" demanded O-Tar. "We do not know that he is there. Did not my chiefs go thither and see nothing of him?"

"But they say that you did not go," pursued E-Thas, "and that they will have none of a coward upon the throne of Manator."

"They said that treason?" O-Tar almost shouted.

"They said that and more, great jeddak," answered the major-domo. "They said that not only did you fear to enter the chambers of O-Mai, but that you feared the slave Turan, and they blame you for your treatment of A-Kor, whom they all believe to have been murdered at your command. They were fond of A-Kor and there are many now who say aloud that A-Kor would have made a wondrous jeddak."

"They dare?" screamed O-Tar. "They dare suggest the name of a slave's bastard for the throne of O-Tar!"

"He is your son, O-Tar," E-Thas reminded him, "nor is there a more beloved man in Manator—I but speak to you of facts which may not be ignored, and I dare do so because only when you realize the truth may you seek a cure for the ills that draw about your throne."

O-Tar had slumped down upon his bench—suddenly he looked shrunken and tired and old. "Cursed be the day," he cried, "that saw those three strangers enter the city of Manator. Would that U-Dor had been spared to me. He was strong—my enemies feared him; but he is gone—dead at the hands of that hateful slave, Turan; may the curse of Issus be upon him!"

"My jeddak, what shall we do?" begged E-Thas. "Cursing the slave will not solve your problems."

"But the great feast and the marriage is but three days off," plead O-Tar. "It shall be a great gala occasion. The warriors and the chiefs all know that—it is the custom. Upon that day gifts and honours shall be bestowed. Tell me, who are most bitter against me? I will send you among them and let it be known that I am planning rewards for their past services to the throne. We will make jeds of chiefs and chiefs of warriors, and grant them palaces and slaves. Eh, E-Thas?"

The other shook his head. "It will not do, O-Tar. They will have nothing of your gifts or honours. I have heard them say as much."

"What do they want?" demanded O-Tar.

"They want a jeddak as brave as the bravest," replied E-Thas, though his knees shook as he said it.

"They think I am a coward?" cried the jeddak.

"They say you are afraid to go to the apartments of O-mai the Cruel."

For a long time O-Tar sat, his head sunk upon his breast, staring blankly at the floor.

"Tell them," he said at last in a hollow voice that sounded not at all like the voice of a great jeddak; "tell them that I will go to the chambers of O-Mai and search for Turan the slave."

Chapter 21

A Risk for Love

"Ey, ey, he is a craven and he called me 'doddering fool'!" The speaker was I-Gos and he addressed a knot of chieftains in one of the chambers of the palace of O-Tar, Jeddak of Manator: "If A-Kor was alive there were a jeddak for us!"

"Who says that A-Kor is dead?" demanded one of the chiefs.

"Where is he then?" asked I-Gos. "Have not others disappeared whom O-Tar thought too well beloved for men so near the throne as they?"

The chief shook his head. "And I thought that, or knew it, rather; I'd join U-Thor at The Gate of Enemies."

"S-s-st," cautioned one; "here comes the licker of feet," and all eyes were turned upon the approaching E-Thas.

"Kaor, friends!" he exclaimed as he stopped among them, but his friendly greeting elicited naught but a few surly nods. "Have you heard the news?" he continued, unabashed by treatment to which he was becoming accustomed.

"What—has O-Tar seen an ulsio and fainted?" demanded I-Gos with broad sarcasm.

"Men have died for less than that, ancient one," E-Thas reminded him.

"I am safe," retorted I-Gos, "for I am not a brave and popular son of the jeddak of Manator."

This was indeed open treason, but E-Thas feigned not to hear it. He ignored I-Gos and turned to the others. "O-Tar goes to the chamber of O-Mai this night in search of Turan the slave," he said. "He sorrows that his warriors have not the courage for so mean a duty and that their jeddak is thus compelled to arrest a common slave," with which taunt E-Thas passed on to spread the word in other parts of the palace. As a matter of fact the latter part of his message was purely original with himself, and he took great delight in delivering it to the discomfiture of his enemies. As he was leaving the little group of men I-Gos called after him. "At what hour does O-Tar intend visiting the chambers of O-Mai?" he asked.

"Toward the end of the eighth zode*," replied the major-domo, and went his way.

"We shall see," stated I-Gos.

"What shall we see?" asked a warrior.

"We shall see whether O-Tar visits the chamber of O-Mai."

"How?" "I shall be there myself and if I see him I will know that he has been there. If I don't see him I will know that he has not," explained the old taxidermist.

"Is there anything there to fill an honest man with fear?" asked a chieftain. "What have you seen?"

"It was not so much what I saw, though that was bad enough, as what I heard," said I-Gos.

"Tell us! What heard and saw you?"

"I saw the dead O-Mai," said I-Gos. The others shuddered.

"And you went not mad?" they asked.

"Am I mad?" retorted I-Gos.

"And you will go again?"

"Yes."

"Then indeed you are mad," cried one.

"You saw the dead O-Mai; but what heard you that was worse?" whispered another.

"I saw the dead O-Mai lying upon the floor of his sleeping chamber with one foot tangled in the sleeping silks and furs upon his couch. I heard horrid moans and frightful screams."

"And you are not afraid to go there again?" demanded several.

"The dead cannot harm me," said I-Gos. "He has lain thus for five thousand years. Nor can a sound harm me. I heard it once and live—I can hear it again. It came from almost at my side where I hid behind the hangings and watched the slave Turan before I snatched the woman away from him."

"I-Gos, you are a very brave man," said a chieftain.

"O-Tar called me 'doddering fool' and I would face worse dangers than lie in the forbidden chambers of O-Mai to know it if he does not visit the chamber of O-Mai. Then indeed shall O-Tar fall!"

The night came and the zodes dragged and the time approached

---

* About 1:00 A. M. Earth Time.

when O-Tar, Jeddak of Manator, was to visit the chamber of O-Mai in search of the slave Turan. To us, who may doubt the existence of malignant spirits, his fear may seem unbelievable, for he was a strong man, an excellent swordsman, and a warrior of great repute; but the fact remained that O-Tar of Manator was nervous with apprehension as he strode the corridors of his palace toward the deserted halls of O-Mai and when he stood at last with his hand upon the door that opened from the dusty corridor to the very apartments themselves he was almost paralyzed with terror. He had come alone for two very excellent reasons, the first of which was that thus none might note his terror-stricken state nor his defection should he fail at the last moment, and the other was that should he accomplish the thing alone or be able to make his chiefs believe that he had, the credit would be far greater than were he to be accompanied by warriors.

But though he had started alone he had become aware that he was being followed, and he knew that it was because his people had no faith in either his courage or his veracity. He did not believe that he would find the slave Turan. He did not very much want to find him, for though O-Tar was an excellent swordsman and a brave warrior in physical combat, he had seen how Turan had played with U-Dor and he had no stomach for a passage at arms with one whom he knew outclassed him.

And so O-Tar stood with his hand upon the door—afraid to enter; afraid not to. But at last his fear of his own warriors, watching behind him, grew greater than the fear of the unknown behind the ancient door and he pushed the heavy skeel aside and entered.

Silence and gloom and the dust of centuries lay heavy upon the chamber. From his warriors he knew the route that he must take to the horrid chamber of O-Mai and so he forced his unwilling feet across the room before him, across the room where the jetan players sat at their eternal game, and came to the short corridor that led into the room of O-Mai. His naked sword trembled in his grasp. He paused after each forward step to listen and when he was almost at the door of the ghost-haunted chamber, his heart stood still within his breast and the cold sweat broke from the clammy skin of his forehead, for from within there came to his affrighted ears the sound of muffled breathing. Then it was that O-Tar of Manator came near to fleeing from the nameless horror that he could not see, but that he knew lay waiting for him in that chamber just ahead. But again came the fear of the wrath and contempt of his warriors and his chiefs. They would degrade him and they would slay him into the bargain. There was no doubt of what his fate would be should he flee the apartments of O-Mai in terror. His only hope, therefore, lay in daring the unknown in preference to the known.

He moved forward. A few steps took him to the doorway. The chamber before him was darker than the corridor, so that he could just indistinctly make out the objects in the room. He saw a sleeping dais near the centre, with a darker blotch of something lying on the marble floor beside it. He moved a step farther into the doorway and the scabbard of his sword scraped against the stone frame. To his horror he saw the sleeping silks and furs upon the central dais move. He saw a figure slowly arising to a sitting posture from the death bed of O-Mai the Cruel. His knees shook, but he gathered all his moral forces, and gripping his sword more tightly in his trembling fingers prepared to leap across the chamber upon the horrid apparition. He hesitated just a moment. He felt eyes upon him—ghoulish eyes that bored through the darkness into his withering heart—eyes that he could not see. He gathered himself for the rush—and then there broke from the thing upon the couch an awful shriek, and O-Tar sank senseless to the floor.

Gahan rose from the couch of O-Mai, smiling, only to swing quickly about with drawn sword as the shadow of a noise impinged upon his keen ears from the shadows behind him. Between the parted hangings he saw a bent and wrinkled figure. It was I-Gos.

"Sheathe your sword, Turan," said the old man. "You have naught to fear from I-Gos."

"What do you here?" demanded Gahan.

"I came to make sure that the great coward did not cheat us. Ey, and he called me 'doddering fool;' but look at him now! Stricken insensible by terror, but, ey, one might forgive him that who had heard your uncanny scream. It all but blasted my own courage. And it was you, then, who moaned and screamed when the chiefs came the day that I stole Tara from you?"

"It was you, then, old scoundrel?" demanded Gahan, moving threateningly toward I-Gos.

"Come, come!" expostulated the old man; "it was I, but then I was your enemy. I would not do it now. Conditions have changed."

"How have they changed? What has changed them?" asked Gahan.

"Then I did not fully realize the cowardice of my jeddak, or the bravery of you and the girl. I am an old man from another age and I love courage. At first I resented the girl's attack upon me, but later I came to see the bravery of it and it won my admiration, as have all her acts. She feared not O-tar, she feared not me, she feared not all the warriors of Manator. And you! Blood of a million sires! how you fight! I am sorry that I exposed you at The Fields of Jetan. I am sorry that I dragged the girl Tara back to O-Tar. I would make amends. I would be your friend. Here is my sword at your feet," and drawing his weapon I-Gos cast it to the floor in front of Gahan.

The Gatholian knew that scarce the most abandoned of knaves would repudiate this solemn pledge, and so he stooped, and picking up the old man's sword returned it to him, hilt first, in acceptance of his friendship.

"Where is the Princess Tara of Helium?" asked Gahan. "Is she safe?"

"She is confined in the tower of the women's quarters awaiting the ceremony that is to make her Jeddara of Manator," replied I-Gos.

"This thing dared think that Tara of Helium would mate with him?" growled Gahan. "I will make short work of him if he is not already dead from fright," and he stepped toward the fallen O-Tar to run his sword through the jeddak's heart.

"No!" cried I-Gos. "Slay him not and pray that he be not dead if you would save your princess."

"How is that?" asked Gahan.

"If word of O-Tar's death reached the quarters of the women the Princess Tara would be lost. They know O-Tar's intention of taking her to wife and making her Jeddara of Manator, so you may rest assured that they all hate her with the hate of jealous women. Only O-Tar's power protects her now from harm. Should O-Tar die they would turn her over to the warriors and the male slaves, for there would be none to avenge her."

Gahan sheathed his sword. "Your point is well taken; but what shall we do with him?"

"Leave him where he lies," counselled I-Gos. "He is not dead. When he revives he will return to his quarters with a fine tale of his bravery and there will be none to impugn his boasts—none but I-Gos. Come! he may revive at any moment and he must not find us here."

I-Gos crossed to the body of his jeddak, knelt beside it for an instant, and then returned past the couch to Gahan. The two quit the chamber of O-Mai and took their way toward the spiral runway. Here I-Gos led Gahan to a higher level and out upon the roof of that portion of the palace from where he pointed to a high tower quite close by. "There," he said, "lies the Princess of Helium, and quite safe she will be until the time of the ceremony."

"Safe, possibly, from other hands, but not from her own," said Gahan. "She will never become Jeddara of Manator—first will she destroy herself."

"She would do that?" asked I-Gos.

"She will, unless you can get word to her that I still live and that there is yet hope," replied Gahan.

"I cannot get word to her," said I-Gos. "The quarters of his women O-Tar guards with jealous hand. Here are his most trusted slaves and warriors, yet even so, thick among them are countless spies, so that no man knows which be which. No shadow falls within those chambers that is not marked by a hundred eyes."

Gahan stood gazing at the lighted windows of the high tower in the upper chambers of which Tara of Helium was confined. "I will find a way, I-Gos," he said.

"There is no way," replied the old man.

For some time they stood upon the roof beneath the brilliant stars and hurtling moons of dying Mars, laying their plans against the time that Tara of Helium should be brought from the high tower to the throne room of O-Tar. It was then, and then alone, argued I-Gos, that any hope of rescuing her might be entertained. Just how far he might trust the other Gahan did not know, and so he kept to himself the knowledge of the plan that he had forwarded to Floran and Val Dor by Ghek, but he assured the ancient taxidermist that if he were sincere in his oft-repeated declaration that O-Tar should be denounced and superseded he would have his opportunity on the night that the jeddak sought to wed the Heliumetic princess.

"Your time shall come then, I-Gos," Gahan assured the other, "and if you have any party that thinks as you do, prepare them for the eventuality that will succeed O-Tar's presumptuous attempt to wed the daughter of The Warlord. Where shall I see you again, and when? I go now to speak with Tara, Princess of Helium."

"I like your boldness," said I-Gos; "but it will avail you naught. You will not speak with Tara, Princess of Helium, though doubtless the blood of many Manatorians will drench the floors of the women's quarters before you are slain."

Gahan smiled. "I shall not be slain. Where and when shall we meet? But you may find me in O-Mai's chamber at night. That seems the safest retreat in all Manator for an enemy of the jeddak in whose palace it lies. I go!"

"And may the spirits of your ancestors surround you," said I-Gos.

After the old man had left him Gahan made his way across the roof to the high tower, which appeared to have been constructed of concrete and afterward elaborately carved, its entire surface being covered with intricate designs cut deep into the stone-like material of which it was composed. Though wrought ages since, it was but little weather-worn owing to the aridity of the Martian atmosphere, the infrequency of rains, and the rarity of dust storms. To scale it, though, presented difficulties and danger that might have deterred the bravest of men—that would, doubtless, have deterred Gahan, had he not felt that the life of the woman he loved depended upon his accomplishing the hazardous feat.

Removing his sandals and laying aside all of his harness and weapons other than a single belt supporting a dagger, the Gatholian essayed the dangerous ascent. Clinging to the carvings with hands and feet he worked himself slowly aloft, avoiding the windows and keeping upon the shadowy side of the tower, away from the light of Thuria and Cluros. The tower rose some fifty feet above the roof of the adjacent part of the palace, comprising five levels or floors with windows looking in every direction. A few of the windows were balconied, and these more than the others he sought to avoid, although, it being now near the close of the ninth zode, there was little likelihood that many were awake within the tower.

His progress was noiseless and he came at last, undetected, to the windows of the upper level. These, like several of the others he had passed at lower levels, were heavily barred, so that there was no possibility of his gaining ingress to the apartment where Tara was confined. Darkness hid the interior behind the first window that he approached. The second opened upon a lighted chamber where he could see a guard sleeping at his post outside a door. Here also was the top of the runway leading to the next level below. Passing still farther around the tower Gahan approached another window, but now he clung to that side of the tower which ended in a courtyard a hundred feet below and in a short time the light of Thuria would reach him. He realized that he must hasten and he prayed that behind the window he now approached he would find Tara of Helium.

Coming to the opening he looked in upon a small chamber dimly lighted. In the centre was a sleeping dais upon which a human form lay beneath silks and furs. A bare arm, protruding from the coverings, lay exposed against a black and yellow striped orluk skin—an arm of wondrous beauty about which was clasped an armlet that Gahan knew. No other creature was visible within the chamber, all of which was exposed to Gahan's view. Pressing his face to the bars the Gatholian whispered her dear name. The girl stirred, but did not awaken. Again he called, but this time louder. Tara sat up and looked about and at the same instant a huge eunuch leaped to his feet from where he had been lying on the floor close by that side of the dais farthest from Gahan. Simultaneously the brilliant light of Thuria flashed full upon the window where Gahan clung silhouetting him plainly to the two within.

Both sprang to their feet. The eunuch drew his sword and leaped for the window where the helpless Gahan would have fallen an easy victim to a single thrust of the murderous weapon the fellow bore, had not Tara of Helium leaped upon her guard dragging him back. At the same time she drew the slim dagger from its hiding place in her harness and even as the eunuch sought to hurl her aside its keen point found his heart. Without a sound he died and lunged forward to the floor. Then Tara ran to the window.

"Turan, my chief!" she cried. "What awful risk is this you take to seek me here, where even your brave heart is powerless to aid me."

"Be not so sure of that, heart of my heart," he replied. "While I bring but words to my love, they be the forerunner of deeds, I hope, that will give her back to me forever. I feared that you might destroy yourself, Tara of Helium, to escape the dishonour that O-Tar would do you, and so I came to give you new hope and to beg that you live for me through whatever may transpire, in the knowledge that there is yet a way and that if all goes well we shall be freed at last. Look for me in the throne room of O-Tar the night that he would wed you. And now, how may we dispose of this fellow?" He pointed to the dead eunuch upon the floor.

"We need not concern ourselves about that," she replied. "None dares harm me for fear of the wrath of O-Tar—otherwise I should have been dead so soon as ever I entered this portion of the palace, for the women hate me. O-Tar alone may punish me, and what cares O-Tar for the life of a eunuch? No, fear not upon this score."

Their hands were clasped between the bars and now Gahan drew her nearer to him.

"One kiss," he said, "before I go, my princess," and the proud daughter of Dejah Thoris, Princess of Helium, and The Warlord of Barsoom whispered: "My chieftain!" and pressed her lips to the lips of Turan, the common panthan.

Chapter 22

At the Moment of Marriage

The silence of the tomb lay heavy about him as O-Tar, Jeddak of Manator, opened his eyes in the chamber of O-Mai. Recollection of the frightful apparition that had confronted him swept to his consciousness. He listened, but heard naught. Within the range of his vision there was nothing apparent that might cause alarm. Slowly he lifted his head and looked about. Upon the floor beside the couch lay the thing that had at first attracted his attention and his eyes closed in terror as he recognized it for what it was; but it moved not, nor spoke. O-Tar opened his eyes again and rose to his feet. He was trembling in every limb. There was nothing on the dais from which he had seen the thing arise.

O-Tar backed slowly from the room. At last he gained the outer corridor. It was empty. He did not know that it had emptied rapidly as the loud scream with which his own had mingled had broken upon the startled ears of the warriors who had been sent to spy upon him. He looked at the timepiece set in a massive bracelet upon his left forearm. The ninth zode was nearly half gone. O-Tar had lain for an hour unconscious. He had spent an hour in the chamber of O-Mai and he was not dead! He had looked upon the face of his predecessor and was still sane! He shook himself and smiled. Rapidly he subdued his rebelliously shaking nerves, so that by the time he reached the tenanted portion of the palace he had gained control of himself. He walked with chin high and something of a swagger. To the banquet hall he went, knowing that his chiefs awaited him there and as he entered they arose and upon the faces of many were incredulity and amaze, for they had not thought to see O-Tar the jeddak again after what the spies had told them of the horrid sounds issuing from the chamber of O-Mai. Thankful was O-Tar that he had gone alone to that chamber of fright, for now no one could deny the tale that he should tell.

E-Thas rushed forward to greet him, for E-Thas had seen black looks directed toward him as the tals slipped by and his benefactor failed to return.

"O brave and glorious jeddak!" cried the major-domo. "We rejoice at your safe return and beg of you the story of your adventure."

"It was naught," exclaimed O-Tar. "I searched the chambers carefully and waited in hiding for the return of the slave, Turan, if he were temporarily away; but he came not. He is not there and I doubt if he ever goes there. Few men would choose to remain long in such a dismal place."

"You were not attacked?" asked E-Thas. "You heard no screams, nor moans?"

"I heard hideous noises and saw phantom figures; but they fled before me so that never could I lay hold of one, and I looked upon the face of O-Mai and I am not mad. I even rested in the chamber beside his corpse."

In a far corner of the room a bent and wrinkled old man hid a smile behind a golden goblet of strong brew.

"Come! Let us drink!" cried O-Tar and reached for the dagger, the pommel of which he was accustomed to use to strike the gong which summoned slaves, but the dagger was not in its scabbard. O-Tar was puzzled. He knew that it had been there just before he entered the chamber of O-Mai, for he had carefully felt of all his weapons to make sure that none was missing. He seized instead a table utensil and struck the gong, and when the slaves came bade them bring the strongest brew for O-Tar and his chiefs. Before the dawn broke many were the expressions of admiration bellowed from drunken lips—admiration for the courage of their jeddak; but some there were who still looked glum.

★ ★ ★ ★ ★

Came at last the day that O-Tar would take the Princess Tara of Helium to wife. For hours slaves prepared the unwilling bride. Seven perfumed baths occupied three long and weary hours, then her whole body was anointed with the oil of pimalia blossoms and massaged by the deft fingers of a slave from distant Dusar. Her harness, all new and wrought for the occasion was of the white hide of the great white apes of Barsoom, hung heavily with platinum and diamonds—fairly encrusted with them. The glossy mass of her jet hair had been built into a coiffure of stately and becoming grandeur, into which diamond-headed pins were stuck until the whole scintillated as the stars in heaven upon a moonless night.

But it was a sullen and defiant bride that they led from the high tower toward the throne room of O-Tar. The corridors were filled with slaves and warriors, and the women of the palace and the city who had been commanded to attend the ceremony. All the power and pride, wealth and beauty of Manator were there.

Slowly Tara, surrounded by a heavy guard of honour, moved along the marble corridors filled with people. At the entrance to The Hall of Chiefs E-Thas, the major-domo, received her. The Hall was empty except for its ranks of dead chieftains upon their dead mounts. Through this long chamber E-Thas escorted her to the throne room which also was empty, the marriage ceremony in Manator differing from that of other countries of Barsoom. Here the bride would await the groom at the foot of the steps leading to the throne. The guests followed her in and took their places, leaving the central aisle from The Hall of Chiefs to the throne clear, for up this O-Tar would approach his bride alone after a short solitary communion with the dead behind closed doors in The Hall of Chiefs. It was the custom.

The guests had all filed through The Hall of Chiefs; the doors at both ends had been closed. Presently those at the lower end of the hall opened and O-Tar entered. His black harness was ornamented with rubies and gold; his face was covered by a grotesque mask of the precious metal in which two enormous rubies were set for eyes, though below them were narrow slits through which the wearer could see. His crown was a fillet supporting carved feathers of the same metal as the mask. To the least detail his regalia was that demanded of a royal bridegroom by the customs of Manator, and now in accordance with that same custom he came alone to The Hall of Chiefs to receive the blessings and the council of the great ones of Manator who had preceded him.

As the doors at the lower end of the Hall closed behind him O-Tar the Jeddak stood alone with the great dead. By the dictates of ages no mortal eye might look upon the scene enacted within that sacred chamber. As the mighty of Manator respected the traditions of Manator, let us, too, respect those traditions of a proud and sensitive people. Of what concern to us the happenings in that solemn chamber of the dead?

Five minutes passed. The bride stood silently at the foot of the throne. The guests spoke together in low whispers until the room was filled with the hum of many voices. At length the doors leading into The Hall of Chiefs swung open, and the resplendent bridegroom stood framed for a moment in the massive opening. A hush fell upon the wedding guests. With measured and impressive step the groom approached the bride. Tara felt the muscles of her heart contract with the apprehension that had been growing upon her as the coils of Fate settled more closely about her and no sign came from Turan. Where was he? What, indeed, could he accomplish now to save her? Surrounded by the power of O-Tar with never a friend among them, her position seemed at last without vestige of hope.

"I still live!" she whispered inwardly in a last brave attempt to combat the terrible hopelessness that was overwhelming her, but her fingers stole for reassurance to the slim blade that she had managed to transfer, undetected, from her old harness to the new. And now the groom was at her side and taking her hand was leading her up the steps to the throne, before which they halted and stood facing the gathering below. Came then, from the back of the room a procession headed by the high dignitary whose office it was to make these two man and wife, and directly behind him a richly-clad youth bearing a silken pillow on which lay the golden handcuffs connected by a short length of chain-of-gold with which the ceremony would be concluded when the dignitary clasped a handcuff about the wrist of each symbolizing their indissoluble union in the holy bonds of wedlock.

Would Turan's promised succour come too late? Tara listened to the long, monotonous intonation of the wedding service. She heard the virtues of O-Tar extolled and the beauties of the bride. The moment was approaching and still no sign of Turan. But what could he accomplish should he succeed in reaching the throne room, other than to die with her? There could be no hope of rescue.

The dignitary lifted the golden handcuffs from the pillow upon which they reposed. He blessed them and reached for Tara's wrist. The time had come! The thing could go no further, for alive or dead, by all the laws of Barsoom she would be the wife of O-Tar of Manator the instant the two were locked together. Even should rescue come then or later she could never dissolve those bonds and Turan would be lost to her as surely as though death separated them.

Her hand stole toward the hidden blade, but instantly the hand of the groom shot out and seized her wrist. He had guessed her intention. Through the slits in the grotesque mask she could see his eyes upon her and she guessed the sardonic smile that the mask hid. For a tense moment the two stood thus. The people below them kept breathless silence for the play before the throne had not passed un-noticed.

Dramatic as was the moment it was suddenly rendered trebly so by the noisy opening of the doors leading to The Hall of Chiefs.

All eyes turned in the direction of the interruption to see another figure framed in the massive opening—a half-clad figure buckling the half-adjusted harness hurriedly in place—the figure of O-Tar, Jeddak of Manator.

"Stop!" he screamed, springing forward along the aisle toward the throne. "Seize the impostor!"

All eyes shot to the figure of the groom before the throne. They saw him raise his hand and snatch off the golden mask, and Tara of Helium in wide-eyed incredulity looked up into the face of Turan the panthan.

"Turan the slave," they cried then. "Death to him! Death to him!"

"Wait!" shouted Turan, drawing his sword, as a dozen warriors leaped forward.

"Wait!" screamed another voice, old and cracked, as I-Gos, the ancient taxidermist, sprang from among the guests and reached the throne steps ahead of the foremost warriors.

At sight of the old man the warriors paused, for age is held in great veneration among the peoples of Barsoom, as is true, perhaps, of all peoples whose religion is based to any extent upon ancestor worship. But O-Tar gave no heed to him, leaping instead swiftly toward the throne. "Stop, coward!" cried I-Gos.

The people looked at the little old man in amazement. "Men of Manator," he cackled in his thin, shrill voice, "wouldst be ruled by a coward and a liar?"

"Down with him!" shouted O-Tar.

"Not until I have spoken," retorted I-Gos. "It is my right. If I fail my life is forfeit—that you all know and I know. I demand therefore to be heard. It is my right!"

"It is his right," echoed the voices of a score of warriors in various parts of the chamber.

"That O-Tar is a coward and a liar I can prove," continued I-Gos. "He said that he faced bravely the horrors of the chamber of O-Mai and saw nothing of the slave Turan. I was there, hiding behind the hangings, and I saw all that transpired. Turan had been hiding in the chamber and was even then lying upon the couch of O-Mai when O-Tar, trembling with fear, entered the room. Turan, disturbed, arose to a sitting position at the same time voicing a piercing shriek. O-Tar screamed and swooned."

"It is a lie!" cried O-Tar.

"It is not a lie and I can prove it," retorted I-Gos. "Didst notice the night that he returned from the chambers of O-Mai and was boasting of his exploit, that when he would summon slaves to bring wine he reached for his dagger to strike the gong with its pommel as is always his custom? Didst note that, any of you? And that he had no dagger? O-Tar, where is the dagger that you carried into the chamber of O-Mai? You do not know; but I know. While you lay in the swoon of terror I took it from your harness and hid it among the sleeping silks upon the couch of O-Mai. There it is even now, and if any doubt it let them go thither and there they will find it and know the cowardice of their jeddak."

"But what of this impostor?" demanded one. "Shall he stand with impunity upon the throne of Manator whilst we squabble about our ruler?"

"It is through his bravery that you have learned the cowardice of O-Tar," replied I-Gos, "and through him you will be given a greater jeddak."

"We will choose our own jeddak. Seize and slay the slave!" There were cries of approval from all parts of the room. Gahan was listening intently, as though for some hoped-for sound. He saw the warriors approaching the dais, where he now stood with drawn sword and with one arm about Tara of Helium. He wondered if his plans had miscarried after all. If they had it would mean death for him, and he knew that Tara would take her life if he fell. Had he, then, served her so futilely after all his efforts?

Several warriors were urging the necessity for sending at once to the chamber of O-Mai to search for the dagger that would prove, if found, the cowardice of O-Tar. At last three consented to go. "You need not fear," I-Gos assured them. "There is naught there to harm you. I have been there often of late and Turan the slave has slept there for these many nights. The screams and moans that frightened you and O-Tar were voiced by Turan to drive you away from his hiding place." Shame-facedly the three left the apartment to search for O-Tar's dagger.

And now the others turned their attention once more to Gahan. They approached the throne with bared swords, but they came slowly for they had seen this slave upon the Field of Jetan and they knew the prowess of his arm. They had reached the foot of the steps when from far above there sounded a deep boom, and another, and another, and Turan smiled and breathed a sigh of relief. Perhaps, after all, it had not come too late. The warriors stopped and listened as did the others in the chamber. Now there broke upon their ears a loud rattle of musketry and it all came from above as though men were fighting upon the roofs of the palace.

"What is it?" they demanded, one of the other.

"A great storm has broken over Manator," said one.

"Mind not the storm until you have slain the creature who dares stand upon the throne of your jeddak," demanded O-Tar. "Seize him!"

Even as he ceased speaking the arras behind the throne parted and a warrior stepped forth upon the dais. An exclamation of surprise and dismay broke from the lips of the warriors of O-Tar. "U-Thor!" they cried. "What treason is this?"

"It is no treason," said U-Thor in his deep voice. "I bring you a new jeddak for all of Manator. No lying poltroon, but a courageous man whom you all love."

He stepped aside then and another emerged from the corridor hidden by the arras. It was A-Kor, and at sight of him there rose exclamations of surprise, of pleasure, and of anger, as the various factions recognized the *coup d'etat* that had been arranged so cunningly. Behind A-Kor came other warriors until the dais was crowded with them—all men of Manator from the city of Manatos.

O-Tar was exhorting his warriors to attack, when a bloody and dishevelled padwar burst into the chamber through a side entrance. "The city has fallen!" he cried aloud. "The hordes of Manatos pour through The Gate of Enemies. The slaves from Gathol have arisen and destroyed the palace guards. Great ships are landing warriors upon the palace roof and in the Fields of Jetan. The men of Helium and Gathol are marching through Manator. They cry aloud for the Princess of Helium and swear to leave Manator a blazing funeral pyre consuming the bodies of all our people. The skies are black with ships. They come in great processions from the east and from the south."

And then once more the doors from The Hall of Chiefs swung wide and the men of Manator turned to see another figure standing upon the threshold—a mighty figure of a man with white skin, and black hair, and grey eyes that glittered now like points of steel and behind him The Hall of Chiefs was filled with fighting men wearing the harness of far countries. Tara of Helium saw him and her heart leaped in exultation, for it was John Carter, Warlord of Barsoom, come at the head of a victorious host to the rescue of his daughter, and at his side was Djor Kantos to whom she had been betrothed.

The Warlord eyed the assemblage for a moment before he spoke. "Lay down your arms, men of Manator," he said. "I see my daughter and that she lives, and if no harm has befallen her no blood need be shed. Your city is filled with the fighting men of U-Thor, and those from Gathol and from Helium. The palace is in the hands of the slaves from Gathol, beside a thousand of my own warriors who fill the halls and chambers surrounding this room. The fate of your jeddak lies in your own hands. I have no wish to interfere. I come only for my daughter and to free the slaves from Gathol. I have spoken!" and without waiting for a reply and as though the room had been filled with his own people rather than a hostile band he strode up the broad main aisle toward Tara of Helium.

The chiefs of Manator were stunned. They looked to O-Tar; but he could only gaze helplessly about him as the enemy entered from The Hall of Chiefs and circled the throne room until they had surrounded the entire company. And then a dwar of the army of Helium entered.

"We have captured three chiefs," he reported to The Warlord, "who beg that they be permitted to enter the throne room and report to their fellows some matter which they say will decide the fate of Manator."

"Fetch them," ordered The Warlord.

They came, heavily guarded, to the foot of the steps leading to the throne and there they stopped and the leader turned toward the others of Manator and raising high his right hand displayed a jewelled dagger. "We found it," he said, "even where I-Gos said that we would find it," and he looked menacingly upon O-Tar.

"A-Kor, jeddak of Manator!" cried a voice, and the cry was taken up by a hundred hoarse-throated warriors.

"There can be but one jeddak in Manator," said the chief who held the dagger; his eyes still fixed upon the hapless O-Tar he crossed to where the latter stood and holding the dagger upon an outstretched palm proffered it to the discredited ruler. "There can be but one jeddak in Manator," he repeated meaningly.

O-Tar took the proffered blade and drawing himself to his full height plunged it to the guard into his breast, in that single act redeeming himself in the esteem of his people and winning an eternal place in The Hall of Chiefs.

As he fell all was silence in the great room, to be broken presently by the voice of U-Thor. "O-Tar is dead!" he cried. "Let A-Kor rule until the chiefs of all Manator may be summoned to choose a new jeddak. What is your answer?"

"Let A-Kor rule! A-Kor, Jeddak of Manator!" The cries filled the room and there was no dissenting voice.

A-Kor raised his sword for silence. "It is the will of A-Kor," he said, "and that of the Great Jed of Manatos, and the commander of the fleet from Gathol, and of the illustrious John Carter, Warlord of Barsoom, that peace lie upon the city of Manator and so I decree that the men of Manator go forth and welcome the fighting men of these our allies as guests and friends and show them the wonders of our ancient city and the hospitality of Manator. I have spoken." And U-Thor and John Carter dismissed their warriors and bade them accept the hospitality of Manator. As the room emptied Djor Kantos reached the side of Tara of Helium. The girl's happiness at rescue had been blighted by sight of this man whom her virtuous heart told her she had wronged. She dreaded the ordeal that lay before her and the dishonour that she must admit before she could hope to be freed from the understanding that had for long existed between them. And now Djor Kantos approached and kneeling raised her fingers to his lips.

"Beautiful daughter of Helium," he said, "how may I tell you the thing that I must tell you—of the dishonour that I have all unwittingly done you? I can but throw myself upon your generosity for forgiveness; but if you demand it I can receive the dagger as honourably as did O-Tar."

"What do you mean?" asked Tara of Helium. "What are you talking about—why speak thus in riddles to one whose heart is already breaking?"

Her heart already breaking! The outlook was anything but promising, and the young padwar wished that he had died before ever he had had to speak the words he now must speak.

"Tara of Helium," he continued, "we all thought you dead. For a long year have you been gone from Helium. I mourned you truly and then, less than a moon since, I wed with Olvia Marthis." He stopped and looked at her with eyes that might have said: "Now, strike me dead!"

"Oh, foolish man!" cried Tara. "Nothing you could have done could have pleased me more. Djor Kantos, I could kiss you!"

"I do not think that Olvia Marthis would mind," he said, his face now wreathed with smiles. As they spoke a body of men had entered the throne room and approached the dais. They were tall men trapped in plain harness, absolutely without ornamentation. Just as their leader reached the dais Tara had turned to Gahan, motioning him to join them.

"Djor Kantos," she said, "I bring you Turan the panthan, whose loyalty and bravery have won my love."

John Carter and the leader of the new come warriors, who were standing near, looked quickly at the little group. The former smiled an inscrutable smile, the latter addressed the Princess of Helium. "'Turan the panthan!'" he cried. "Know you not, fair daughter of Helium, that this man you call panthan is Gahan, Jed of Gathol?"

For just a moment Tara of Helium looked her surprise; and then she shrugged her beautiful shoulders as she turned her head to cast her eyes over one of them at Gahan of Gathol.

"Jed or panthan," she said; "what difference does it make what one's slave has been?" and she laughed roguishly into the smiling face of her lover.

* * * * *

His story finished, John Carter rose from the chair opposite me, stretching his giant frame like some great forest-bred lion.

"You must go?" I cried, for I hated to see him leave and it seemed that he had been with me but a moment.

"The sky is already red beyond those beautiful hills of yours," he replied, "and it will soon be day."

"Just one question before you go," I begged.

"Well?" he assented, good-naturedly.

"How was Gahan able to enter the throne room garbed in O-Tar's trappings?" I asked.

"It was simple—for Gahan of Gathol," replied The Warlord. "With the assistance of I-Gos he crept into The Hall of Chiefs before the ceremony, while the throne room and Hall of Chiefs were vacated to receive the bride. He came from the pits through the corridor that opened behind the arras at the rear of the throne, and passing into The Hall of Chiefs took his place upon the back of a riderless thoat, whose warrior was in I-Gos' repair room. When O-Tar entered and came near him Gahan fell upon him and struck him with the butt of a heavy spear. He thought that he had killed him and was surprised when O-Tar appeared to denounce him."

"And Ghek? What became of Ghek?" I insisted.

"After leading Val Dor and Floran to Tara's disabled flier which they repaired, he accompanied them to Gathol from where a message was sent to me in Helium. He then led a large party including A-Kor and U-Thor from the roof, where our ships landed them, down a spiral runway into the palace and guided them to the throne room. We took him back to Helium with us, where he still lives, with his single rykor which we found all but starved to death in the pits of Manator. But come! No more questions now."

I accompanied him to the east arcade where the red dawn was glowing beyond the arches.

"Good-bye!" he said.

"I can scarce believe that it is really you," I exclaimed. "Tomorrow I will be sure that I have dreamed all this."

He laughed and drawing his sword scratched a rude cross upon the concrete of one of the arches.

"If you are in doubt tomorrow," he said, "come and see if you dreamed this."

A moment later he was gone.

Appendix

Jetan, or Martian Chess

For those who care for such things, and would like to try the game, I give the rules of Jetan as they were given me by John Carter. By writing the names and moves of the various pieces on bits of paper and pasting them on ordinary checkermen the game may be played quite as well as with the ornate pieces used upon Mars.

The Board: Square board consisting of one hundred alternate black and orange squares.

The Pieces: In order, as they stand upon the board in the first row, from left to right of each player.

WARRIOR:
2 feathers; 2 spaces straight in any direction or combination.

PADWAR:
2 feathers; 2 spaces diagonal in any direction or combination.

DWAR:
3 feathers; 3 spaces straight in any direction or combination.

FLIER:
3 bladed propellor; 3 spaces diagonal in any direction or combination; and may jump intervening pieces.

CHIEF:
Diadem with ten jewels; 3 spaces in any direction; straight or diagonal or combination.

PRINCESS:
Diadem with one jewel; same as Chief, except may jump intervening pieces.

FLIER: See above.

DWAR: See above.

PADWAR: See above.

WARRIOR: See above.

And in the second row from left to right:

THOAT: Mounted warrior 2 feathers; 2 spaces, one straight and one diagonal in any direction.

PANTHANS: (8 of them): 1 feather; 1 space, forward, side, or diagonal, but not backward.

THOAT: See above.

The game is played with twenty black pieces by one player and twenty orange by his opponent, and is presumed to have originally represented a battle between the Black race of the south and the Yellow race of the north. On Mars the board is usually arranged so that the Black pieces are played from the south and the Orange from the north.

The game is won when any piece is placed on same square with opponent's Princess, or a Chief takes a Chief.

The game is drawn when either Chief is taken by a piece other than the opposing Chief, or when both sides are reduced to three pieces, or less, of equal value and the game is not won in the ensuing ten moves, five apiece.

The Princess may not move onto a threatened square, nor may she take an opposing piece. She is entitled to one ten-space move at any time during the game. This move is called the escape.

Two pieces may not occupy the same square except in the final move of a game where the Princess is taken.

When a player, moving properly and in order, places one of his pieces upon a square occupied by an opponent piece, the opponent piece is considered to have been killed and is removed from the game.

The moves explained. Straight moves mean due north, south, east, or west; diagonal moves mean northeast, southeast, southwest, or northwest. A Dwar might move straight north three spaces, or north one space and east two spaces, or any similar combination of straight moves, so long as he did not cross the same square twice in a single move. This example explains combination moves.

The first move may be decided in any way that is agreeable to both players; after the first game the winner of the preceding game moves first if he chooses, or may instruct his opponent to make the first move.

Gambling: The Martians gamble at Jetan in several ways. Of course the outcome of the game indicates to whom the main stake belongs; but they also put a price upon the head of each piece, according to its value, and for each piece that a player loses he pays its value to his opponent.

The Sixth Adventure

Mastermind of Mars

A Letter

Helium, June 8th, 1925

My Dear Mr. Burroughs:

It was in the Fall of nineteen seventeen at an officers' training camp that I first became acquainted with John Carter, War Lord of Barsoom, through the pages of your novel "A Princess of Mars." The story made a profound impression upon me and while my better judgment assured me that it was but a highly imaginative piece of fiction, a suggestion of the verity of it pervaded my inner consciousness to such an extent that I found myself dreaming of Mars and John Carter, of Dejah Thoris, of Tars Tarkas and of Woola as if they had been entities of my own experience rather than the figments of your imagination.

It is true that in those days of strenuous preparation there was little time for dreaming, yet there were brief moments before sleep claimed me at night and these were my dreams. Such dreams! Always of Mars, and during my waking hours at night my eyes always sought out the Red Planet when he was above the horizon and clung there seeking a solution of the seemingly unfathomable riddle he has presented to the Earthman for ages.

Perhaps the thing became an obsession. I know it clung to me all during my training camp days, and at night, on the deck of the transport, I would he on my back gazing up into the red eye of the god of battle—my god—and wishing that, like John Carter, I might be drawn across the great void to the haven of my desire.

And then came the hideous days and nights in the trenches—the rats, the vermin, the mud—with an occasional glorious break in the monotony when we were ordered over the top. I loved it then and I loved the bursting shells, the mad, wild chaos of the thundering guns, but the rats and the vermin and the mud—God! how I hated them. It sounds like boasting, I know, and I am sorry; but I wanted to write you just the truth about myself. I think you will understand.

And it may account for much that happened afterwards.

There came at last to me what had come to so many others upon those bloody fields. It came within the week that I had received my first promotion and my captaincy, of which I was greatly proud, though humbly so; realizing as I did my youth, the great responsibility that it placed upon me as well as the opportunities it offered, not only in service to my country but, in a personal way, to the men of my command. We had advanced a matter of two kilometres and with a small detachment I was holding a very advanced position when I received orders to fall back to the new line. That is the last that I remember until I regained consciousness after dark. A shell must have burst among us. What became of my men I never knew. It was cold and very dark when I awoke and at first, for an instant, I was quite comfortable—before I was fully conscious, I imagine—and then I commenced to feel pain. It grew until it seemed unbearable. It was in my legs. I reached down to feel them, but my hand recoiled from what it found, and when I tried to move my legs I discovered that I was dead from the waist down. Then the moon came out from behind a cloud and I saw that I lay within a shell hole and that I was not alone—the dead were all about me.

It was a long time before I found the moral courage and the physical strength to draw myself up upon one elbow that I might view the havoc that had been done me.

One look was enough, I sank back in an agony of mental and physical anguish—my legs had been blown away from midway between the hips and knees. For some reason I was not bleeding excessively, yet I know that I had lost a great deal of blood and that I was gradually losing enough to put me out of my misery in a short time if I were not soon found; and as I lay there on my back, tortured with pain, I prayed that they would not come in time, for I shrank more from the thought of going maimed through life than I shrank from the thought of death.

Then my eyes suddenly focussed upon the bright red eye of Mars and there surged through me a sudden wave of hope. I stretched out my arms towards Mars, I did not seem to question or to doubt for an instant as I prayed to the god of my vocation to reach forth and succour me. I knew that he would do it, my faith was complete, and yet so great was the mental effort that I made to throw off the hideous bonds of my mutilated flesh that I felt a momentary qualm of nausea and then a sharp click as of the snapping of a steel wire, and suddenly I stood naked upon two good legs looking down upon the bloody, distorted thing that had been I. Just for an instant did I stand thus before I turned my eyes aloft again to my star of destiny and with outstretched arms stand there in the cold of that French night—waiting.

Suddenly I felt myself drawn with the speed of thought through the trackless wastes of interplanetary space. There was an instant of extreme cold and utter darkness, then—But the rest is in the manuscript that, with the aid of one greater than either of us, I have found the means to transmit to you with this letter. You and a few others of the chosen will believe in it—for the rest it matters not as yet.

The time will come—but why tell you what you already know?

My salutations and my congratulations—the latter on your good fortune in having been chosen as the medium through which Earthmen shall become better acquainted with the manners and customs of Barsoom, against the time that they shall pass through space as easily as John Carter, and visit the scenes that he has described to them through you, as have I.

Your sincere friend,

Ulysses Paxton

Late Captain, —th Inf., U.S. Army.

Chapter 1

The House Of The Dead

I must have closed my eyes involuntarily during the transition for when I opened them I was lying flat on my back gazing up into a brilliant, sun-lit sky, while standing a few feet from me and looking down upon me with the most mystified expression was as strange a looking individual as my eyes ever had rested upon.

He appeared to be quite an old man, for he was wrinkled and withered beyond description. His limbs were emaciated; his ribs showed distinctly beneath his shrunken hide; his cranium was large and well developed, which, in conjunction with his wasted limbs and torso, lent him the appearance of top heaviness, as though he had a head beyond all proportion to his body, which was, I am sure, really not the case.

As he stared down upon me through enormous, many lensed spectacles I found the opportunity to examine him as minutely in return. He was, perhaps, five feet five in height, though doubtless he had been taller in youth, since he was somewhat bent; he was naked except for some rather plain and well-worn leather harness which supported his weapons and pocket pouches, and one great ornament a collar, jewel studded, that he wore around his scraggy neck—such a collar as a dowager empress of pork or real estate might barter her soul for, if she had one. His skin was red, his scant locks grey. As he looked at me his puzzled expression increased in intensity, he grasped his chin between the thumb and fingers of his left hand and slowly raising his right hand he scratched his head most deliberately. Then he spoke to me, but in a language I did not understand.

At his first words I sat up and shook my head. Then I looked about me. I was seated upon a crimson sward within a high walled enclosure, at least two, and possibly three, sides of which were formed by the outer walls of a structure that in some respects resembled more closely a feudal castle of Europe than any familiar form of architecture that comes to my mind. The facade presented to my view was ornately carved and of most irregular design, the roof line being so broken as to almost suggest a ruin, and yet the whole seemed harmonious and not without beauty. Within the enclosure grew a number of trees and shrubs, all weirdly strange and all, or almost all, profusely flowering. About them wound walks of coloured pebbles among which scintillated what appeared to be rare and beautiful gems, so lovely were the strange, unearthly rays that leaped and played in the sunshine.

The old man spoke again, peremptorily this time, as though repeating a command that had been ignored, but again I shook my head. Then he laid a hand upon one of his two swords, but as he drew the weapon I leaped to my feet, with such remarkable results that I cannot even now say which of us was the more surprised. I must have sailed ten feet into the air and back about twenty feet from where I had been sitting; then I was sure that I was upon Mars (not that I had for one instant doubted it), for the effects of the lesser gravity, the colour of the sward and the skin-hue of the red Martians I had seen described in the manuscripts of John Carter, those marvellous and as yet unappreciated contributions to the scientific literature of a world. There could be no doubt of it, I stood upon the soil of the Red Planet, I had come to the world of my dreams—to Barsoom.

So startled was the old man by my agility that he jumped a bit himself, though doubtless involuntarily, but, however, with certain results. His spectacles tumbled from his nose to the sward, and then it was that I discovered that the pitiful old wretch was practically blind when deprived of these artificial aids to vision, for he got to his knees and commenced to grope frantically for the lost glasses, as though his very life depended upon finding them in the instant.

Possibly he thought that I might take advantage of his helplessness and slay him. Though the spectacles were enormous and lay within a couple of feet of him he could not find them, his hands, seemingly afflicted by that strange perversity that sometimes confounds our simplest acts, passing all about the lost object of their search, yet never once coming in contact with it.

As I stood watching his futile efforts and considering the advisability of restoring to him the means that would enable him more readily to find my heart with his sword point, I became aware that another had entered the enclosure.

Looking towards the building I saw a large red-man running rapidly towards the little old man of the spectacles. The newcomer was quite naked, he carried a club in one hand, and there was upon his face such an expression as unquestionably boded ill for the helpless husk of humanity grovelling, mole-like, for its lost spectacles.

My first impulse was to remain neutral in an affair that it seemed could not possibly concern me and of which I had no slightest knowledge upon which to base a predilection towards either of the parties involved; but a second glance at the face of the club-bearer aroused a question as to whether it might not concern me after all.

There was that in the expression upon the man's face that betokened either an inherent savageness of disposition or a maniacal cast of mind which might turn his evidently murderous attentions upon me after he had dispatched his elderly victim, while, in outward appearance at least, the latter was a sane and relatively harmless individual. It is true that his move to draw his sword against me was not indicative of a friendly disposition towards me, but at least, if there were any choice, he seemed the lesser of two evils.

He was still groping for his spectacles and the naked man was almost upon him as I reached the decision to cast my lot upon the side of the old man. I was twenty feet away, naked and unarmed, but to cover the distance with my Earthly muscles required but an instant, and a naked sword lay by the old man's side where he had discarded it the better to search for his spectacles. So it was that I faced the attacker at the instant that he came within striking distance of his victim, and the blow which had been intended for another was aimed at me. I side-stepped it and then I learned that the greater agility of my Earthly muscles had its disadvantages as well as its advantages, for, indeed, I had to learn to walk at the very instant that I had to learn to fight with a new weapon against a maniac armed with a bludgeon, or at least, so I assumed him to be and I think that it is not strange that I should have done so, what with his frightful show of rage and the terrible expression upon his face.

As I stumbled about endeavouring to accustom myself to the new conditions, I found that instead of offering any serious opposition to my antagonist I was hard put to it to escape death at his hands, so often did I stumble and fall sprawling upon the scarlet sward; so that the duel from its inception became but a series of efforts, upon his part to reach and crush me with his great club, and upon mine to dodge and elude him. It was mortifying but it is the truth.

However, this did not last indefinitely, for soon I learned, and quickly too under the exigencies of the situation, to command my muscles, and then I stood my ground and when he aimed a blow at me, and I had dodged it, I touched him with my point and brought blood along with a savage roar of pain. He went more cautiously then, and taking advantage of the change I pressed him so that he fell back. The effect upon me was magical, giving me new confidence, so that I set upon him in good earnest, thrusting and cutting until I had him bleeding in a half-dozen places, yet taking good care to avoid his mighty swings, any one of which would have felled an ox.

In my attempts to elude him in the beginning of the duel we had crossed the enclosure and were now fighting at a considerable distance from the point of our first meeting. It now happened that I stood facing towards that point at the moment that the old man regained his spectacles, which he quickly adjusted to his eyes. Immediately he looked about until he discovered us, whereupon he commenced to yell excitedly at us at the same time running in our direction and drawing his short-sword as he ran. The red-man was pressing me hard, but I had gained almost complete control of myself, and fearing that I was soon to have two antagonists instead of one I set upon him with redoubled intensity. He missed me by the fraction of an inch, the wind in the wake of his bludgeon fanning my scalp, but he left an opening into which I stepped, running my word fairly through his heart. At least I thought that I had pierced his heart but I had forgotten what I had once read in one of John Carter's manuscripts to the effect that all the Martian internal organs are not disposed identically with those of Earthmen. However, the immediate results were quite as satisfactory as though I had found his heart for the wound was sufficiently grievous to place him hors de combat, and at that instant the old gentleman arrived. He found me ready, but I had mistaken his intentions. He made no unfriendly gestures with his weapon, but seemed to be trying to convince me that he had no intention of harming me. He was very excited and apparently tremendously annoyed that I could not understand him, and perplexed, too. He hopped about screaming strange sentences at me that bore the tones of peremptory commands, rabid invective and impotent rage. But the fact that he had returned his sword to its scabbard had greater significance than all his jabbering, and when he ceased to yell at me and commenced to talk in a sort of pantomime I realized that he was making overtures of peace if not of friendship, so I lowered my point and bowed. It was all that I could think of to assure him that I had no immediate intention of spitting him.

He seemed satisfied and at once turned his attention to the fallen man. He examined his pulse and listened to his heart, then, nodding his head, he arose and taking a whistle from one of his pocket pouches sounded a single loud blast.

There emerged immediately from one of the surrounding buildings a score of naked red-men who came running towards us. None was armed. To these he issued a few curt orders, whereupon they gathered the fallen one in their arms and bore him off. Then the old man started towards the building, motioning me to accompany him. There seemed nothing else for me to do but obey. Wherever I might be upon Mars, the chances were a million to one that I would be among enemies; and so I was as well off here as elsewhere and must depend upon my own resourcefulness, skill and agility to make my way upon the Red Planet.

The old man led me into a small chamber from which opened numerous doors, through one of which they were just bearing my late antagonist. We followed into a large, brilliantly lighted chamber wherein there burst upon my astounded vision the most gruesome scene that I ever had beheld. Rows upon rows of tables arranged in parallel lines filled the room and with few exceptions each table bore a similar grisly burden, a partially dismembered or otherwise mutilated human corpse. Above each table was a shelf bearing containers of various sizes and shapes, while from the bottom of the shelf depended numerous surgical instruments, suggesting that my entrance upon Barsoom was to be through a gigantic medical college.

At a word from the old man, those who bore the Barsoomian I had wounded laid him upon an empty table and left the apartment. Whereupon my host if so I may call him, for certainly he was not as yet my captor, motioned me forward. While he conversed in ordinary tones, he made two incisions in the body of my late antagonist; one, I imagine, in a large vein and one in an artery, to which he deftly attached the ends of two tubes, one of which was connected with an empty glass receptacle and the other with a similar receptacle filled with a colourless, transparent liquid resembling clear water. The connections made, the old gentleman pressed a button controlling a small motor, whereupon the victim's blood was pumped into the empty jar while the contents of the other was forced into the emptying veins and arteries.

The tones and gestures of the old man as he addressed me during this operation convinced me that he was explaining in detail the method and purpose of what was transpiring, but as I understood no word of all he said I was as much in the dark when he had completed his discourse as I was before he started it, though what I had seen made it appear reasonable to believe that I was witnessing an ordinary Barsoomian embalming. Having removed the tubes the old man closed the openings he had made by covering them with bits of what appeared to be heavy adhesive tape and then motioned me to follow him. We went from room to room, in each of which were the same gruesome exhibits. At many of the bodies the old man paused to make a brief examination or to refer to what appeared to be a record of the case, that hung upon a hook at the head of each of the tables.

From the last of the chambers we visited upon the first floor my host led me up an inclined runway to the second floor where there were rooms similar to those below, but here the tables bore whole rather than mutilated bodies, all of which were patched in various places with adhesive tape. As we were passing among the bodies in one of these rooms a Barsoomian girl, whom I took to be a servant or slave, entered and addressed the old man, whereupon he signed me to follow him and together we descended another runway to the first floor of another building.

Here, in a large, gorgeously decorated and sumptuously furnished apartment an elderly red-woman awaited us. She appeared to be quite old and her face was terribly disfigured as by some injury. Her trappings were magnificent and she was attended by a score of women and armed warriors, suggesting that she was a person of some consequence, but the little old man treated her quite brusquely, as I could see, quite to the horror of her attendants.

Their conversation was lengthy and at the conclusion of it, at the direction of the woman, one of her male escort advanced and opening a pocket pouch at his side withdrew a handful of what appeared to me to be Martian coins. A quantity of these he counted out and handed to the little old man, who then beckoned the woman to follow him, a gesture which included me. Several of her women and guard started to accompany us, but these the old man waved back peremptorily; whereupon there ensued a heated discussion between the woman and one of her warriors on one side and the old man on the other, which terminated in his proffering the return of the woman's money with a disgusted air. This seemed to settle the argument, for she refused the coins, spoke briefly to her people and accompanied the old man and myself alone.

He led the way to the second floor and to a chamber which I had not previously visited. It closely resembled the others except that all the bodies therein were of young women, many of them of great beauty. Following closely at the heels of the old man the woman inspected the gruesome exhibit with painstaking care.

Thrice she passed slowly among the tables examining their ghastly burdens. Each time she paused longest before a certain one which bore the figure of the most beautiful creature I had ever looked upon; then she returned the fourth time to it and stood looking long and earnestly into the dead face. For awhile she stood there talking with the old man, apparently asking innumerable questions, to which he returned quick, brusque replies, then she indicated the body with a gesture and nodded assent to the withered keeper of this ghastly exhibit.

Immediately the old fellow sounded a blast upon his whistle, summoning a number of servants to whom he issued brief instructions, after which he led us to another chamber, a smaller one in which were several empty tables similar to those upon which the corpses lay in adjoining rooms. Two female slaves or attendants were in this room and at a word from their master they removed the trappings from the old woman, unloosed her hair and helped her to one of the tables. Here she was thoroughly sprayed with what I presume was an antiseptic solution of some nature, carefully dried and removed to another table, at a distance of about twenty inches from which stood a second parallel table.

Now the door of the chamber swung open and two attendants appeared bearing the body of the beautiful girl we had seen in the adjoining room. This they deposited upon the table the old woman had just quitted and as she had been sprayed so was the corpse, after which it was transferred to the table beside that on which she lay. The little old man now made two incisions in the body of the old woman, just as he had in the body of the red-man who had fallen to my sword; her blood was drawn from her veins and the clear liquid pumped into them, life left her and she lay upon the polished ersite slab that formed the table top, as much a corpse as the poor, beautiful, dead creature at her side.

The little old man, who had removed the harness down to his waist and been thoroughly sprayed, now selected a sharp knife from among the instruments above the table and removed the old woman's scalp, following the hair line entirely around her head. In a similar manner he then removed the scalp from the corpse of the young woman, after which, by means of a tiny circular saw attached to the end of a flexible, revolving shaft he sawed through the skull of each, following the line exposed by the removal of the scalps. This and the balance of the marvellous operation was so skilfully performed as to baffle description.

Suffice it to say that at the end of four hours he had transferred the brain of each woman to the brain pan of the other, deftly connected the severed nerves and ganglia, replaced the skulls and scalps and bound both heads securely with his peculiar adhesive tape, which was not only antiseptic and healing but anaesthetic, locally, as well.

He now reheated the blood that he had withdrawn from the body of the old woman, adding a few drops of some clear chemical solution, withdrew the liquid from the veins of the beautiful corpse, replacing it with the blood of the old woman and simultaneously administering a hypodermic injection.

During the entire operation he had not spoken a word. Now he issued a few instructions in his curt manner to his assistants, motioned me to follow him, and left the room. He led me to a distant part of the building or series of buildings that composed the whole, ushered me into a luxurious apartment, opened the door to a Barsoomian bath and left me in the hands of trained servants.

Refreshed and rested I left the bath after an hour of relaxation to find harness and trappings awaiting me in the adjoining chamber. Though plain, they were of good material, but there were no weapons with them.

Naturally I had been thinking much upon the strange things I had witnessed since my advent upon Mars, but what puzzled me most lay in the seemingly inexplicable act of the old woman in paying my host what was evidently a considerable sum to murder her and transfer to the inside of her skull the brain of a corpse. Was it the outcome of some horrible religious fanaticism, or was there an explanation that my Earthly mind could not grasp?

I had reached no decision in the matter when I was summoned to follow a slave to another and near-by apartment where I found my host awaiting me before a table loaded with delicious foods, to which, it is needless to say, I did ample justice after my long fast and longer weeks of rough army fare.

During the meal my host attempted to converse with me, but, naturally, the effort was fruitless of results. He waxed quite excited at times and upon three distinct occasions laid his hand upon one of his swords when I failed to comprehend what he was saying to me, an action which resulted in a growing conviction upon my part that he was partially demented; but he evinced sufficient self-control in each instance to avert a catastrophe for one of us.

The meal over he sat for a long time in deep meditation, then a sudden resolution seemed to possess him. He turned suddenly upon me with a faint suggestion of a smile and dove headlong into what was to prove an intensive course of instruction in the Barsoomian language. It was long after dark before he permitted me to retire for the night, conducting me himself to a large apartment, the same in which I had found my new harness, where he pointed out a pile of rich sleeping silks and furs, bid me a Barsoomian good night and left me, locking the door after him upon the outside, and leaving me to guess whether I were more guest or prisoner.

Chapter 2

Preferment

Three weeks passed rapidly. I had mastered enough of the Barsoomian tongue to enable me to converse with my host in a reasonably satisfactory manner, and I was also progressing slowly in the mastery of the written language of his nation, which is different, of course, from the written language of all other Barsoomian nations, though the spoken language of all is identical. In these three weeks I had teamed much of the strange place in which I was half guest and half prisoner and of my remarkable host-jailer, Ras Thavas, the old surgeon of Toonol, whom I had accompanied almost constantly day after day until gradually there had unfolded before my astounded faculties an understanding of the purposes of the institution over which he ruled and in which he laboured practically alone; for the slaves and attendants that served him were but hewers of wood and carriers of water. It was his brain alone and his skill that directed the sometimes beneficent, the sometimes malevolent, but always marvellous activities of his life's work.

Ras Thavas himself was as remarkable as the things he accomplished. He was never intentionally cruel; he was not, I am sure, intentionally wicked. He was guilty of the most diabolical cruelties and the basest of crimes; yet in the next moment he might perform a deed that if duplicated upon Earth would have raised him to the highest pinnacle of man's esteem. Though I know that I am safe in saying that he was never prompted to a cruel or criminal act by base motives, neither was he ever urged to a humanitarian one by high motives. He had a purely scientific mind entirely devoid of the cloying influences of sentiment, of which he possessed none. His was a practical mind, as evidenced by the enormous fees he demanded for his professional services; yet I know that he would not operate for money alone and I have seen him devote days to the study of a scientific problem the solution of which could add nothing to his wealth, while the quarters that he furnished his waiting clients were overflowing with wealthy patrons waiting to pour money into his coffers.

His treatment of me was based entirely upon scientific requirements. I offered a problem. I was either, quite evidently, not a Barsoomian at all, or I was of a species of which he had no knowledge. It therefore best suited the purposes of science that I be preserved and studied. I knew much about my own planet. It pleased Ras Thavas' scientific mind to milk me of all I knew in the hope that he might derive some suggestion that would solve one of the Barsoomian scientific riddles that still baffle their savants; but he was compelled to admit that in this respect I was a total loss, not alone because I was densely ignorant upon practically all scientific subjects, but because the learned sciences on Earth have not advanced even to the swaddling-clothes stage as compared with the remarkable progress of corresponding activities on Mars. Yet he kept me by him, training me in many of the minor duties of his vast laboratory. I was entrusted with the formula of the "embalming fluid" and taught how to withdraw a subject's blood and replace it with this marvellous preservative that arrests decay without altering in the minutest detail the nerve or tissue structure of the body. I learned also the secret of the few drops of solution which, added to the rewarmed blood before it is returned to the veins of the subject revitalizes the latter and restores to normal and healthy activity each and every organ of the body.

He told me once why he had permitted me to learn these things that he had kept a secret from all others, and why he kept me with him at all times in preference to any of the numerous individuals of his own race that served him and me in lesser capacities both day and night.

"Vad Varo," he said, using the Barsoomian name that he had given me because he insisted that my own name was meaningless and impractical, "for many years I have needed an assistant, but heretofore I have never felt that I had discovered one who might work here for me wholeheartedly and disinterestedly without ever having reason to go elsewhere or to divulge my secrets to others. You, in all Barsoom, are unique—you have no other friend or acquaintance than myself. Were you to leave we you would find yourself in a world of enemies, for all are suspicious of a stranger. You would not survive a dozen dawns and you would be cold and hungry and miserable—a wretched outcast in a hostile world. Here you have every luxury that the mind of man can devise or the hand of man produce, and you are occupied with work of such engrossing interest that your every hour must be fruitful of unparalleled satisfaction. There is no selfish reason, therefore, why you should leave me and there is every reason why you should remain. I expect no loyalty other than that which may be prompted by egoism. You make an ideal assistant, not only for the reasons I have just given you, but because you are intelligent and quick-witted, and now I have decided, after observing you carefully for a sufficient time, that you can serve me in yet another capacity—that of personal bodyguard.

"You may have noticed that I alone of all those connected with my laboratory am armed. This is unusual upon Barsoom, where people of all classes, and all ages and both sexes habitually go unarmed. But many of these people I could not trust armed as they would slay me; and were I to give arms to those whom I might trust, who knows but that the others would obtain possession of them and slay me, or even those whom I had trusted turn against me, for there is not one who might not wish to go forth from this place back among his own people—only you, Vad Varo, for there is no other place for you to go. So I have decided to give you weapons.

"You saved my life once. A similar opportunity might again present itself. I know that being a reasoning and reasonable creature, you will not slay me, for you have nothing to gain and everything to lose by my death, which would leave you friendless and unprotected in a world of strangers where assassination is the order of society and natural death one of the rarest of phenomena. Here are your arms." He stepped to a cabinet which he unlocked, displaying an assortment of weapons, and selected for me a long-sword, a short-sword, a pistol and a dagger.

"You seem sure of my loyalty, Ras Thavas," I said.

He shrugged his shoulders. "I am only sure that I know perfectly where your interests lie—sentimentalists have words: love, loyalty, friendship, enmity, jealousy, hate, a thousand others; a waste of words—one word defines them all: self-interest. All men of intelligence realize this. They analyse an individual and by his predilections and his needs they classify him as friend or foe, leaving to the weak-minded idiots who like to be deceived the drooling drivel of sentiment."

I smiled as I buckled my weapons to my harness, but I held my peace. Nothing could be gained by arguing with the man and, too, I felt quite sure that in any purely academic controversy I should get the worst of it; but many of the matters of which he had spoken had aroused my curiosity and one had reawakened in my mind a matter to which I had given considerable thought. While partially explained by some of his remarks I still wondered why the red-man from whom I had rescued him had seemed so venomously bent upon slaying him the day of my advent upon Barsoom, and so, as we sat chatting after our evening meal, I asked him.

"A sentimentalist," he said. "A sentimentalist of the most pronounced type. Why that fellow hated me with a venom absolutely unbelievable by any of the reactions of a trained, analytical mind such as mine; but having witnessed his reactions I become cognizant of a state of mind that I cannot of myself even imagine. Consider the facts. He was the victim of assassination—a young warrior in the prime of life, possessing a handsome face and a splendid physique. One of my agents paid his relatives a satisfactory sum for the corpse and brought it to me. It is thus that I obtain practically all of my material. I treated it in the manner with which you are familiar. For a year the body lay in the laboratory, there being no occasion during that time that I had use for it; but eventually a rich client came, a not overly prepossessing man of considerable years. He had fallen desperately in love with a young woman who was attended by many handsome suitors. My client had more money than any of them, more brains, more experience, but he lacked the one thing that each of the others had that always weighs heavily with the undeveloped, unreasoning, sentiment-ridden minds of young females—good looks."

"Now 378-J-493811-P had what my client lacked and could afford to purchase."

Quickly we reached an agreement as to price and I transferred the brain of my rich client to the head of 378-J-493811-P and my client went away and for all I know won the hand of the beautiful moron; and 378-J-493811-P might have rested on indefinitely upon his ersite slab until I needed him or a part of him in my work, had I not, merely by chance, selected him for resurgence because of an existing need for another male slave.

"Mind you now, the man had been murdered. He was dead. I bought and paid for the corpse and all there was in it. He might have lain dead forever upon one of my ersite slabs had I not breathed new life into his dead veins. Did he have the brains to view the transaction in a wise and dispassionate manner? He did not."

His sentimental reactions caused him to reproach me because I had given him another body, though it seemed to me that, looking at the matter from a standpoint of sentiment, if one must, he should have considered me as a benefactor for having given him life again In a perfectly healthy, if somewhat used, body.

"He had spoken to me upon the subject several times, begging me to restore his body to him, a thing of which, of course, as I explained to him, was utterly out of the question unless chance happened to bring to my laboratory the corpse of the client who had purchased his carcass—a contingency quite beyond the pale of possibility for one as wealthy as my client. The fellow even suggested that I permit him to go forth and assassinate my client bringing the body back that I might reverse the operation and restore his body to his brain. When I refused to divulge the name of the present possessor of his body he grew sulky, but until the very hour of your arrival, when he attacked me, I did not suspect the depth of his hate complex.

"Sentiment is indeed a bar to all progress. We of Toonol are probably less subject to its vagaries than most other nations upon Barsoom, but yet most of my fellow countrymen are victims of it in varying degrees. It has its rewards and compensations, however. Without it we could preserve no stable form of government and the Phundahlians, or some other people, would overrun and conquer us; but enough of our lower classes have sentiment to a sufficient degree to give them loyalty to the Jeddak of Toonol and the upper classes are brainy enough to know that it is to their own best interests to keep him upon his throne.

"The Phundahlians, upon the other hand, are egregious sentimentalists, filled with crass stupidities and superstitions, slaves to every variety of brain withering conceit. Why the very fact that they keep the old termagant, Xaxa, on the throne brands them with their stupid idiocy. She is an ignorant, arrogant, selfish, stupid, cruel virago, yet the Phundahlians would fight and die for her because her father was Jeddak of Phundahl. She taxes them until they can scarce stagger beneath their burden, she misrules them, exploits them, betrays them, and they fall down and worship at her feet. Why? Because her father was Jeddak of Phundahl and his father before him and so on back into antiquity; because they are ruled by sentiment rather than reason; because their wicked rulers play upon this sentiment.

"She had nothing to recommend her to a sane person—not even beauty. You know, you saw her."

"I saw her?" I demanded.

"You assisted me the day that we gave her old brain a new casket—the day you arrived from what you call your Earth."

"She! That old woman was Jeddara of Phundahl?"

"That was Xaxa," he assured me.

"Why, you did not accord her the treatment that one of the Earth would suppose would be accorded a ruler, and so I had no idea that she was more than a rich old woman."

"I am Ras Thavas," said the old man. "Why should I incline the head to any other? In my world nothing counts but brain and in that respect and without egotism, I may say that I acknowledge no superior."

"Then you are not without sentiment," I said, smiling. "You acknowledge pride in your intellect!" "It is not pride," he said, patiently, for him, "it is merely a fact that I state. A fact that I should have no difficulty in proving. In all probability I have the most highly developed and perfectly functioning mind among all the learned men of my acquaintance, and reason indicates that this fact also suggests that I possess the most highly developed and perfectly functioning mind upon Barsoom. From what I know of Earth and from what I have seen of you, I am convinced that there is no mind upon your planet that may even faintly approximate in power that which I have developed during a thousand years of active study and research. Rasoom (Mercury) or Cosoom (Venus) may possibly support intelligences equal to or even greater than mine. While we have made some study of their thought waves, our instruments are not yet sufficiently developed to more than suggest that they are of extreme refinement, power and flexibility."

"And what of the girl whose body you gave to the Jeddara?" I asked, irrelevantly, for my mind could not efface the memory of that sweet body that must, indeed, have possessed an equally sweet and fine brain.

"Merely a subject! Merely a subject!" he replied with a wave of his hand.

"What will become of her?' I insisted.

"What difference does it make?" he demanded. "I bought her with a batch of prisoners of war. I do not even recall from what country my agent obtained them, or from whence they originated. Such matters are of no import."

"She was alive when you bought her?" I demanded.

"Yes. Why?"

"You-er-ah-killed her, then?"

"Killed her! No; I preserved her. That was some ten years ago. Why should I permit her to grow old and wrinkled? She would no longer have the same value then, would she? No, I preserved her. When Xaxa bought her she was just as fresh and young as the day she arrived. I kept her a long time. Many women looked at her and wanted her face and figure, but it took a Jeddara to afford her. She brought the highest price that I have ever been paid."

"Yes, I kept her a long time, but I knew that some day she would bring my price."

She was indeed beautiful and so sentiment has its uses—were it not for sentiment there would be no fools to support this work that I am doing, thus permitting me to carry on investigations of far greater merit. You would be surprised, I know, were I to tell you that I feel that I am almost upon the point of being able to produce rational human beings through the action upon certain chemical combinations of a group of rays probably entirely undiscovered by your scientists, if I am to judge by the paucity of your knowledge concerning such things."

"I would not be surprised," I assured him. "I would not be surprised by anything that you might accomplish."

Chapter 3

Valla Dia

I lay awake a long time that night thinking of 4296-E-2631-H, the beautiful girl whose perfect body had been stolen to furnish a gorgeous setting for the cruel brain of a tyrant. It seemed such a horrid crime that I could not rid my mind of it and I think that contemplation of it sowed the first seed of my hatred and loathing for Ras Thavas. I could not conjure a creature so utterly devoid of bowels of compassion as to even consider for a moment the frightful ravishing of that sweet and lovely body for even the holiest of purposes, much less one that could have been induced to do so for filthy pelf.

So much did I think upon the girl that night that her image was the first to impinge upon my returning consciousness at dawn, and after I had eaten, Ras Thavas not having appeared, I went directly to the storage room where the poor thing was. Here she lay, identified only by a small panel, bearing a number: 4296-E-2631-H. The body of an old woman with a disfigured face lay before me in the rigid immobility of death; yet that was not the figure that I saw, but instead, a vision of radiant loveliness whose imprisoned soul lay dormant beneath those greying locks.

The creature here with the face and form of Xaxa was not Xaxa at all, for all that made the other what she was had been transferred to this cold corpse. How frightful would be the awakening, should awakening ever come! I shuddered to think of the horror that must overwhelm the girl when first she realized the horrid crime that had been perpetrated upon her. Who was she? What story lay locked in that dead and silent brain? What loves must have been hers whose beauty was so great and upon whose fair face had lain the indelible imprint of graciousness! Would Ras Thavas ever arouse her from this happy semblance of death?—far happier than any quickening ever could be for her. I shrank from the thought of her awakening and yet I longed to hear her speak, to know that that brain lived again, to learn her name, to listen to the story of this gentle life that had been so rudely snatched from its proper environment and so cruelly handled by the hand of Fate. And suppose she were awakened! Suppose she were awakened and that I—A hand was laid upon my shoulder and I turned to look into the face of Ras Thavas.

You seem interested in this subject," he said.

"I was wondering," I replied, "what the reaction this girl's brain would be were she to awaken to the discovery that she had become an old, disfigured woman."

He stroked his chin and eyed me narrowly. "An interesting experiment," he mused.

"I am gratified to discover that you are taking a scientific interest in the labours that I am carrying on. The psychological phases of my work I have, I must confess, rather neglected during the past hundred years or so, though I formerly gave them a great deal of attention. It would be interesting to observe and study several of these cases. This one, especially, might prove of value to you as an initial study, it being simple and regular. Later we will let you examine into a case where a man's brain has been transferred to a woman's skull, and a woman's brain to a man's. There are also the interesting cases where a portion of diseased or injured brain has been replaced by a portion of the brain from another subject, and, for experimental purposes alone, those human brains that have been transplanted to the craniums of beasts, and vice versa, offer tremendous opportunities for observation. I have in mind one case in which I transferred half the brain of an ape to the skull of a man, after having removed half of his brain, which I grafted upon the remaining part of the brain in the ape's skull. That was a matter of several years ago and I have often thought that I should like to recall these two subjects and note the results. I shall have to have a look at them—as I recall it they are in vault L-42-X, beneath building 4-J-21. We shall have to have a look at them someday soon—it has been years since I have been below. There must be some very interesting specimens there that have escaped my mind. But come! let us recall 4296-E-2631-H."

"No!" I exclaimed, laying a hand upon his arm. "It would be horrible."

He turned a surprised look upon me and then a nasty, sneering smile curled his lips. "Maudlin, sentimental fool!" he cried. "Who dare say no to me?"

I laid a hand upon the hilt of my long-sword and looked him steadily in the eye.

"Ras Thavas," I said, "you are master in your own house; but while I am your guest treat me with courtesy."

He returned my look for a moment but his eyes wavered. "I was hasty," he said. "Let it pass." That, I let answer for an apology—really it was more than I had expected—but the event was not unfortunate. I think he treated me with far greater respect thereafter; but now he turned immediately to the slab bearing the mortal remains of 4296-E-2631-H.

"Prepare the subject for revivification," he said, "and make what study you can of all its reactions." With that he left the room.

I was now fairly adept at this work which I set about with some misgivings but with the assurance that I was doing right in obeying Ras Thavas while I remained a member of his entourage. The blood that had once flowed through the veins of the beautiful body that Ras Thavas had sold to Xaxa reposed in an hermetically sealed vessel upon the shelf above the corpse. As I had before done in other cases beneath the watchful eyes of the old surgeon I now did for the first time alone. The blood heated, the incisions made, the tubes attached and the few drops of life-giving solution added to the blood, I was now ready to restore life to that delicate brain that had lain dead for ten years. As my finger rested upon the little button that actuated the motor that was to send the revivifying liquid into those dormant veins, I experienced such a sensation as I imagined no mortal man has ever felt.

I had become master of life and death, and yet at this moment that I stood there upon the point of resurrecting the dead I felt more like a murderer than a saviour. I tried to view the procedure dispassionately through the cold eye of science, but I failed miserably. I could only see a stricken girl grieving for her lost beauties. With a muffled oath I turned away. I could not do it! And then, as though an outside force had seized upon me, my finger moved unerringly to the button and pressed it. I cannot explain it, unless upon the theory of dual mentality, which may explain many things. Perhaps my subjective mind directed the act. I do not know. Only I know that I did it, the motor started, the level of the blood in the container commenced gradually to lower.

Spell-bound, I stood watching. Presently the vessel was empty. I shut off the motor, removed the tubes, sealed the openings with tape. The red glow of life tinged the body, replacing the sallow, purplish hue of death. The breasts rose and fell regularly, the head turned slightly and the eyelids moved. A faint sigh issued from between the parting lips. For a long time there was no other sign of life, then, suddenly, the eyes opened. They were dull at first, but presently they commenced to fill with questioning wonderment. They rested on me and then passed on about that portion of the room that was visible from the position of the body. Then they came back to me and remained steadily fixed upon my countenance after having once surveyed me up and down. There was still the questioning in them, but there was no fear.

"Where am I?" she asked. The voice was that of an old woman—high and harsh. A startled expression filled her eyes. "What is the matter with me? What is wrong with my voice? What has happened?"

I laid a hand upon her forehead. "Don't bother about it now," I said, soothingly. "Wait until sometime when you are stronger. Then I will tell you."

She sat up. "I am strong," she said, and then her eyes swept her lower body and limbs and a look of utter horror crossed her face. "What has happened to me? In the name of my first ancestor, what has happened to me?"

The shrill, harsh voice grated upon me. It was the voice of Xaxa and Xaxa now must possess the sweet musical tones that alone would have harmonized with the beautiful face she had stolen. I tried to forget those strident notes and think only of the pulchritude of the envelope that had once graced the soul within this old and withered carcass.

She extended a hand and laid it gently upon mine. The act was beautiful, the movements graceful. The brain of the girl directed the muscles, but the old, rough vocal cords of Xaxa could give forth no sweeter notes. "Tell me, please!" she begged. There were tears in the old eyes, I'll venture for the first time in many years. "Tell me! You do not seem unkind."

And so I told her. She listened intently and when I was through she sighed.

"After all," she said, "it is not so dreadful, now that I really know. It is better than being dead." That made me glad that I had pressed the button. She was glad to be alive, even draped in the hideous carcass of Xaxa. I told her as much.

"You were so beautiful," I told her.

"And now I am so ugly?" I made no answer.

"After all, what difference does it make?" she inquired presently. "This old body cannot change me, or make me different from what I have always been. The good in me remains and whatever of sweetness and kindness, and I can be happy to be alive and perhaps to do some good. I was terrified at first, because I did not know what had happened to me. I thought that maybe I had contracted some terrible disease that had so altered me—that horrified me; but now that I know—pouf! what of it?"

"You are wonderful," I said. "Most women would have gone mad with the horror and grief of it—to lose such wondrous beauty as was yours—and you do not care."

"Oh, yes, I care, my friend," she corrected me, "but I do not care enough to ruin my life in all other respects because of it, or to cast a shadow upon the lives of those around me. I have had my beauty and enjoyed it. It is not an unalloyed happiness I can assure you. Men killed one another because of it; two great nations went to war because of it; and perhaps my father lost his throne or his life—I do not know, for I was captured by the enemy while the war still raged. It may be raging yet and men dying because I was too beautiful. No one will fight for me now, though," she added, with a rueful smile.

"Do you know how long you have been here?" I asked.

"Yes," she replied. "It was the day before yesterday that they brought me hither."

"It was ten years ago," I told her.

"Ten years! Impossible."

I pointed to the corpses around us. "You have lain like this for ten years," I explained. "There are subjects here who have lain thus for fifty, Ras Thavas tells me."

"Ten years! Ten years! What may not have happened in ten years! It is better thus. I should fear to go back now. I should not want to know that my father, my mother too, perhaps, were gone. It is better thus. Perhaps you will let me sleep again? May I not?"

"That remains with Ras Thavas," I replied; "but for a while I am to observe you."

"Observe me?"

"Study you—your reactions."

"Ah! and what good will that do?"

"It may do some good in the world."

"It may give this horrid Ras Thavas some new ideas for his torture chamber—some new scheme for coining money from the suffering of his victims," she said, her harsh voice saddened.

"Some of his works are good," I told her. "The money he makes permits him to maintain this wonderful establishment where he constantly carries on countless experiments. Many of his operations are beneficent. Yesterday a warrior was brought in whose arm was crushed beyond repair. Ras Thavas gave him a new arm. A demented child was brought. Ras Thavas gave her a new brain. The arm and the brain were taken from two who had met violent deaths. Through Ras Thavas they were permitted, after death, to give life and happiness to others."

She thought for a moment. "I am content," she said. "I only hope that you will always be the observer."

Presently Ras Thavas came and examined her. "A good subject," he said. He looked at the chart where I had made a very brief record following the other entries relative to the history of Case No. 4296-E-2631-H. Of course this is, naturally, a rather free translation of this particular identification number. The Barsoomians have no alphabet such as ours and their numbering system is quite different. The thirteen characters above were represented by four Toonolian characters, yet the meaning was quite the same—they represented, in contracted form, the case number, the room, the table and the building.

"The subject will be quartered near you where you may regularly observe it," continued Ras Thavas. "There is a chamber adjoining yours. I will see that it is unlocked. Take the subject there. When not under your observation, lock it in."

It was only another case to him.

I took the girl, if I may so call her, to her quarters. On the way I asked her her name, for it seemed to me an unnecessary discourtesy always to address her and refer to her as 4296-E-2631-H, and this I explained to her.

"It is considerate of you to think of that," she said, "but really that is all that I am here—just another subject for vivisection."

"You are more than that to me," I told her. "You are friendless and helpless. I want to be of service to you—to make your lot easier if I can."

"Thank you again," she said. "My name is Valla Dia, and yours?"

"Ras Thavas calls me Vad Varo," I told her.

But that is not your name?"

"My name is Ulysses Paxton."

"It is a strange name, unlike any that I have ever heard, but you are unlike any man I have ever seen—you do not seem Barsoomian. Your colour is unlike that of any race."

"I am not of Barsoom, but from Earth, the planet you sometimes call Jasoom. That is why I differ in appearance from any you have known before."

"Jasoom! There is another Jasoomian here whose fame has reached to the remotest corners of Barsoom, but I never have seen him."

"John Carter?" I asked.

"Yes, The War Lord. He was of Helium and my people were not friendly with those of Helium. I never could understand how he came here. And now there is another from Jasoom—how can it be? How did you cross the great void?"

I shook my head. "I cannot even guess," I told her.

"Jasoom must be peopled with wonderful men," she said. It was a pretty compliment.

"As Barsoom is with beautiful women," I replied.

She glanced down ruefully at her old and wrinkled body.

"I have seen the real you," I said gently.

"I hate to think of my face," she said. "I know it is a frightful thing."

"It is not you, remember that when you see it and do not feel too badly."

"Is it as bad as that?" she asked.

I did not reply. "Never mind," she said presently. "If I had not beauty of the soul, I was not beautiful, no matter how perfect my features may have been; but if I possessed beauty of soul then I have it now. So I can think beautiful thoughts and perform beautiful deeds and that, I think, is the real test of beauty, after all."

"And there is hope," I added, almost in a whisper.

"Hope? No, there is no hope, if what you mean to suggest is that I may some time regain my lost self. You have told me enough to convince me that that can never be."

"We will not speak of it," I said, "but we may think of it and sometimes thinking a great deal of a thing helps us to find a way to get it, if we want it badly enough."

"I do not want to hope," she said, "for it will but mean disappointment for me. I shall be happy as I am. Hoping, I should always be unhappy."

I had ordered food for her and after it was brought Ras Thavas sent for me and I left her, locking the door of her chamber as the old surgeon had instructed. I found Ras Thavas in his office, a small room which adjoined a very large one in which were a score of clerks arranging and classifying reports from various departments of the great laboratory. He arose as I entered.

"Come with me, Vad Varo," he directed. "We will have a look at the two cases in L-42-X, the two of which I spoke."

"The man with half a simian brain and the ape with a half human brain?" I asked.

He nodded and preceded me towards the runway that led to the vaults beneath the building. As we descended, the corridors and passageways indicated long disuse.

The floors were covered with an impalpable dust, long undisturbed; the tiny radium bulbs that faintly illuminated the sub-Barsoomian depths were likewise coated. As we proceeded, we passed many doorways on either side, each marked with its descriptive hieroglyphic. Several of the openings had been tightly sealed with masonry. What gruesome secrets were hid within? At last we came to L-42-X. Here the bodies were arranged on shelves, several rows of which almost completely filled the room from floor to ceiling, except for a rectangular space in the centre of the chamber, which accommodated an ersite topped operating table with its array of surgical instruments, its motor and other laboratory equipment.

Ras Thavas searched out the subjects of his strange experiment and together we carried the human body to the table. While Ras Thavas attached the tubes I returned for the vessel of blood which reposed upon the same shelf with the corpse. The now familiar method of revivification was soon accomplished and presently we were watching the return of consciousness to the subject.

The man sat up and looked at us, then he cast a quick glance about the chamber; there was a savage light in his eyes as they returned to us. Slowly he backed from the table to the floor, keeping the former between us.

"We will not harm you," said Ras Thavas.

The man attempted to reply, but his words were unintelligible gibberish, then he shook his head and growled. Ras Thavas took a step towards him and the man dropped to all fours, his knuckles resting on the floor, and backed away, growling.

"Come!" cried Ras Thavas. "We will not harm you." Again he attempted to approach the subject, but the man only backed quickly away, growling more fiercely; and then suddenly he wheeled and climbed quickly to the top of the highest shelf, where he squatted upon a corpse and gibbered at us.

"We shall have to have help," said Ras Thavas and, going to the doorway, he blew a signal upon his whistle.

"What are you blowing that for?" demanded the man suddenly. "Who are you? What am I doing here? What has happened to me?"

"Come down," said Ras Thavas. "We are friends."

Slowly the man descended to the floor and came towards us, but he still moved with his knuckles to the pavement He looked about at the corpses and a new light entered his eyes.

"I am hungry!" he cried. "I will eat!" and with that he seized the nearest corpse and dragged it to the floor.

"Stop! Stop!" cried Ras Thavas, leaping forward. "You will ruin the subject," but the man only backed away, dragging the corpse along the floor after him. It was then that the attendants came and with their help we subdued and bound the poor creature. Then Ras Thavas had the attendants bring the body of the ape and he told them to remain, as we might need them.

The subject was a large specimen of the Barsoomian white ape, one of the most savage and fearsome denizens of the Red Planet, and because of the creature's great strength and ferocity Ras Thavas took the precaution to see that it was securely bound before resurgence.

It was a colossal creature about ten or fifteen feet tall, standing erect, and had an intermediary set of arms or legs midway between its upper and lower limbs. The eyes were close together and non-protruding; the ears were high set, while its snout and teeth were strikingly like those of our African gorilla.

With returning consciousness the creature eyed us questioningly. Several times it seemed to essay to speak but only inarticulate sounds issued from its throat.

Then it lay still for a period.

Ras Thavas spoke to it. "If you understand my words, nod your head." The creature nodded.

"Would you like to be freed of your bonds?" asked the surgeon.

Again the creature nodded an affirmative.

"I fear that you will attempt to injure us, or escape," said Ras Thavas.

The ape was apparently trying very hard to articulate and at last there issued from its lips a sound that could not be misunderstood. It was the single word no.

"You will not harm us or try to escape?" Ras Thavas repeated his question.

"No," said the ape, and this time the word was clearly enunciated.

"We shall see," said Ras Thavas. "But remember that with our weapons we may dispatch you quickly if you attack us."

The ape nodded, and then, very laboriously: "I will not harm you."

At a sign from Ras Thavas the attendants removed the bonds and the creature sat up. It stretched its limbs and slid easily to the floor, where it stood erect upon two feet, which was not surprising, since the white ape goes more often upon two feet than six; a fact of which I was not cognizant at the time, but which Ras Thavas explained to we later in commenting upon the fact that the human subject had gone upon all fours, which, to Ras Thavas, indicated a reversion to type in the fractional ape-brain transplanted to the human skull.

Ras Thavas examined the subject at considerable length and then resumed his examination of the human subject which continued to evince more simian characteristics than human, though it spoke more easily than the ape, because, undoubtedly, of its more perfect vocal organs. It was only by exerting the closest attention that the diction of the ape became understandable at all.

"There is nothing remarkable about these subjects," said Ras Thavas, after devoting half a day to them. "They bear out what I had already determined years ago in the transplanting of entire brains; that the act of transplanting stimulates growth and activity of brain cells. You will note that in each subject the transplanted portions of the brains are more active—they, in a considerable measure, control. That is why we have the human subject displaying distinctly simian characteristics, while the ape behaves in a more human manner; though if longer and closer observation were desirable you would doubtless find that each reverted at times to his own nature—that is the ape would be more wholly an ape and the human more manlike—but it is not worth the time, of which I have already given too much to a rather unprofitable forenoon. I shall leave you now to restore the subjects to anaesthesia while I return to the laboratories above. The attendants will remain here to assist you, if required."

The ape, who had been an interested listener, now stepped forward. "Oh, please, I pray you," it mumbled, "do not again condemn me to these horrid shelves. I recall the day that I was brought here securely bound, and though I have no recollection of what has transpired since I can but guess from the appearance of my own skin and that of these dusty corpses that I have lain here long. I beg that you will permit me to live and either restore me to my fellows or allow me to serve in some capacity in this establishment, of which I saw something between the time of my capture and the day that I was carried into this laboratory, bound and helpless, to one of your cold, ersite slabs."

Ras Thavas made a gesture of impatience. "Nonsense!" he cried. "You are better off here, where you can be preserved in the interests of science."

"Accede to his request," I begged, "and I will myself take over all responsibility for him while I profit by the study that he will afford me."

"Do as you are directed," snapped Ras Thavas as he quit the room.

I shrugged my shoulders. "There is nothing for it, then," I said.

"I might dispatch you all and escape," mused the ape, aloud, "but you would have helped me. I could not kill one who would have befriended me—yet I shrink from the thought of another death. How long have I lain here?"

I referred to the history of his case that had been brought and suspended at the head of the table. "Twelve years," I told him.

"And yet, why not?" he demanded of himself. "This man would slay me—why should I not slay him first."

"It would do you no good," I assured him, "for you could never escape. Instead you would be really killed, dying a death from which Ras Thavas would probably think it not worth while ever to recall you, while I, who might find the opportunity at some later date and who have the inclination, would be dead at your hands and thus incapable of saving you."

I had been speaking in a low voice, close to his ear, that the attendants might not overhear me. The ape listened intently.

"You will do as you suggest?" he asked.

"At the first opportunity that presents itself," I assured him.

"Very well," he said, "I will submit, trusting to you."

A half hour later both subjects had been returned to their shelves.

Chapter 4

The Compact

Days ran into weeks, weeks into months, as day by day I laboured at the side of Ras Thavas, and more and more the old surgeon took me into his confidence, more and more he imparted to me the secrets of his skill and his profession.

Gradually he permitted me to perform more and more important functions in the actual practice of his vast laboratory. I started transferring limbs from one subject to another, then internal organs of the digestive tract. Then he entrusted to me a complete operation upon a paying client I removed the kidneys from a rich old man, replacing them with healthy ones from a young subject The following day I gave a stunted child new thyroid glands. A week later I transferred two hearts and then, at last, came the great day for me—unassisted, with Ras Thavas standing silently beside me, I took the brain of an old man and transplanted it within the cranium of a youth.

When I had done Ras Thavas laid a hand upon my shoulder. "I could not have done better myself," he said. He seemed much elated and I could not but wonder at this unusual demonstration of emotion upon his part, he who so prided himself upon his lack of emotionalism. I had often pondered the purpose which influenced Ras Thavas to devote so much time to my training, but never had I hit upon any more satisfactory explanation than that he had need of assistance in his growing practice. Yet when I consulted the records, that were now open to me, I discovered that his practice was no greater than it had been for many years; and even had it been there was really no reason why he should have trained me in preference to one of his red-Martian assistants, his belief in my loyalty not being sufficient warrant, in my mind, for this preferment when he could, as well as not have kept me for a bodyguard and trained one of his own kind to aid him in his surgical work.

But I was presently to learn that he had an excellent reason for what he was doing—Ras Thavas always had an excellent reason for whatever he did. One night after we had finished our evening meal he sat looking at me intently as he so often did, as though he would read my mind, which, by the way, he was totally unable to do, much to his surprise and chagrin; for unless a Martian is constantly upon the alert any other Martian can read clearly his every thought; but Ras Thavas was unable to read mine. He said that it was due to the fact that I was not a Barsoomian. Yet I could often read the minds of his assistants, when they were off their guard, though never had I read aught of Ras Thavas' thoughts, nor, I am sure, had any other read them. He kept his brain sealed like one of his own blood jars, nor was he ever for a moment found with his barriers down.

He sat looking at me this evening for a long time, nor did it in the least embarrass me, so accustomed was I to his peculiarities. "Perhaps," he said presently, "one of the reasons that I trust you is due to the fact that I cannot ever, at any time, fathom your mind; so, if you harbour traitorous thoughts concerning me I do not know it, while the others, every one of them, reveal their inmost souls to my searching mind and in each one there is envy, jealousy or hatred of me. Them, I know, I cannot trust. Therefore I must accept the risk and place all my dependence upon you, and my reason tells me that my choice is a wise one—I have told you upon what grounds it based my selection of you as my bodyguard. The same holds true in my selection of you for the thing I have in mind. You cannot harm me without harming yourself and no man will intentionally do that; nor is there any reason why you should feel any deep antagonism towards me.

"You are, of course, a sentimentalist and doubtless you look with horror upon many of the acts of a sane, rational, scientific mind; but you are also highly intelligent and can, therefore, appreciate better than another, even though you may not approve them, the motives that prompt me to do many of those things of which your sentimentality disapproves. I may have offended you, but I have never wronged you, nor have I wronged any creature for which you might have felt some of your so-called friendship or love. Are my premises incorrect, or my reasoning faulty?"

I assured him to the contrary.

"Very well! Now let me explain why I have gone to such pains to brain you as no other human being, aside from myself, has ever been trained. I am not ready to use you yet, or rather you are not ready; but if you know my purpose you will realize the necessity for bending your energy to the consummation of my purpose, and to that end you will strive even more diligently than you have to perfect yourself in the high, scientific art I am imparting to you.

"I am a very old man," he continued after a brief pause, "even as age goes upon Barsoom. I have lived more than a thousand years. I have passed the allotted natural span of life, but I am not through with my life's work—I have but barely started it. I must not die. Barsoom must not be robbed of this wondrous brain and skill of mine. I have long had in mind a plan to thwart death, but it required another with skill equal to mine—two such might live for ever. I have selected you to be that other, for reasons that I already have explained—they are undefiled by sentimentalism. I did not choose you because I love you, or because I feel friendship for you, or because I think that you love me, or feel friendship towards me. I chose you because I knew that of all the inhabitants of a world you were the one least likely to fail me. For a time you will have my life in your hands. You will understand now why I have not been able to choose carelessly.

"This plan that I have chosen is simplicity itself provided that I can count upon just two essential factors—skill and self-interested loyalty in an assistant. My body is about worn out. I must have a new one. My laboratory is filled with wonderful bodies, young and complete with potential strength and health. I have but to select one of these and have my skilled assistant transfer my brain from this old carcass to the new one." He paused.

"I understand now, why you have trained me," I said. "It has puzzled me greatly."

"Thus and thus only may I continue my labours," he went on, "and thus may Barsoom be assured a continuance practically indefinitely, of the benefits that my brain may bestow upon her children. I may live for ever, provided I always have a skilled assistant, and I may assure myself of such by seeing to it that he never dies; when he wears out one organ, or his whole body, I can replace either from my great storehouse of perfect parts, and for me he can perform the same service. Thus may we continue to live indefinitely; for the brain, I believe, is almost deathless, unless injured or attacked by disease.

"You are not ready as yet to be entrusted with this important task. You must transfer many more brains and meet with and overcome the various irregularities and idiosyncrasies that constitute the never failing differences that render no two operations identical. When you gain sufficient proficiency I shall be the first to know it and then we shall lose no time in making Barsoom safe for posterity."

The old man was far from achieving hatred of himself. However, his plan was an excellent one, both for himself and for me. It assured us immortality—we might live for ever and always with strong, healthy, young bodies. The outlook was alluring—and what a wonderful position it placed me in. If the old man could be assured of my loyalty because of self-interest, similarly might I depend upon his loyalty; for he could not afford to antagonize the one creature in the world who could assure him immortality, or withhold it from him. For the first time since I had entered his establishment I felt safe.

As soon as I had left him I went directly to Valla Dia's apartment, for I wanted to tell her his wonderful news. In the weeks that had passed since her resurrection I had seen much of her and in our daily intercourse there had been revealed to me little by little the wondrous beauties of her soul, until at last I no longer saw the hideous, disfigured face of Xaxa when I looked upon her, but the eyes of my heart penetrated deeper to the loveliness that lay within that sweet mind. She had become my confidante, as I was hers, and this association constituted the one great pleasure of my existence upon Barsoom.

Her congratulations, when I told her of what had come to me, were very sincere and lovely. She said that she hoped I would use this great power of mine to do good in the world. I assured her that I would and that among the first things that I should demand of Ras Thavas was that he should give Valla Dia a beautiful body; but she shook her head.

"No, my friend," she said, "if I may not have my own body this old one of Xaxa's is quite as good for me as another. Without my own body I should not care to return to my native country; while were Ras Thavas to give me the beautiful body of another, I should always be in danger of the covetousness of his clients, any one of whom might see and desire to purchase it, leaving to me her old husk, conceivably one quite terribly diseased or maimed. No, my friend, I am satisfied with the body of Xaxa, unless I may again possess my own, for Xaxa at least bequeathed me a tough and healthy envelope, however ugly it may be; and for what do looks count here? You, alone, are my friend—that I have your friendship is enough. You admire me for what I am, not for what I look like, so let us leave well enough alone."

"If you could regain your own body and return to your native country, you would like that?" I demanded.

"Oh, do not say it!" she cried. "The simple thought of it drives me mad with longing. I must not harbour so hopeless a dream that at best may only tantalize me into greater abhorrence of my lot."

"Do not say that it is hopeless," I urged. "Death, only, renders hope futile."

"You mean to be kind," she said, "but you are only hurting me. There can be no hope."

"May I hope for you, then?" I asked. "For I surely see a way; however slight a possibility for success it may have, still, it is a way."

She shook her head. "There is no way," she said, with finality. "No more will Duhor know me."

"Duhor?" I repeated. "Your—someone you care for very much?"

"I care for Duhor very much," she answered with a smile, "but Duhor is not someone—Duhor is my home, the country of my ancestors."

"How came you to leave Duhor?" I asked. "You have never told me, Valla Dia."

"It was because of the ruthlessness of Jal Had, Prince of Amhor," she replied.

"Hereditary enemies were Duhor and Amhor; but Jal Had came disguised into the city of Duhor, having heard, they say, of the great beauty attributed to the only daughter of Kor San, Jeddak of Duhor, and when he had seen her he determined to possess her. Returning to Amhor he sent ambassadors to the court of Kor San to sue for the hand of the Princess of Duhor; but Kor San, who had no son, had determined to wed his daughter to one of his own Jeds, that the son of this union, with the blood of Kor San in his veins, might rule over the people of Duhor; and so the offer of Jal Had was declined.

"This so incensed the Amhorian that he equipped a great fleet and set forth to conquer Duhor and take by force that which he could not win by honourable methods. Duhor was, at that time, at war with Helium and all her forces were far afield in the south, with the exception of a small army that had been left behind to guard the city. Jal Had, therefore, could not have selected a more propitious time for an attack. Duhor fell, and while his troops were looting the fair city Jal Had, with a picked force, sacked the palace of the Jeddak and searched for the princess; but the princess had no mind to go back with him as Princess of Amhor. From the moment that the vanguard of the Amhorian fleet was seen in the sky she had known, with the others of the city, the purpose for which they came, and so she used her head to defeat that purpose.

"There was in her retinue a cosmetologist whose duty it was to preserve the lustrous beauty of the princess' hair and skin and prepare her for public audiences, for fetes and for the daily intercourse of the court. He was a master of his art; he could render the ugly pleasant to look upon, he could make the plain lovely, and he could make the lovely radiant. She called him quickly to her and commanded him to make the radiant ugly, and when he had done with her none might guess that she was the Princess of Duhor, so deftly had he wrought with his pigments and his tiny brushes.

"When Jal Had could not find the princess within the palace, and no amount of threat or torture could force a statement of her whereabouts from the loyal lips of her people, the Amhorian ordered that every woman within the palace be seized and taken to Amhor; there to be held as hostages until the Princess of Duhor should be delivered to him in marriage. We were, therefore, all seized and placed upon an Amhorian war ship which was sent back to Amhor ahead of the balance of the fleet, which remained to complete the sacking of Duhor.

"When the ship, with its small convoy, had covered some four thousand of the five thousand haads that separate Duhor from Amhor, it was sighted by a fleet from Phundahl which immediately attacked. The convoying ships were destroyed or driven off and that which carried us was captured. We were taken to Phundahl where we were put upon the auction block and I fell to the bid of one of Ras Thavas' agents. The rest you know."

"And what became of the princess?" I asked.

"Perhaps she died—her party was separated in Phundahl—but death could not more definitely prevent her return to Duhor. The Princess of Duhor will never again see her native country."

"But you may!" I cried, for I had suddenly hit upon a plan. "Where is Duhor?"

"You are going there?" she asked, laughingly.

"Yes!" "You are mad, my friend," she said. "Duhor lies a full seven thousand, eight hundred haads from Toonol, upon the opposite side of the snow-clad Artolian Hills. You, a stranger and alone, could never reach it; for between lie the Toonolian Marshes, wild hordes, savage beasts and warlike cities. You would but die uselessly within the first dozen haads, even could you escape from the island upon which stands the laboratory of Ras Thavas; and what motive is there to prompt you to such a useless sacrifice?"

I could not tell her. I could not look upon that withered figure and into that hideous and disfigured face and say: "it is because I love you, Valla Dia." But that, alas, was my only reason. Gradually, as I had come to know her through the slow revealment of the wondrous beauty of her mind and soul, there had crept into my heart a knowledge of my love; and yet, explain it I cannot, I could not speak the words to that frightful old hag. I had seen the gorgeous mundane tabernacle that had housed the equally gorgeous spirit of the real Valla Dia—that I could love; her heart and soul and mind I could love; but I could not love the body of Xaxa. I was torn, too, by other emotions, induced by a great doubt—could Valla Dia return my love. Habilitated in the corpse of Xaxa, with no other suitor, nay, with no other friend she might, out of gratitude or through sheer loneliness, be attracted to me; but once again were she Valla Dia the beautiful and returned to the palace of her king, surrounded by the great nobles of Duhor, would she have either eyes or heart for a lone and friendless exile from another world? I doubted it—and yet that doubt did not deter me from my determination to carry out, as far as Fate would permit, the mad scheme that was revolving in my brain.

"You have not answered my question, Vad Varo," she interrupted my surging thoughts. "Why would you do this thing?"

"To right the wrong that has been done you, Valla Dia," I said.

She sighed. "Do not attempt it, please," she begged. "You would but rob me of my one friend, whose association is the only source of happiness remaining to me. I appreciate your generosity and your loyalty, even though I may not understand them; your unselfish desire to serve me at such suicidal risk touches me more deeply than I can reveal, adding still further to the debt I owe you; but you must not attempt it—you must not."

"If it troubles you, Valla Dia," I replied, "we will not speak of it again; but know always that it is never from my thoughts. Some day I shall find a way, even though the plan I now have fails me."

The days moved on and on, the gorgeous Martian nights, filled with her hurtling moons, followed one upon another. Ras Thavas spent more and more time in directing my work of brain transference. I had long since become an adept; and I realized that the time was rapidly approaching when Ras Thavas would feel that he could safely entrust to my hands and skill his life and future. He would be wholly within my power and he knew that I knew it. I could slay him; I could permit him to remain for ever in the preserving grip of his own anaesthetic; or I could play any trick upon him that I chose, even to giving him the body of a calot or a part of the brain of an ape; but he must take the chance and that I knew, for he was failing rapidly. Already almost stone blind, it was only the wonderful spectacles that he had himself invented that permitted him to see at all;

long deaf, he used artificial means for hearing; and now his heart was showing symptoms of fatigue that he could not longer ignore.

One morning I was summoned to his sleeping apartment by a slave. I found the old surgeon lying, a shrunken, pitiful heap of withered skin and bones.

"We must hasten, Vad Varo," he said in a weak whisper. "My heart was like to have stopped a few tals ago. It was then that I sent for you." He pointed to a door leading from his chamber. "There," he said, "you will find the body I have chosen. There, in the private laboratory I long ago built for this very purpose, you will perform the greatest surgical operation that the universe has ever known, transferring its most perfect brain to the most beautiful and perfect body that ever has passed beneath these ancient eyes. You will find the head already prepared to receive my brain; the brain of the subject having been removed and destroyed—totally destroyed by fire. I could not possibly chance the existence of a brain desiring and scheming to regain its wondrous body. No, I destroyed it. Call slaves and have them bear my body to the ersite slab."

"That will not be necessary," I told him; and lifting his shrunken form in my arms as he had been an earthly babe, I carried him into the adjoining room where I found a perfectly lighted and appointed laboratory containing two operating tables, one of which was occupied by the body of a red-man. Upon the surface of the other, which was vacant, I laid Ras Thavas, then I turned to look at the new envelope he had chosen. Never, I believe, had I beheld so perfect a form, so handsome a face—Ras Thavas had indeed chosen well for himself. Then I turned back to the old surgeon. Deftly, as he had taught me, I made the two incisions and attached the tubes. My finger rested upon the button that would start the motor pumping his blood from his veins and his marvellous preservative-anaesthetic into them. Then I spoke.

"Ras Thavas," I said, "You have long been training me to this end. I have laboured assiduously to prepare myself that there might be no slightest cause for apprehension as to the outcome. You have, coincidentally, taught me that one's every act should be prompted by self-interest only. You are satisfied, therefore, that I am not doing this for you because I love you, or because I feel any friendship for you; but you think that you have offered me enough in placing before me a similar opportunity for immortality.

"Regardless of your teaching I am afraid that I am still somewhat of a sentimentalist I crave the redressing of wrongs. I crave friendship and love. The price you offer is not enough. Are you willing to pay more that this operation may be successfully concluded?"

He looked at me steadily for a long minute. "What do you want?" he asked. I could see that he was trembling with anger, but he did not raise his voice.

"Do you recall 4296-E-2631-H?" I inquired.

"The subject with the body of Xaxa? Yes, I recall the case. What of it?"

"I wish her body returned to her. That is the price you must pay for this operation."

He glared at me. "It is impossible. Xaxa has the body. Even if I cared to do so, I could never recover it. Proceed with the operation!"

"When you have promised me," I insisted.

"I cannot promise the impossible—I cannot obtain Xaxa. Ask me something else. I am not unwilling to grant any reasonable request."

"That is all I wish—just that; but I do not insist that you obtain the body. If I bring Xaxa here will you make the transfer?"

"It would mean war between Toonol and Phundahl," he fumed.

"That does not interest me," I said. "Quick! Reach a decision. In five tals I shall press this button. If you promise what I ask, you shall be restored with a new and beautiful body; if you refuse you shall lie here in the semblance of death for ever."

"I promise," he said slowly, "that when you bring the body of Xaxa to me I will transfer to that body any brain that you select from among my subjects."

"Good!" I exclaimed, and pressed the button.

Chapter 5

Danger

Ras Thavas awakened from the anaesthetic a new and gorgeous creature—a youth of such wondrous beauty that he seemed of heavenly rather than worldly origin; but in that beautiful head was the hard, cold, thousand-year-old brain of the master surgeon. As he opened his eyes he looked upon me coldly.

"You have done well," he said.

"What I have done, I have done for friendship—perhaps for love," I said, "so you can thank the sentimentalism you decry for the success of the transfer."

He made no reply.

"And now," I continued, "I shall look to you for the fulfilment of the promise you have made me."

"When you bring Xaxa's body I shall transfer to it the brain of any of my subjects you may select," he said, "but were I you, I would not risk my life in such an impossible venture—you cannot succeed. Select another body—there are many beautiful ones—and I will give it the brain of 4296-E-2631-H."

"None other than the body now owned by the Jeddara Xaxa will fulfil your promise to me," I said.

He shrugged and there was a cold smile upon his handsome lips. "Very well," he said, "fetch Xaxa. When do you start?"

"I am not yet ready. I will let you know when I am."

"Good and now begone—but wait! First go to the office and see what cases await us and if there be any that do not require my personal attention, and they fall within your skill and knowledge, attend to them yourself."

As I left him I noticed a crafty smile of satisfaction upon his lips. What had aroused that? I did not like it and as I walked away I tried to conjure what could possibly have passed through that wondrous brain to call forth at that particular instant so unpleasant a smile. As I passed through the doorway and into the corridor beyond I heard him summon his personal slave and body servant, Yamdor, a huge fellow whose loyalty he kept through the bestowal of lavish gifts and countless favours. So great was the fellow's power that all feared him, as a word to the master from the lips of Yamdor might easily send any of the numerous slaves or attendants to an ersite slab for eternity. It was rumoured that he was the result of an unnatural experiment which had combined the brain of a woman with the body of a man, and there was much in his actions and mannerisms to justify this general belief. His touch, when he worked about his master, was soft and light, his movements graceful, his ways gentle, but his mind was jealous, vindictive and unforgiving.

I believe that he did not like me, through jealousy of the authority I had attained in the establishment of Ras Thavas; for there was no questioning the fact that I was a lieutenant, while he was but a slave; yet he always accorded me the utmost respect. He was, however, merely a minor cog in the machinery of the great institution presided over by the sovereign mind of Ras Thavas, and as such I had given him little consideration; nor did I now as I bent my steps towards the office.

I had gone but a short distance when I recalled a matter of importance upon which it was necessary for me to obtain instructions from Ras Thavas immediately; and so I wheeled about and retraced my way towards his apartments, through the open doorway of which, as I approached, I heard the new voice of the master surgeon. Ras Thavas had always spoken in rather loud tones, whether as a vocal reflection of his naturally domineering and authoritative character, or because of his deafness, I do not know; and now, with the fresh young vocal cords of his new body, his words rang out clearly and distinctly in the corridor leading to his room.

"You will, therefore, Yamdor," he was saying, "go at once and, selecting two slaves in whose silence and discretion you may trust, take the subject from the apartments of Vad Varo and destroy it—let no vestige of body or brain remain. Immediately after, you will bring the two slaves to the laboratory F-30-L, permitting them to speak to no one, and I will consign them to silence and forgetfulness for eternity. Vad Varo will discover the absence of the subject and report the matter to me."

"During my investigation you will confess that you aided 4296-E-2631-H to escape, but that you have no idea where it intended going. I will sentence you to death as punishment, but at last explaining how urgently I need your services and upon your solemn promise never to transgress again, I will defer punishment for the term of your continued good behaviour. Do you thoroughly understand the entire plan?"

"Yes, master," replied Yamdor.

"Then depart at once and select the slaves who are to assist you."

Quickly and silently I sped along the corridor until the first intersection permitted me to place myself out of sight of anyone coming from Ras Thavas' apartment; then I went directly to the chamber occupied by Valla Dia. Unlocking the door I threw it open and beckoned her to come out. "Quick! Valla Dia!" I cried. "No time is to be lost. In attempting to save you I have but brought destruction upon you. First we must find a hiding place for you, and that at once—afterwards we can plan for the future."

The place that first occurred to me as affording adequate concealment was the half forgotten vaults in the pits beneath the laboratories, and towards these I hastened Valla Dia. As we proceeded I narrated all that had transpired, nor did she once reproach me; but, instead, expressed naught but gratitude for what she was pleased to designate as my unselfish friendship. That it had miscarried, she assured me, was no reflection upon me and she insisted that she would rather die in the knowledge that she possessed one such friend than to live on indefinitely, friendless.

We came at last to the chamber I sought—vault L-42-X, in building 4-J-21, where reposed the bodies of the ape and the man, each of which possessed half the brain of the other. Here I was forced to leave Valla Dia for the time, that I might hasten to the office and perform the duties imposed upon me by Ras Thavas, lest his suspicions be aroused when Yamdor reported that he had found her apartment vacant.

I reached the office without it being discovered by anyone who might report the fact to Ras Thavas that I had been a long time coming from his apartment. To my relief, I found there were no cases. Without appearing in any undue haste, I nevertheless soon found an excuse to depart and at once made my way towards my own quarters, moving in a leisurely and unconcerned manner and humming, as was my wont (a habit which greatly irritated Ras Thavas), snatches from some song that had been popular at the time that I quit Earth. In this instance it was "Oh, Frenchy."

I was thus engaged when I met Yamdor moving hurriedly along

the corridor leading from my apartment, in company with two male slaves. I greeted him pleasantly, as was my custom, and he returned my greeting; but there was an expression of fear and suspicion in his eyes. I went at once to my quarters, opened the door leading to the chamber formerly occupied by Valla Dia and then hastened immediately to the apartment of Ras Thavas, where I found him conversing with Yamdor. I rushed in apparently breathless and simulating great excitement.

"Ras Thavas," I demanded, "what have you done with 4296-E-2631-H? She has disappeared; her apartment is empty; and as I was approaching it I met Yamdor and two other slaves coming from that direction." I turned then upon Yamdor and pointed an accusing finger at him. "Yamdor!" I cried. "What have you done with this woman?"

Both Ras Thavas and Yamdor seemed genuinely puzzled and I congratulated myself that I had thus readily thrown them off the track. The master surgeon declared that he would make an immediate investigation; and he at once ordered a thorough search of the ground and of the island outside the enclosure. Yamdor denied any knowledge of the woman and I, at least, was aware of the sincerity of his protestations, but not so Ras Thavas. I could see a hint of suspicion in his eyes as he questioned his body servant; but evidently he could conjure no motive for any such treasonable action on the part of Yamdor as would have been represented by the abduction of the woman and the consequent gross disobedience of orders.

Ras Thavas' investigation revealed nothing. I think as it progressed that he became gradually more and more imbued with a growing suspicion that I might know more about the disappearance of Valla Dia than my attitude indicated, for I presently became aware of a delicately concealed espionage. Up to this time I had been able to smuggle food to Valla Dia every night, after Ras Thavas had retired to his quarters. Then, on one occasion, I suddenly became subconsciously aware that I was being followed, and instead of going to the vaults I went to the office, where I added some observations to my report upon a case I had handled that day. Returning to my room I hummed a few bars from "Over There," that the suggestion of my unconcern might be accentuated. From the moment that I quit my quarters until I returned to them I was sure that eyes had been watching my every move. What was I to do? Valla Dia must have food, without it she would die; and were I to be followed to her hiding place while taking it to her, she would die; Ras Thavas would see to that.

Half the night I lay awake, racking my brains for some solution to the problem.

There seemed only one way—I must elude the spies. If I could do this but one single time I could carry out the balance of a plan that had occurred to me, and which was, I thought, the only one feasible that might eventually lead to the resurrection of Valla Dia in her own body. The way was long, the risks great; but I was young, in love and utterly reckless of consequences in so far as they concerned me; it was Valla Dia's happiness alone that I could not risk too greatly, other than under dire stress. Well, the stress existed and I must risk that even as I risked my life.

My plan was formulated and I lay awake upon my sleeping silks and furs in the darkness of my room, awaiting the time when I might put it into execution. My window, which was upon the third floor, overlooked the walled enclosure, upon the scarlet sward of which I had made my first bow to Barsoom. Across the open casement I had watched Cluros, the farther moon, take his slow deliberate way.

He had already set. Behind him, Thuria, his elusive mistress, fled through the heavens. In five xats (about 15 minutes) she would set; and then for about three and three quarters Earth hours the heavens would be dark, except for the stars.

In the corridor, perhaps, lurked those watchful eyes. I prayed God that they might not be elsewhere as Thuria sank at last beneath the horizon and I swung to my window ledge, in my hand a long rope fabricated from braided strips torn from my sleeping silks while I had awaited the setting of the moons. One end I had fastened to a heavy sorapus bench which I had drawn close to the window. I dropped the free end of the rope and started my descent. My Earthly muscles, untried in such endeavours, I had not trusted to the task of carrying me to my window ledge in a single leap, when I should be returning. I felt that they would, but I did not know; and too much depended upon the success of my venture to risk any unnecessary chance of failure. And so I had prepared the rope.

Whether I was being observed I did not know. I must go on as though none were spying upon me. In less then four hours Thuria would return (just before the sudden Barsoomian dawn) and in the interval I must reach Valla Dia, persuade her of the necessity of my plan and carry out its details, returning to my chamber before Thuria could disclose me to any accidental observer. I carried my weapons with me and in my heart was unbending determination to slay whoever might cross my path and recognize me during the course of my errand, however innocent of evil intent against me he might be.

The night was quiet except for the usual distant sounds that I had heard ever since I had been here—sounds that I had interpreted as the cries of savage beasts. Once I had asked Ras Thavas about them, but he had been in ill humour and had ignored my question. I reached the ground quickly and without hesitation moved directly to the nearest entrance of the building, having previously searched out and determined upon the route I would follow to the vault. No one was visible and I was confident, when at last I reached the doorway, that I had come through undetected. Valla Dia was so happy to see me again that it almost brought the tears to my eyes.

"I thought that something had happened to you," she cried, "for I knew that you would not remain away so long of your own volition."

I told her of my conviction that I was being watched and that it would not be possible for me longer to bring food to her without incurring almost certain detection, which would spell immediate death for her.

"There is a single alternative," I said, "and that I dread even to suggest and would not were there any other way. You must be securely hidden for a long time, until Ras Thavas' suspicions have been allayed; for as long as he has me watched I cannot possibly carry out the plans I have formulated for your eventual release, the restoration of your own body and your return to Duhor."

"Your will shall be my law, Vad Varo."

I shook my head. "It will be harder for you than you imagine."

"What is the way?" she asked.

I pointed, to the ersite topped table. "You must pass again though that ordeal that I may hide you away in this vault until the time is ripe for the carrying out of my plans. Can you endure it?"

She smiled. "Why not?" she asked. "It is only sleep—if it lasts for ever I shall be no wiser."

I was surprised that she did not shrink from the idea, but I was very glad since I knew that it was the only way that we had a chance for success. Without my help she disposed herself upon the ersite slab.

"I am ready, Vad Varo," she said, bravely; "but first promise me that you will take no risks in this mad venture. You cannot succeed. When I close my eyes I know that it will be for the last time if my resurrection depends upon the successful outcome of the maddest venture that ever man conceived; yet I am happy, because I know that it is inspired by the greatest friendship with which any mortal woman has ever been blessed."

As she talked I had been adjusting the tubes and now I stood beside her with my finger upon the starting button of the motor.

"Good-bye, Vad Varo," she whispered.

"Not good-bye, Valla Dia, but only a sweet sleep for what to you will be the briefest instant. You will seem but to close your eyes and open them again. As you see me now, I shall be standing here beside you as though I never had departed from you. As I am the last that you look upon to-night before you close your eyes, so shall I be the first that you shall look upon as you open them on that new and beautiful morning; but you shall not again look forth through the eyes of Xaxa, but from the limpid depths of your own beautiful orbs."

She smiled and shook her head. Two tears formed beneath her lids. I pressed her hand in mine and touched the button.

Chapter 6

Suspicions

In so far as I could know I reached my apartment without detection. Hiding my rope where I was sure it would not be discovered, I sought my sleeping silks and furs and was soon asleep.

The following morning as I emerged from my quarters I caught a fleeting glimpse of a figure in a nearby corridor and from then on for a long time I had further evidence that Ras Thavas suspicioned me. I went at once to his quarters, as had been my habit. He seemed restless, but he gave me no hint that he held any assurance that I had been responsible for the disappearance of Valla Dia, and I think that he was far from positive of it. It was simply that his judgment pointed to the fact that I was the only person who might have any reason for interfering in any way with this particular subject, and he was having me watched to either prove or disprove the truth of his reasonable suspicions. His restlessness he explained to me himself.

"I have often studied the reaction of others who have undergone brain transference," he said, "and so I am not wholly surprised at my own. Not only has my brain energy been stimulated, resulting in an increased production of nervous energy, but I also feel the effects of the young tissue and youthful blood of my new body. They are affecting my consciousness in a way that my experiment had vaguely indicated, but which I now see must be actually experienced to be fully understood. My thoughts, my inclinations, even my ambitions have been changed, or at least coloured, by the transfer. It will take some time for me to find myself."

Though uninterested, I listened politely until he was through and then I changed the subject "Have you located the missing woman?" I asked.

He shook his head, negatively.

"You must appreciate, Ras Thavas," I said, "that I fully realize that you must have known that the removal or destruction of that woman would entirely frustrate my entire plan. You are master here. Nothing that passes is without your knowledge."

"You mean that I am responsible for the disappearance of the woman?" he demanded.

"Certainly. It is obvious. I demand that she be restored."

He lost his temper. "Who are you to demand?" he shouted. "You are naught but a slave. Cease your impudence or I shall erase you—erase you. It will be as though you never had existed."

I laughed in his face. "Anger is the most futile attribute of the sentimentalist," I reminded him. "You will not erase me, for I alone stand between you and mortality."

"I can train another," he parried.

"But you could not trust him," I pointed out.

"But you bargained with me for my life when you had me in your power," he cried.

"For nothing that it would have harmed you to have granted willingly. I did not ask anything for myself. Be that as it may, you will trust me again. You will trust, for no other reason than that you will be forced to trust me. So why not win my gratitude and my loyalty by returning the woman to me and carrying out in spirit as well as in fact the terms of our agreement?"

He turned and looked steadily at me. "Vad Varo," he said, "I give you the word of honour of a Barsoomian noble that I know absolutely nothing concerning the whereabouts of 4296-E-2631-H."

"Perhaps Yamdor does," I persisted.

"Nor Yamdor. Of my knowledge no person in any way connected with me knows what became of it. I have spoken the truth."

Well, the conversation was not as profitless as it might appear, for I was sure that it had almost convinced Ras Thavas that I was equally as ignorant of the fate of Valla Dia as was he. That it had not wholly convinced him was evidenced by the fact that the espionage continued for a long time, a fact which determined me to use Ras Thavas' own methods in my own defence. I had had allotted to me a number of slaves, and these I had won over by kindness and understanding until I knew that I had the full measure of their loyalty. They had no reason to love Ras Thavas and every reason to hate him; on the other hand they had no reason to hate me, and I saw to it that they had every reason to love me.

The result was that I had no difficulty in enlisting the services of a couple of them to spy upon Ras Thavas' spies, with the result that I was soon apprised that my suspicions were well founded—I was being constantly watched every minute that I was out of my apartments, but the spying did not come beyond my outer chamber walls. That was why I had been successful in reaching the vault in the manner that I had, the spies having assumed that I would leave my chamber only by its natural exit, had been content to guard that and permit my windows to go unwatched.

I think it was about two of our months that the spying continued and then my men reported that it seemed to have ceased entirely. All that time I was fretting at the delay, for I wanted to be about my plans which would have been absolutely impossible for me to carry out if I were being watched. I had spent the interval in studying the geography of the north-eastern Barsoomian hemisphere where my activities were to be carried on, and also in scanning a great number of case histories and inspecting the subjects to which they referred; but at last, with the removal of the spies, it began to look as though I might soon commence to put my plans in active operation.

Ras Thavas had for some time permitted me considerable freedom in independent investigation and experiment, and this I determined to take advantage of in every possible way that might forward my plans for the resurrection of Valla Dia. My study of the histories of many of the cases had been with the possibility in mind of discovering subjects that might be of assistance to me in my venture. Among those that had occupied my careful attention were, quite naturally, the cases with which I had been most familiar, namely: 378-J-493811-P, the red-man from whose vicious attack I had saved Ras Thavas upon the day of my advent upon Mars; and he whose brain had been divided with an ape.

The former, 378-J-493811-P, had been a native of Phundahl—a young warrior attached to the court of Xaxa, Jeddara of Phundahl—and a victim of assassination. His body had been purchased by a Phundahlian noble for the purpose, as Ras Thavas had narrated, of winning the favour of a young beauty. I felt that I might possibly enlist his services, but that would depend upon the extent of his loyalty towards Xaxa, which I could only determine by reviving and questioning him.

He whose brain had been divided with an ape had originated in Ptarth, which lay at a considerable distance to the west of Phundahl and a little south and about an equal distance from Duhor, which lay north and a little west of it. An inhabitant of Ptarth, I reasoned, would know much of the entire country included in the triangle formed by

Phundahl, Ptarth and Duhor; the strength and ferocity of the great ape would prove of value in crossing beast infested wastes; and I felt that I could hold forth sufficient promise to the human half of the great beast's brain, which really now dominated the creature, to win its support and loyalty. The third subject that I had tentatively selected had been a notorious Toonolian assassin, whose audacity, fearlessness and swordsmanship had won for him a reputation that had spread far beyond the boundaries of his country.

Ras Thavas, himself a Toonolian, had given me something of the history of this man whose grim calling is not without honour upon Barsoom, and which Gor Hajus had raised still higher in the esteem of his countrymen through the fact that he never struck down a woman or a good man and that he never struck from behind.

His killings were always the results of fair fights in which the victim had every opportunity to defend himself and slay his attacker; and he was famous for his loyalty to his friends. In fact this very loyalty had been a contributing factor in his downfall which had brought him to one of Ras Thavas' ersite slabs some years since, for he had earned the enmity of Vobis Kan, Jeddak of Toonol, through his refusal to assassinate a man who once had befriended Gor Hajus in some slight degree; following which Vobis Kan conceived the suspicion that Gor Hajus had him marked for slaying. The result was inevitable: Gor Hajus was arrested and condemned to death; immediately following the execution of the sentence an agent of Ras Thavas had purchased the body.

These three, then, I had chosen to be my partners in my great adventure. It is true that I had not discussed the matter with any one of them, but my judgment assured me that I would have no difficulty in enlisting their services and loyalty in return for their total resurrection.

My first task lay in renewing the organs of 378-J-493811-P and of Gor Hajus which had been injured by the wounds that had laid them low; the former requiring a new lung and the latter a new heart, his executioner having run him through with a short-sword. I hesitated to ask Ras Thavas' permission to experiment on these subjects for fear of the possibility of arousing his suspicions, in which event he would probably have them destroyed, and so I was forced to accomplish my designs by subterfuge and stealth. To this end I made it a practice for weeks to carry my regular laboratory work far into the night, often requiring the services of various assistants that all might become accustomed to the sight of me at work at unusual hours. In my selection of these assistants I made it a point to choose two of the very spies that Ras Thavas had set to watching me. While it was true that they were no longer employed in this particular service, I had hopes that they would carry word of my activities to their master; and I was careful to see that they received from me the proper suggestions that would mould their report in language far from harmful to me. By the merest suggestion I carried to them the idea that I worked thus late purely for the love of the work itself and the tremendous interest in it that Ras Thavas had awakened within my mind. Some nights I worked with assistants and as often I did not, but always I was careful to assure myself that the following morning those in the office were made aware that I had laboured far into the preceding night.

This groundwork carefully prepared, I had comparatively little fear of the results of actual discovery when I set to work upon the warrior of Phundahl and the assassin of Toonol. I chose the former first. His lung was badly injured where my blade had passed through it, but from the laboratory where were kept fractional bodies I brought a perfect lung, with which I replaced the one that I had ruined. The work occupied but half the night. So anxious was I to complete my task that I immediately opened up the breast of Gor Hajus, for whom I had selected an unusually strong and powerful heart and by working rapidly I succeeded in completing the transference before dawn. Having known the nature of the wounds that had dispatched these two men, I had spent weeks in performing similar operations that I might perfect myself especially in this work; and having encountered no unusual pathological conditions in either subject, the work had progressed smoothly and with great rapidity. I had completed what I had feared would be the most difficult part of my task and now, having removed as far as possible all signs of the operation except the therapeutic tape which closed the incisions, I returned to my quarters for a few minutes of much needed rest, praying that Ras Thavas would not by any chance examine either of the subjects upon which I had been working, although I had fortified myself against such a contingency by entering full details of the operation upon the history card of each subject that, in the event of discovery, any suspicion of ulterior motives upon my part might be allayed by my play of open frankness.

I arose at the usual time and went at once to Ras Thavas' apartment, where I was met with a bombshell that nearly wrecked my composure. He eyed me closely for a long minute before he spoke.

"You worked late last night, Vad Varo," he said.

"I often do," I replied, lightly; but my heart was heavy as a stone.

"And what might it have been that so occupied your interest?" he inquired.

I felt as a mouse with which the cat is playing. "I have been doing quite a little lung and heart transference of late," I replied, "and I became so engrossed with my work that I did not note the passage of time."

"I have known that you worked late at night. Do you think it wise?"

At that moment I felt that it had been very unwise, yet I assured him to the contrary.

"I was restless," he said. "I could not sleep and so I went to your quarters after midnight, but you were not there. I wanted someone with whom to talk, but your slaves knew only that you were not there—where you were they did not know—so I set out to search for you." My heart went into my sandals. "I guessed that you were in one of the laboratories, but though I visited several I did not find you." My heart arose with the lightness of a feather. "Since my own transference I have been cursed with restlessness and sleeplessness, so that I could almost wish for the return of my old corpse—the youth of my body harmonizes not with the antiquity of my brain. It is filled with latent urges and desires that comport illy with the serious subject matter of my mind."

"What your body needs," I said, "is exercise. It is young, strong, virile. Work it hard and it will let your brain rest at night."

"I know that you are right," he replied. "I have reached that same conclusion myself. In fact, not finding you, I walked in the gardens for an hour or more before returning to my quarters, and then I slept soundly. I shall walk every night when I cannot sleep, or I shall go into the laboratories and work as do you."

This news was most disquieting. Now I could never be sure but that Ras Thavas was wandering about at night and I had one more very important night's work to do, perhaps two. The only way that I could be sure of him was to be with him.

"Send for me when you are restless," I said, "and I will walk and work with you. You should not go about thus at night alone."

"Very well," he said, "I may do that occasionally."

I hoped that he would do it always, for then I would know that when he failed to send for me he was safe in his own quarters. Yet I saw that I must henceforth face the menace of detection; and knowing this I determined to hasten the completion of my plans and to risk everything on a single bold stroke.

That night I had no opportunity to put it into action as Ras Thavas sent for me early and informed me that we would walk in the gardens until he was tired. Now, as I needed a full night for what I had in mind and as Ras Thavas walked until midnight, I was compelled to forego everything for that evening, but the following morning I persuaded him to walk early on the pretext that I should like to go beyond the enclosure and see something of Barsoom beside the inside of his laboratories and his gardens. I had little confidence that he would grant my request, yet he did so. I am sure he never would have done it had he possessed his old body; but thus greatly had young blood changed Ras Thavas.

I had never been beyond the buildings, nor had I seen beyond, since there were no windows in the outside walls of any of the structures and upon the garden side the trees had grown to such a height that they obstructed all view beyond them. For a time we walked in another garden just inside the outer wall, and then I asked Ras Thavas if I might go even beyond this.

"No," he said. "It would not be safe."

"And why not?" I asked.

"I will show you and at the same time give you a much broader view of the outside world than you could obtain by merely passing through the gate. Come, follow me!" He led me immediately to a lofty tower that rose at the corner of the largest building of the group that comprised his vast establishment. Within was a circular runway which led not only upward, but down as well. This we ascended, passing openings at each floor, until we came at last out upon its lofty summit.

About me spread the first Barsoomian landscape of any extent upon which my eyes had yet rested during the long months that I had spent upon the Red Planet. For almost an Earthly year I had been immured within the grim walls of Ras Thavas' bloody laboratory, until, such creatures of habit are we, the weird life there had grown to seem quite natural and ordinary; but with this first glimpse of open country there surged up within me an urge for freedom, for space, for room to move about, such as I knew would not be long denied.

Directly beneath lay an irregular patch of rocky land elevated perhaps a dozen feet or more above the general level of the immediately surrounding country. Its extent was, at a rough guess, a hundred acres. Upon this stood the buildings and grounds, which were enclosed in a high wall. The tower upon which we stood was situated at about the centre of the total area enclosed. Beyond the outer wall was a strip of rocky ground on which grew a sparse forest of fair sized trees interspersed with patches of a jungle growth, and beyond all, what appeared to be an oozy marsh through which were narrow water courses connecting occasional open water—little lakes, the largest of which could have comprised scarce two acres. This landscape extended as far as the eye could reach, broken by occasional islands similar to that upon which we were and at a short distance by the skyline of a large city, whose towers and domes and minarets glistened and sparkled in the sun as though plated with shining metals and picked out with precious gems.

This, I knew, must be Toonol and all about us the Great Toonolian Marshes which extend nearly eighteen hundred Earth miles east and west and in some places have a width of three hundred miles. Little is known about them in other portions of Barsoom as they are frequented by fierce beasts, afford no landing places for fliers and are commanded by Phundahl at their western end and Toonol at the east, inhospitable kingdoms that invite no intercourse with the outside world and maintain their independence alone by their inaccessibility and savage aloofness.

As my eyes returned to the island at our feet I saw a huge form emerge from one of the nearby patches of jungle a short distance beyond the outer wall. It was followed by a second and a third. Ras Thavas saw that the creatures had attracted my notice.

"There," he said, pointing to them, "are three of a number of similar reasons why it would not have been safe for us to venture outside the enclosure."

They were great white apes of Barsoom, creatures so savage that even that fierce Barsoomian lion, the banth, hesitates to cross their path.

"They serve two purposes," explained Ras Thavas. "They discourage those who might otherwise creep upon me by night from the city of Toonol, where I am not without many good enemies, and they prevent desertion upon the part of my slaves and assistants."

"But how do your clients reach you?" I asked. "How are your supplies brought in?"

He tuned and pointed down toward the highest portion of the irregular roof of the building below us. Built upon it was a large, shed-like structure. "There," he said, "I keep three small ships. One of them goes every day to Toonol."

I was overcome with eagerness to know more about these ships, in which I thought I saw a much needed means of escape from the island; but I dared not question him for fear of arousing his suspicions.

As we turned to descend the tower runway I expressed interest in the structure which gave evidence of being far older than any of the surrounding buildings.

"This tower," said Ras Thavas, "was built some twenty-three thousand years ago by an ancestor of mine who was driven from Toonol by the reigning Jeddak of the time. Here, and upon other islands, he gathered a considerable following, dominated the surrounding marshes and defended himself successfully for hundreds of years. While my family has been permitted to return to Toonol since, this has been their home; to which, one by one, have been added the various buildings which you see about the tower, each floor of which connects with the adjacent building from the roof to the lowest pits beneath the ground."

This information also interested me greatly since I thought that I saw where it too might have considerable bearing upon my plan of escape, and so, as we descended the runway, I encouraged Ras Thavas to discourse upon the construction of the tower, its relation to the other buildings and especially its accessibility from the pits. We walked again in the outer garden and by the time we returned to Ras Thavas' quarters it was almost dark and the master surgeon was considerably fatigued.

"I feel that I shall sleep well to-night," he said as I left him.

"I hope so, Ras Thavas," I replied.

Chapter 7

Escape

It was usually about three hours after the evening meal, which was served immediately after dark, that the establishment quieted down definitely for the night. While I should have preferred waiting longer before undertaking that which I had in mind, I could not safely do so, since there was much to be accomplished before dawn. So it was that with the first indications that the occupants of the building in which my work was to be performed had retired for the night, I left my quarters and went directly to the laboratory, where, fortunately for my plans, the bodies of Gor Hajus, the assassin of Toonol, and 378-J-493811-P both reposed. It was the work of a few minutes to carry them to adjoining tables, where I quickly strapped them securely against the possibility that one or both of them might not be willing to agree to the proposition I was about to make them, and thus force me to anaesthetize them again. At last the incisions were made, the tubes attached and the motors started. 378-J-493811-P, whom I shall hereafter call by his own name, Dar Tarus, was the first to open his eyes; but he had not regained full consciousness when Gor Hajus showed signs of life.

I waited until both appeared quite restored. Dar Tarus was eyeing me with growing recognition that brought a most venomous expression of hatred to his countenance. Gor Hajus was frankly puzzled. The last he remembered was the scene in the death chamber at the instant that his executioner had run a sword through his heart. It was I who broke the silence.

"In the first place" I said, "let me tell you where you are, if you do not already know."

"I know well enough where I am," growled Dar Tarus.

"Ah!" exclaimed Gor Hajus, whose eyes had been roaming about the chamber. "I can guess where I am. What Toonolian has not heard of Ras Thavas? So they sold my corpse to the old butcher did they? And what now? Did I just arrive?"

"You have been here six years," I told him, "and you may stay here for ever unless we three can reach an agreement within the next few minutes, and that goes for you too, Dar Tarus."

"Six years!" mused Gor Hajus. "Well, out with it, man. What do you want? If it is to slay Ras Thavas, no! He has saved me from utter destruction; but name me some other, preferably Vobis Kan, Jeddak of Toonol. Find me a blade and I will slay a hundred to regain life."

"I seek the life of none unless he stands in the way of the fulfilment of my desire in this matter that I have in hand. Listen! Ras Thavas had here a beautiful Duhorian girl. He sold her body to Xaxa, Jeddara of Phundahl, transplanting the girl's brain to the wrinkled and hideous body of the Jeddara. It is my intention to regain the body, restore it to its own brain and return the girl to Duhor."

Gor Hajus grinned. "You have a large contract on your hands," he said, "but I can see that you are a man after my own heart and I am with you. It will give freedom and fighting, and all that I ask is a chance for one thrust at Vobis Kan."

"I promise you life," I replied; "but with the understanding that you serve me faithfully and none other, undertaking no business of your own, until mine has been carried to a successful conclusion."

"That means that I shall have to serve you for life," he replied, "for the thing you have undertaken you can never accomplish; but that is better than lying here on a cold ersite slab waiting for old Ras Thavas to come along and carve out my gizzard. I am yours! Let me up, that I may feel a good pair of legs under me again."

"And you?" I asked, turning to Dar Tarus as I released the bonds that held Gor Hajus. For the first time I now noticed that the ugly expression that I had first noted upon the face of Dar Tarus had given place to one of eagerness.

"Strike off my bonds!" he cried. "I will follow you to the ends of Barsoom and the way leads thus far to the fulfilment of your design; but it will not. It will lead to Phundahl and to the chamber of the wicked Xaxa, where, by the generosity of my ancestors, I may be given the opportunity to avenge the hideous wrong the creature did me. You could not have chosen one better fitted for your mission than Dar Tarus, one time soldier of the Jeddara's Guard, whom she had slain that in my former body one of her rotten nobles might woo the girl I loved."

A moment later the two men stood at my side, and without more delay I led them towards the runway that descended to the path beneath the building. As we went, I described to them the creature I had chosen to be the fourth member of our strange party. Gor Hajus questioned the wisdom of my choice, saying that the ape would attract too much attention to us. Dar Tarus, however, behaved that it might be helpful in many respects, since it was possible that we might be compelled to spend some time among the islands of the marshes which were often infested with these creatures; while, once in Phundahl, the ape might readily be used in the furtherance of our plans and would cause no considerable comment in a city where many of these beasts are held in captivity and often are seen performing for the edification of street crowds. We went at once to the vault where the ape lay and where I had concealed the anaesthetized body of Valla Dia. Here I revived the great anthropoid and to my great relief found that the human half of its brain still was dominant. Briefly I explained my plan as I had to the other two and won the hearty promise of his support upon my engaging to restore his brain to its rightful place upon the completion of our venture.

First we must get off the island, and I outlined two plans I had in mind. One was to steal one of Ras Thavas' three fliers and set out directly for Phundahl, and the other, in the event that the first did not seem feasible, was to secrete ourselves aboard one of them on the chance that we might either overpower the crew and take over the ship after we had left the island, or escape undetected upon its arrival in Toonol. Dar Tarus liked the first plan; the ape, whom we now called by the name belonging to the human half of his brain, Hovan Du, preferred the first alternative of the second plan; and Gor Hajus the second alternative.

Dar Tarus explained that as our principal objective was Phundahl, the quicker we got there the better. Hovan Du argued that by seizing the ship after it had left the island we would have longer time in which to make our escape before the ship was missed and pursuit instituted, than by seizing it now in the full knowledge that its absence would be discovered within a few hours. Gor Hajus thought that it would be better if we could come into Toonol secretly and there, through one of his friends, secure arms and a flier of our own. It would never do, he insisted, to attempt to go far without arms for himself and Dar Tarus, nor could we hope to reach Phundahl without being overhauled by pursuers; for we must plan on the hypothesis that Ras Thavas would immediately discover my absence; that he would at once investigate; that he would find Dar Tarus and Gor Hajus missing and thereupon lose no time in advising Vobis Kan, Jeddak of Toonol, that Gor Hajus the assassin was at large, whereupon the Jeddak's best ships would be sent in pursuit.

Gor Hajus' reasoning was sound and coupled with my recollection that Ras Thavas had told me that his three ships were slow, I could readily foresee that our liberty would be of short duration were we to steal one of the old surgeon's fliers.

As we discussed the matter we had made our way through the Pits and I had found the exit to the tower. Silently we passed upward along the runway and out upon the roof. Both moons were winging low through the heavens and the scene was almost as light as day. If anyone was about discovery was certain. We hastened towards the hangar and were soon within it where, for a moment at least, I breathed far more easily than I had beneath those two brilliant moons upon the exposed roof.

The fliers were peculiar looking contrivances, low, squat, with rounded bows and stems and covered decks, their every line proclaiming them as cargo carriers built for anything but speed. One was much smaller than the other two and a second was evidently undergoing repairs. The third I entered and examined carefully. Gor Hajus was with me and pointed out several places where we might hide with little likelihood of discovery unless it were suspected that we might be aboard, and that of course constituted a very real danger; so much so that I had about decided to risk all aboard the small flier, which Gor Hajus assured me would be the fastest of the three, when Dar Tarus stuck his head into the ship and motioned me to come quickly.

"There is someone about," he said when I reached his side.

"Where?" I demanded.

"Come," he said, and led me to the rear of the hangar, which was flush with the wall of the building upon which it stood, and pointed through one of the windows into the inner garden where, to my consternation, I saw Ras Thavas walking slowly to and fro. For an instant I was sick with despair, for I knew that no ship could leave that roof unseen while anyone was abroad in the garden beneath, and Ras Thavas least of all people in the world; but suddenly a great light dawned upon me. I called the three close to me and explained my plan.

Instantly they grasped the possibilities in it and a moment later we had run the small flier out upon the roof and turned her nose toward the east, away from Toonol. Then Gor Hajus entered her, set the various controls as we had decided, opened the throttle, slipped back to the roof. The four of us hastened into the hangar and ran to the rear window where we saw the ship moving slowly and gracefully out over the garden and the head of Ras Thavas, whose ears must instantly have caught the faint purring of the motor, for he was looking up by the time we reached the window.

Instantly he hailed the ship and stepping back from the window that he might not see me I answered: "Good-bye, Ras Thavas! It is I, Vad Varo, going out into a strange world to see what it is like. I shall return. The spirits of your ancestors be with you until then."

That was a phrase I had picked up from reading in Ras Thavas' library and I was quite proud of it.

"Come back at once," he shouted up in reply, "or you will be with the spirits of your own ancestors before another day is done."

I made no reply. The ship was now at such a distance that I feared my voice might no longer seem to come from it and that we should be discovered. Without more delay we concealed ourselves aboard one of the remaining fliers, that upon which no work was being done, and there commenced as long and tiresome a period of waiting as I can recall ever having passed through.

I had at last given up any hope of the ship's being flown that day when I heard voices in the hangar, and presently the sound of footsteps aboard the flier. A moment later a few commands were given and almost immediately the ship moved slowly out into the open.

The four of us were crowded into a small compartment built into a tiny space between the forward and aft starboard buoyancy tanks. It was very dark and poorly ventilated, having evidently been designed as a storage closet to utilize otherwise waste space. We dared not converse for fear of attracting attention to our presence, and for the same reason we moved about as little as possible, since we had no means of knowing but that some member of the crew might be just beyond the thin door that separated us from the main cabin of the ship.

Altogether we were most uncomfortable; but the distance to Toonol is not so great but that we might hope that our situation would soon be changed—at least if Toonol was to be the destination of the ship. Of this we soon had cheering hope. We had been out but a short time when, faintly, we heard a hail and then the motors were immediately shut down and the ship stopped.

"What ship?" we heard a voice demand, and from aboard our own came the reply: "The Vosar, Tower of Thavas for Toonol." We heard a scraping as the other ship touched ours.

"We are coming aboard to search you in the name of Vobis Kan, Jeddak of Toonol. Make way!" shouted one from the other ship. Our cheer had been of short duration. We heard the shuffling of many feet and Gor Hajus whispered in my ear.

"What shall we do?" he asked.

I slipped my short-sword into his hand. "Fight!" I replied.

"Good, Vad Varo," he replied, and then I handed him my pistol and told him to pass it on to Dar Tarus. We heard the voices again, but nearer now.

"What ho!" cried one. "It is Bal Zak himself, my old friend Bal Zak!" "None other," replied a deep voice. "And whom did you expect to find in command of the Vosar other than Bal Zak?"

"Who could know but that it might have been this Vad Varo himself, or even Gor Hajus," said the other, "and our orders are to search all ships."

"I would that they were here," replied Bal Zak, "for the reward is high. But how could they, when Ras Thavas himself with his own eyes saw them fly off in the Pinsar before dawn this day and disappear in the east?"

"Right you are, Bal Zak," agreed the other, "and it were a waste of time to search your ship. Come men! to our own!" I could feel the muscles about my heart relax with the receding footfalls of Vobis Kan's warriors as they quitted the deck of the Vosar for their own ship, and my spirits rose with the renewed purring of our own motor as Ras Thavas' flier again got under way. Gor Hajus bent his lips close to my ear.

"The spirits of our ancestors smile upon us," he whispered. "It is night and the darkness will aid in covering our escape from the ship and the landing stage."

"What makes you think it is night?" I asked.

"Vobis Kan's ship was close by when it hailed and asked our name. By daylight it could have seen what ship we were."

He was right. We had been locked in that stuffy hole since before dawn, and while I had thought that it had been for a considerable time, I also had realized that the darkness and the inaction and the nervous strain would tend to make it seem much longer than it really had been; so that I would not have been greatly surprised had we made Toonol by daylight.

The distance from the Tower of Thavas to Toonol is inconsiderable, so that shortly after Vobis Kan's ship had spoken to us we came to rest upon the landing stage at our destination. For a long time we waited, listening to the sounds of movement aboard the ship and wondering, upon my part at least, as to what the intentions of the captain might be. It was quite possible that Bal Zak might return to Thavas this same night, especially if he had come to Toonol to fetch a rich or powerful patient to the laboratories; but if he had come only for supplies he might well lie here until the morrow. This much I had learned from Gor Hajus, my own knowledge of the movements of the fliers of Ras Thavas being considerably less than nothing; for, though I had been months a lieutenant of the master surgeon, I had learned only the day before of the existence of his small fleet, it being according to the policy of Ras Thavas to tell me nothing unless the telling of it coincided with and furthered his own plans.

Questions which I asked he always answered, if he reasoned that the effects would not be harmful to his own interests, but he volunteered nothing that he did not particularly wish me to know; and the fact that there were no windows in the outside walls of the building facing towards Toonol, that I had never before the previous day been upon the roof and that I never had seen a ship sail over the inner court towards the east all tended to explain my ignorance of the fleet and its customary operations.

We waited quietly until silence fell upon the ship, betokening either that the crew had retired for the night or that they had gone down into the city. Then, after a whispered consultation with Gor Hajus, we decided to make an attempt to leave the flier. It was our purpose to seek a hiding place within the tower of the landing stage from which we might investigate possible avenues of escape into the city, either at once or upon the morrow when we might more easily mix with the crowd that Gor Hajus said would certainly be in evidence from a few hours after sunrise.

Cautiously I opened the door of our closet and looked into the main cabin beyond. It lay in darkness. Silently we filed out. The silence of the tomb lay upon the flier, but from far below arose the subdued noises of the city. So far, so good! Then, without sound, without warning, a burst of brilliant light illuminated the interior of the cabin. I felt my fingers tighten upon my sword-hilt as I glanced quickly about.

Directly opposite us, in the narrow doorway of a small cabin, stood a tall man whose handsome harness betokened the fact that he was no common warrior. In either hand he held a heavy Barsoomian pistol, into the muzzles of which we found ourselves staring.

Chapter 8

Hands Up!

In quiet tones he spoke the words of the Barsoomian equivalent of our Earthly hands up! The shadow of a grim smile touched his lips, and as he saw us hesitate to obey his commands he spoke again.

"Do as I tell you and you will be well off. Keep perfect silence. A raised voice may spell your doom; a pistol shot most assuredly."

Gor Hajus raised his hands above his head and we others followed his example.

"I am Bal Zak," announced the stranger. My heart slumped.

"Then you had better commence firing," said Gor Hajus, "for you will not take us alive and we are four to one."

"Not so fast, Gor Hajus," admonished the captain of the Vosar, until you learn what is in my mind."

"That, we already know for we heard you speak of the large reward that awaited the captor of Vad Varo and Gor Hajus," snapped the assassin of Toonol.

"Had I craved that reward so much I could have turned you over to the dwar of Vobis Kan's ship when he boarded us," said Bal Zak.

"You did not know we were aboard the Vosar," I reminded him.

"Ah, but I did."

Gor Hajus snorted his disbelief.

"How then," Bal Zak reminded us, "was I able to be ready upon this very spot when you emerged from your hiding place? Yes, I knew that you were aboard."

"But how?" demanded Dar Tarus.

"It is immaterial," replied Bal Zak, "but to satisfy your natural curiosity I will tell you that I have quarters in a small room in the Tower of Thavas, my windows overlook the roof and the hangar. My long life spent aboard fliers has made me very sensitive to every sound of a ship-motors changing their speed will awaken me in the dead of night, as quickly as will their starting or their stopping. I was awakened by the starting of the motors of the Pinsar; I saw three of you upon the roof and the fourth drop from the deck of the flier as she started and my judgment told me that the ship was being sent out unmanned for some reason of which I had no knowledge. It was too late for me to prevent the act and so I waited in silence to learn what would follow. I saw you hasten into the hangar and I heard Ras Thavas' hail and your reply, and then I saw you board the Vosar. Immediately I descended to the roof and ran noiselessly to the hangar, apprehending that you intended making away with this ship; but there was no one about the controls; and from a tiny port in the control room, through which one has a view of the main cabin, I saw you enter the closet. I was at once convinced that your only purpose was to stow away for Toonol and consequently, aside from keeping an eye upon your hiding place, I went about my business as usual."

"And you did not advise Ras Thavas?" I asked.

"I advised no one," he replied. "Years ago I learned to mind my own business, to see all, to hear all and to tell nothing unless it profited me to do so."

"But you said that the reward is high for our apprehension," Gor Hajus reminded him. "Would it not be profitable to collect it?"

"There are in the breasts of honourable men," replied Bal Zak, "forces that rise superior to the lust for gold, and while Toonolians are supposedly a people free from the withering influences of sentiment yet I for one am not totally unconscious of the demand of gratitude. Six years ago, Gor Hajus, you refused to assassinate my father, holding that he was a good man, worthy to live and one that had once befriended you slightly. To-day, through his son, you reap your reward and in some measure are repaid for the punishment that was meted out to you by Vobis Kan because of your refusal to slay the sire of Bal Zak. I have sent my crew away that none aboard the Vosar but myself might have knowledge of your presence. Tell me your plans and command me in what way I may be of further service to you."

"We wish to reach the streets, unobserved," replied Gor Hajus. "Can you but help us in that we shall not put upon your shoulders further responsibility for our escape. You have our gratitude and in Toonol, I need not remind you, the gratitude of Gor Hajus is a possession that even the Jeddak has craved."

"Your problem is complicated," said Bal Zak, after a moment of thought, "by the personnel of your party. The ape would immediately attract attention and arouse suspicion. Knowing much of Ras Thavas' experiments I realized at once this morning, after watching him with you, that he had the brain of a man; but this very fact would attract to him and to you the closer attention of the masses."

"I do not need acquaint them with the fact," growled Hovan Du. "To them I need be but a captive ape. Are such unknown in Toonol?"

"Not entirely, though they are rare," replied Bal Zak. "But there is also the white skin of Vad Varo! Ras Thavas appears to have known nothing of the presence of the ape with you; but he full well knew of Vad Varo, and your description has been spread by every means at his command. You would be recognized immediately by the first Toonolian that lays eyes upon you, and then there is Gor Hajus. He has been as dead for six years, yet I venture there is scarce a Toonolian that broke the shell prior to ten years ago who does not know the face of Gor Hajus as well as he knows that of his own mother. The Jeddak himself was not better known to the people of Toonol than Gor Hajus. That leaves but one who might possibly escape suspicion and detection in the streets of Toonol."

"If we could but obtain weapons for these others," I suggested, "we might even yet reach the house of Gor Hajus' friend."

"Fight your way through the city of Toonol?" demanded Bal Zak.

"If there is no other way we should have to," I replied.

"I admire the will," commented the commander of the Vosar, "but fear that the flesh is without sufficient strength. Wait! there is a way—perhaps. On the stage just below this there is a public depot where equilibrimotors are kept and rented. Could we find the means to obtain four of these there would be a chance, at least, for you to elude the air patrols and reach the house of Gor Hajus' friend; and I think I see a way to the accomplishment of that. The landing tower is closed for the night but there are several watchmen distributed through it at different levels. There is one at the equilibrimotor depot and, as I happen to know, he is a devotee of jetan. He would rather play jetan than attend to his duties as watchman. I often remain aboard the Vosar at night and occasionally he and I indulge in a game. I will ask him up to-night and while he is thus engaged you may go to the depot, help yourselves to equilibrimotors and pray to your ancestors that no air patrol suspects you as you cross the city towards your destination. What think you of this plan, Gor Hajus?"

"It is splendid," replied the assassin. "And you, Vad Varo?"

"If I knew what an equilibrimotor is I might be in a better position to judge the merits of the plan," I replied. "However, I am satisfied to abide by the judgment of Gor Hajus. I can assure you, Bal Zak, of our great appreciation, and as Gor Hajus has put the stamp of his approval upon your plan I can only urge you to arrange that we may put it into effect with as little delay as possible."

"Good!" exclaimed Bal Zak. "Come with me and I will conceal you until I have lured the watchman to the jetan game within my cabin. After that your fate will be in your own hands."

We followed him from the ship on to the deck of the landing stage and close under the side of the Vosar opposite that from which the watchman must approach the ship and enter it. Then, bidding us good luck, Bal Zak departed.

From the summit of the landing tower I had my first view of a Martian city.

Several hundred feet below me lay spread the broad, well-lighted avenues of Toonol, many of which were crowded with people. Here and there, in this central district, a building was raised high upon its supporting, cylindrical metal shaft; while further out, Where the residences predominated, the city took on the appearance of a colossal and grotesque forest. Among the larger palaces only an occasional suite of rooms was thus raised high above the level of the others, these being the sleeping apartments of the owners, their servants or their guests; but the smaller homes were raised in their entirety, a precaution necessitated by the constant activities of the followers of Gor Hajus' ancient profession that permitted no man to be free from the constant menace of assassination. Throughout the central district the sky was pierced by the lofty towers of several other landing stages; but, as I was later to learn, these were comparatively few in number. Toonol is in no sense a flying nation, supporting no such enormous fleets of merchant ships and vessels of war as, for example, the twin cities of Helium or the great capital of Ptarth.

A peculiar feature of the street lighting of Toonol, and in fact the same condition applies to the fighting of other Barsoomian cities I have visited, I noted for the first time that night as I waited upon the landing stage for the return of Bal Zak with the watchman. The luminosity below me seemed confined directly to the area to be lighted; there was no diffusion of light upward or beyond the limits the lamps were designed to light This was effected, I was told, by lamps designed upon principles resulting from ages of investigation of the properties of light waves and the laws governing them which permit Barsoomian scientists to confine and control light as we confine and control matter. The light waves leave the lamp, pass along a prescribed circuit and return to the lamp. There is no waste nor, strange this seemed to me, are there any dense shadows when lights are properly installed and adjusted, for the waves in passing around objects to return to the lamp, illuminate all sides of them.

The effect of this lighting from the great height of the tower was rather remarkable. The night was dark, there being no moons at that hour upon this night, and the effect was that obtained when sitting in a darkened auditorium and looking upon a brilliantly lighted stage. I was still intent upon watching the life and colour beneath when we heard Bal Zak returning. That he had been successful in his mission was apparent from the fact that he was conversing with another.

Five minutes later we crept quietly from our hiding place and descended to the stage below where lay the equilibrimotor depot. As theft is practically unknown upon Barsoom, except for purposes entirely disassociated from a desire to obtain pecuniary profit through the thing stolen, no precautions are taken against theft. We therefore found the doors of the depot open and Gor Hajus and Dar Tarus quickly selected four equilibrimotors and adjusted them upon us. They consist of a broad belt, not unlike the life belt used aboard trans-oceanic liners upon Earth; these belts are filled with the eighth Barsoomian ray, or ray of propulsion, to a sufficient degree to just about equalize the pull of gravity and thus to maintain a person in equilibrium between that force and the opposite force exerted by the eighth ray. Permanently attached to the back of the belt is a small radium motor, the controls for which are upon the front of the belt.

Rigidly attached to and projecting from each side of the upper rim of the belt is a strong, light wing with small hand levers for quickly altering its position.

Gor Hajus quickly explained the method of control, but I could apprehend that there might be embarrassment and trouble awaiting me before I mastered the art of flying in an equilibrimotor. He showed me how to tilt the wings downward in walking so that I would not leave the ground at every step, and thus he led me to the edge of the landing stage.

"We will rise here," he said, "and keeping in the darkness of the upper levels seek to reach the house of my friend without being detected. If we are pursued by air patrols we must separate; and later those who escape may gather just west of the city wall where you will find a small lake with a deserted tower upon its northern rim—this tower will be our rendezvous in event of trouble. Follow me!" He started his motor and rose gracefully into the air.

Hovan Du followed him and then it was my turn. I rose beautifully for about twenty feet, floating out over the city which lay hundreds of feet below, and then, quite suddenly, I turned upside down. I had done something wrong—I was quite positive of it. It was a most startling sensation, I can assure you, floating there with my head down, quite helpless; while below me lay the streets of a great city and no softer, I was sure, than the streets of Los Angeles or Paris. My motor was still going, and as I manipulated the controls which operated the wings I commenced to describe all sorts of strange loops and spirals and spins; and then Dar Tarus came to my rescue. First he told me to lie quietly and then directed the manipulation of each wing until I had gained an upright position. After that I did fairly well and was soon rising in the wake of Gor Hajus and Hovan Du.

I need not describe in detail the hour of flying, or rather floating, that ensued. Gor Hajus led us to a considerable altitude and there, through the darkness above the city, our slow motors drove us towards a district of magnificent homes surrounded by spacious grounds; and here, as we hovered over a large palace, we were suddenly startled by a sharp challenge coming from directly above us.

"Who flies by night?" a voice demanded.

"Friends of Mu Tel, Prince of the House of Kan," replied Gor Hajus: quickly.

"Let me see your night flying permit and your flier's licence," ordered the one above us, at the same time swooping suddenly to our level and giving me my first sight of a Martian policeman. He was equipped with a much swifter and handier equilibrimotor than ours. I think that was the first fact to impress us deeply, and it demonstrated the futility of flight; for he could have given us ten minutes start and overhauled each of us within another ten minutes, even though we had elected to fly in different directions. The fellow was a warrior rather than a policeman, though detailed to duty such as our Earthly police officers perform; the city being patrolled both day and night by the warriors of Vobis Kan's army.

He dropped now close to the assassin of Toonol, again demanding permit and licence and at the same time flashing a light in the face of my comrade.

"By the sword of the Jeddak!" he cried. "Fortune heaps her favours upon me. Who would have thought an hour since that it would be I who would collect the reward for the capture of Gor Hajus?"

"Any other fool might have thought it," returned Gor Hajus, "but he would have been as wrong as you," and as he spoke he struck with the short-sword I had loaned him.

The blow was broken by the wing of the warrior's equilibrimotor, which it demolished, yet it inflicted a severe wound in the fellow's shoulder. He tried to back off, but the damaged wing caused him only to wheel around erratically; and then he seized upon his whistle and attempted to blow a mighty blast that was cut short by another blow from Gor Hajus' sword that split the man's head open to the bridge of his nose.

"Quick!" cried the assassin. "We must drop into the gardens of Mu Tel, for that signal will bring a swarm of air patrols about our heads."

The others I saw falling rapidly towards the ground, but again I had trouble.

Depress my wings as I would I moved only slightly downward and upon a path that, if continued, would have landed me at a considerable distance from the gardens of Mu Tel. I was approaching one of the elevated portions of the palace, what appeared to be a small suite that was raised upon its shining metal shaft far above the ground. From all directions I could hear the screaming whistles of the air patrols answering the last call of their comrade whose corpse floated just above me, a guide even in death to point the way for his fellows to search us out. They were sure to discover him and then I would be in plain view, of them and my fate sealed.

Perhaps I could find ingress to the apartment looming darkly near! There I might hide until the danger had passed, provided I could enter, undetected. I directed my course towards the structure; an open window took form through the darkness and then I collided with a fine wire netting—I had run into a protecting curtain that fends off assassins of the air from these high-flung sleeping apartments. I felt that I was lost. If I could but reach the ground I might find concealment among the trees and shrubbery that I had seen vaguely outlined beneath me in the gardens of this Barsoomian prince; but I could not drop at a sufficient angle to bring me to ground within the garden, and when I tried to spiral down I turned over and started up again. I thought of ripping open my belt and letting the eighth ray escape; but in my unfamiliarity with this strange force I feared that such an act might precipitate me to the ground with too great violence, though I was determined to have recourse to it as a last alternative if nothing less drastic presented itself.

In my last attempt to spiral downward I rose rapidly feet foremost to a sudden and surprising collision with some object above me. As I frantically righted myself, fully expecting to be immediately seized by a member of the air patrol, I found myself face to face with the corpse of the warrior Gor Hajus had slain.

The whistling of the air patrols sounded ever nearer—it could be only a question of seconds now before I was discovered—and with the stern necessity that confronted me, with death looking me in the face, there burst upon me a possible avenue of escape from my dilemma.

Seizing tightly with my left hand the harness of the dead Toonolian, I whipped out my dagger and slashed his buoyancy belt a dozen times. Instantly, as the rays escaped, his body started to drag me downward, Our descent was rapid, but not precipitate, and it was but a matter of seconds before we landed gently upon the scarlet sward of the gardens of Mu Tel, Prince of the House of Kan, close beside a clump of heavy shrubbery. Above me sounded the whistles of the circling patrols as I dragged the corpse of the warrior into the concealing depth of the foliage. Nor was I an instant too soon for safety, as almost immediately the brilliant rays of a searchlight shot downward from the deck of a small patrol ship, illuminating the open spaces of the garden all about me. A hurried glance through the branches and the leaves of my sanctuary revealed nothing of my companions and I breathed a sigh of relief in the thought that they, too, had found concealment.

The light played for a short time about the gardens and then passed on, as did the sound of the patrol's whistles, as the search proceeded elsewhere; thus giving me the assurance that no suspicion was directed upon our hiding place.

Left in darkness I appropriated such of the weapons of the dead warrior as I coveted, after having removed my equilibrimotor, which I was first minded to destroy, but which I finally decided to moor to one of the larger shrubs against the possibility that I might again have need for it; and now, secure in the conviction that the danger of discovery by the air patrol had passed, I left my concealment and started in search of my companions.

Keeping well in the shadows of the trees and shrubs I moved in the direction of the main building, which loomed darkly near at hand; for in this direction I believed Gor Hajus would lead the others as I knew that the palace of Mu Tel was to have been our destination. As I crept along, moving with utmost stealth, Thuria, the nearer moon, shot suddenly above the horizon, illuminating the night with her brilliant rays. I was close to the building's ornately carved wall at the moment; beside me was a narrow niche, its interior cast in deepest shadow by

Thuria's brilliant rays; to my left was an open bit of lawn upon which, revealed in every detail of its terrifying presence, stood as fearsome a creature as my Earthly eyes ever had rested upon. It was a beast about the size of a Shetland pony, with ten short legs and a terrifying head that bore some slight resemblance to that of a frog, except that the jaws were equipped with three rows of long, sharp tusks.

The thing had its nose in the air and was sniffing about, while its great pop eyes moved swiftly here and there, assuring me, beyond the shadow of a doubt, that it was searching for someone. I am not inclined to be egotistical, yet I could not avoid the conviction that it was searching for me. It was my first experience of a Martian watch dog; and as I sought concealment within the dark shadows of the niche behind me, at the very instant that the creature's eyes alighted upon me, and heard his growl and saw him charge straight towards me, I had a premonition that it might prove my last experience with one.

I drew my long-sword as I backed into the niche, but with a sense of the utter inadequacy of the unaccustomed weapon in the face of this three or four hundred pounds of ferocity incarnate. Slowly I backed away into the shadows as the creature bore down upon me and then, as it entered the niche, my back collided with a solid obstacle that put an end to further retreat.

CHAPTER 9

The Palace Of Mu Tel

As the calot entered the niche I experienced, I believe, all of the reactions of the cornered rat, and I certainly know that I set myself to fight in that proverbial manner. The beast was almost upon me and I was metaphorically kicking myself for not having remained in the open where there were many tall trees when the support at my back suddenly gave way, a hand reached out of the darkness behind me and seized my harness and I was drawn swiftly into inky blackness. A door slammed and the silhouette of the calot against the moonlit entrance to the niche was blotted out.

A gruff voice spoke in my ear. "Come with me!" it said. A hand found mine and thus I was led along through the darkness of what I soon discovered was a narrow corridor from the constantly recurring collisions I had first with one side of it and then with the other.

Ascending gradually, the corridor turned abruptly at right angles and I saw beyond my guide a dim luminosity that gradually increased until another turn brought us to the threshold of a brilliantly lighted chamber—a magnificent apartment, the gorgeous furnishings and decorations of which beggar the meagre descriptive powers of my native tongue. Cold, ivory, precious stones, marvellous woods, resplendent fabrics, gorgeous furs and startling architecture combined to impress upon my earthly vision such a picture as I had never even dreamed of dreaming; and in the centre of this room, surrounded by a little group of Martians, were my three companions.

My guide conducted me towards the party, the members of which had turned towards us as we entered the chamber, and stopped before a tall Barsoomian, resplendent in jewel encrusted harness.

"Prince," he said, "I was scarce a tal too soon. In fact, as I opened the door to step out into the garden in search of him, as you directed, there he was upon the opposite side with one of the calots of the garden almost upon him."

"Good!" exclaimed he who had been addressed as prince, and then he turned to Gor Hajus. "This is he, my friend, of whom you told me?"

"This is Vad Varo, who claims to be from the planet Jasoom," replied Gor Hajus; "and this, Vad Varo, is Mu Tel, Prince of the House of Kan."

I bowed and the prince advanced and placed his right hand upon my left shoulder in true Barsoomian acknowledgment of an introduction; when I had done similarly, the ceremony was over. There was no silly pleased-to-meet-you, how-do-you-do? or it's-a-pleasure-I-assure-you.

At Mu Tel's request I narrated briefly what had befallen me between the time I had become separated from my companions and the moment that one of his officers had snatched me from impending disaster. Mu Tel gave instructions that all traces of the dead patrol be removed before dawn lest their discovery bring upon him the further suspicion of his uncle, Vobis Kan, Jeddak of Toonol, whom it seemed had long been jealous of his nephew's growing popularity and fearful that he harboured aspirations for the throne.

It was later in the evening, during one of those elaborate meals for which the princes of Barsoom are justly famous, when mellowed slightly by the rare vintages with which he delighted his guests, that Mu Tel discoursed with less restraint upon his imperial uncle.

"The nobles have long been tired of Vobis Kan," he said, "and the people are tiring of him—he is a conscienceless tyrant—but he is our hereditary ruler, and so they hesitate to change. We are a practical people, little influenced by sentiment; yet there is enough to keep the masses loyal to their Jeddak even after he has ceased to deserve their loyalty, while the fear of the wrath of the masses keeps the nobles loyal. There is also the natural suspicion that I, the next in line for succession, would make them no less tyrannical a Jeddak than has Vobis Kan, while, having youth, I might be much more active in cruel and nefarious practices.

"For myself, I would not hesitate to destroy my uncle and seize his throne were I sure of the support of the army, for with the warriors of Vobis Kan at my back I might defy the balance of Toonol. It is because of this that I long since offered my friendship to Gor Hajus; not that he might slay my uncle, but that when I had slain him in fair fight Gor Hajus might win to me the loyalty of the Jeddak's warriors, for great is the popularity of Gor Hajus among the soldiers, who ever look up to such a great fighter with reverence and devotion. I have offered Gor Hajus a high place in the affairs of Toonol should he cast his lot with me; but he tells me that he has first to fulfil his obligations to you, Vad Varo, and for the furtherance of your adventure he has asked me to give you what assistance I may. This I offer gladly, from purely practical motives, since your early success will hasten mine. Therefore I propose to place at your disposal a staunch flier that will carry you and your companions to Phundahl."

This offer I naturally accepted, after which we fell to discussing plans for our departure which we finally decided to attempt early the following night, at a time when neither of the moons would be in the heavens. After a brief discussion of equipment we were, at my request, permitted to retire since I had not slept for more than thirty-six hours and my companions for twenty-four.

Slaves conducted us to our sleeping apartments, which were luxuriously furnished, and arranged magnificent sleeping silks and furs for our comfort.

After they had left us Gor Hajus touched a button and the room rose swiftly upon its metal shaft to a height of forty or fifty feet; the wire netting automatically dropped about us, and we were safe for the night.

The following morning, after our apartment had been lowered to its daylight level and before I was permitted to leave it, a slave was sent to me by Mu Tel with instructions to stain my entire body the beautiful copper-red of my Barsoomian friends; furnishing me with a disguise which I well knew to be highly essential to the success of my venture, since my white skin would have drawn unpleasant notice upon me in any city of Barsoom. Another slave brought harness and weapons for Gor Hajus, Dar Tarus and myself, and a collar and chain for Hovan Du, the ape-man. Our harness, while of heavy material, and splendid workmanship, was quite plain, being free of all insignia either of rank or service—such harness as is customarily worn by the Barsoomian panthan, or soldier of fortune, at such times as he is not definitely in the service of any nation or individual. These panthans are virtually men without a country, being roving mercenaries ready to sell their swords to the highest bidder. Although they have no organization they are ruled by a severe code of ethics and while in the employ of a master are, almost without exception, loyal to him. They are generally supposed to be men who have flown from the wrath of their own Jeddaks or the justice of their own courts, but there is among them a sprinkling of adventurous souls who have adopted their calling because of the thrills and excitement it offers. While they are well paid, they are also great gamblers and notorious spenders, with the result that they are almost always without funds and often reduced to strange expedients for the gaining of their livelihood between engagements; a fact which gave great plausibility to our possession of a trained ape, which upon Mars would appear no more remarkable than would to us the possession of a monkey or parrot by an old salt just returned, from a long cruise, to one of our Earthly ports.

This day that I stayed in the palace of Mu Tel I spent much in the company of the prince, who found pleasure in questioning me concerning the customs, the politics, the civilization and the geography of Earth, with much of which, I was surprised to note, he seemed quite familiar; a fact which he explained was due to the marvellous development of Barsoomian astronomical instruments, wireless photography and wireless telephony; the last of which has been brought to such a state of perfection that many Barsoomian savants have succeeded in learning several Earthly languages, notably Urdu, English and Russian, and, a few, Chinese also. These have doubtless been the first languages to attract their attention because of the fact that they are spoken by great numbers of people over large areas of the world.

Mu Tel took me to a small auditorium in his palace that reminded me somewhat of private projection rooms on Earth. It had, I should say, a capacity of some two hundred persons and was built like a large camera obscura; the audience sitting within the instrument, their backs towards the lens and in front of them, filling one entire end of the room, a large ground glass upon which is thrown the image to be observed.

Mu Tel seated himself at a table upon which was a chart of the heavens. Just above the chart was a movable arm carrying a pointer. This pointer Mu Tel moved until it rested upon the planet Earth, then he switched off the light in the room and immediately there appeared upon the ground glass plate a view such as one might obtain from an airplane riding at an elevation of a thousand feet.

There was something strangely familiar about the scene before me. It was of a desolate, wasted country. I saw shattered stumps whose orderly arrangement proclaimed that here once an orchard had blossomed and borne fruit. There were great, unsightly holes in the earth and over and across all a tangle of barbed wire. I asked Mu Tel how we might change the picture to another locality. He lighted a small radio bulb between us and I saw a globe there, a globe of Earth, and a small pointer fixed over it.

"The side of this globe now presented to you represents the face of the Earth turned towards us," explained Mu Tel. "You will note that the globe is slowly revolving. Place this pointer where you will upon the globe and that portion of Jasoom will be revealed for you."

I moved the pointer very slowly and the picture changed. A ruined village came into view. I saw some people moving among its ruins. They were not soldiers. A little further on I came upon trenches and dug-outs—there were no soldiers here, either. I moved the pointer rapidly north and south along a vast line of trenches. Here and there in villages there were soldiers, but they were all French soldiers and never were they in the trenches. There were no German soldiers and no fighting. The war was over, then! I moved the pointer to the Rhine and across. There were soldiers in Germany—French soldiers, English soldiers, American soldiers. We had won the war! I was glad, but it seemed very far away and quite unreal—as though no such world existed and no such peoples had ever fought—it was as though I were recalling through its illustrations a novel that I had read a long time since.

"You seem much interested in that war torn country," remarked Mu Tel.

"Yes," I explained, "I fought in that war. Perhaps I was killed. I do not know."

"And you won?" he asked.

"Yes, my people won," I replied. "We fought for a great principle and for the peace and happiness of a world. I hope that we did not fight in vain."

"If you mean that you hope that your principle will triumph because you fought and won, or that peace will come, your hopes are futile. War never brought peace—it but brings more and greater wars. War is Nature's natural state—it is folly to combat it. Peace should be considered only as a time for preparation for the principal business of man's existence. Were it not for constant warring of one form of life upon another, and even upon itself, the planets would be so overrun with life that it would smother itself out. We found upon Barsoom that long periods of peace brought plagues and terrible diseases that killed more than the wars killed and in a much more hideous and painful way. There is neither pleasure nor thrill nor reward of any sort to be gained by dying in bed of a loathsome disease. We must all die—let us therefore go out and die in a great and exciting game, and make room for the millions who are to follow us. We have tried it out upon Barsoom and we would not be without war."

Mu Tel told me much that day about the peculiar philosophy of Toonolians. They believe that no good deed was ever performed except for a selfish motive; they have no god and no religion; they believe, as do all educated Barsoomians, that man came originally from the Tree of Life, but unlike most of their fellows they do not believe that an omnipotent being created the Tree of Life. They hold that the only sin is failure—success, however achieved, is meritorious; and yet, paradoxical as it may seem, they never break their given word. Mu Tel explained that they overcame the baneful results of this degrading weakness—this sentimental bosh—by seldom, if ever, binding themselves to loyalty to another, and then only for a definitely prescribed period.

As I came to know them better, and especially Gor Hajus, I began to realize that much of their flaunted contempt of the finer sensibilities was specious. It is true that generations of inhibition had to some extent atrophied those characteristics of heart and soul which the noblest among us so highly esteem; that friendships ties were lax and that blood kinship awakened no high sense of responsibility or love even between parents and children; yet Gor Hajus was essentially a man of sentiment, though he would doubtless have run through the heart any who had dared accuse him of it, thus perfectly proving the truth of the other's accusation. His pride in his reputation for integrity and loyalty proved him a man of heart as truly as did his jealousy of his reputation for heartlessness prove him a man of sentiment; and in all this he was but typical of the people of Toonol. They denied deity, and in the same breath worshipped the fetish of science that they had permitted to obsess them quite as harmfully as do religious fanatics accept the unreasoning rule of their imaginary gods; and so, with all their vaunted knowledge, they were unintelligent because unbalanced.

As the day drew to a close I became the more anxious to be away. Far to the west across desolate leagues of marsh lay Phundahl, and in Phundahl the beauteous body of the girl I loved and that I was sworn to restore to its rightful owner.

The evening meal was over and Mu Tel himself had conducted us to a secret hangar in one of the towers of his palace. Here artisans had prepared a flier for us, having removed during the day all signs of its real ownership, even to slightly altering its lines; so that in the event of capture Mu Tel's name might in no way be connected with the expedition. Provisions were stored, including plenty of raw meat for Hovan Du, and, as the farther moon sank below the horizon and darkness fell, a panel of the tower wall, directly in front of the flier's nose, slid aside. Mu Tel wished us luck and the ship slipped silently out into the night. The flier, like many of her type, was without cockpit or cabin; a low, metal hand-rail surmounted her gunwale; heavy rings were set substantially in her deck and to these her crew was supposed to cling or attach themselves by means of their harness hooks provided for this and similar purposes; a low wind shield, with a rakish slant afforded some protection from the wind; the motor and controls were all exposed, as all the space below decks was taken up by the buoyancy tanks. In this type everything is sacrificed to speed; there is no comfort aboard. When moving at high speed each member of the crew lies extended at full length upon the deck, each in his allotted place to give the necessary trim, and hangs on for dear life. These Toonolian crafts, however, are not overly fast, so I was told, being far outstripped in speed by the fliers of such nations as Helium and Ptarth who have for ages devoted themselves to the perfection of their navies; but this one was quite fast enough for our purposes, to the consummation of which it would be pitted against fliers of no higher rating, and it was certainly fast enough for me. In comparison with the slow moving Vosar, it seemed to shoot through the air like an arrow.

We wasted no time in strategy or stealth, but opened her wide as soon as we were in the clear, and directed her straight towards the west and Phundahl. Scarcely had we passed over the gardens of Mu Tel when we met with our first adventure.

We shot by a solitary figure floating in the air and almost simultaneously there shrilled forth the warning whistle of an air patrol. A shot whistled above us harmlessly and we were gone; but within a few seconds I saw the rays of a searchlight shining down from above and moving searchingly to and fro through the air.

"A patrol boat!" shouted Gor Hajus in my ear. Hovan Du growled savagely and shook the chain upon his collar. We raced on, trusting to the big gods and the little gods and all our ancestors that the relentless eye of light would not find us out; but it did. Within a few seconds it fell full upon our deck from above and in front of us and there it clung as the patrol boat dropped rapidly towards us while it maintained a high rate of speed upon a course otherwise identical with ours. Then, to our consternation, the ship opened fire on us with explosive bullets. These projectiles contain a high explosive that is detonated by light rays when the opaque covering of the projectile is broken by impact with the target. It is therefore not at all necessary to make a direct hit for a shot to be effective. If the projectile strikes the ground or the deck of a vessel or any solid substance near its target, it does considerably more damage when fired at a group of men than if it strikes but one of them, since it will then explode if its outer shell is broken and kill or wound several; while if it enters the body of an individual the light rays cannot reach it and it accomplishes no more than a non-explosive bullet. Moonlight is not powerful enough to detonate this explosive and so projectiles fired at night, unless touched by the powerful rays of searchlights, detonate at sunrise the following morning, making a battlefield a most unsafe place at that time even though the contending forces are no longer there. Similarly they make the removal of the unexploded projectiles from the bodies of the wounded a most ticklish operation which may well result in the instant death of both the patient and the surgeon.

Dar Tarus, at the controls, turned the nose of our flier upward directly towards the patrol boat and at the same time shouted to us to concentrate our fire upon her propellers. For myself, I could see little but the blinding eye of the searchlight, and at that I fired with the strange weapon to which I had received my first introduction but a few hours since when it was presented to me by Mu Tel. To me that all searching eye represented the greatest menace that confronted us, and could we blind it the patrol boat would have no great advantage over us. So I kept my rifle straight upon it my finger on the button that controlled the fire, and prayed for a hit.

Gor Hajus knelt at my side, his weapon spitting bullets at the patrol boat. Dar Tarus' hands were busy with the controls and Hovan Du squatted in the bow and growled.

Suddenly Dar Tarus voiced an exclamation of alarm. "The controls are hit!" he shouted. "We can't alter our course—the ship is useless." Almost the same instant the searchlight was extinguished—one of my bullets evidently having found it. We were quite close to the enemy now and heard their shout of anger.

Our own craft, out of control, was running swiftly towards the other. It seemed that if there was not a collision we would pass directly beneath the keel of the air patrol. I asked Dar Tarus if our ship was beyond repair.

"We could repair it if we had time," he replied, "but it would take hours and while we were thus delayed the whole air patrol force of Toonol would be upon us."

"Then we must have another ship," I said. Dar Tarus laughed. "You are right, Vad Varo," he replied, "but where shall we find it?"

I pointed to the patrol boat. "We shall not have to look far."

Dar Tarus shrugged his shoulders. "Why not!" he exclaimed. "It would be a glorious fight and a worthy death."

Gor Hajus slapped me on the shoulder. "To the death, my captain!" he cried.

Hovan Du shook his chain and roared.

The two ships were rapidly approaching one another. We had stopped firing now for fear that we might disable the craft we hoped to use for our escape; and for some reason the crew of the patrol ship had ceased firing at us—I never learned why. We were moving in a line that would bring us directly beneath the other ship. I determined to board her at all costs. I could see her keel boarding tackle slung beneath her, ready to be lowered to the deck of a quarry when once her grappling hooks had seized the prey. Doubtless they were already manning the latter, and as soon as we were beneath her the steel tentacles would reach down and seize us as her crew swarmed down the board tackle to our deck.

I called Hovan Du and he crept back to my side where I whispered my instructions in his ear. When I was done he nodded his head with a low growl. I cast off the harness hook that held me to the deck, and the ape and I moved to our bow after I had issued brief, whispered instructions to Gor Hajus and Dar Tarus. We were now almost directly beneath the enemy craft; I could see the grappling hooks being prepared for lowering. Our bow ran beneath the stern of the other ship and the moment was at hand for which I had been waiting. Now those upon the deck of the patrol boat could not see Hovan Du or me. The boarding tackle of the other ship swung fifteen feet above our heads; I whispered a word of command to the ape and simultaneously we crouched and sprang for the tackle. It may sound like a mad chance—failure meant almost certain death—but I felt that if two of us could reach the deck of the patrol boat while her crew was busy with the grappling gear it would be well worth the risk.

Gor Hajus had assured me that there would not be more than six men aboard the patrol ship; that one would be at the controls and the others manning the grappling hooks. It would be a most propitious time to gain a footing on the enemy's deck.

Hovan Du and I made our leaps and Fortune smiled upon us, though the huge ape but barely reached the tackle with one outstretched hand, while my Earthly muscles carried me easily to my goal. Together we made our way rapidly towards the bow of the patrol craft and without hesitation, and as previously arranged, he clambered quickly up the starboard side and I the port. If I were the more agile jumper Hovan Du far outclassed me in climbing, with the result that he reached the rail and was clambering over while my eyes were still below the level of the deck, which was, perhaps, a fortunate thing for me since, by chance, I had elected to gain the deck directly at a point where, unknown to me, one of the crew of the ship was engaged with the grappling hooks. Had his eyes not been attracted elsewhere by the shout of one of his fellows who was first to see Hovan Du's savage face rise above the gunwale, he could have dispatched me with a single blow before ever I could have set foot upon the deck The ape had also come up directly in front of a Toonolian warrior and this fellow had let out a yell of surprise and sought to draw his sword, but the ape, for all his great bulk, was too quick for him; and as my eyes topped the rail I saw the mighty anthropoid seize the unfortunate man by the harness, drag him to the side and hurl him to destruction far below. Instantly we were both over the rail and squarely on deck while the remaining members of the craft's crew, abandoning their stations, ran forward to overpower us. I think that the sight of the great, savage beast must have had a demoralizing effect upon them, for they hesitated, each seeming to be willing to accord his fellow the honour of first engaging us; but they did come on, though slowly. This hesitation I was delighted to see, for it accorded perfectly with the plan that I had worked out, which depended largely upon the success which might attend the efforts of Gor Hajus and Dar Tarus to reach the deck of the patrol when our craft had risen sufficiently close beneath the other to permit them to reach the boarding tackle, which we were utilizing with reverse English, as one might say.

Gor Hajus had cautioned me to dispatch the man at the controls as quickly as possible, since his very first act would be to injure them the instant that there appeared any possibility that we might be successful in our attempt to take his ship, and so I ran quickly towards him and before he could draw I cut him down. There were now four against us and we waited for them to advance that we might gain time for our fellows to reach the deck.

The four moved slowly forward and were almost within striking distance when I saw Gor Hajus' head appear above the stern rail, quickly followed by that of Dar Tarus.

"Look!" I cried to the enemy, "and surrender," and I pointed astern.

One of them turned to look and what he saw brought an exclamation of surprise to his lips. "It is Gor Hajus," he cried, and then, to me: "What is your purpose with us if we surrender?"

"We have no quarrel with you," I replied. "We but wish to leave Toonol and go our way in peace—we shall not harm you."

He turned to his fellows while, at a sign from me, my three companions stopped their advance and waited. For a few minutes the four warriors conversed in low tones, then he who had first spoken addressed me.

"There are few Toonolians," he said, "who would not be glad to serve Gor Hajus, whom we had thought long dead, but to surrender our ship to you would mean certain death for us when we reported our defeat at our headquarters. On the other hand were we to continue our defence most of us here upon the deck of this flier would be killed. If you can assure us that your plans are not aimed at the safety of Toonol I can make a suggestion that will afford an avenue of escape and safety for us all."

"We only wish to leave Toonol," I replied. "No harm can come to Toonol because of what I seek to accomplish."

"Good!" and where do you wish to go?"

"That I may not tell you."

"You may trust us, if you accept my proposal," he assured me, "which is that we convey you to your destination, after which we can return to Toonol and report that we engaged you and that after a long running fight, in which two of our number were killed, you eluded us in the darkness and escaped."

"Can we trust these men?" I asked, addressing Gor Hajus, who assured me that we could, and thus the compact was entered into which saw us speeding rapidly towards Phundahl aboard one of Vobis Kan's own fliers.

CHAPTER 10

Phundahl

The following night the Toonolian crew set us down just inside the wall of the city of Phundahl, following the directions of Dar Tarus who was a native of the city, had been a warrior of the Jeddara's Guard and, prior to that seen service in Phundahl's tiny navy. That he was familiar with every detail of Phundahl's defences and her systems of patrols was evidenced by the fact that we landed without detection and that the Toonolian ship rose and departed apparently unnoticed.

Our landing place had been the roof of a low building built within and against the city wall. From this roof Dar Tarus led us down an inclined runway to the street, which, at this point, was quite deserted. The street was narrow and dark, being flanked upon one side by the low buildings built against the city wall and upon the other by higher buildings, some of which were windowless and none showing any light. Dar Tarus explained that he had chosen this point for our entrance because it was a district of storage houses, and while a hive of industry during the day, was always deserted at night, not even a watchman being required owing to the almost total absence of thievery upon Barsoom.

By devious and roundabout ways he led us finally to a section of second-rate shops, eating places and hotels such as are frequented by the common soldiers, artisans and slaves, where the only attention we attracted was due to the curiosity aroused by Hovan Du. As we had not eaten since leaving Mu Tel's palace, our first consideration was food. Mu Tel had furnished Gor Hajus with money, so that we had the means to gratify our wants. Our first stop was at a small shop where Gor Hajus purchased four or five pounds of thoat steak for Hovan Du, and then we repaired to an eating place of which Dar Tarus knew. At first the proprietor would not let us bring Hovan Du inside, but finally, after much argument, he permitted us to lock the great ape in an inner room where Hovan Du was forced to remain with his thoat meat while we sat at a table in the outer room.

I will say for Hovan Du that he played his role well, nor was there once when the proprietor of the place, or any of his patrons, or the considerable crowd that gathered to listen to the altercation, could have guessed that the body of the great savage beast was animated by a human brain. It was really only when feeding or fighting that the simian half of Hovan Du's brain appeared to exercise any considerable influence upon him; yet there seemed little doubt that it always coloured all his thoughts and actions to some extent, accounting for his habitual taciturnity and the quickness with which he was aroused to anger, as well as to the fact that he never smiled, nor appeared to appreciate in any degree the humour of a situation. He assured me, however, that the human half of his brain not only appreciated but greatly enjoyed the lighter episodes and occurrences of our adventure and the witty stories and anecdotes related by Gor Hajus, the Assassin, but that his simian anatomy had developed no muscles wherewith to evidence physical expression of his mental reactions.

We dined heartily, though upon rough and simple fare, but were glad to escape the prying curiosity of the garrulous and gossipy proprietor, who plied us with so many questions as to our past performances and future plans that Dar Tarus, who was our spokesman here, was hard put to it to quickly fabricate replies that would be always consistent. However, escape we did at last, and once again in the street, Dar Tarus set out to lead us to a public lodging house of which he knew. As we went we approached a great building of wondrous beauty in and out of which constant streams of people were pouring, and when we were before it Dar Tarus asked us to wait without as he must enter. When I asked him why, he told me that this was a temple of Tur, the god worshipped by the people of Phundahl.

"I have been away for a long time," he said, "and have had no opportunity to do honour to my god. I shall not keep you waiting long. Gor Hajus, will you loan me a few pieces of gold?"

In silence the Toonolian took a few pieces of money from one of his pocket pouches and handed them to Dar Tarus, but I could see that it was only with difficulty that he hid an expression of contempt, since the Toonolians are atheists.

I asked Dar Tarus if I might accompany him into the temple, which seemed to please him very much; and so we fell in with the stream approaching the broad entrance. Dar Tarus gave me two of the gold pieces that he had borrowed from Gor Hajus and told me to follow directly behind him and do whatever I saw him doing.

Directly inside the main entrance, and spread entirely across it at intervals that permitted space for the worshippers to pass between them, was a line of priests, their entire bodies, including their heads and faces, covered by a mantle of white cloth. In front of each was a substantial stand upon which rested a cash drawer. As we approached one of these we handed him a piece of gold which he immediately changed into many pieces of lesser value, one of which we dropped into a box at his side; whereupon he made several passes with his hands above our heads, dipped one of his fingers into a bowl of dirty water which he rubbed upon the ends of our noses, mumbled a few words which I could not understand and turned to the next in line as we passed on into the interior of the great temple. Never have I seen such a gorgeous display of wealth and lavish ornamentation as confronted my eyes in this, the first of the temples of Tur that it was my fortune to behold.

The enormous floor was unbroken by a single pillar and arranged upon it at regular intervals were carven images resting upon gorgeous pedestals. Some of these images were of men and some of women and many of them were beautiful; and there were others of beasts and of strange, grotesque creatures and many of these were hideous indeed. The first we approached was that of a beautiful female figure; and about the pedestal of this lay a number of men and women prone upon the floor against which they bumped their heads seven times and then arose and dropped a piece of money into a receptacle provided for that purpose, moving on then to another figure. The next that Dar Tarus and I visited was that of a man with a body of a silian, about the pedestal of which was arranged a series of horizontal wooden bars in concentric circles. The bars were about five feet from the floor and hanging from them by their knees were a number of men and women, repeating monotonously, over and over again, something that sounded to me like, bibble-babble-blup.

Dar Tarus and I swung to the bars like the others and mumbled the meaningless phrase for a minute or two, then we swung down, dropped a coin into the box, and moved on. I asked Dar Tarus what the words were that we had repeated and what they meant, but he said he did not know. I asked him if anyone knew, but he appeared shocked and said that such a question was sacrilegious and revealed a marked lack of faith. At the next figure we visited the people were all upon their hands and knees crawling madly in a circle about the pedestal.

Seven times around they crawled and then they arose and put some money in a dish and went their ways. At another the people rolled about, saying, "Tur is Tur; Tur is Tur; Tur is Tur," and dropping money in a golden bowl when they were done.

"What god was that?" I whispered to Dar Tarus when we had quit this last figure, which had no head, but eyes, nose and mouth in the centre of its belly.

"There is but one god," replied Dar Tarus solemnly, "and he is Tur!"

"Was that Tur?" I inquired.

"Silence, man," whispered Dar Tarus. "They would tear you to pieces were they to hear such heresy."

"Oh, I beg your pardon," I exclaimed. "I did not mean to offend. I see now that that is merely one of your idols."

Dar Tarus clapped a hand over my mouth. "S-s-s-t!" he cautioned to silence. "We do not worship idols—there is but one god and he is Tur!" "Well, what are these?" I insisted, with a sweep of a hand that embraced the several score images about which were gathered the thousands of worshippers.

"We must not ask," he assured me. "It is enough that we have faith that all the works of Tur are just and righteous. Come! I shall soon be through and we may join our companions."

He led me next to the figure of a monstrosity with a mouth that ran entirely around its head. It had a long tail and the breasts of a woman. About this image were a great many people, each standing upon his head. They also were repeating, over and over, "Tur is Tur; Tur is Tur; Tur is Tur." When we had done this for a minute or two, during which I had a devil of a time maintaining my equilibrium, we arose, dropped a coin into the box by the pedestal and moved on.

"We may go now," said Dar Tarus. "I have done well in the sight of Tur."

"I notice," I remarked, "that the people repeated the same phrase before this figure that they did at the last—Tur is Tur."

"Oh, no," exclaimed Dar Tarus. "On the contrary they said just exactly the opposite from what they said at the other. At that they said, Tur is Tur; while at this they absolutely reversed it and said, Tur is Tur. Do you not see? They turned it right around backwards, which makes a very great difference."

"It sounded the same to me," I insisted.

"That is because you lack faith," he said sadly, and we passed out of the temple, after depositing the rest of our money in a huge chest, of which there were many standing about almost filled with coins.

We found Gor Hajus and Hovan Du awaiting us impatiently, the centre of a large and curious throng among which were many warriors in the metal of Xaxa, the Jeddara of Phundahl. They wanted to see Hovan Du perform, but Dar Tarus told them that he was tired and in an ugly mood.

"To-morrow," he said, "when he is rested I shall bring him out upon the avenues to amuse you."

With difficulty we extricated ourselves, and passing into a quieter avenue, took a round-about way to the lodging place, where Hovan Du was confined in a small chamber while Gor Hajus, Dar Tarus and I were conducted by slaves to a large sleeping apartment where sleeping silks and furs were arranged for us upon a low platform that encircled the room and was broken only at the single entrance to the chamber. Here were already sleeping a considerable number of men, while two armed slaves patrolled the aisle to guard the guests from assassins.

It was still early and some of the other lodgers were conversing in low whispers so I sought to engage Dar Tarus in conversation relative to his religion, about which I was curious.

"The mysteries of religions always fascinate me, Dar Tarus," I told him.

"Ah, but that is the beauty of the religion of Tur," he exclaimed, "it has no mysteries. It is simple, natural, scientific and every word and work of it is susceptible of proof through the pages of Turgan, the great book written by Tur himself.

"Tur's home is upon the sun. There, one hundred thousand years ago, he made Barsoom and tossed it out into space. Then he amused himself by creating man in various forms and two sexes; and later he fashioned animals to be food for man and each other, and caused vegetation and water to appear that man and the animals might live. Do you not see how simple and scientific it all is?"

But it was Gor Hajus who told me most about the religion of Tur one day when Dar Tarus was not about. He said that the Phundahlians maintained that Tur still created every living thing with his own hands. They denied vigorously that man possessed the power to reproduce his kind and taught their young that all such belief was vile; and always they hid every evidence of natural procreation, insisting to the death that even those things which they witnessed with their own eyes and experienced with their own bodies in the bringing forth of their young never transpired.

Turgan taught them that Barsoom is flat and they shut their minds to every proof to the contrary. They would not leave Phundahl far for fear of failing off the edge of the world; they would not permit the development of aeronautics because should one of their ships circumnavigate Barsoom it would be a wicked sacrilege in the eyes of Tur who made Barsoom flat.

They would not permit the use of telescopes, for Tur taught them that there was no other world than Barsoom and to look at another would be heresy; nor would they permit the teaching in their schools of any history of Barsoom that antedated the creation of Barsoom by Tur, though Barsoom has a well authenticated written history that reaches back more than one hundred thousand years; nor would they permit any geography of Barsoom except that which appears in Turgan, nor any scientific researches along biological lines. Turgan is their only text book—if it is not in Turgan it is a wicked lie.

Much of all this and a great deal more I gathered from one source or another during my brief stay in Phundahl, whose people are, I believe, the least advanced in civilization of any of the red nations upon Barsoom. Giving, as they do, all their best thought to religious matters, they have become ignorant, bigoted and narrow, going as far to one extreme as the Toonolians do to the other.

However, I had not come to Phundahl to investigate her culture but to steal her queen, and that thought was uppermost in my mind when I awoke to a new day—my first in Phundahl. Following the morning meal we set out in the direction of the palace to reconnoitre, Dar Tarus leading us to a point from which he might easily direct us the balance of the way, as he did not dare accompany us to the immediate vicinity of the royal grounds for fear of recognition, the body he now possessed having formerly belonged to a well-known noble.

It was arranged that Gor Hajus should act as spokesman and I as keeper of the ape. This arranged, we bade farewell to Dar Tarus and set forth, the three of us, along a broad and beautiful avenue that led directly to the palace gates. We had been planning and rehearsing the parts that we were to play and which we hoped would prove so successful that they would open the gates to us and win us to the presence of the Jeddara.

As we strolled with seeming unconcern along the avenue, I had ample opportunity to enjoy the novel and beautiful sights of this rich boulevard of palaces. The sun shone down upon vivid scarlet lawns, gorgeous flowered pimalia and a score of other rarely beautiful Barsoomian shrubs and trees, while the avenue itself was shaded by almost perfect specimens of the magnificent sorapus. The sleeping apartments of the buildings had all been lowered to their daytime level, and from a hundred balconies gorgeous silks and furs were airing in the sun. Slaves were briskly engaged with their duties about the grounds, while upon many a balcony women and children sat at their morning meal. Among the children we aroused considerable enthusiasm, or at least Hovan Du did, nor was he without interest to the adults. Some of them would have detained us for an exhibition, but we moved steadily on towards the palace, for nowhere else had we business or concern within the walls of Phundahl.

Around the palace gates was the usual crowd of loitering curiosity seekers; for after all human nature is much the same everywhere, whether skins be black or white, red or yellow or brown, upon Earth or upon Mars. The crowd before Xaxa's gates were largely made up of visitors from the islands of that part of the Great Toonolian Marshes which owes allegiance to Phundahl's queen, and like all provincials eager for a glimpse of royalty; though none the less to be interested by the antics of a simian, wherefore we had a ready made audience awaiting our arrival. Their natural fear of the great brute caused them to fall back a little at our approach so that we had a clear avenue to the very gates themselves, and there we halted while the crowds closed in behind, forming a half circle about us. Gor Hajus addressed them in a loud tone of voice that might be overheard by the warriors and their officers beyond the gates, for it was really them we had come to entertain, not the crowds in which we had not the slightest interest.

"Men and women of Phundahl," cried Gor Hajus, "behold two poor panthans, who, risking their lives, have captured and trained one of the most savage and ferocious and at the same time most intelligent specimens of the great white ape of Barsoom ever before seen in captivity and at great expense have brought it to Phundahl for your entertainment and edification. My friends, this wonderful ape is endowed with human intelligence; he understands every word that is spoken to him. With your kind attention, my friends, I will endeavour to demonstrate the remarkable intelligence of this ferocious, man-eating beast—an intelligence that has entertained the crowned heads of Barsoom and mystified the minds of her most learned savants."

I thought Gor Hajus did pretty well as a bally-hoo artist. I had to smile as I listened, here upon Mars, to the familiar lines that I had taught him out of my Earthly experience of county fairs and amusement parks, so highly ludicrous they sounded falling from the lips of the Assassin of Toonol; but they evidently interested his auditors and impressed them, too, for they craned their necks and stood in earnest eyed silence awaiting the performance of Hovan Du. Even better, several members of the Jeddara's Guard pricked up their ears and sauntered towards the gates; and among them was an officer.

Gor Hajus caused Hovan Du to be down at word of command, to get up, to stand upon one foot, and to indicate the number of fingers that Gor Hajus held up by growling once for each finger, thus satisfying the audience that he could count; but these simple things were only by way of leading up to the more remarkable achievements which we hoped would win an audience before the Jeddara. Gor Hajus borrowed a set of harness and weapons from a man in the crowd and had Hovan Du don it and fence with him, and then indeed did we hear exclamations of amazement.

The warriors and the officer of Xaxa had drawn near the gates and were interested spectators, which was precisely what we wished, and now Gor Hajus was ready for the final, astounding revelation of Hovan Du's intelligence.

"These things that you have witnessed are as nothing," he cried. "Why this wonderful beast can even read and write. He was captured in a deserted city near Ptarth and can read and write the language of that country. Is there among you one who, by chance, comes from that distant country?"

A slave spoke up. "I am from Ptarth."

"Good!" said Gor Hajus. "Write some simple instructions and hand them to the ape. I will turn my back that you may know that I cannot assist him in any way."

The slave drew forth a tablet from a pocket pouch and wrote briefly. What he wrote he handed to Hovan Du. The ape read the message and without hesitation moved quickly to the gate and handed it to the officer standing upon the other side, the gate being constructed of wrought metal in fanciful designs that offered no obstruction to the view or to the passage of small articles. The officer took the message and examined it.

"What does it say?" he demanded of the slave that had penned it.

"It says," replied the latter: "Take this message to the officer who stands just within the gates."

There were exclamations of surprise from all parts of the crowd and Hovan Du was compelled to repeat his performance several times with different messages which directed him to do various things, the officer always taking a great interest in the proceedings.

"It is marvellous," said he at last "The Jeddara would be amused by the performance of this beast. Wait here, therefore, until I have sent word to her that she may, if she so desires, command your presence."

Nothing could have better suited us and so we waited with what patience we might for the messenger to return; and while we waited Hovan Du continued to mystify his audience with new proofs of his great intelligence.

Chapter 11
Xaxa

The officer returned, the gates swung out and we were commanded to enter the courtyard of the palace of Xaxa, Jeddara of Phundahl. After that events transpired with great rapidity—surprising and totally unexpected events. We were led through an intricate maze of corridors and chambers until I became suspicious that we were purposely being confused, and convinced that whether such was the intention or not the fact remained that I could no more have retraced my steps to the outer courtyard than I could have flown without wings.

We had planned that, in the event of gaining admission to the palace, we would carefully note whatever might be essential to a speedy escape; but when, in a whisper, I asked Gor Hajus if he could find his way out again he assured me that he was as confused as I.

The palace was in no sense remarkable nor particularly interesting, the work of the Phundahlian artists being heavy and oppressing and without indication of high imaginative genius. The scenes depicted were mostly of a religious nature illustrating passages from Turgan, the Phundahlian bible, and, for the most part, were a series of monotonous repetitions. There was one, which appeared again and again, depicting Turgan creating a round, flat Mars and hurling it into Space, that always reminded me of a culinary artist turning a flap jack in a child's window.

There were also numerous paintings of what appeared to be court scenes delineating members of the Phundahlian royal line in various activities; it was noticeable that the more recent ones in which Xaxa appeared had had the principal figure repainted so that there confronted me from time to time portraits, none too well done, of the beautiful face and figure of Valla Dia in the royal trappings of a Jeddara. The effect of these upon me is not easy of description. They brought home to me the fact that I was approaching, and should presently be face to face with, the person of the woman to whom I had consecrated my love and my life, and yet in that same person I should be confronting one whom I loathed and would destroy.

We were halted at last before a great door and from the number of warriors and nobles congregated before it I was confident that we were soon to be ushered into the presence of the Jeddara. As we waited those assembled about us eyed us with, it seemed to me, more of hostility than curiosity and when the door swung open they accompanied us, with the exception of a few warriors, into the chamber beyond. The room was of medium size and at the farther side, behind a massive table, sat Xaxa. About her were grouped a number of heavily armed nobles. As I looked them over I wondered if among them was he for whom the body of Dar Tarus had been filched; for we had promised him that if conditions were favourable we would attempt to recover it.

Xaxa eyed us coldly as we were halted before her. "Let us see the beast perform," she commanded, and then suddenly: "What mean you by permitting strangers to enter my presence bearing arms?" she cried. "Sag Or, see that their weapons are removed!" and she turned to a handsome young warrior standing near her.

Sag Or! That was the name. Before me stood the noble for whom Dar Tarus had suffered the loss of his liberty, his body and his love. Gor Hajus had also recognized the name and Hovan Du, too; I could tell by the way they eyed the man as he advanced. Curtly he instructed us to hand our weapons to two warriors who advanced to receive them. Gor Hajus hesitated. I admit that I did not know what course to pursue.

Everyone seemed hostile and yet that might be, and doubtless was, but a reflection of their attitude towards all strangers. If we refused to disarm we were but three against a room full, if they chose to resort to force; or if they turned us out of the palace because of it we would be robbed of this seemingly god given opportunity to win to the very heart of Xaxa's palace and to her very presence, where we must eventually win before we could strike. Would such an opportunity ever be freely offered us again? I doubted it and felt that we had better assume a vague risk now than, by refusing their demand, definitely arm their suspicions. So I quietly removed my weapons and handed them to the warrior waiting to receive them; and following my example, Gor Hajus did likewise, though I can imagine with what poor grace.

Once again Xaxa signified that she would see Hovan Du perform. As Gor Hajus put him through his antics she watched listlessly; nor did anything that the ape did arouse the slightest flicker of interest among the entire group assembled about the Jeddara. As the thing dragged on I became obsessed with apprehensions that all was not right. It seemed to me that an effort was being made to detain us for some purpose—to gain time. I could not understand, for instance, why Xaxa required that we repeat several times the least interesting of the ape's performances. And all the time Xaxa sat playing with a long, slim dagger, and I saw that she watched me quite as much as she watched Hovan Du, while I found it difficult to keep my eyes averted from that perfect face, even though I knew that it was but a stolen mask behind which lurked the cruel mind of a tyrant and a murderess.

At last came an interruption to the performance. The door opened and a noble entered, who went directly to the Jeddara whom he addressed briefly and in a low tone. I saw that she asked him several questions and that she seemed vexed by his replies. Then she dismissed him with a curt gesture and turned towards us.

"Enough of this!" she cried. Her eyes rested upon mine and she pointed her slim dagger at me. "Where is the other?" she demanded.

"What other?" I inquired.

"There were three of you, besides the ape. I know nothing about the ape, nor where, nor how you acquired it; but I do know all about you, Vad Varo, and Gor Hajus, the Assassin of Toonol, and Dar Tarus. Where is Dar Tarus?" her voice was low and musical and entirely beautiful—the voice of Valla Dia—but behind it I knew was the terrible personality of Xaxa, and I knew too that it would be hard to deceive her, for she must have received what information she had directly from Ras Thavas. It had been stupid of me not to foresee that Ras Thavas would immediately guess the purpose of my mission and warn Xaxa. I perceived instantly that it would be worse than useless to deny our identity, rather I must explain our presence—if I could.

"Where is Dar Tarus?" she repeated.

"How should I know?" I countered. "Dar Tarus has reasons to believe that he would not be safe in Phundahl and I imagine that he is not anxious that anyone should know his whereabouts—myself included. He helped me to escape from the Island of Thavas, for which his liberty was to be his reward. He has not chosen to accompany me further upon my adventures."

Xaxa seemed momentarily disarmed that I did not deny my identity—evidently she had supposed that I would do so.

"You admit then," she said, "that you are Vad Varo, the assistant of Ras Thavas?"

"Have I ever sought to deny it?"

"You have disguised yourself as a red-man of Barsoom."

"How could I travel in Barsoom otherwise, where every man's hand is against a stranger?"

"And why would you travel in Barsoom?" Her eyes narrowed as she waited for my reply.

"As Ras Thavas has doubtless sent you word, I am from another world and I would see more of this one," I told her. "Is that strange?"

"And you come to Phundahl and seek to gain entrance to my presence and bring with you the notorious Assassin of Toonol that you may see more of Barsoom?"

"Gor Hajus may not return to Toonol," I explained, "and so he must seek service for his sword at some other court than that of Vobis Kan—in Phundahl perhaps, or if not here he must move on. I hope that he will decide to accompany me as I am a stranger in Barsoom, unaccustomed to the manners and ways of her people. I would fare ill without a guide and mentor."

"You shall fare ill," she cried. "You have seen all of Barsoom that you are destined to see—you have reached the end of your adventure. You think to deceive me, eh? You do not know, perhaps, that I have heard of your infatuation for Valla Dia or that I am fully conversant with the purpose of your visit to Phundahl." Her eyes left me and swept her nobles and her warriors. "To the pits with them!" she cried. "Later we shall choose the manner of their passing."

Instantly we were surrounded by a score of naked blades. There was no escape for Gor Hajus or me, but I thought that I saw an opportunity for Hovan Du to get away. I had had the possibility of such a contingency in mind from the first and always I had been on the look-out for an avenue of escape for one of us, and so the open windows at the right of the Jeddara had not gone unnoticed, nor the great trees growing in the courtyard beneath. Hovan Du was close beside me as Xaxa spoke.

"Go!" I whispered. "The windows are open. Go, and tell Dar Tarus what has happened to us," and then I fell back away from him and dragged Gor Hajus with me as though we would attempt to resist arrest; and while I thus distracted their attention from him Hovan Du turned towards an open window. He had taken but a few steps when a warrior attempted to halt him; with that the ferocious brain of the anthropoid seemed to seize dominion over the great creature. With a hideous growl he leaped with the agility of a cat upon the unfortunate Phundahlian, swung him high in giant hands and using his body as a flail tumbled his fellows to right and left as he cut a swath towards the open window nearest him.

Instantly pandemonium reigned in the apartment. The attention of all seemed centred upon the great ape and even those who had been confronting us turned to attack Hovan Du. And in the midst of the confusion I saw Xaxa step to some heavy hangings directly behind her desk, part them and disappear.

"Come!" I whispered to Gor Hajus. Apparently intent only upon watching the conflict between the ape and the warriors I moved forward with the fighters but always to the left towards the desk that Xaxa had just quitted. Hovan Du was giving a good account of himself. He had discarded his first victim and one by one had seized others as they came within range of his long arms and powerful hands, sometimes four at a time as he stood well braced upon two of his hand-like feet and fought with the other four. His shock of bristling hair stood erect upon his skull and his fierce eyes blazed with rage as, towering high above his antagonists, he fought for his life—the most feared of all the savage creatures of Barsoom. Perhaps his greatest advantage lay in the inherent fear of him that was a part of every man in that room who faced him, and it forwarded my quickly conceived plan, too, for it kept every eye turned upon Hovan Du, so that Gor Hajus and I were able to work our way to the rear of the desk. I think Hovan Du must have sensed my intention then, for he did the one thing best suited to attract every eye from us to him and, too, he gave me notice that the human half of his brain was still alert and watchful of our welfare.

Heretofore the Phundahlians must have looked upon him as a remarkable specimen of great ape, marvellously trained, but now, of a sudden, he paralyzed them with awe, for his roars and growls took the form of words and he spoke with the tongue of a human. He was near the window now. Several of the nobles were pushing bravely forward. Among them was Sag Or. Hovan Du reached forth and seized him, wrenching his weapons from him. "I go," he cried, "but let harm befall my friends and I shall return and tear the heart from Xaxa. Tell her that, from the Great Ape of Ptarth."

For an instant the, warriors and the nobles stood transfixed with awe. Every eye was upon Hovan Du as he stood there with the struggling figure of Sag Or in his mighty grasp. Gor Hajus and I were forgotten. And then Hovan Du turned and leaped to the sill of the window and from there lightly to the branches of the nearest tree; and with him went Sag Or, the favourite of Xaxa, the Jeddara. At the same instant I drew Gor Hajus with me between the hangings in the rear of Xaxa's desk, and as they fell behind us we found ourselves in the narrow mouth of a dark corridor.

Without knowledge of where the passage led we could only follow it blindly, urged on by the necessity for discovering a hiding place or an avenue of escape from the palace before the pursuit which we knew would be immediately instituted, overtook us. As our eyes became accustomed to the gloom, which was partially dispelled by a faint luminosity, we moved more rapidly and presently came to a narrow spiral runway which descended into a dark hole below the level of the corridor and also arose into equal darkness above.

"Which way?" I asked Gor Hajus.

"They will expect us to descend," he replied, "for in that direction lies the nearest avenue of escape."

"Then we will go up."

"Good!" he exclaimed. "All we seek now is a place to hide until night has fallen, for we may not escape by day."

We had scarcely started to ascend before we heard the first sound of pursuit—the clank of accoutrements in the corridor beneath. Yet, even with this urge from behind, we were forced to move with great caution, for we knew not what lay before. At the next level there was a doorway, the door closed and locked, but there was no corridor, nor anywhere to hide, and so we continued on upward. The second level was identical with that just beneath, but at the third a single corridor ran straight off into darkness and at our right was a door, ajar. The sounds of pursuit were appreciably nearer now and the necessity for concealment seemed increasing as the square of their growing proportions until every other consideration was overwhelmed by it. Nor is this so strange when the purpose of my adventure is considered and that discovery now must assuredly spell defeat and blast for ever the slender ray of hope that remained for the resurrection of Valla Dia in her own flesh.

There was scarce a moment for consideration. The corridor before us was shrouded in darkness—it might be naught but a blind alley. The door was close and ajar.

I pushed it gently inward. An odour of heavy incense greeted our nostrils and through the small aperture we saw a portion of a large chamber garishly decorated. Directly before us, and almost wholly obstructing our view of the entire chamber, stood a colossal statue of a squatting man-like figure. Behind us we heard voices—our pursuers already were ascending the spiral—they would be upon us in a few seconds. I examined the door and discovered that it fastened with a spring lock. I looked again into the chamber and saw no one within the range of our vision, and then I motioned Gor Hajus to follow me and stepping into the room closed the door behind us. We had burned our bridges. As the door closed the lock engaged with a sharp, metallic click.

"What was that?" demanded a voice, originating, seemingly, at the far end of the chamber.

Gor Hajus looked at me and shrugged his shoulders in resignation (he must have been thinking what I was thinking—that with two avenues we had chosen the wrong one) but he smiled and there was no reproach in his eyes.

"It sounded from the direction of the Great Tur," replied a second voice.

"Perhaps someone is at the door," suggested the first speaker.

Gor Hajus and I were flattened against the back of the statue that we might postpone as long as possible our inevitable discovery should the speakers decide to investigate the origin of the noise that had attracted their suspicions. I was facing against the polished stone of the figure's back, my hands outspread upon it. Beneath my fingers were the carven bits of its ornamental harness—jutting protuberances that were costly gems set in these trappings of stone, and there were gorgeous inlays of gold filigree; but these things I had no eyes for now. We could hear the two conversing as they came nearer. Perhaps I was nervous, I do not know. I am sure I never shrank from an encounter when either duty or expediency called; but in this instance both demanded that we avoid conflict and remain undiscovered. However that may be, my fingers must have been moving nervously over the jewelled harness of the figure when I became vaguely, perhaps subconsciously, aware that one of the gems was loose in its setting. I do not recall that this made any impression upon my conscious mind, but I do know that it seemed to catch the attention of my wandering fingers and they must have paused to play with the loosened stone.

The voices seemed quite close now—it could be but a matter of seconds before we should be confronted by their owners. My muscles seemed to tense for the anticipated encounter and unconsciously I pressed heavily upon the loosened setting—whereat a portion of the figure's back gave noiselessly inward revealing to us the dimly lighted interior of the statue. We needed no further invitation; simultaneously we stepped across the threshold and in almost the same movement I turned and closed the panel gently behind us. I think that there was absolutely no sound connected with the entire transaction; and following it we remained in utter silence, motionless—scarce breathing. Our eyes became quickly accustomed to the dim interior which we discovered was lighted through numerous small orifices in the shell of the statue, which was entirely hollow, and through these same orifices every outside sound came clearly to our ears.

We had scarcely closed the opening when we heard the voices directly outside it and simultaneously there came a hammering on the door by which we had entered the apartment from the corridor. "Who seeks entrance to Xaxa's Temple?" demanded one of the voices within the room.

"'Tis I, dwar of the Jeddara's Guard," boomed a voice from without. "We are seeking two who came to assassinate Xaxa."

"Came they this way?"

"Think you, priest, that I should be seeking them here had they not?"

"How long since?"

"Scarce twenty tals since," replied the dwar.

"Then they are not here," the priest assured him, "for we have been here for a full zode* and no other has entered the temple during that time. Look quickly to Xaxa's apartments above and to the roof and the hangars, for if you followed them up the spiral there is no other where they might flee."

"Watch then the temple carefully until I return," shouted the warrior and we heard him and his men moving on up the spiral.

Now we heard the priests conversing as they moved slowly past the statue.

"What could have caused the noise that first attracted our attention?" asked one.

"Perhaps the fugitives tried the door," suggested the other.

"It must have been that, but they did not enter or we should have seen them when they emerged from behind the Great Tur, for we were facing him at the time, nor have once turned our eyes from this end of the temple."

"Then at least they are not within the temple."

"And where else they may be is no concern of ours."

---

*A tal is about one second, and a zode approximately two and one-half hours, Earth time.

"No, nor if they reached Xaxa's apartment, if they did not pass through the temple."

"Perhaps they did reach it."

"And they were assassins!" "Worse things might befall Phundahl."

"Hush! the gods have ears."

"Of stone."

"But the ears of Xaxa are not of stone and they hear many things that are not intended for them."

"The old she-banth!" "She is Jeddara and High Priestess."

"Yes, but-" the voices passed beyond the range of our ears at the far end of the temple, yet they had told me much—that Xaxa was feared and hated by the priesthood and that the priests themselves had none too much reverence for their deity as evidenced by the remark of one that the gods have ears of stone. And they had told us other things, important things, when they conversed with the dwar of the Jeddara's Guard.

Gor Hajus and I now felt that we had fallen by chance upon a most ideal place of concealment, for the very guardians of the temple would swear that we were not, could not be, where we were. Already had they thrown the pursuers off our track.

Now, for the first time, we had an opportunity to examine our hiding place. The interior of the statue was hollow and far above us, perhaps forty feet, we could see the outside light shining through the mouth, ears and nostrils, just below which a circular platform could be discerned running around the inside of the neck. A ladder with flat rungs led upward from the base to the platform. Thick dust covered the floor on which we stood, and the extremity of our position suggested a careful examination of this dust, with the result that I was at once impressed by the evidence that it revealed; which indicated that we were the first to enter the statue for a long time, possibly for years, as the fine coating of almost impalpable dust that covered the floor was undisturbed. As I searched for this evidence my eyes fell upon something lying huddled close to the base of the ladder and approaching nearer I saw that it was a human skeleton, while a closer examination revealed that the skull was crushed and one arm and several ribs broken. About it lay, dust covered, the most gorgeous trappings I had ever seen. Its position at the foot of the ladder, as well as the crushed skull and broken bones, appeared quite conclusive evidence of the manner in which death had come—the man had fallen head foremost from the circular platform forty feet above, carrying with him to eternity, doubtless, the secret of the entrance to the interior of the Great Tur.

I suggested this to Gor Hajus who was examining the dead man's trappings and he agreed with me that such must have been the manner of his death.

"He was a high priest of Tur," whispered Gor Hajus, "and probably a member of the royal house—possibly a Jeddak. He has been dead a long time."

"I am going up above," I said. "I will test the ladder. If it is safe, follow me up. I think we shall be able to see the interior of the temple through the mouth of Tur."

"Go carefully," Gor Hajus admonished. "The ladder is very old."

I went carefully, testing each rung before I trusted my weight to it, but I found the old sorapus wood of which it was constructed sound and as staunch as steel. How the high priest came to his death must always remain a mystery, for the ladder or the circular platform would have carried the weight of a hundred red-men.

From the platform I could see through the mouth of Tur. Below me was a large chamber along the sides of which were ranged other, though lesser, idols. They were even more grotesque than those I had seen in the temple in the city and their trappings were rich beyond the conception of man—Earthman—for the gems of Barsoom scintillate with rays unknown to us and of such gorgeous and blinding beauty as to transcend description. Directly in front of the Great Tur was an altar of palthon, a rare and beautiful stone, blood red, in which are traced in purest white Nature's most fanciful designs; the whole vastly enhanced by the wondrous polish which the stone takes beneath the hand of the craftsman.

Gor Hajus joined me and together we examined the interior of the temple. Tall windows lined two sides, letting in a flood of light. At the far end, opposite the Great Tur, were two enormous doors, closing the main entrance to the chamber, and here stood the two priests whom we had heard conversing. Otherwise the temple was deserted. Incense burned upon tiny altars before each of the minor idols, but whether any burned before the Great Tur we could not see.

Having satisfied our curiosity relative to the temple, we returned our attention to a further examination of the interior of Tur's huge head and were rewarded by the discovery of another ladder leading upward against the rear wall to a higher and smaller platform that evidently led to the eyes. It did not take me long to investigate and here I found a most comfortable chair set before a control that operated the eyes, so that they could be made to turn from side to side, or up or down, according to the whim of the operator; and here too was a speaking-tube leading to the mouth. This again I must needs investigate and so I returned to the lower platform and there I discovered a device beneath the tongue of the idol, and this device, which was in the nature of an amplifier, was connected with the speaking-tube from above. I could not repress a smile as I considered these silent witnesses to the perfidy of man and thought of the broken thing lying at the foot of the ladder. Tur, I could have sworn, had been silent for many years.

Together Gor Hajus and I returned to the higher platform and again I made a discovery—the eyes of Tur were veritable periscopes. By turning them we could see any portion of the temple and what we saw through the eyes was magnified.

Nothing could escape the eyes of Tur and presently, when the priests began to talk again, we discovered that nothing could escape Tur's ears, for every slightest sound in the temple came clearly to us. What a valuable adjunct to high priesthood this Great Tur must have been in the days when that broken skeleton lying below us was a thing of blood and life!

Chapter 12

The Great Tur

The day dragged wearily for Gor Hajus and me. We watched the various priests who came in pairs at intervals to relieve those who had preceded them, and we listened to their prattle, mostly idle gossip of court scandals. At times they spoke of us and we learned that Hovan Du had escaped with Sag Or, nor had they been located as yet, nor had Dar Tarus. The whole court was mystified by our seemingly miraculous disappearance. Three thousand people, the inmates and attaches of the palace, were constantly upon the look-out for us. Every part of the palace and the palace grounds had been searched and searched again. The pits had been explored more thoroughly than they had been explored within the memory of the oldest retainer, and it seemed that queer things had been unearthed there—things of which not even Xaxa dreamed, and the priests whispered that at least one great and powerful house would fall because of what a dwar of the Jeddak's Guard had discovered in a remote precinct of the pits.

As the sun dropped below the horizon and darkness came, the interior of the temple was illuminated by a soft white light, brilliantly but without the glare of Earthly artificial illumination. More priests came and many young girls, priestesses. They performed before the idols, chanting meaningless gibberish.

Gradually the chamber filled with worshippers, nobles of the Jeddara's court with their women and their retainers, forming in two lines along either side of the temple before the lesser idols, leaving a wide aisle from the great entrance to the foot of the Great Tur and towards this aisle they all faced, waiting. For what were they waiting? Their eyes were turned expectantly towards the closed doors of the great entrance and Gor Hajus and I felt our eyes held there too, fascinated by the suggestion that they were about to open and reveal some stupendous spectacle.

And presently the doors did swing slowly open and all we saw was what appeared to be a great roll of carpet lying upon its side across the opening. Twenty slaves, naked but for their scant leather harness, stood behind the huge roll; and as the doors swung fully open they rolled the carpet inward to the very feet of the altar before the Great Tur, covering the wide aisle from the entranceway almost to the idol with a thick, soft rug of gold and white and blue. It was the most beautiful thing in the temple where all else was blatant, loud and garish or hideous, or grotesque. And then the doors closed and again we waited; but not for long. Bugles sounded from without, the sound increasing as they neared the entrance. Once more the doors swung in. Across the entrance stood a double rank of gorgeously trapped nobles. Slowly they entered the temple and behind them came a splendid chariot drawn by two banths, the fierce Barsoomian lion, held in leash by slaves on either side. Upon the chariot was a litter and in the litter, reclining at ease, lay Xaxa. As she entered the temple the people commenced to chant her praises in a monotonous sing-song. Chained to the chariot and following on foot was a red warrior and behind him a procession composed of fifty young men and an equal number of young girls.

Gor Hajus touched my arm. "The prisoner," he whispered, "do you recognize him?"

"Dar Tarus!" I exclaimed.

It was Dar Tarus—they had discovered his hiding place and arrested him, but what of Hovan Du? Had they taken him, also? If they had it must have been only after slaying him, for they never would have sought to capture the fierce beast, nor would he have brooked capture. I looked for Sag Or, but he was nowhere to be seen within the temple and this fact gave me hope that Hovan Du might be still at liberty.

The chariot was halted before the altar and Xaxa alighted; the lock that held Dar Tarus' chain to the vehicle was opened and the banths were led away by their attendants to one side of the temple behind the lesser idols. Then Dar Tarus was dragged roughly to the altar and thrown upon it and Xaxa, mounting the steps at its base, came close to his side and with bands outstretched above him looked up at the Great Tur towering above her. How beautiful she was! How richly trapped! Ah, Valla Dia! that your sweet form should be debased to the cruel purposes of the wicked mind that now animates you!

Xaxa's eyes now rested upon the face of the Great Tur. "O, Tur, Father of Barsoom," she cried, "behold the offering we place before you, All-seeing, All-knowing, All-powerful One, and frown no more upon us in silence. For a hundred years you have not deigned to speak aloud to your faithful slaves; never since Hora San, the high priest, was taken away by you on that long-gone night of mystery have you unsealed your lips to your people. Speak, Great Tur! Give us some sign, ere we plunge this dagger into the heart of our offering, that our works are pleasing in thine eyes. Tell us whither went the two who came here to-day to assassinate your high priestess; reveal to us the fate of Sag Or. Speak Great Tur, ere I strike," and she raised her slim blade above the heart of Dar Tarus and looked straight upward into the eyes of Tur.

And then, as a bolt from the blue, I was struck by the great inspiration. My hand sought the lever controlling the eyes of Tur and I turned them until they completed a full circuit of the room and rested again upon Xaxa. The effect was magical. Never before had I seen a whole room full of people so absolutely stunned and awestruck as were these. As the eyes returned to Xaxa she seemed turned to stone and her copper skin to have taken on an ashen purple hue. Her dagger remained stiffly poised above the heart of Dar Tarus. Not for a hundred years had they seen the eyes of the Great Tur move. Then I placed the speaking-tube to my lips and the voice of Tur rumbled through the chamber. As from one great throat a gasp arose from the crowded temple floor and the people fell upon their knees and buried their faces in their hands.

"Judgment is mine!" I cried. "Strike not lest ye be struck! To Tur is the sacrifice!" I was silent then, attempting to plan how best to utilize the advantage I had gained. Fearfully, one by one, the bowed heads were raised and frightened eyes sought the face of Tur. I gave them another thrill by letting the god's eyes wander slowly over the upturned faces, and while I was doing this I had another inspiration, which I imparted to Gor Hajus in a low whisper. I could hear him chuckle as he started down the ladder to carry my new plan into effect. Again I had recourse to the speaking-tube.

"The sacrifice is Tur's," I rumbled. "Tur will strike with his own hand. Extinguish the lights and let no one move under pain of instant death until Tur gives the word. Prostrate yourselves and bury your eyes in your palms, for whosoever sees shall be blinded when the spirit of Tur walks among his people."

Down they went again and one of the priests hurriedly extinguished the lights, leaving the temple in total darkness; and while Gor Hajus was engaged with his part of the performance I tried to cover any accidental noise he might make by keeping up a running fire of celestial revelation.

"Xaxa, the high priestess, asks what has become of the two whom she believed came to assassinate her. I, Tur took them to myself. Vengeance is Tur's! And Sag Or I took, also. In the guise of a great ape I came and took Sag Or and none knew me; though even a fool might have guessed, for who is there ever heard a great ape speak with tongue of man unless he was animated by the spirit of Tur?"

I guess that convinced them, it being just the sort of logic suited to their religion, or it would have convinced them if they had not already been convinced. I wondered what might be passing in the mind of the doubting priest who had remarked that the gods had ears of stone.

Presently I heard a noise upon the ladder beneath me and a moment later someone climbed upon the circular landing.

"All's well," whispered the voice of Gor Hajus. "Dar Tarus is with me."

"Light the temple!" I commanded through the speaking-tube. "Rise and look upon your altar."

The lights flashed on and the people rose, trembling, to their feet. Every eye was bent upon the altar and what they saw there seemed to crush them with terror. Some of the women screamed and fainted. It all impressed me with the belief that none of them had taken this god of theirs with any great amount of seriousness, and now when they were confronted with absolute proof of his miraculous powers they were swept completely off their feet. Where, a few moments before, they had seen a live sacrifice awaiting the knife of the high priestess they saw now only a dust-covered human skull. I grant you that without an explanation it might have seemed a miracle to almost anyone so quickly had Gor Hajus run from the base of the idol with the skull of the dead high priest and returned again leading Dar Tarus with him. I had been a bit concerned as to what the attitude of Dar Tarus might be, who was no more conversant with the hoax than were the Phundahlians, but Gor Hajus had whispered "For Valla Dia" in his ear and he had understood and come quickly.

"The Great Tur," I now announced, "is angry with his people. For a long time they had denied him in their hearts even while they made open worship of him. The Great Tur is angry with Xaxa. Only through Xaxa may the people of Phundahl be saved from destruction, for the Great Tur is angry. Go then from the temple and the palace leaving no human being here other than Xaxa, the high priestess of Tur. Leave her here in solitude beside the altar. Tur would speak with her alone."

I could see Xaxa fairly shrivel in fright.

"Is the Jeddara Xaxa, High Priestess of the Great God Tur, afraid to meet her master?" I demanded. The woman's jaw trembled so that she could not reply.

"Obey! or Xaxa and all her people shall be struck dead!" I fairly screamed at them.

Like cattle they turned and fled towards the entrance and Xaxa, her knees shaking so that she could scarce stand erect, staggered after them. A noble saw her and pushed her roughly back, but she shrieked and ran after him when he had left her. Then others dragged her to the foot of the altar and threw her roughly down and one menaced her with his sword, but at that I called aloud that no harm must befall the Jeddara if they did not wish the wrath of Tur to fall upon them all. They left her lying there and so weak from fright was she that she could not rise, and a moment later the temple was empty, but not until I had shouted after them to clear the whole palace within a quarter zode, for my plan required a free and unobstructed as well as unobserved field of action.

The last of them was scarce out of sight ere we three descended from the head of Tur and stepped out upon the temple floor behind the idol. Quickly I ran towards the altar, upon the other side of which Xaxa had dropped to the floor in a swoon. She still lay there and I gathered her into my arms and ran quickly back to the door in the wall behind the idol—the doorway through which Gor Hajus and I had entered the temple earlier in the day.

Preceded by Gor Hajus and followed by Dar Tarus, I ascended the runway towards the roof where the conversation of the priests had informed us were located the royal hangars. Had Hovan Du and Sag Or been with us my cup of happiness would have been full, for within half a day, what had seemed utter failure and defeat had been turned almost to assured success. At the landing where lay Xaxa's apartments we halted and looked within, for the long night voyage I contemplated would be cold and the body of Valla Dia must be kept warm with suitable robes even though it was inhabited by the spirit of Xaxa. Seeing no one we entered and soon found what we required. As I was adjusting a heavy robe of orluk about the Jeddara she regained consciousness. Instantly she recognized me and then Gor Hajus and finally Dar Tarus. Mechanically she felt for her dagger, but it was not there and when she saw my smile she paled with anger. At first she must have jumped to the conclusion that she had been the victim of a hoax, but presently a doubt seemed to enter her mind—she must have been recalling some of the things that had transpired within the temple of the Great Tur, and these, neither she nor any other mortal might explain.

"Who are you?" she demanded.

"I am Tur," I replied, brazenly.

"What is your purpose with me?"

"I am going to take you away from Phundahl," I replied.

"But I do not wish to go. You are not Tur. You are Vad Varo. I shall call for help and my guards will come and slay you."

"There is no one in the palace," I reminded her. "Did I, Tur, not send them away?" "I shall not go with you," she announced firmly. "Rather would I die."

"You shall go with me, Xaxa," I replied, and though she fought and struggled we carried her from her apartment and up the spiral runway to the roof where, I prayed, I should find the hangars and the royal fliers; and as we stepped out into the fresh night air of Mars we did see the hangars before us, but we saw something else—a group of Phundahlian warriors of the Jeddara's Guard whom they had evidently failed to notify of the commands of Tur. At sight of them Xaxa cried aloud in relief.

"To me! To the Jeddara!" she cried. "Strike down these assassins and save me!" There were three of them and there were three of us, but they were armed and between us we had but Xaxa's slender dagger. Gor Hajus carried that. Victory seemed turned to defeat as they rushed towards us; but it was Gor Hajus who gave them pause. He seized Xaxa and raised the blade, its point above her heart.

"Halt!" he cried, "or I strike."

The warriors hesitated; Xaxa was silent, stricken with fear. Thus we stood in stalemate when, just beyond the three Phundahlian warriors, I saw a movement at the roof's edge. What was it? In the dim light I saw something that seemed a human head, and yet unhuman, rise slowly above the edge of the roof, and then, silently, a great form followed, and then I recognized it—Hovan Du, the great white ape.

"Tell them," I cried to Xaxa in a loud voice that Hovan Du might hear, "that I am Tur, for see, I come again in the semblance of a white ape!" and I pointed to Hovan Du. "I would not destroy these poor warriors. Let them lay down their weapons and go in peace."

The men turned, and seeing the great ape standing there behind them, materialized, it might have been, out of thin air, were shaken.

"Who is he, Jeddara?" demanded one of the men.

"It is Tur," replied Xaxa in a weak voice; "but save me from him!

Save me from him!" "Throw down your weapons and your harness and fly!" I commanded, "or Tur will strike you dead. Heard you not the people rushing from the palace at Tur's command? How think you we brought Xaxa hither with a lesser power than Tur's when all her palace was filled with her fighting men? Go, while yet you may in safety."

One of them unbuckled his harness and threw it with his weapons upon the roof, and as he started at a run for the spiral his companions followed his example.

Then Hovan Du approached us.

"Well done, Vad Varo," he growled, "though I know not what it is all about."

"That you shall know later," I told him, "but now we must find a swift flier and be upon our way. Where is Sag Or? Does he still live?"

"I have him securely bound and safely hidden in one of the high towers of the palace," replied the ape. "It will be easy to get him when we have launched a flier."

Xaxa was eyeing us ragefully. "You are not Tur!" she cried. "The ape has exposed you."

"But too late to profit you in any way, Jeddara," I assured her. "Nor could you convince one of your people who stood in the temple this night that I am not Tur. Nor do you, yourself, know that I am not. The ways of Tur, the all-powerful, all-knowing, are beyond the conception of mortal man. To you then, Jeddara, I am Tur, and you will find me all-powerful enough for my purposes."

I think she was still perplexed as we found and dragged forth a flier, aboard which we placed her, and turned the craft's nose towards a lofty tower where Hovan Du told us lay Sag Or.

"I shall be glad to see myself again," said Dar Tarus, with a laugh.

"And you shall be yourself again, Dar Tarus," I told him, "as soon as ever we can come again to the pits of Ras Thavas."

"Would that I might be reunited with my sweet Kara Vasa," he sighed. Then, Vad Varo, the last full measure of my gratitude would be yours."

"Where may we find her?"

"Alas, I do not know. It was while I was searching for her that I was apprehended by the agents of Xaxa. I had been to her father's palace only to learn that he had been assassinated and his property confiscated. The whereabouts of Kara Vasa they either did not know or would not divulge; but they held me there upon one pretext or another until a detachment of the Jeddara's Guard could come and arrest me."

"We shall have to make inquiries of Sag Or," I said.

We were now coming to a stop alongside a window of the tower Hovan Du had indicated, and he and Dar Tarus leaped to the sill and disappeared within. We were all armed now, having taken the weapons discarded by the three warriors at the hangars, and with a good flier beneath our feet and all our little company reunited, with Xaxa and Sag Or, whom they were now conducting aboard, we were indeed in high spirits.

As we got under way again, setting our nose towards the east, I asked Sag Or if he knew what had become of Kara Vasa, but he assured me, in surly tones, that he did not.

"Think again, Sag Or," I admonished him, "and think hard, for perhaps upon your answer your life depends."

"What chance have I for life?" he sneered, casting an ugly look towards Dar Tarus.

"You have every chance," I replied. "Your life lies in the hollow of my hand; and you serve me well it shall be yours, though in your own body and not in that belonging to Dar Tarus."

"You do not intend destroying me?"

"Neither you nor Xaxa," I answered. "Xaxa shall live on in her own body and you in yours."

"I do not wish to live in my own body," snapped the Jeddara.

Dar Tarus stood looking at Sag Or—looking at his own body like some disembodied soul—as weird a situation as I have ever encountered.

"Tell me, Sag Or," he said, "what has become of Kara Vasa. When my body has been restored to me and yours to you I shall hold no enmity against you if you have not harmed Kara Vasa and will tell me where she be."

"I cannot tell you, for I do not know. She was not harmed, but the day after you were assassinated she disappeared from Phundahl. We were positive that she was spirited away by her father, but from him we could learn nothing. Then he was assassinated," the man glanced at Xaxa, "and since, we have learned nothing. A slave told us that Kara Vasa, with some of her father's warriors, had embarked upon a flier and set out for Helium, where she purposed placing herself under the protection of the great War Lord of Barsoom; but of the truth of that we know nothing. This is the truth. I, Sag Or, have spoken!" It was futile then to search Phundahl for Kara Vasa and so we held our course towards the east and the Tower of Thavas.

Chapter 13

Back To Thavas

All that night we sped beneath the hurtling moons of Mars, as strange a company as was ever foregathered upon any planet, I will swear. Two men, each possessing the body of the other, an old and wicked empress whose fair body belonged to a youthful damsel beloved by another of this company, a great white ape dominated by half the brain of a human being, and I, a creature of a distant planet, with Gor Hajus, the Assassin of Toonol, completed the mad roster.

I could scarce keep my eyes from the fair form and face of Xaxa, and it is well that I was thus fascinated for I caught her in the act of attempting to hurl herself overboard, so repugnant to her was the prospect of living again in her own old and hideous corpse. After that I kept her securely bound and fastened to the deck though it hurt me to see the bonds upon those fair limbs.

Dar Tarus was almost equally fascinated by the contemplation of his own body, which he had not seen for many years.

"By my first ancestor," he ejaculated. "It must be that I was the least vain of fellows, for I give you my word I had no idea that I was so fair to look upon. I can say this now without seeming egotism, since I am speaking of Sag Or," and he laughed aloud at his little joke.

But the fact remained that the body and face of Dar Tarus were beautiful indeed, though there was a hint of steel in the eyes and the set of the jaw that betokened fighting blood. Little wonder, then, that his own, which Dar Tarus now possessed, was marked by dissipation and age; nor that Dar Tarus yearned to come again into his own.

Just before dawn we dropped to one of the numerous small islands that dot the Great Toonolian Marshes and nosing the ship between the boles of great trees we came to rest upon the surface of the ground, half buried in the lush and gorgeous jungle grasses, well hidden from the sight of possible pursuers. Here Hovan Du found fruits and nuts for us which the simian section of his brain pronounced safe for human consumption, and instinct led him to a nearby spring from which there bubbled delicious water. We four were half famished and much fatigued, so that the food and water were most welcome to us; nor did Xaxa and Sag Or refuse them. Having eaten, three of us lay down upon the ship's deck to sleep, after securely chaining our prisoners, while the fourth stood watch. In this way, taking turns, we slept away most of the day and when night fell, rested and refreshed, we were ready to resume our flight.

Making a wide detour to the south we avoided Toonol and about two hours before dawn we sighted the high Tower of Thavas. I think we were all keyed up to the highest pitch of excitement, for there was not one aboard that flier but whose whole life would be seriously affected by the success or failure of our venture.

As a first precaution we secured the hands of Xaxa and Sag Or behind their backs and placed gags in their mouths, lest they succeed in giving warning of our approach.

Cluros had long since set and Thuria was streaming towards the horizon as we stopped our motor and drifted without lights a mile or two south of the tower while we waited impatiently for Thuria to leave the heavens to darkness and the world to us. To the northwest the lights of Toonol shone plainly against the dark background of the windows of the great laboratory of Ras Thavas, but the tower itself was dark from plinth to pinnacle.

And now the nearer moon dropped plummetlike beneath the horizon and left the scene to darkness and to us. Dar Tarus started the motor, the wonderful, silent motor of Barsoom, and we moved slowly, close to the ground, towards Ras Thavas' island, with no sound other than the gentle whirring of our propeller; nor could that have been heard scarce a hundred feet so slowly was it turning. Close off the island we came to a stop behind a cluster of giant trees and Hovan Du, going into the bow, uttered a few low growls. Then we stood waiting in silence, listening. There was a rustling in the dense undergrowth upon the shore. Again Hovan Du voiced his low, grim call and this time there came an answer from the black shadows. Hovan Du spoke in the language of the great apes and the invisible creature replied.

For five minutes, during which time we were aware from the different voices that others had joined in the conversation from the shore, the apes conversed, and then Hovan Du turned to me.

"It is arranged," he said. "They will permit us to hide our ship beneath these trees and they will permit us to pass out again when we are ready and board her, nor will they harm us in any way. All they ask is that when we are through we shall leave the gate open that leads to the inner court."

"Do they understand that while an ape goes in with us none will return with us?"

I asked.

"Yes; but they will not harm us."

"Why do they wish the gate left open?" "Do not inquire too closely, Vad Varo," replied Hovan Du. "It should be enough that the great apes make it possible for you to restore Valla Dia's body to her brain and escape with her from this terrible place."

"It is enough," I replied. "When may we land?"

"At once. They will help us drag the ship beneath the trees and make her fast."

"But first we must top the wall to the inner court," I reminded him.

"Yes, true—I had forgotten that we cannot open the gate from this side."

He spoke again, then, to the apes, whom we had not yet seen; and then he told us that all was arranged and that he and Dar Tarus would return with the ship after landing us inside the wall.

Again we got under way and rising slowly above the outer wall dropped silently to the courtyard beyond. The night was unusually dark, clouds having followed Thuria and blotted out the stars after the moon had set. No one could have seen the ship at a distance of fifty feet, and we moved almost without noise. Quietly we lowered our prisoners over the side and Gor Hajus and I remained with them while Dar Tarus and Hovan Du rose again and piloted the ship back to its hiding place.

I moved at once to the gate and, unlatching it, waited. I heard nothing. Never, I think, have I endured such utter silence. There came no sound from the great pile rising behind me, nor any from the dark jungle beyond the wall. Dimly I could see the huddled forms of Gor Hajus, Xaxa and Sag Or beside me—otherwise I might have been alone in the darkness and immensity of space.

It seemed an eternity that I waited there before I heard a soft scratching on the panels of the heavy gate. I pushed it open and Dar Tarus and Hovan Du stepped silently within as I closed and relatched it. No one spoke. All had been carefully planned so that there was no need of speech. Dar Tarus and I led the way, Gor Hajus and Hovan

Du brought up the rear with the prisoners. We moved directly to the entrance to the tower, found the runway and descended to the pits. Every fortune seemed with us. We met no one, we had no difficulty in finding the vault we sought, and once within we secured the door so that we had no fear of interruption—that was our first concern—and then I hastened to the spot where I had hidden Valla Dia behind the body of a large warrior, tucked far back against the wall in a dark corner. My heart stood still as I dragged aside the body of the warrior, for always had I feared that Ras Thavas, knowing my interest in her and guessing the purpose of my venture, would cause every chamber and pit to be searched and every body to be examined until he found her for whom he sought; but my fears had been baseless, for there lay the body of Xaxa, the old and wrinkled casket of the lovely brain of my beloved, where I had hidden it against this very night. Gently I lifted it out and bore it to one of the two ersite topped tables. Xaxa, standing there bound and gagged, looked on with eyes that shot hate and loathing at me and at that hideous body to which her brain was so soon to be restored.

As I lifted her to the adjoining slab she tried to wriggle from my grasp and hurl herself to the floor, but I held her and soon had strapped her securely in place. A moment later she was unconscious and the re-transference was well under way. Gor Hajus, Sag Or and Hovan Du were interested spectators, but to Dar Tarus, who stood ready to assist me, it was an old story, for he had worked in the laboratory and seen more than enough of similar operations. I will not bore you with a description of it—it was but a repetition of what I had done many times in preparation for this very event.

At last it was completed and my heart fairly stood still as I replaced the embalming fluid with Valla Dia's own life blood and saw the colour mount to her cheeks and her rounded bosom rise and fall to her gentle breathing. Then she opened her eyes and looked up into mine.

"What has happened, Vad Varo?" she asked. "Has something gone amiss that you have recalled me so soon, or did I not respond to the fluid?"

Her eyes wandered past me to the faces of the others standing about. "What does it mean?" she asked. "Who are these?"

I raised her gently in my arms and pointed at the body of Xaxa lying deathlike on the ersite slab beside her. Valla Dia's eyes went wide. "It is done?" she cried, and clapped her hands to her face and felt of all her features and of the soft, delicate contours of her smooth neck; and yet she could scarce believe it and asked for a glass and I took one from Xaxa's pocket pouch and handed it to her. She looked long into it and the tears commenced to roll down her cheeks, and then she looked up at me through the mist of them and put her dear arms about my neck and drew my face down to hers. "My chieftain," she whispered—that was all. But it was enough. For those two words I had risked my life and faced unknown dangers, and gladly would I risk my life again for that same reward and always, for ever.

Another night had fallen before I had completed the restoration of Dar Tarus and Hovan Du. Xaxa, and Sag Or and the great ape I left sleeping the death-like sleep of Ras Thavas' marvellous anaesthetic. The great ape I had no intention of restoring, but the others I felt bound to return to Phundahl, though Dar Tarus, now resplendent in his own flesh and the gorgeous trappings of Sag Or, urged me not to inflict them again upon the long suffering Phundahlians.

"But I have given my word," I told him.

"Then they must be returned," he said.

"Though what I may do afterward is another matter," I added, for there had suddenly occurred to me a bold scheme.

I did not tell Dar Tarus what it was nor would I have had time, for at the very instant we heard someone without trying the door and then we heard voices and presently the door was tried again, this time with force. We made no noise, but just waited. I hoped that whoever it was would go away. The door was very strong and when they tried to force it they must soon have realized the futility of it because they quickly desisted and we heard their voices for only a short time thereafter and then they seemed to have gone away.

"We must leave," I said, "before they return."

Strapping the hands of Xaxa and Sag Or behind them and placing gags in their mouths I quickly restored them to life, nor ever did I see two less grateful.

The looks they cast upon me might well have killed could looks do that, and with what disgust they viewed one another was writ plain in their eyes.

Cautiously unbolting the door I opened it very quietly, a naked sword in my right hand and Dar Tarus, Gor Hajus and Hovan Du ready with theirs at my shoulder, and as it swung back it revealed two standing in the corridor watching—two of Ras Thavas' slaves; and one of them was Yamdor, his body servant. At sight of us the fellow gave a loud cry of recognition and before I could leap through the doorway and prevent them, they had both turned and were flying up the corridor as fast as their feet would carry them.

Now there was no time to be lost—everything must be sacrificed to speed.

Without thought of caution or silence we hastened through the pits towards the runway in the tower; and when we stepped into the inner court it was night again, but the farther moon was in the heavens and there were no clouds. The result was that we were instantly discovered by a sentry, who gave the alarm as he ran forward to intercept us.

What was a sentry doing in the courtyard of Ras Thavas? I could not understand.

And what were these? A dozen armed warriors were hurrying across the court on the heels of the sentry.

"Toonolians!" shouted Gor Hajus. "The warriors of Vobis Kan, Jeddak of Toonol!" Breathlessly we raced for the gate. If we could but reach it first! But we were handicapped by our prisoners, who held back the moment they discovered how they might embarrass us, and so it was that we all met in front of the gate. Dar Tarus and Gor Hajus and Hovan Du and I put Valla Dia and our prisoners behind us and fought the twenty warriors of Toonol with the odds five to one against us; but we had more heart in the fight than they and perhaps that gave us an advantage, though I am sure that Gor Hajus was as ten men himself so terrible was the effect of his name alone upon the men of Toonol.

"Gor Hajus!" cried one, the first to recognize him.

"Yes, it is Gor Hajus," replied the assassin. "Prepare to meet your ancestors!" and he drove into them like a racing propeller, and I was upon his right and Hovan Du and Dar Tarus upon his left.

It was a pretty fight, but it must eventually have gone against us, so greatly were we outnumbered, had I not thought of the apes and the gate beside us.

Working my way to it I threw it open and there upon the outside, attracted by the noise of the conflict, stood a full dozen of the great beasts. I called to Gor Hajus and the others to fall back beside the gate, and as the apes rushed in I pointed to the Toonolian warriors.

I think the apes were at a loss to know which were friends and which were foes, but the Toonolians apprised them by attacking them, while we stood aside with our points upon the ground. Just a moment we stood thus waiting. Then as the apes rushed among the Toonolian warriors, we slipped into the darkness of the jungle beyond the outer wall and sought our flier. Behind us we could hear the growls and the roars of the beasts mingled with the shouts and the curses of the men;

and the sound still rose from the courtyard as we clambered aboard the flier and pushed off into the night.

As soon as we felt that we were safely escaped from the Island of Thavas I removed the gags from the mouths of Xaxa and Sag Or and I can tell you that I immediately regretted it, for never in my life had I been subjected to such horrid abuse as poured from the wrinkled old lips of the Jeddara; and it was only when I started to gag her again that she promised to desist.

My plans were now well laid and they included a return to Phundahl since I could not start for Duhor with Valla Dia without provisions and fuel; nor could I obtain these elsewhere than in Phundahl, since I felt that I held the key that would unlock the resources of that city to me; whereas all Toonol was in arms against us owing to Vobis Kan's fear of Gor Hajus.

So we retraced our way towards Phundahl as secretly as we had come, for I had no mind to be apprehended before we had gained entrance to the palace of Xaxa.

Again we rested over daylight upon the same island that had given us sanctuary two days before, and at dark we set out upon the last leg of our journey to Phundahl. If there had been pursuit we had seen naught of it, and that might easily be explained by the great extent of the uninhabited marshes across which we flew and the far southerly course that we followed close above the ground.

As we neared Phundahl I caused Xaxa and Sag Or to be again gagged, and further, I had their heads bandaged so that none might recognize them; and then we sailed straight over the city towards the palace, hoping that we would not be discovered and yet ready in the event that we should be.

But we came to the hangars on the roof apparently unseen and constantly I coached each upon the part he was to play. As we were settling slowly to the roof Dar Tarus, Hovan Du and Valla Dia quickly bound Gor Hajus and me and wrapped our heads in bandages, for we had seen below the figures of the hangar guard. Had we found the roof unguarded the binding of Gor Hajus and me had been unnecessary.

As we dropped nearer one of the guard hailed us. "What ship?" he cried.

"The royal flier of the Jeddara of Phundahl," replied Dar Tarus, "returning with Xaxa and Sag Or."

The warriors whispered among themselves as we dropped nearer and I must confess that I felt a bit nervous as to the outcome of our ruse;

but they permitted us to land without a word and when they saw Valla Dia they saluted her after the manner of Barsoom, as, with the regal carriage of an empress, she descended from the deck of the flier.

"Carry the prisoners to my apartments!" she commanded, addressing the guard, and with the help of Hovan Du and Dar Tarus the four bound and muffled figures were carried from the flier down the spiral runway to the apartments of Xaxa, Jeddara, of Phundahl. Here excited slaves hastened to do the bidding of the Jeddara. Word must have flown through the palace with the speed of light that Xaxa had returned, for almost immediately court functionaries began to arrive and be announced, but Valla Dia sent word that she would see no one for a while.

Then she dismissed her slaves, and at my suggestion Dar Tarus investigated the apartments with a view to finding a safe hiding place for Gor Hajus, me, and the prisoners. This he soon found in a small antechamber directly off the main apartment of the royal suite; the bonds were removed from the assassin and myself and together we carried Xaxa and Sag Or into the room.

The entrance here was furnished with a heavy door over which there were hangings that completely hid it. I bade Hovan Du, who, like the rest of us, wore Phundahlian harness, stand guard before the hangings and let no one enter but members of our own party. Gor Hajus and I took up our positions just within the hangings through which we cut small holes that permitted us to see all that went on within the main chamber, for I was greatly concerned for Valla Dia's safety while she posed as Xaxa, whom I knew to be both feared and hated by her people and therefore always liable to assassination.

Valla Dia summoned the slaves and bade them admit the officials of the court, and as the doors opened fully a score of nobles entered. They appeared ill at ease and I could guess that they were recalling the episode in the temple when they had deserted their Jeddara and even hurled her roughly at the feet of the Great Tur, but Valla Dia soon put them at their ease.

"I have summoned you," she said, "to hear the word of Tur. Tur would speak again to his people. Three days and three nights have I spent with Tur. His anger against Phundahl is great. He bids me summon all the higher nobles to the temple after the evening meal to-night, and all the priests, and the commanders and dwars of the Guard, and as many of the lesser nobles as be in the palace; and then shall the people of Phundahl hear the word and the law of Tur and all those who shall obey shall live and all those who shall not obey shall die; and woe be to him who, having been summoned, shall not be in the temple this night. I, Xaxa, Jeddara of Phundahl, have spoken! Go!" They went and they seemed glad to go. Then Valla Dia summoned the odwar of the Guard, who would be in our world a general, and she told him to clear the palace of every living being from the temple level to the roof an hour before the evening meal, nor to permit any one to enter the temple or the levels above it until the hour appointed for the assembling in the temple to hear the word of Tur, excepting however those who might be in her own apartments, which were not to be entered upon pain of death. She made it all very clear and plain and the odwar understood and I think he trembled a trifle, for all were in great fear of the Jeddara Xaxa; and then he went away and the slaves were dismissed and we were alone.

Chapter 14

John Carter

Half an hour before the evening meal we carried Xaxa and Sag Or down the spiral runway and placed them in the base of the Great Tur and Gor Hajus and I took our places on the upper platform behind the eyes and voice of the idol. Valla Dia, Dar Tarus and Hovan Du remained in the royal apartments. Our plans were well formulated. There was no one between the door at the rear of the Great Tur and the flier that lay ready on the roof in the event that we were forced to flee through any miscarriage of our mad scheme.

The minutes dragged slowly by and darkness fell. The time was approaching. We heard the doors of the temple open and beyond we saw the great corridor brilliantly lighted. It was empty except for two priests who stood hesitating nervously in the doorway. Finally one of them mustered up sufficient courage to enter and switch on the lights. More bravely now they advanced and prostrated themselves before the altar of the Great Tur. When they arose and looked up into the face of the idol I could not resist the temptation to turn those huge eyes until they had rolled completely about the interior of the chamber and rested again upon the priests; but I did not speak and I think the effect of the awful silence in the presence of the living god was more impressive than would words have been. The two priests simply collapsed. They slid to the floor and lay there trembling, moaning and supplicating Tur to have mercy on them, nor did they rise before the first of the worshippers arrived.

Thereafter the temple filled rapidly and I could see the word of Tur had been well and thoroughly disseminated. They came as they had before; but there were more this time, and they ranged upon either side of the central aisle and there they waited, their eyes divided between the doorway and the god. About the time that I thought the next scene was about to be enacted I let Tur's eyes travel over the assemblage that they might be keyed to the proper pitch for what was to follow. They reacted precisely as had the priests, falling upon the floor and moaning and supplicating; and there they remained until the sounds of bugles announced the coming of the Jeddara. Then they rose unsteadily to their feet.

The great doors swung open and there was the carpet and the slaves behind it. As they rolled it down towards the altar the bugles sounded louder and the head of the royal procession came into view. I had ordered it thus to permit of greater pageantry than was possible when the doors opened immediately upon the head of the procession. My plan permitted the audience to see the royal retinue advancing down the long corridor and the effect was splendid. First came the double rank of nobles and behind these the chariot drawn by the two banths, bearing the litter upon which reclined Valla Dia. Behind her walked Dar Tarus, but all within that room thought they were looking upon the Jeddara Xaxa and her favourite, Sag Or. Hovan Du walked behind Sag Or and following came the fifty young men and the fifty maidens.

The chariot halted before the altar and Valla Dia descended and knelt and the voices that had been chanting the praises of Xaxa were stilled as the beautiful creature extended her hands towards the Great Tur and looked up into his face.

"We are ready, Master!" she cried. "Speak! We await the word of Tur!" A gasp arose from the kneeling assemblage, a gasp that ended in a sob. I felt that they were pretty well worked up and that everything ought to go off without a hitch. I placed the speaking tube to my lips.

"I am Tur!" I thundered and the people trembled. "I come to pass judgment on the men of Phundahl. As you receive my word so shall you prosper or so shall you perish. The sins of the people may be atoned by two who have sinned most in my sight." I let the eyes of Tur rove about over the audience and then brought them to rest upon Valla Dia. "Xaxa, are you ready to atone for your sins and for the sins of your people?"

Valla Dia bowed her beautiful head. "Thy will is law, Master!" she replied.

"And Sag Or," I continued, "you have sinned. Are you prepared to pay?"

"As Tur shall require," said Dar Tarus.

"Then it is my will," I boomed, "that Xaxa and Sag Or shall give back to those from whom they stole them, the beautiful bodies they now wear; that he from whom Sag Or took this body shall become Jeddak of Phundahl and High Priest of Tur; and that she from whom Xaxa stole her body shall be returned in pomp to her native country. I have spoken. Let any who would revolt against my word speak now or for ever hold his peace."

There was no objection voiced. I had felt pretty certain that there would not be. I doubt if any god ever looked down upon a more subdued and chastened flock.

As I had talked, Gor Hajus had descended to the base of the idol and removed the bonds from the feet and legs of Xaxa and Sag Or.

"Extinguish the lights!" I commanded. A trembling priest did my bidding.

Valla Dia and Dar Tarus were standing side by side before the altar when the lights went out. In the next minute they and Gor Hajus must have worked fast, for when I heard a low whistle from the interior of the idol's base, the prearranged signal that Gor Hajus had finished his work, and ordered the lights on again, there stood Xaxa and Sag Or where Valla Dia and Dar Tarus: had been, and the latter were nowhere in sight. I think the dramatic effect of that transformation upon the people there was the most stupendous thing I have ever seen. There was no cord or gag upon either Xaxa or Sag Or, nothing to indicate that they had been brought hither by force—no one about who might have so brought them. The illusion was perfect—it was a gesture of omnipotence that simply staggered the intellect. But I wasn't through.

"You have heard Xaxa renounce her throne," I said, "and Sag Or submit to the judgment of Tur."

"I have not renounced my throne!" cried Xaxa. "It is all a——" "Silence!" I thundered. "Prepare to greet the new Jeddak, Dar Tarus of Phundahl!" I turned my eyes towards the great doors and the eyes of the assemblage followed mine. They swung open and there stood Dar Tarus, resplendent in the trappings of Hora San, the long dead Jeddak and high priest, whose bones we had robbed in the base of the idol an hour earlier. How Dar Tarus had managed to make the change so quickly is beyond me, but he had done it and the effect was colossal. He looked every inch a Jeddak as he moved with slow dignity up the wide aisle along the blue and gold and white carpet. Xaxa turned purple with rage. "Impostor!" she shrieked. "Seize him! Kill him!" and she ran forward to meet him as though she would slay him with her bare hands.

"Take her away," said Dar Tarus in a quiet voice, and at that Xaxa fell foaming to the floor. She shrieked and gasped and then lay still—a wicked old woman dead of apoplexy. And when Sag Or saw her lying there he must have been the first to realize that she was dead and that there was now no one to protect him from the hatreds that are levelled always at the person of a ruler's favourite. He looked wildly about for an instant and then threw himself at the feet of Dar Tarus.

"You promised to protect me!" he cried.

"None shall harm you," replied Dar Tarus. "Go your way and live in peace." Then he turned his eyes upward towards the face of the Great Tur. "What is thy will, Master?" he cried. "Dar Tarus, thy servant, awaits thy commands!" I permitted an impressive silence before I replied.

"Let the priests of Tur, the lesser nobles and a certain number of the Jeddara's Guard go forth into the city and spread the word of Tur among the people that they may know that Tur smiles again upon Phundahl and that they have a new Jeddak who stands high in the favour of Tur. Let the higher nobles attend presently in the chambers that were Xaxa's and do honour to Valla Dia in whose perfect body their Jeddara once ruled them, and effect the necessary arrangements for her proper return to Duhor, her native city. There also will they find two who have served Tur well and these shall be accorded the hospitality and friendship of every Phundahlian—Gor Hajus of Toonol and Vad Varo of Jasoom. Go! and when the last has gone let the temple be darkened. I, Tur, have spoken!" Valla Dia had gone directly to the apartments of the former Jeddara and the moment that the lights were extinguished Gor Hajus and I joined her. She could not wait to hear the outcome of our ruse, and when I assured her that there had been no hitch the tears came to her eyes for very joy.

"You have accomplished the impossible, my chieftain," she murmured, "and already can I see the hills of Duhor and the towers of my native city. Ah, Vad Varo, I had not dreamed that life might again hold for me such happy prospects. I owe you life and more than life."

We were interrupted by the coming of Dar Tarus, and with him were Hovan Du and a number of the higher nobles. The latter received us pleasantly, though I think they were mystified as to just how we were linked with the service of their god, nor, I am sure, did one of them ever learn. They were frankly delighted to be rid of Xaxa; and while they could not understand Tur's purpose in elevating a former warrior of the Guard to the throne, yet they were content if it served to relieve them from the wrath of their god, now a very real and terrible god, since the miracles that had been performed in the temple. That Dar Tarus had been of a noble family relieved them of embarrassment, and I noted that they treated him with great respect. I was positive that they would continue to treat him so, for he was also high priest and for the first time in a hundred years he would bring to the Great Tur in the royal temple the voice of god, for Hovan Du had agreed to take service with Dar Tarus, and Gor Hajus as well, so that there would never be lacking a tongue wherewith Tur might speak. I foresaw great possibilities for the reign of Dar Tarus, Jeddak of Phundahl.

At the meeting held in the apartments of Xaxa it was decided that Valla Dia should rest two days in Phundahl while a small fleet was preparing to transport her to Duhor. Dar Tarus assigned Xaxa's apartments for her use and gave her slaves from different cities to attend upon her, all of whom were to be freed and returned with Valla Dia to her native land.

It was almost dawn before we sought our sleeping silks and furs and the sun was high before we awoke. Gor Hajus and I breakfasted with Valla Dia, outside whose door we had spread our beds that we might not leave her unprotected for a moment that it was not necessary. We had scarce finished our meal when a messenger came from Dar Tarus summoning us to the audience chamber, where we found some of the higher officers of the court gathered about the throne upon which Dar Tarus sat, looking every inch an emperor. He greeted us kindly, rising and descending from his dais to receive Valla Dia and escort her to one of the benches be had placed beside the throne for her and for me.

"There is one," he said to me, "who has come to Phundahl over night and now begs audience of the Jeddak—one whom I thought you might like to meet again," and he signed to one of his attendants to admit the petitioner; and when the doors at the opposite end of the room opened I saw Ras Thavas standing there. He did not recognize me or Valla Dia or Gor Hajus until he was almost at the foot of the throne, and when he did he looked puzzled and glanced again quickly at Dar Tarus.

"Ras Thavas of the Tower of Thavas, Toonol," announced an officer.

"What would Ras Thavas of the Jeddak of Phundahl?" asked Dar Tarus.

"I came seeking audience of Xaxa," replied Ras Thavas, "not knowing of her death or your accession until this very morning; but I see Sag Or upon Xaxa's throne and beside him one whom I thought was Xaxa, though they tell me Xaxa is dead, and another who was my assistant at Thavas and one who is the Assassin of Toonol, and I am confused, Jeddak, and do not know whether I be among friends or foes."

"Speak as though Xaxa still sat upon the throne of Phundahl," Dar Tarus told him, "for though I am Dar Tarus, whom you wronged, and not Sag Or, yet need you have no fear in the court of Phundahl."

"Then let me tell you that Vobis Kan, Jeddak of Toonol, learning that Gor Hajus had escaped me, swore that I had set him free to assassinate him, and he sent warriors who took my island and would have imprisoned me had I not been warned in time to escape; and I came hither to Xaxa to beg her to send warriors to drive the men of Toonol from my island and restore it to me that I may carry on my scientific labours."

Dar Tarus turned to me. "Vad Varo, of all others you are most familiar with the work of Ras Thavas. Would you see him again restored to his island and his laboratory?"

"Only on condition that he devote his great skill to the amelioration of human suffering," I replied, "and no longer prostitute it to the foul purposes of greed and sin." This led to a discussion which lasted for hours, the results of which were of far-reaching significance. Ras Thavas agreed to all that I required and Dar Tarus commissioned Gor Hajus to head an army against Toonol.

But these matters, while of vast interest to those most directly concerned, have no direct bearing upon the story of my adventures upon Barsoom, as I had no part in them, since upon the second day I boarded a flier with Valla Dia and, escorted by a Phundahlian fleet, set out towards Duhor. Dar Tarus accompanied us for a short distance. When the fleet was stopped at the shore of the great marsh he bade us farewell, and was about to step to the deck of his own ship and return to Phundahl when a shout arose from the deck of one of the other ships and word was soon passed that a lookout had sighted what appeared to be a great fleet far to the south-west. Nor was it long before it became plainly visible to us all and equally plain that it was headed for Phundahl.

Dar Tarus told me then that as much as he regretted it, there seemed nothing to do but return at once to his capital with the entire fleet, since he could not spare a single ship or man if this proved an enemy fleet, nor could Valla Dia or I interpose any objection; and so we turned about and sped as rapidly as the slow ships of Phundahl permitted back towards the city.

The stranger fleet had sighted us at about the same time that we had sighted it, and we saw it change its course and bear down upon us; and as it came nearer it fell into single file and prepared to encircle us. I was standing at Dar Tarus' side when the colours of the approaching fleet became distinguishable and we first learned that it was from Helium.

"Signal and ask if they come in peace," directed Dar Tarus.

"We seek word with Xaxa, Jeddara of Phundahl." came the reply. "The question of peace or war will be hers to decide."

"Tell them that Xaxa is dead and that I, Dar Tarus, Jeddak of Phundahl, will receive the commander of Helium's fleet in peace upon the deck of this ship, or that I will receive him in war with all my guns. I, Dar Tarus, have spoken!" From the bow of a great ship of Helium there broke the flag of truce and when Dar Tarus' ship answered it in kind the other drew near and presently we could see the men of Helium upon her decks. Slowly the great flier came alongside our smaller ship and when the two had been made fast a party of officers boarded us.

They were fine looking men, and at their head was one whom I recognized immediately though I never before had laid eyes upon him. I think he was the most impressive figure I have ever seen as he advanced slowly across the deck towards us—John Carter, Prince of Helium, Warlord of Barsoom.

"Dar Tarus," he said, "John Carter greets you and in peace, though it had been different, I think, had Xaxa still reigned."

"You came to war upon Xaxa?" asked Dar Tarus.

"We came to right a wrong," replied the Warlord. "But from what we know of Xaxa that could have been done only by force."

"What wrong has Phundahl done Helium?" demanded Dar Tarus.

"The wrong was against one of your own people—even against you in person."

"I do not understand," said Dar Tarus.

"There is one aboard my ship who may be able to explain to you, Dar Tarus," replied John Carter, with a smile. He turned and spoke to one of his aides in a whisper, and the man saluted and returned to the deck of his own ship. "You shall see with your own eyes, Dar Tarus." Suddenly his eyes narrowed. "This is indeed Dar Tarus who was a warrior of the Jeddara's Guard and supposedly assassinated by her command?"

"It is," replied Dar Tarus.

"I must be certain," said the Warlord.

"There is no question about it, John Carter," I spoke up in English.

His eyes went wide, and when they fell upon me and he noted my lighter skin, from which the dye was wearing away, he stepped forward and held out his hand.

"A countryman?" he asked.

"Yes, an American," I replied.

"I was almost surprised," he said. "Yet why should I be? I have crossed—there is no reason why others should not. And you have accomplished it! You must come to Helium with me and tell me all about it."

Further conversation was interrupted by the return of the aide, who brought a young woman with him. At sight of her Dar Tarus uttered a cry of joy and sprang forward, and I did not need to be told that this was Kara Vasa.

There is little more to tell that might not bore you in the telling—of how John Carter himself took Valla Dia and me to Duhor after attending the nuptials of Dar Tarus and Kara Vasa; and of the great surprise that awaited me in Duhor, where I learned for the first time that Kor San, Jeddak of Duhor, was the father of Valla Dia; and of the honours and the great riches that he heaped upon me when Valla Dia and I were wed.

John Carter was present at the wedding and we initiated upon Barsoom a good old American custom, for the Warlord acted as best man; and then he insisted that we follow that up with a honeymoon and bore us off to Helium, where I am writing this.

Even now it seems like a dream that I can look out of my window and see the scarlet and the yellow towers of the twin cities of Helium; that I have met, and see daily, Carthoris, Thuvia of Ptarth, Tara of Helium, Gahan of Gathol and that peerless creature, Dejah Thoris, Princess of Mars. Though to me, beautiful as she is, there is another even more beautiful—Valla Dia, Princess of Duhor—Mrs. Ulysses Paxton

LEONAUR

ALSO FROM LEONAUR
AVAILABLE IN SOFTCOVER OR HARDCOVER WITH DUST JACKET

THE COLLECTED SCIENCE FICTION AND FANTASY OF STANLEY G. WEINBAUM: INTERPLANETARY ODYSSEYS—Classic Tales of Interplanetary Adventure Including: A Martian Odyssey, its Sequel Valley of Dreams, the Complete 'Ham' Hammond Stories and Others.

THE COLLECTED SCIENCE FICTION AND FANTASY OF STANLEY G. WEINBAUM: OTHER EARTHS—Classic Futuristic Tales Including: Dawn of Flame & its Sequel The Black Flame, plus The Revolution of 1960 & Others.

THE COLLECTED SCIENCE FICTION AND FANTASY OF STANLEY G. WEINBAUM: STRANGE GENIUS—Classic Tales of the Human Mind at Work Including the Complete Novel The New Adam, the 'van Manderpootz' Stories and Others.

THE COLLECTED SCIENCE FICTION AND FANTASY OF STANLEY G. WEINBAUM: THE BLACK HEART—Classic Strange Tales Including: the Complete Novel The Dark Other, Plus Proteus Island and Others.

DARKNESS AND DAWN 1: THE VACANT WORLD *by George Allen England*—A Novel of a future New York.

DARKNESS AND DAWN 2: BEYOND THE GREAT OBLIVION *by George Allen England*—A Novel of a future America.

DARKNESS AND DAWN 3: THE AFTER GLOW *by George Allen England*—A Novel of a future America.

CARSON OF VENUS VOLUME 1: PIRATES OF VENUS & LOST ON VENUS—*by Edgar Rice Burroughs*—Two full length novels.

JOHN CARTER OF MARS VOLUME 1: THE PRINCESS OF MARS & THE GODS OF MARS—*by Edgar Rice Burroughs*—Two full length novels.

PELLUCIDAR - THE INNER WORLD VOLUME 1: AT THE EARTH'S CORE - PELLUCIDAR—*by Edgar Rice Burroughs*—Two full length novels.

BEFORE ADAM & OTHER STORIES—*by Jack London*—Includes the novel Before Adam + The Scarlet Plague A Relic of the Pliocene When the World Was Young and others.

THE IRON HEEL & OTHER STORIES—*by Jack London*—Includes the novel The Iron Heel + The Enemy of All the World The Shadow and the Flash The Strength of the Strong The Unparalleled Invasion The Dream of Debs.

AVAILABLE ONLINE AT
www.leonaur.com
AND OTHER GOOD BOOK STORES

CLASSIC SF FROM LEONAUR
AVAILABLE IN SOFTCOVER OR HARDCOVER WITH DUST JACKET

SF7 CLASSIC SCIENCE FICTION SERIES
INTERPLANETARY ODYSSEYS
by Stanley G. Weinbaum

Classic Tales of Interplanetary Adventure Including: A Martian Odyssey, its Sequel Valley of Dreams & Others

SOFTCOVER : **ISBN 1-84677-060-2**
HARDCOVER : **ISBN 1-84677-070-X**

SF8 CLASSIC SCIENCE FICTION SERIES
OTHER EARTHS
by Stanley G. Weinbaum

Classic Futuristic Tales Including: Dawn of Flame & its Sequel The Black Flame, plus The Revolution of 1960 & Others

SOFTCOVER : **ISBN 1-84677-062-9**
HARDCOVER : **ISBN 1-84677-072-6**

SF9 CLASSIC SCIENCE FICTION SERIES
STRANGE GENIUS
by Stanley G. Weinbaum

Classic Tales of the Human Mind at Work Including the Complete Novel The New Adam, the 'van Manderpootz' Stories & More

SOFTCOVER : **ISBN 1-84677-048-3**
HARDCOVER : **ISBN 1-84677-055-6**

SF10 CLASSIC SCIENCE FICTION SERIES
THE BLACK HEART
by Stanley G. Weinbaum

Classic Strange Tales Including: the Complete Novel The Dark Other, Plus Proteus Island and Others

SOFTCOVER : **ISBN 1-84677-049-1**
HARDCOVER : **ISBN 1-84677-054-8**

AVAILABLE ONLINE AT
www.leonaur.com
AND OTHER GOOD BOOK STORES

CLASSIC SF FROM LEONAUR
AVAILABLE IN SOFTCOVER OR HARDCOVER WITH DUST JACKET

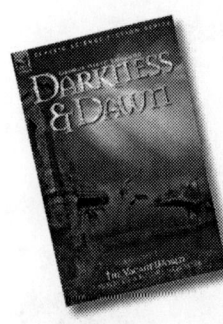

SF4 CLASSIC SCIENCE FICTION SERIES
DARKNESS & DAWN 1: The Vacant World
by George Allen England

SOFTCOVER : ISBN 1-84677-027-0
HARDCOVER : ISBN 1-84677-034-3

New York City – the end of the 3rd millennium. Buildings in ruins. Central Park a jungle peopled by sub-humans. A huge black shape moving across the night sky. Civilization has vanished along with humankind. Into this hostile new world two survivors of our enlightened age awaken from 1000 years of slumber - to fall victims to a world gone wild? - or to give mankind a second chance?

SF5 CLASSIC SCIENCE FICTION SERIES
DARKNESS & DAWN 2: Beyond the Great Oblivion by George Allen England

SOFTCOVER : ISBN 1-84677-028-9
HARDCOVER : ISBN 1-84677-036-X

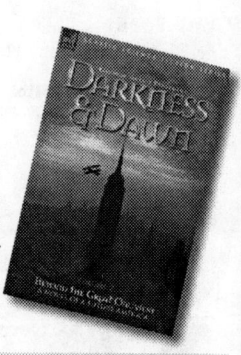

The distant future - exotic flora and fauna thrive - savage tribes of cannibalistic sub-humans fight for dominance. New York is a place of little hope! The last vestiges of humanity set out across America's devastated landscape in search of their dream, enticed onward by a mysterious and vast black chasm 500 miles deep - does the future threaten extinction for mankind? - or offer one last chance of redemption?

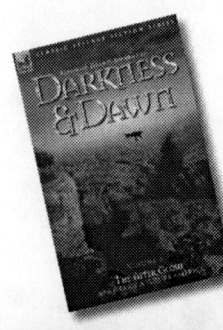

SF6 CLASSIC SCIENCE FICTION SERIES
DARKNESS & DAWN 3: The After Glow
by George Allen England

SOFTCOVER : ISBN 1-84677-029-7
HARDCOVER : ISBN 1-84677-038-6

Near the Great Lakes, 1000 years from now. Below our planet's surface tribes of albino warriors eke out an existence in a hostile environment. They tell stories of a golden age; but such tales are mere myths - until a man and a woman with god-like abilities arrive and promise to lead them towards the surface, towards the light and to a new life of plenty.

AVAILABLE ONLINE AT
www.leonaur.com
AND OTHER GOOD BOOK STORES

Printed in the United States
105003LV00003B/88/A